THE R

"Ya bother me, preacher, like an itch I cain't git to." Mason eased his rifle from his saddle and aimed it at Cordell without moving the weapon to his shoulder. "Lion Graham keeps a'tellin' us that you really is Rule Cordell. Says he knew you in one o' them Bible places somewhars. What 'bout that, preacher?"

"Oh hell, Mason," Lester said. "Who cares? More important, preacher . . . you hit me . . . in the face." The narrow-faced Regulator studied the stoic minister with renewed suspicion. "I don't like . . . getting hit . . . in the face."

"Wal, ya kin call it crazy if'n ya want—but now he's a'wearin' a flower an' sportin' outlaw-fast hoss flesh. Thar's only one man I hear tell that liked wearin' hisse'f a flower. Rule Cordell." The blond Regulator cocked the hammer on his rifle. "Just who the hell are you anyway, preacher-man?"

The narrow-faced man's hand curled around the rifle across his saddle and added, "I think . . . you'd better pull your hands outta . . . your pockets . . . an' get down."

"Sure, boys, anything you want." Cordell leaned back and raised his pockets toward them, as if freeing his hands. Instead, orange blasts erupted from the coat. . . .

Other *Leisure* books by Cotton Smith:

SPIRIT RIDER
BROTHERS OF THE GUN
BEHOLD A RED HORSE
PRAY FOR TEXAS
DARK TRAIL TO DODGE

SONS OF THUNDER

COTTON SMITH

LEISURE BOOKS  NEW YORK CITY

To Maggie, Sam, and Betty

LEISURE BOOKS®

September 2003

Published by

Dorchester Publishing Co., Inc.
200 Madison Avenue, Suite 2000
New York, NY 10016

ISBN 0-8439-5113-3

Printed in the United States of America.

SONS OF THUNDER

Chapter One

Faint sounds of galloping horses caught the ears of the faithful inside the tiny church. Almost as quickly, the distant thunder went away. Just a cattleman working on the Lord's Day, someone muttered with a knowing smile. But a few minutes later, the sounds came again. Louder and closer.

Horses pounded to a stop outside the adobe warehouse a few miles outside of Clark Springs, nestled in the Texas hill country. It was a church only on Sunday. Barrels and boxes were pushed aside for worship services; long planks were stretched over boxes to make pews. James Rule Langford, part-time preacher, had started the church the year before; the rest of the time he trained horses on his small ranch.

Both tasks gave him great joy. Better having services in a warehouse than a saloon, like many towns did, he told himself often. That was always followed by a chuckle and the observation that God wanted him to go where he was needed—and that would definitely be a saloon. Still, he much preferred this simple gathering place, in spite of having to make room for people each Sunday.

Curses of dismounting riders and snorts of their agitated mounts tore into the comforting rhythm of worship. Shrill commands grabbed at the courage of every parishioner. Even the children realized it wasn't late-comers to Sunday services and looked at their parents for reassurance. From a middle pew, Mrs. Tomlinson caught the young minister's attention and mouthed "no vices," a reminder of her weekly request that he give a sermon about vices. Her particular set included no use of tobacco or whiskey, no cardplaying, base-ball, or reading books.

Reverend Langford glanced at his best friend, Ian Taullery, sitting with his young wife, Mary, and their just-baptized baby son, Rule Christian Taullery. Typically, the tall handsome man with the well-groomed blond beard was more concerned about his appearance than anything else. He straightened his cravat, pulled on his vest, and picked a strand of hair from his coat sleeve. But his expression was easy to read. He thought the interruption was definitely someone's fault. But nothing was quite perfect enough to suit him anymore. He mouthed "Regulators," and Reverend Langford nodded.

However, Mary Taullery's panicked expression was easy to ignore. She had the same reaction to a hangnail as she did to a tornado: Everything was a sheer disaster; there were no degrees of concern. Anything out of her mouth came loudly. A whisper was an unknown form of communication. And only full-out dispair for anything that was viewed as a problem or a distraction. It was hard for the minister to understand what Taullery saw in her, except that she came from a wealthy family.

Reverend Langford's gaze quickly sought his beautiful wife, Aleta, seated next to the Taullerys. Her eyes made love with his and her smile was more reassuring than she felt. Her stunning figure was demurely presented in a light-blue print dress; her long black hair was tightly pulled back against her head and held in a bun at the back.

She little resembled the brash hellcat with a quick pistol and a sharp tongue who rode with outlaws sought by every Federal trooper and state policeman in Texas. To the parish, she was the warm and caring wife of their minister and, according to the current gossip, born of Spanish nobility and educated at the finest European schools. Aleta would have laughed that wonderful deep laugh if she had heard such a tale. But she accepted with pride compliments about her teaching the community's children.

"My brothers and sisters, join our voices in glorious tribute to the Lord with 'Let Us Gather at the River.' You'll find it on page twenty-four of the fine new hymnals, thanks to the generous contribution of Ian and Mary Taullery," Reverend James Rule Langford announced, trying to drown out the cursing and heavy-booted advance on the wooden steps leading to the parish door. His shoulders rose and fell in anticipation of trouble, swaying the black robe given him by the congregation.

The minister's dark eyes studied the congregation in front of him as if willing them courage with his gaze. Langford's chiseled face gave no indication of concern. Instead, a warm smile harvested his countenance, an act of sheer will. Lying on his chest was a simple silver cross, held around his neck by a long leather cord, a wedding gift from Aleta. He touched it unconsciously.

Under the Christian cloak was a different kind of spiritual symbolism: a tiny buckskin pouch, also on a leather thong, a long-ago gift of spirit medicine from an aging Comanche shaman before the young soldier left Texas for the War. The medicine pouch had been good enough to protect him from the haunting memories of his evil minister father—and the piercing reality of Union bullets—and guide him back to God. A God his own minister father never saw or wanted to.

His fingers slid from the cross to the comforting pouch and back again as he burst into song. He hoped his own enthusiasm would comfort the tense faces in front of him. Joining the singing with gusto, Taullery opened the right side of his tailored, three-piece suitcoat, indicating to his minister friend that he wasn't armed. Reverend Langford frowned at the suggestion that he was even thinking of a gun, not the lack of a weapon itself. His devotion to bringing the Word to the prairie was as fierce and committed as his earlier devotion to the Confederacy and its dashing cavalry leader, General Jeb Stuart.

He had no intention of returning to the man of the gun he had once been. No matter what. His life now was Aleta, horses, and this would-be church. No one else in the congregation—or the little community itself, for that matter—knew their preacher was actually Rule Cordell, the former Confederate cavalry hero and Texas pistol-fighter. If asked, all would have said the outlaw Rule Cordell was killed in a Union army ambush a year before, along with the deadly Johnny Cat Carlson and his wild band of Rebel warriors.

Part of the story was true: Carlson and his men were cut down. Rule Cordell had already left the gang, finally realizing they were fighting for themselves and not for Texas or the rebirth of the Confederacy. Excited Federal troopers mistook the body of another guerrilla for the famous gunfighter and the story spread.

Aleta, too, had been a part of the gang and Johnny

Cat's woman, leaving to find the man she loved and saving Cordell's life in the process. Taullery's too. Cordell's announced death was a blessing, allowing him to disappear into Reverend James Rule Langford. He kept "Rule" as a middle name to cover any inadvertent use of that name by friends.

For all of his friends and former comrades in arms, it was a time of aching sadness. The soul of Texas was empty and her lands occupied by Northern conquerors who ruled with gun and greed and unrelenting vindictiveness. By Eastern newspaper accounts, the War had been over some two years back and the country was well on the way to mending itself whole again. Texas hadn't heard that news—and would have spit at the words if it did.

But spitting wouldn't help anyone now. Both Rule Cordell, now known as Reverend Langford, and Taullery recognized one voice in particular. Cutting through the door were the shrill demands of Captain Alfred McPherson Padgett. The arrogant leader's militia served as the carpetbagger governor's enforcement arm. Known as the "Regulators," the state police served authorized hell to the state, beset with postwar destruction, poverty, and grief. Sadly, they had replaced the Texas Rangers, who had been forced to disband after the War.

This was in addition to what was left of Sherman's army stationed along the Rio Grande. Originally a force of 51,000, it was now reduced to a much smaller size. Supposedly, the show of Union force, right after the War ended, was to put a preemptive end to any designs the Mexican government might have on Texas soil. Most Texans saw the real motive: to have an at-hand force ready to pound any sign of Confederate resurrection into the ground. Even now, the governor was an appointed puppet of Sherman, all courts were military, and all positions of authority taken by Yankees or their sympathizers.

Reverend Langford knew the battle for attention was already lost. Aleta, Ian and Mary Taullery, and Widow Bauer, on the front row, were the only people singing as the fifty-some parishioners turned in unison to see who would be coming into the adobe-walled building. Fear had already told them it was Regulators.

" 'Shall we gather at the river . . . the beautiful, beautiful riv—" The planked door burst open, and even Aleta stopped singing. Her flashing dark eyes went to the back and then returned to her husband. Reverend Langford paused a few words later. His clear voice echoed off the gray walls and slipped between the candlelit shadows. A vanguard of timid sunlight led the dozen men with rifles pouring inside. Some were dressed in remmants of Yankee uniforms; one wore Confederate trousers; the rest were in long coats and vests. Three were Negroes. A shiny state police badge was the only visible thing this string of armed men had in common, other than holstered revolvers and brandished rifles. They filed along the back of the church, leaving open the doorway for Captain Padgett's grand appearance. Outside, another dozen state police stood at the ready.

Mary Taullery stage-whispered, "My God, it's Regulators! Ohmygod, Ian, what's happening?"

Taullery quieted her. "It'll be all right, Mary. Be quiet."

"My God, we'll all be killed."

"Dammit, Mary, that's *enough*. Shut up."

Like a king expecting adulation, Captain Padgett entered the hushed room in a wheelchair. One stray sunbeam curled back to dance on the shiny wheel rims. A rail-thin militiaman was assigned the task of pushing, and, clearly, it was taxing the limit of his strength. Beaded-cuff gauntlets in Padgett's fist slapped at trail dust on his still legs. Captain Padgett studied the filled church with obvious relish, his beady eyes flashing hatred.

A tall man with well-trimmed, graying mustache and sideburns, the Regulator leader was outfitted immaculately in a uniform of his own design, adorned with gold buttons, piping, and epaulets. His face was a hatchet, now puffy from excess of food, drink, and little exercise. Two gold-plated, pearl-handled revolvers in matching beaded holsters hung from the chair, one over each wooden arm.

On the second row, a one-armed former Confederate, still wearing faded and patched buttermilk pants, whispered to the farmer next to him that he'd never seen so much gold on a man in his life, " 'ceptin' one of them fanciful foreign prince fellers." The farmer squinted his reaction and coughed to relieve the chuckle that wanted to follow in spite of the fear in his belly.

Three rows in front of them, a heavyset townsman responded to his wife's hushed question that Padgett had been injured by Rebel gunfire during the First Battle of Manassas and hated everything Southern for what they did to him. She then wanted to know how he traveled with his men. Rolling his eyes at the continuing questioning, the husband dutifully responded that a special wagon had been built just for Padgett and paid for out of tax funds. A grimace trailed the statement.

Oblivious to the danger of being overheard by the Regulators, she wanted to know what kind of "special wagon" it was. Keeping his eyes on the armed men spreading out behind the last pews, he told her it was a buckboard with sides reinforced by heavy planks to make a movable fort. Men could stand behind its "walls" and shoot through rifle holes. A fold-down ramp allowed the wheelchair to be pushed into the wagon bed. Once there, the wheels were bolted into place.

Near the driver's seat, a Gatling gun was mounted on a raised platform, where a militiaman was stationed. The fearsome weapon could be pivoted and fired in all directions, including over the head of the driver and a team of eight matched black mules. "A war wagon," she said. He shook his ahead in agreement, and a shiver followed.

"Gentlemen, this is a house of worship. We welcome strangers to our service. You are invited to leave your guns outside, remove your hats and join us. We are singing the hymn on page twenty-four of the hymnal, 'Let Us Gather at the River.' Perhaps you've sung it before—in your own churches." Reverend Langford stood in the center of the opened area beyond the line of rough-hewed plank pews.

Long brown hair covered his ears and touched his white collar, the only remaining sign of his earlier wildness. Even the Cheyenne stone earring had been removed. His evenly moderated voice belied the desire to attack the intruders with his bare fists. He hadn't yet tried to restart the congregation's singing and knew it would be futile at the moment. Fear painted their faces, mixed with traces of bitterness and touches of anger. All were justified emotions, but none would matter to Padgett and his men.

"Shut up, Bible-thumper," Captain Padgett bellowed, and waved the fistful of gloves in Langford's direction. "We aren't here for any of your windies. We're here to arrest a traitor to the United States."

Padgett's eyes examined the scared expressions turned toward him, as well as the backs of those few parishers defiantly choosing to face the minister. He didn't see the hatred that crossed Langford's face and disappeared into his mind once more. Aleta's whispered "Be careful, Rule" reached him, but he didn't acknowledge the warning. Interruptions like this were familiar stories throughout Texas.

Chapter Two

It seemed like every week Regulators arrested civilians without cause and took their homes and lands. Innocent men were shot or hanged. Northern revenge expressed itself in destroyed ranches and burned buildings, confiscated herds and stolen crops. There wasn't much one man could do to stop this mindless destruction, especially not a man whose only weapon now was the Good Book.

Slipping through the door and taking his place beside Padgett was a gray shadow of a man wearing wire-rimmed spectacles. Reverend Langford knew who he was immediately. So did others in the church, as indicated by the gasps. Lion David Graham. His reputation as a killer of men had murmured its way through Texas. His name was mentioned in the same hushed sentence as were Clay Allison, Cullen Baker, John Wesley Hardin, and the late Rule Cordell. During the War, he had been a Union sniper; in the years following, he hired out his gun to anyone who could pay. It had been rumored that Padgett had recently employed him to assist in his regulatory duties. Here was proof of the awful thought.

Unlike the others with the Regulator leader, Lion Graham wore no badge on his gray, three-piece suit with matching derby. A short cape rested on his shoulders. Around his waist was a gray silk sash holding two black-handled revolvers. His countenance matched his clothing; a gray pallor to his skin reminded many of death. A black goatee and thin eyebrows set off a razor-thin face with a carrot for a nose. It was said he rarely smiled, never drank or smoke, and didn't like women. There was one particularly harsh tale about him putting a man's eyes out with bullets at point-blank range—while laughing hysterically.

Lion Graham's mouth flickered at the corner. He rolled his neck from side to side, as if embarrassed by the attention his appearance had created. He stared at Reverend Langford, pushing his glasses against his nose. A slight puzzled look visited Graham's face momentarily and vanished.

Under his breath, Reverend Langford muttered, " 'There is a lion in the way; a lion is in the streets.' Psalms Twenty-six, Thirteen." Would Graham recognize him? Surely not, they had played together as boys before Graham's parents moved away.

Reverend Langford's shoulders rose and fell, and he addressed Padgett again. "Sir, there are no traitors here, only souls wishing to talk with their Lord. I ask that you step outside if you don't wish to join our service."

Reverend Langford's eyes sought Captain Padgett's gaze, and the crippled leader was surprised at their unyielding intensity. Padgett blinked and studied his men to assess the correctness of their alignment before responding. His glance included a negative nod to Graham, who continued to study the minister.

"I'll do the ordering around here, preacher," Padgett said, not returning his eyes to Reverend Langford's continuing stare. "The man we want is Douglas Harper."

A woman's wild cry followed the announcement and a short, stocky man jumped to his feet in the middle of the assembled group. "What do ya be wantin' me fer, Padgett? I ain't dun nothin' to nobody. Jes' a man workin' hard to turn his land into somethin' fer his family." Two children beside their mother whimpered, and she tried to comfort them in spite of her own terror. Douglas Harper squeezed her outstretched hand and gently let it go.

Padgett's smile didn't reach his eyes. "Harper, you're under arrest for treason. You will be hanged. Take him, men. Shoot anyone who interferes with justice. Sergeant Limon, your patrol."

Immediately, a sergeant and five Regulator riflemen marched toward the standing Harper. In concert, the remaining militiamen pointed their guns arbitrarily at people throughout the church. Seated on the aisle of Harper's pew, a broad-shouldered man in an ill-fitting coat stood to stop the advancing Regulators. A rifle butt to his head dropped the well-intentioned neighbor and he flopped to the floor, a gash in his forehead blossoming blood.

Harper's mouth was a grim stripe across his white face. He hadn't moved, standing at attention in the middle of the pew and staring at the grinning Captain Padgett. Graham folded his arms and muttered something under his breath that made Padgett chuckle and say, "Not yet."

Realizing Harper wasn't coming his way, the sergeant shrugged his shoulders and began easing through the crowded plank to get to the former Confederate. He apologized to each couple as he moved past tucked-in knees and moved-aside legs. Behind him came his men, one at a time, like a line of awkward dancers.

When Sergeant Limon passed in front of Harper's wife, she grabbed for him and shoved the startled militiaman against the seated parishioners in front of them. His rifle clattered on the hard earthen floor. Overreacting to the impact, a woman screamed and fell forward. Her husband went to his knees to comfort her, not daring to look at the reason for the sudden violence against their backs.

Frantically, the sergeant clubbed the Harper woman with his forearm and elbow. Harper reached for the man to pull him away, landing an overhand haymaker that stunned him. Rifle-butt blows to Harper's rib cage and lower back from the closest Regulator stopped his attack before it was more than started. Harper grabbed for wind that wouldn't return and doubled over.

Now undeterred, Sergeant Limon pounded at Mrs. Harper's face and clawing hands. Her fierceness finally gave way to unconsciousness and she collapsed in front of her sobbing children. The rest of the Regulator patrol closed in, swearing at the seated parishioners to get out of their way, and yanked the stunned Harper to his wobbly feet. Captain Padgett barked at him to come peacefully or his family would be shot where they were. He glanced at Graham, and the gray-suited pistolfighter drew a pistol from his sash.

Harper's shoulders rose and fell. To his unconscious wife, he said, "I love you, Ellena." He stared at each child, fighting to hold back his own tears. "I love ya, Michael. I love ya, Rebecca." Sergeant Limon stepped between him and his children, who wanted to hug their father. The state policeman shoved both children back into the pew and turned around to Harper. The former Confederate's arms rose above his head at the sergeant's command, and they began to file out of the makeshift pew, passing seated neighbors who either wouldn't look at Harper or who muttered regrets with one eye on the Regulators.

William H. Giles, town mayor and owner of two area ranches and the town hotel, stood dramatically from the third pew. In his most mayoral tone, the bulldog-jawed Northerner from Indiana pronounced officiously, "Ladies and gentlemen, please. This is a house of worship, not a brawling establishment. Let the authorities do their job and then we can get on with . . . our worship . . . so ably conducted by Reverend Langford here."

The heavy-jowled man preferred being called "Colonel Giles" or just "Colonel." However, there was no record of his having served in the military on either side. In private, Aleta Langford usually referred to him as "Colonel Bulldog" and expressed a wariness of the man and his motives. The part-time minister took his wife's observations seriously; she had an uncanny sense about most people.

Turning toward the young minister, Mayor Giles nodded affirmatively. "I'm certain you agree, Reverend. The sooner we can return to our service, the better." White spittle settled in the corner of his month.

Reverend Langford's eyes flashed and he declared in a voice inches away from exploding, "Only if that service includes Mr. Harper."

Giles's expression blinked into pure hatred at the rebuff, then returned to its normal placid state. His long, sprawling eyebrows jumped with a life of their own as his faced churned with the decision about what to say next. He glanced at Padgett, then at Lion Graham. A gentle pull on his coat caused him to look down at his wife.

Dressed as if she were attending a New Orleans ball and wearing layers of makeup, the pudgy woman whispered to her husband, "Colonel, you can't let them take that nice Mister Harper. He's a good man. Tell those awful men to leave."

Giles gave a condescending smile. "Don't get involved in what you don't understand, Lillibeth."

Straightening his coat and vest to continue his plea for understanding, Giles was stunned to see Reverend Langford drop his hymnal and head toward the back of the church. Aleta's urgent plea for him to stay out of it went unheeded or unheard. Mary Taullery screamed. The new hymnal bounced off the floor and came to rest against one of the boxes supporting the closest plank. Widow Attles picked it up and held the leather-bound book to her chest, afraid to watch. Mayor Giles shrugged his shoulders, glanced again at Padgett, and sat down. His wife immediately began to talk, and he told her to be quiet as he watched.

Taullery started to rise, but his wife held his arm and loudly demanded that he stay where he was. Returning to his seat, Taullery couldn't keep his eyes off Lion Graham. But so far Graham was only watching, his drawn pistol at his side. Mary stage-whispered that Reverend Langford should stay out of it too. Spinning around, Aleta told her to mind her own business and finished with a flourish of Spanish no one understood.

"No! I will vouch for Douglas Harper. He's an innocent, law-abiding citizen. You can't do this!" Reverend Langford shouted as he ran toward the Regulators; his black robe floated behind him, turning him into a dark angel.

"Stay out of this, preacher—I won't warn you again." Padgett's threat was a machete in the still room.

Langford's wild advance surprised the six Regulators surrounding Harper, and they turned toward him too slowly. The minister slammed between the sergeant and Douglas Harper and said, "Take me, instead. I'm Rule Cordell. I've killed Union soldiers everywhere. Take me." He raised his hands above his head in surrender.

At the sound of the name "Rule Cordell," Lion David Graham turned his head slowly to the right and examined the minister again. Something resembling a smile flickered at his mouth and vanished. Sergeant Limon's eyebrows arched, and he looked at Padgett. The crippled leader's own face was stunned by the admission, then he broke into a wide smile and a wicked laugh. "Yeah, and I'm Robert E. Lee. Shoot the lyin' Bible-thumper. Rule Cordell's long dead an' rotted. Get on with it, men."

As Padgett's words sank into Sergeant Limon's mind, Langford's right fist drove savagely into the sergeant's face. Bones cracked and blood spewed onto the closest parishioners. An eyeblink later, Reverend Langford's vicious uppercut followed and drove the militiaman up and sideways into the lap of an older woman. She spat at his unseeing face and pushed his limp frame onto the floor.

Three other Regulators grabbed for the raging minister, driving the butts of their rifles into his head and shoulders as he swung wildly and missed. Two more grabbed him from the back and held his arms. His kick caught an advancing rifleman in the groin. Grabbing for the intense pain, the Regulator dropped to his knees and vomited. But the tallest Regulator landed a blow to Langford's unprotected stomach, then a second. Langford gagged, but managed to yank his right arm free and parry the third strike.

Screaming in Spanish, Aleta ran toward the fight, hurling herself at the nearest Regulator, who stood next to the darkened church wall. The man staggered backwards from the impact as her head barreled into his stomach. Breath popped from his lungs and he fought desperately to find the air necessary to live. Her fist clipped his chin, but he had recovered enough to stop her assault. Holding his rifle with both hands in front of him, he shoved the weapon against her face and slammed her against the wall of the church. Her head thudded against it and she slid unseeing to the floor. She didn't hear Mary Taullery say they should have stayed out of it.

Catching a glimpse of his wife's futile advance only enraged the fiery minister further. His fist freed, he drove it into the face of the leering, thin-faced Regulator who held his left arm and broke loose of the hold. Langford spun to receive the attack of the remaining militiamen. A pistol popped across the back of his skull. He staggered and collapsed in the lap of a farmer. He cried and patted the minister's head as blood began to crawl across the farmer's worn pants.

Barely conscious, Reverend Langford tried to stand, stumbling against another parishioner. His eyes were wild with pain. He took one spasmodic step and fell to the floor next to the bloodstained farmer. Taullery was suddenly beside Langford and held his friend down, not letting his little remaining strength and his unrelenting fury carry the fight further to his death.

Standing five feet away, Lion David Graham held a short-barreled revolver in each hand, hammers back, and aimed at the downed minister. Barely heard, he declared with an arrogant grin, "I knew you weren't dead. Remember, I killed you in another life. It is my destiny to do it it again."

Padgett waved the killer off with a nonchalant motion. "Smart man. You just saved your preacher's life."

Peering through his glasses at the crippled Regulator leader, Graham's eyes were cold and narrowed. Ignoring Padgett's motion, he glanced toward the third pew and saw Giles shaking his head negatively. Graham snorted, eased the hammers into place, and pushed the guns into his sash. He spun and left the church without looking back. Padgett laughed and followed his men as they dragged Harper out of the church. The door slammed shut behind the militiaman pushing Padgett's wheelchair, not quite cutting off Harper's choked cry of "Long live the Confederacy."

The following silence was broken by Mayor Giles's authoritative voice: "My friends, this has been a most unfortunate morning. Such things always are, to discover a neighbor is guilty of crimes against us all. Let us not leave this place in such a terrible state." He stood and slid through the crowded pew and walked to the front of the makeshift church. "Although I am unworthy, I will attempt to lead us in worship. Shall we try 'Let Us Gather at the River' again? I know it's one of your favorites, Mrs. Bauer."

Chapter Three

A warm breeze teased the hair on Reverend James Rule Langford's forehead, introduced a gentle dance to the rest of his face, and playfully wiggled the half-faded mirror above the nearby washstand. Suddenly, the wounded minister was awake. It was the morning of the third day since the attack in his church, the first time he was fully conscious. He was weak—and very, very hungry.

Sliding his bare feet over the side of the bed, he paused to let the glaze lift from his mind. He was naked except for a nightshirt and the medicine pouch around his neck. Dull pain in the back of his head reintroduced itself, and he touched that spot gingerly. A long welt lay under the tightly wrapped bandage. Crusts of dried blood along the soft cloth marked its passage. He winced and shook his head to clear it. But that only brought a dizziness, and he grabbed on to the bed to keep from floating away.

The stark room's lone window was open, allowing glittering jewels of morning sunlight to adorn the framed bed and the dark, scratched dresser with its white pitcher and bowl. A mud wasp joined the sunlight and entered through the window. Becoming entangled in the faded curtains, it angrily attacked the containment to no avail. A breeze flipped open the curtain's edge so the insect could again join the outside world.

Outside, streaks of violet, rose, and gold signaled the morning's completed arrival to his small adobe-and-timber home. The small ranch had been built by a Mexican vaquero killed in a saloon brawl; Rule Cordell and Aleta had bought it from his widow, who wanted to return to Mexico. It was Aleta's idea. Combined with a sturdy barn, a well-built corral, a windmill that consistently produced springwater, and close proximity to an expanding settlement, the place offered a perfect beginning for their new life together. She understood and nourished his need to preach, even though her preferences were inclined toward more practical decisions.

He wanted to give himself full-time to spreading the Word. But she told him that turning the other cheek wasn't very effective in these turbulent times. At least, she wasn't convinced of its ability to feed them—and the children they both wanted. She wished he would think of building a steady income of some kind. One night, she even suggested they rob a Yankee bank. After that, he had accepted the idea of preaching part-time while training and selling horses, and she would teach. In spite of an occasional Spanish word or phrase slipping into her instruction, the classroom was a natural environment for her.

He struggled with the dead sleep in his head. Remnants of dreams battled for control, mostly nightmares. A stern face returned to his mind, one that he had managed to close off for some time. His father, Reverend

Aaron Cordell, was a man who used the pulpit to justify the cruel and evil things he did as divine rights directly from God. The young minister's nightmare brought his self-righteous father back into his life, even though he hadn't seen him in more than a year. As far as he knew, Reverend Cordell continued to dominate churchgoers in Waco, a five-day ride to the northeast. The younger Cordell didn't plan on seeing him again. Ever.

In his dreams, just before waking, he felt again the savage slaps across his young face as a boy and felt the layered welts from a leather strap. He saw again the cruel man punish his wife, the boy's mother, for some imagined offense. He saw again his own father trying to kill him as Rule Cordell tried to break his friend, Ian Taullery, from a Waco jail, a confinement owing to the fact that Taullery had come home with some money after the War—and Reverend Aaron Cordell's accusation that Taullery knew his son and, therefore, must be a part of the Johnny Cat Carlson outlaw gang.

How ironic it was that Rule Cordell would follow in his father's footsteps, at least in the sense that he became a minister. Only he was a minister more closely resembling Moon, the aging Comanche shaman, than anything like his tyrannical father. In many ways, his single day with the old man in the Comanche camp had affected him far more than a young lifetime with his father. But that was in 1862, on the way to battle, and he was a far different man, carrying the hate of his father within him all the way to Virginia and back.

So often, the words of Moon became words in his sermons, words about caring for others, looking for miracles in everyday things, and that God was everywhere and in everything. It certainly wasn't the usual doctrine of the plains preacher—no fire and brimstone, no righteous wrath. His growing faithful loved his comforting way of preaching. Of course, his ministry was only a

Sunday thing; his everyday job was producing quality horses on their small ranch—although finding buyers with money was difficult, unless they were Yankees.

Rule Cordell had presented the old shaman with a Bible that had been a gift from his mother and prayed the Lord's Prayer, the only thing he could think of at the time. It had been the old man's dying wish that Cordell talk with the white man's God so that he might enter the next world with all the spirits at his side. He had looked into the future and it did not bode well for the Comanche, and he feared Comanche spirits were therefore growing weak.

Moon had given him a stone earring and a small medicine pouch with a leather neck thong. The small pebble was a piece of Mother Moon to protect him in battle; he no longer wore it, but Aleta had packed the spirit tribute away in a small box. In the bundle was the medicine of the owl, the shaman's personal messenger to the spirits. The tiny leather pouch, discolored by the sweat of years, lay quietly on his chest even now. He never figured out how the dying Comanche knew his father was a minister—and an evil one—but he did. His fingers touched the pouch. "It is a morning of miracles, Moon," he muttered, and smiled.

Sometimes he felt Moon's spirit was close. It was easy to imagine that a shadow was more than darkness. His Comanche friends knew both were so. Since his rebirth as a minister, Cordell had spent considerable time learning their approach to life. It was his way to pay Moon for making him think and change. He loved the fact that they called themselves *Noomah*; it meant "The Real People" or "True Humans."

It was also a way to move on. Rule Cordell was dead, or so the newspapers said. He was James Rule Langford, a different man with a different calling. A miracle of resurrection, Moon would have told him, just like a dead warrior returning. Whatever. He was a man of God, not a man of the gun. A man of good horses, not of fierce violence.

Of course, the young minister had no organized theological training, nor claimed any. Instead, he explained that he had studied privately and had been ordained a minister several years earlier. He never said where, exactly. If pushed, he might have said, "By God, just outside of Waco, while on my knees praying." But no one asked. Directly. Taullery had planted most of the misinformation about his background, including the idea that his ordination had been in Houston. It didn't really matter. Cordell's command of the Bible and worship services in general had long since dispelled any concern about his calling to preach.

His mind gradually recalled a more recent happening, one that seemed unbelievable as the memory of it passed through his consciousness. He was certain that yesterday he was in church. *Aleta? Aleta was hurt! And Douglas Harper? Oh my God, they took him. What . . .*

He jumped to his feet, and the throbbing pain brought him to his knees. A trembling hand pushed against the side of the bed, and he stood again. Long, deep breaths sought to regain control of his body, driving the weakness into the shadows of his mind. Soft noises were coming from the main room of the log-framed house. From where he stood, he could see the banked stone fireplace and the southern edge of kitchen shelves.

"Aleta?"

No answer. His memory raced to the church to determine how badly hurt she had been, fearing what he might find. But all he could recall was a frantic battle against too many Regulators. *If only I had a gun.* The thought sped through his mind faster than a bullet and slammed itself against his conscience. *Forgive me, Lord, I didn't mean that.*

"Good morning, preacher. Thought you were going to sleep all the way to next Sunday." Around the corner came a smiling Ian Taullery with cups of steaming coffee in both fists. "How are you feeling, Rule?"

As usual, Taullery was dressed nattily in a three-piece suit with a fresh collar and carefully tied cravat. A gold stickpin was centered exactly three inches above the V in his vest—where it always was. Cordell couldn't remember when his friend wasn't obsessed with detail, especially when it came to figuring out how to get something he wanted. Yet when they were together, it was like nothing had changed since childhood. They were simply best friends, Ian Taullery and Rule Cordell—not storekeeper and part-time minister with a phony name.

"Good to see you, too, Ian." Cordell accepted the mug and sipped its hot contents, but his mind was on Aleta. "Where's Aleta? Hey, that's good. Who made it?"

"Well, who do you think? I made it. Mighty tasty, I'd say. Although I like to grind the beans a bit more than Aleta does." Taullery chuckled at his own presentation. "Aleta's doin' fine. Got conked on the head real good—but came around pretty quick. You, on the other hand . . ."

"Where is she?"

Taullery sipped some of his own coffee. He rolled the hot liquid around in his mouth before swallowing. A frown collected on his forehead, and his eyes found refuge at the window. "She's at the school. Mary went with her. After school, the plans are to be . . . with Missus Harper. All of us are, if you're up to it." He swallowed the coffee and coughed. "They have to get off their land today. Taxes are due. Regulators are comin' at noon. Haven't heard who the new owner is. Some carpetbagger, I'm sure. You know, that's good land."

Cordell stared at his friend as the meaning of the answer fully sank into him. "They hanged Douglas." It wasn't a question.

"Big as you please. Strung him up . . . at the old cottonwood by the creek. Soon as they left the church. Padgett had one of his boys play 'Dixie' on a harmonica while they all watched—an' laughed. That killer, Lion Graham, he shot Harper's brother when he came to help. Shot him in the heart four times from thirty feet. Only one man I've ever known could handle a pistol like that."

"That man is dead."

Taullery's face reddened and his eyes narrowed. He was not the fierce warrior that his friend, Rule Cordell, had been. Few were. But his passion for the South ran just as deep—at least, his vision of what it was and should be. Wetness gathered at the corners of his eyes, and he wiped them brusquely with his free hand and tried to return himself to a controlled manner. Everything Ian Taullery did was careful.

Even the simple task of lighting a cigar or eating an apple became a complete ceremony. It didn't matter what it was—apple, cigar, or battle—Ian Taullery rarely did anything without thinking through all the steps first. He liked knowing what he was doing before he did it. That wasn't an excuse for not taking action, just a detailed map to follow to the letter. Cordell teased him that he must have written out what he was going to do on his wedding night. Taullery's reply was "only a few notes," followed by a big smile.

His general store in town was already known for carefully displayed merchandise. Actually, just having merchandise was something of a miracle in this ravished country. But that talent had blossomed as the other scouts increasingly depended on him to find food, horses, and bullets. He was known to follow customers around, straightening canned goods and refolding cloth as they shopped. A customer's pause at a can of peaches could yield a thorough assessment of the contents—usually with an enthusiastic description of how it tasted and ranked with similar foods.

Taullery was still thinking about the hanging when Cordell asked where the Harper family would be going. Cordell asked again, this time staring at his coffee: "Where will the Harpers be staying?"

"Huh? Oh, Widow Bauer invited them to stay—as long as they wanted. I think she's lonely. So it worked out. Sort of. She's a real Yankee hater, you know. Says she gets up early just so she can have more time to hate 'em. Quite a lady." Bitterness laced his words, and the laugh that followed was forced.

"What about Douglas's . . . funeral? Did you . . ."

"Well, we buried both him an' his brother—in the town cemetery. No service, though. Figured you could do it when you were up an' around again. That's the way . . . widow Harper wanted it. Virgil Harper didn't have any family—except his brother's."

"About all I'm good for—saying words over the graves of friends." Cordell's chest rose and fell. Fierceness fought for control of his mind.

"The South lost, Rule. We said states had the right to secede; they said no. They won. We're paying for that." Taullery walked to the window and looked out. "Even the mayor is a scalawag—an' the sheriff too. Think on it, Rule. All the way down to li'l old Clark Springs. Yankees control it all. No way any of us are going to get to vote. Or have much of anything. Unless we play smart."

"I never thought it would be this bad. Guess I never thought we'd lose."

"Hard to imagine anything worse. Even your Bible's hell," Taullery said, glancing back at Cordell. "Sorry, didn't mean it that way."

"Man, I forgot about the horses. I—"

"Don't worry. They've been grained, watered, and brushed down," Taullery interrupted. "Aleta and Mary helped me. Say, how's that little brown gelding coming for Mary? She fed him this morning. Thought he looked real cute. But you know if that damn horse so much as hiccups, she'll be complaining for months."

Cordell studied his feet for a moment before answering. His head seemed to be full of disconnected thoughts. "Aleta rode the brown to school all last week. I wanted to make sure it was used to a lady early on. I've seen gentle horses go crazy when a woman gets on them—if they've never been around one before."

"And?"

Cordell chuckled. "Aleta liked the way he handled."

"Well, that's good."

"Not really. Aleta likes fiery horses. You ever ride her paint?"

"No, I guess I haven't." Taullery rubbed his chin. "What are we going to do?"

Cordell looked around. "Where are my pants?"

Taullery pointed in the direction of the chair and asked if his friend was changing the subject. Cordell said he planned to start looking for a mount for Mary after he delivered four head promised to Jacob Evans, a nearby rancher. Taullery laughed and said the rancher wouldn't be able to pay him, except in eggs or something.

"I owe Jacob. He and his boys came over and helped me reroof the barn and fix up the corral when we bought this place. Figured it was the least I could do to repay him," Cordell said, slipping into his pants.

"Four good horses for a little roof repair? That's pretty good pay."

"Without the Evanses' help, we wouldn't be where we are today."

Taullery licked his lower lip and changed the subject. "Man, I like that roan stallion. Where'd he come from?"

"Traded some guns for him. Caleb Shank—you know, 'The Russian'—came by two weeks ago, trailing that big rascal behind his cart. Had papers. He traded a rug and a few pots for it."

"Can he run?"

"Like a Texas storm." Cordell pulled off his nightshirt and poured water in the washstand bowl. "But he's quieter than you'd think. Doesn't act like a bull. Even good around my geldings. Been thinking about breeding him with Aleta's paint mare. Wouldn't that be a colt to have!"

"Reminds me of that big-shouldered roan Billy Rip had . . . when we were in Virginia. Near the end."

"Yeah, I suppose so. Say, that reminds me, have you heard anything from Billy Rip recently? Or Whisper?"

Billy Ripton—or "Billy Rip," as his friends called him—and Whisper Jenson were two of their Rebel friends from the War. The four cavalry scouts had managed to stop a Union division from successfully attacking Longstreet's unsuspecting flank with a ruse of a phantom Confederate army that was still talked about in Rebel circles.

"Not since that letter from Whisper a while back. You know, the one about the Riptons thinking about driving longhorns to where they'd be worth real money. Twenty dollars a head, Whisper said. Crazy talk, just plain crazy." Taullery turned away from the window.

"Maybe not, Ian. I read where Charlie Goodnight and Oliver Loving drove a herd of longhorns all the way to Fort. Sumner over in New Mexico Territory," Cordell responded. "You know, there's been talk of a drive all the way to Abilene, Kansas."

"Yeah, where maybe there's a railroad—and maybe there isn't."

Cordell smiled. He wasn't in the mood to argue.

Taullery's grin was immediate. "How about some breakfast? I'll get it going while you get dressed."

"Best offer I've had today."

"Best you'll get, too."

Taullery's attention was drawn to a dark corner of the room, away from even the most daring sunlight. There, a handmade, waist-high Mexican cabinet, accented with hand-carved flowers, had been turned into a strange display of guns. The sight surprised him, and he swallowed to keep his surprise from appearing on his face. Even to the casual eye, the placement of pistols and rifles was a measured one, almost ceremonial.

On its clawed top, rubbed raw by a half-century of use, lay seven .44 revolvers of mixed origin. Resting on the guns was a Bible. Two were settled in holsters with their belts snugly wrapped around them. Two more were short-barreled, positioned with their noses facing each other. Another brace of guns were silver-plated and pearl-handled. He guessed these were Aleta's; he couldn't imagine his friend using such fancy revolvers.

Propped alongside the seventh, a five-shot Dean & Adams pistol, was a dried rose and a lone rose stem without petals. He recognized them immediately as reminders of the Confederacy and their leader, Jeb Stuart, who liked to wear a rose on his uniform. The rose had also been a trademark of the outlaw Rule Cordell, worn in Stuart's honor. The stem was all that was left from the flower given to him by Stuart's widow at his funeral. Stacked on each side of the cabinet were two Henry carbines. His curiosity badly wanted an explanation about it—and why his friend had risked everything by yelling out his real identity at the church—but something told him not to question his friend about it. At least, not now.

Chapter Four

With a casual "Breakfast will be ready when you are" salutation, Taullery left the bedroom, glancing again at the display as he left Cordell to his toilet and his memories. Billy Ripton and his family had cared for him at their ranch outside of Waco after Cordell's father had shot him during the jail break. "Billy Rip" wasn't yet twenty, having joined the Rebel forces while barely in his teens. Like his father and older brothers, he was husky and strong, but his ways with horses were gentle and that had made him an immediate favorite of both Taullery and Cordell. So far, Riptons had avoided any problems with the Northerners in charge of Texas.

On the other hand, Whisper Jenson was in the thick of the political foray, battling the carpetbaggers and scalawags with his exceptional legal skills. A successful lawyer before the War, Cordell liked him for his hard questioning manner, a style that usually forced better decisions—even if it did embarrass a few foolish officers along the way, or a few Northern bureaucrats.

His raspy voice was the result of a Yankee rifle bullet early in the conflict, and now even his family called him "Whisper" instead of his real name, "Franklin David." At the "mascarade ambush" near the bitter end, he had been severely wounded and lost an arm to amputation. The doctor who did it almost lost his life to an angry Cordell.

Since most of the courts were military tribunals and held little resemblance to courts of law, Jenson's effectiveness was greatly limited. Still, he had already saved a few homesteads from the grasp of unscrupulous bankers and gained the wrath of the men in control. There was a happy tale of Whisper spitting tobacco juice in the face of a government witness who kept lying under oath. Whisper's aim had been a source of wonderment during the Conflict. Taullery often compared Whisper's spitting with Cordell's pistol shooting, and joked that if tobacco juice were gunpowder his friend might have a problem.

If any of the former Rebel soldiers could have voted, Jenson would have been elected almost anything he wanted to run for in the area—even if his brand of oratory was little more than hoarse statements. But the "ironclad oath" required of every voter—that he had not willingly borne arms against the United States of America—omitted most white males, except the very old, from the decision-making process.

Finished with his shaving, Cordell walked toward the gun display that had attracted Taullery earlier. He paused there, and his fingers touched first one gun, then another, then the dried rose, like a bird not daring to light. Finally, his hand reached the Bible and stayed. This had been a daily routine since both he and Aleta had turned away from the outlaw trail. They decided to keep their weapons where they could see them as a reminder of their commitment.

Without saying so, Rule knew that Aleta's decision was based more on the eventuality of needing them again quickly than on any thought of peace through disarmament. That was all right. His decision was anchored to his determination to change. Each day, Rule made a commitment to himself and to God to follow His will and leave violence behind. He never cleaned the weapons, but he knew Aleta did. He smiled to himself, remembering how smitten he had been by this beautiful she-wolf from the very first time he saw her.

His cheeks still stinging from the straight razor's application, Cordell entered the main part of the house, encouraged by the smells of frying salt pork, potatoes and onions, eggs, coffee, and tortillas. Sunlight from the lone kitchen window awaited like a proud conquistador. Freshly made blackberry jam was already on the planked table, along with stoneware plates and heavy iron utensils.

"Man, that smells great! I could eat a horse," Cordell said, rubbing his hands together enthusiastically.

"Not one of yours, I presume. I don't think that roan stallion would let you."

Cordell laughed. His simple black broadcloth suit with the full black vest and white collar was a bit crumpled. Around his neck dangled the familiar silver cross on a leather cord, but Taullery noticed the slight bulge slightly above it and knew the significance. This was the outfit Cordell always wore when traveling on ministry concerns. He liked its stark simplicity. The white bandage surrounding his forehead seemed out of place.

"Well, I can't take too much credit. Aleta made the tortillas before she left. Oh, she also told me to tell you—she loves you," Taullery responded with a lopsided grin. His eyes glanced at Cordell before returning to the two skillets resting on the orange bed of coals in the fireplace.

Cordell returned the grin with only a slight blush reaching his face. He went to the coffeepot and repoured his cup. Aleta was his life, and he missed her fiercely already. Just having her beside him made everything seem right in a land that was harrowed with retribution and harvested hopelessness. Inside he was attacked by a gush of guilt over the hanging of Douglas Harper. Why hadn't he been able to stop it? A sadness seeped into his thoughts, dragging a malaise of spirit that wouldn't go away. He was a minister, a man of God now, a calling he knew was right. Why couldn't he shake off this awful sense of being . . . useless.

"Brought the potatoes and onions from the store. Thought they might taste good to you," Taullery said, shoving an iron spatula under the tantalizing mixture of sliced potatoes and onions. "Eggs came from your chickens in back. Took me a while to find the best ones." He chuckled.

"I'm sure you got them, though."

Taullery glanced back at his friend and asked the question that had been boiling inside him since Sunday. "Rule, why in the world did you shout out your name to Padgett? Lion Graham studied you hard. He had to recognize—"

"I thought it might save Harper's life," Cordell interrupted.

"Well, I'm damn glad Padgett thought you were making it up. Graham was going to kill you, Rule. He was angry as hell when Padgett wouldn't let him."

"I doubt Lion recognized me, Ian. We were just kids when his folks moved away."

"We knew him."

"Of course we did." Cordell sipped the coffee and realized it was too hot to continue. "He's well known. He wasn't expecting to see me—or you." He blew on the black liquid.

"Well, Rule Cordell is a helluva lot better known than Lion David Graham." Taullery flipped over the potatoes and examined them to make sure none were burned.

"Rule Cordell is dead."

"Come on, Rule, aren't you worried about him telling people?"

"Who's going to believe him?"

The discussion wandered backward to childhood adventures and those that included Graham before his family moved to Ohio. Taullery remembered him as always crying about something and always wanting to do whatever Cordell was doing, or be the character Cordell was pretending to be in their make-believe game. He recalled them teasing Graham about his unusual name, Lion, and calling him "Growl" and "Bobcat."

"Remember when we played like we were Roman soldiers? Down by that old creek? There was a whole bunch of us. You, me, Lion, Jimmy Watkins . . . ah, what was his name—oh yeah, Howard Green." Taullery tasted the potatoes and decided to add pepper. "We all took those long creek canes with the sharp roots for spears—and had branches for swords. Man, we played war for days."

"Yeah, I remember you worked on a branch sword every night—to get it just right."

Cordell smiled and tried his coffee again. It was good, and he swallowed eagerly. Dipping his finger in the liquid, he drew a spear on the table with the wetness. What was it about Lion David Graham that bothered him? Was it really that the gun professional suspected who he was? No, it was something he hadn't experienced often.

It was fear. A fear he didn't feel about Captain Padgett. That was only frustrated anger.

Graham had gunned down Luke Robbins in a fair fight, and Robbins was as good with a gun as anyone in Texas. There were fourteen other known killings attributed to Graham. Down deep, was he afraid to face this bespectacled killer? Or was it that he felt the man was going to pull him back to his old life as a gunfighter? Or was it that the evil man reminded him of his own father in some strange way? Or was it all three?

"When I ran into him—in town—a week or so ago, all he could talk about was you." Taullery spread the pepper with his fingers from a canister. "Kept asking me if I really thought you were dead."

"You saw him? When was that? You didn't mention it before." Cordell looked up from his table drawing.

Taullery's face tightened. "Sure I did. You were probably thinking about that roan, or next week's sermon, instead of listening to me."

"Yeah, probably."

"Anyway, Graham talked about that Roman soldier stuff. Only, he sounded like he thought it was real. Said something about killing you—when you were both Roman soldiers. Said it was . . . his, ah, fate . . . to do it again," Taullery said, and waited for a response.

None came, and he returned to cooking, knowing his friend had no intention of discussing the matter further.

"Did you notice the mayor and his wife were in your church Sunday?" Taullery said as he pushed the steaming potatoes and onions onto two plates. "Or did that knock on your head push away all the good stuff like that?"

"How I could I miss him? He practically invited Padgett to hang Harper."

Taullery bristled without turning around. "That's not

the way I saw it, Rule. Giles was doing the smart thing, keeping people from—"

"From protecting Harper?" Cordell interrupted.

"Oh come on, Rule. Mayor Giles, he's an important man around here—and he's going to be even bigger."

"I'm sure he would agree with you."

"What's that mean?" This time Taullery turned toward Cordell.

"Don't overcook my eggs. I like 'em runny." Cordell's eyes twinkled.

Taullery's smile was slow, but it came. "Hey, Rule, I was serious. Giles is a man who can help you—and me."

"I'm sure you're right, Ian. Let's eat."

Talk during breakfast ranged from a former wealthy rancher who was working as a crew hand repairing one of the many dismantled railroads strewn about the South . . . to the thousands of freed slaves traveling across the land in search of something, anything . . . to the constant worry that debt would swallow the entire South . . . to speculation about the money Charlie Goodnight and Oliver Loving made from driving a herd of longhorns all the way to Fort Sumner in New Mexico Territory. There was talk of a drive all the way to Abilene or Baxter Springs, Kansas, where the railroad was supposed to be. Taullery was mostly concerned about his own store and the need to start turning down requests for food without some form of payment.

"Last week, Issac Roark came in with a big sack full of old bullets and scrap metal. Picked them out of his land when he was plowing. Wanted to trade for some canned goods." Taullery rubbed his hands together and studied the interaction before continuing. "I agreed. Don't have the faintest idea of what I'm going to do with that sack, though."

"Yeah, that's tough. Any more blacks bring in things

to trade?" Cordell asked between mouthfuls of potatoes and onions.

"Every week some Negro is at my door with something. I don't know why they keep coming to me. I'm sure most of it's stolen. I don't want to do business with 'em. Ignorant black bastards should know their place."

Cordell didn't respond—partly because his mouth was full and partly because he was remembering something. Swallowing the last of the potatoes, he told his friend about a black newspaper he'd read that was filled with requests by former slaves trying to find lost loved ones. It grieved him to think of their anguish, and he wondered what they could do to help. Taullery warned him that he should be careful about his sermons concerning the treatment of blacks and the sin of slavery. Cordell reminded him that he had fought for the South but that didn't mean he supported slavery. He hated the whole idea of it—but he thought a state had a right to decide what it wanted to do.

Taullery knew better than to press the matter further; his friend might wear a collar of the ministry on Sundays now, but he used to be one of the most dangerous pistol-fighters in Texas and, before that, a daring Confederate cavalry officer. The storekeeper tried hard to push that old image of his friend away, but every time he saw Reverend James Rule Langford, he always first saw the intense Confederate warrior Rule Cordell.

He saw a wild man with four or five revolvers shoved into his belt. A chiseled face hardened by war, winter, and starvation. Dark eyes that cut into a man's soul peered from under a wide-brimmed cavalry hat with an eagle feather instead of a cavalry plume. Long dark hair brushed along his strong shoulders, barely hiding a Comanche stone earring.

But the thing that said the most about his friend was the dried stem of a rose, pinned to his uniform collar. A tribute to General Stuart, the dramatic cavalry officer who liked to wear a red rose on his jacket. At his funeral, Stuart's widow gave a rose to Cordell and several others. Rule Cordell never took his off, even after it became nothing more than a shriveled stick. Taullery's mind tiptoed back to the dried rose lying on the altar of guns in Rule's bedroom. His thoughts stayed there to wonder.

Taullery was brought back to the kitchen table by Cordell's harsh observation that Harper was the third former Confederate soldier hanged and his lands taken in the past month. Taullery agreed that Padgett and his men were getting ever bolder, pretext for their actions becoming nothing more than a dare to be stopped. Cordell said he heard that things were worse in Atlanta, Richmond, Mobile, and other Southern cities to the east. They lay in absolute ruins. He stood and went to the fireplace to prepare a second helping of eggs and potatoes.

Taullery watched his friend and said, "You know, the papers are full of stories about secret bands of Texans going after all these Yanks—and Negroes too. 'Knights of the Rising Sun,' they call themselves." He took a sip of coffee, waiting for a response from Cordell. Not getting one, he continued, "Got 'em all over the South, you know. Secret bands an' all. Started in Tennessee right after Lee's surrender, they tell me. Some got a real strange name. Ku Klux Klan. Fancy sounding, I suppose. Don't know what that means. Latin, I guess. All kinds of secret rituals and rules, like a college fraternity, you know. Hear tell they're forming one around here, too. Long overdue, I'd say."

He stared at his friend, but Cordell didn't comment as he returned to the table, concentrating instead on adding a spoonful of blackberry jam to a tortilla.

"Heard anything about a pardon for Marse Robert or

Jeff Davis?" Cordell's question came just before he bit into the rolled tortilla. He studied the end to make sure the jam didn't escape out the end, then decided it would be safer to fold the edge into a flap.

Realizing that Cordell didn't want to talk about the Knights of the Rising Sun, Taullery wanted to ask if there had been any news about a pardon for them—and all the others who fought for the Confederacy. Instead, he decided to say only that he hadn't heard anything new about either Robert E. Lee or Jefferson Davis. Davis had been released on bail and promised a speedy trial for treason. But so far nothing had happened. He reminded his friend that Union generals had stepped in to keep Lee from further Federal harassment. Cordell wondered what would have happened to Jeb Stuart if he had lived.

"They hate us, you know. Them damn Yanks. They'd like us all dead so they can give over everything—to the Negroes." Taullery put down his fork on a cleaned plate and swallowed the rest of his coffee. He stared at the plate, then rearranged the utensils.

Cordell finished his tortilla and wiped his chin with the back of his hand. "It's way past time for the blacks to have their own, Ian. I didn't fight for slavery. I thought we had the right to be our own country. We were—for a while. Now we're not. Maybe we were on the wrong side, ever think about that? All men are the same under God. Maybe that's why the North won."

"Don't give me that crap. The North won because they had more guns, more supplies and more men, that's all. Besides, I have to deal with those ignorant Negroes all the time, and you don't. They were better off as slaves. I fought for the Stars and Bars, an' I'm damn proud of it." Taullery straightened the fork twice more before he was satisfied.

Cordell shook his head and bit his lower lip. Sensing

a need to change subjects, Taullery said he read where the North was blossoming with industrial growth and railroads were springing up everywhere. The words were a snarl.

A knock at the door interrupted their conversation.

"Wonder who that is?" Cordell asked.

"Probably some poor soul in need of saving," Taullery teased.

Cordell frowned at his friend's remark and stood slowly. At the door was a black man.

Chapter Five

Swinging open the door, Cordell smiled broadly and put out his hand. "Jacob Henry Eliason, it's been too long. Come in, Suitcase. Come in."

"Thank ya, Reverend Langford. It's mighty good to see ya too. How's the sweet missus? She sure be a sight for these old eyes." Jacob Henry "Suitcase" Eliason stepped inside and extended his open right hand, keeping the hat in his left at his side.

Nearly bald with a full, graying beard, he was about Cordell's height, wearing a navy blue three-piece suit with a gray silk cravat. A gold chain crossed his vest. His matching hat was in his hands. Behind him was a black buggy pulled by two gray mules. In the back seat was a large leather suitcase, heavily marked and scratched from much wear. Friends knew Eliason kept his legal papers there, close at hand, as well as clothes. A double-barreled shotgun rested within easy reach when he drove.

Cordell shook Eliason's hand enthusiastically and asked, "Had any breakfast? Ian and I are just sittin' down at the table. Got some of Aleta's good tortillas. Plenty of eggs and potatoes. Jam, too."

"Already broke the fast, but I'd sur 'nuff have some of that coffee. Smells fine."

"Hey, Ian, guess what? Jacob's here."

From around the corner came a friendly greeting. "Suitcase, you old rascal! What business have you bought today?"

"Hey, Ian, how's that store doin' these days?"

"Just fair, Suitcase. Hard to find folks with any cash money."

Jacob Henry Eliason was one of the more fortunate former slaves. As a teenager, he had escaped from a Texas ranch on the underground railway and been educated by a sympathetic white family and later graduated from Knox College in Illinois. After the War, he returned to Texas and shrewdly began buying bankrupt businesses and turning them into successful enterprises. He was well connected with Northern bureacrats who liked to point to him as an example of how well a freed slave could do.

Eliason's true feelings about the carpetbaggers were kept to himself—or, occasionally, to friends like Cordell and Taullery. He despised their interference in Texas but had no illusions about how it could help him. He had done a good job of cultivating the Northern controllers, and it was paying off with opportunities like these.

His nickname, Suitcase, had stuck with him because he apparently had no place of residence, even though he was wealthy enough to buy most any home in Texas. He preferred to sleep at one of his businesses and carry his few belongings, and all of his legal papers, with him. No one was certain where he kept his money, and it was well known he was handy with a gun and a knife.

"You menfolk dun run off all your pretty ladies?"

Cordell chuckled. "Not if we're lucky. Aleta and Mary are at the school, then they're going to be with the Harper woman. You heard . . ."

"Yessuh, I did. Awful, Reverend. Lord a' Mercy, what's gonna happen to us all?"

"I wish I knew the answer to that. All I know is God has a plan."

"Sur do wish the ol' boy would up an' let us in on it." Eliason's eyes twinkled, and he patted Cordell's shoulder. Cordell laughed.

Cordell and Eliason entered the small kitchen, and Taullery offered the black man a hot cup of coffee and asked again about having some breakfast. Eliason enthusiastically received the coffee but again declined eating. Cordell went directly to the counter, retrieved the plate of tortillas, and brought them to the sitting Eliason. He smiled and said, "Well now, I bin eyein' that jam—an' I do think it would be a mighty fine thing to taste."

"Please do," Cordell said. "Think I'll have one."

"That'll be three already, Rule," Taullery said with a grin.

"Who's counting?" Cordell answered, and dipped his spoon into the jam jar after Eliason finished filling his tortilla.

When the black businessman leaned forward to take a bite of his rolled treat, sunlight twinkled off the silver-plated, pearl-handled revolver carried in a shoulder holster. He also carried two derringers, one in each vest pocket. His lean frame and gentle manner belied a man who could handle himself well in a dangerous situation, whether political or physical. Rumors said he had killed three men in self-defense. Taullery thought the black man had likely started the story himself, just to add a threatening dimension to his presence for the sake of protection.

Conversation resumed easily among the three men, mostly about a small boot-making company Eliason had bought from the county for back taxes and was trying to get reopened. Eliason, Cordell, and Taullery had been friends for more than a year, a friendship that began after Cordell stopped eight Rebels from hanging a black man because he was riding a mule. He followed that with a sermon about black people being God's children, equal in his sight, and deserving of help in finding jobs and getting educated—a sermon that cost him some churchgoers.

"Heard a bunch of Negroes took over a ranch way north of here," Taullery said, avoiding Cordell's frown. "Word is they just up an' marched into the big house—and told the white folks there to get out."

"Yeah, I heard that too." Eliason sipped the coffee and shook his head with pleasure. "My, my, your lady can sure make fine jam, Reverend."

Cordell smiled at Eliason's smooth dismissal of Taullery's racial concern, thanked him for the compliment, and asked, "How's the new boot factory coming?"

"Pretty good. Hired back some folks that used to work there. Really know how to make good boots. Got real pride in it. I like that. Yes sir, I do."

"White folks?" Taullery's question had an edge.

Eliason's wide smile pushed his cheeks as if something inside his mouth extended them. "Well, yes, Mister Taullery. They be the only folks that know how to make boots." He paused and added, "For now."

Cordell glanced at Taullery and frowned again. The storekeeper wanted to ask more questions concerning the changing labor situation but decided against it. He and Cordell had disagreed on the subject of slavery long before the War. Taullery thought the condition had a proper place in the social and economic way of things, although he didn't condone mistreatment of slaves. Cordell had hated the very thought of one man presuming to own another from the time he understood the situation. His fight for the South had been to defend its right to leave the Union—and a love of battle, even though he would never have admitted it. If he was honest with himself, it was also a way to strike back at his evil father without actually doing so.

Eyeing the young minister carefully, Eliason put down his coffee cup and said, "I came to ask a favor. A big one, Reverend."

"I'm not preaching about boots." Cordell's smile stretched across his tanned face and he rose to get more coffee. "What do you need?"

"Would you and the missus find it in your hearts to teach schoolin' to some black kids over in the next county?" Eliason ran his fingers along the edge of the saucer. "I can pay. Cash money."

Taullery coughed to hide his surprise, but Cordell merely turned and refilled their cups before answering. "I thought the Freedman's Bureau was running schools for black children."

"Yes sir, they be doin' that. 'Cept some white folks ran off the last three teachers." Eliason nodded his thanks for the coffee.

"I'm not a teacher, Suitcase."

"Nobody's gonna run you off. I'll start with that."

Taullery wondered if Eliason knew who his minister friend actually was, but that wasn't his question to ask. He added a spoonful of sugar to his own coffee and stirred it twelve times, counting to himself, and was careful not to connect with Cordell's gaze.

"Suitcase, we'd be happy to help. But Aleta's got her regular school every day. You need her more than you need me. She's a good teacher."

"I know all of that. How about three nights a week?" Eliason continued. "Would ten dollars a week be fair?"

Aleta Langford conducted a school for white children to help provide for their income. Ten dollars a month for five months of the year; the children were needed on their parents' land the rest of the time. The school itself was actually a converted chicken coop. But she enjoyed teaching as much as he did preaching, although her Spanish accent occasionally caused confusion among the students.

"I'll have to ask Aleta, but it sounds fine to me if she agrees."

"Oh my, that's sweet music to this black man's ears," Eliason said, and added, "You know, most of my people don't even know what money is. They haven't eaten with forks and spoons. Haven't bought a railroad ticket or just walked through a town. The government may say they're free—but ignorance be a worse master than one with chains and a whip."

Cordell nodded agreement. His dark eyes flickered and his mouth was a line of intensity.

Eliason drew an imaginary line on the table with his dark finger. "At least most around here are getting paid to work—or gettin' a share of the crop. That's a start. But them Yanks are swarmin' around, gettin' into their pockets every which way. All the time smilin' and sayin' they want to help 'em. The bastards."

Taullery tried to hide his discomfort at Cordell accepting the black school job. It wouldn't sit well with most of the white people in town, and especially not his parish. He also knew it was useless to bring up those objections to Cordell; they would only serve to make him more determined.

Discussion about the schooling continued between Eliason and Cordell, with decisions made to start next week and to hold it at the boot-making plant. Eliason would take care of getting the word out and insisted on paying Cordell in gold for books and supplies for all the children. Talk wandered to the subject of food, and Eliason volunteered that the Freedman's Bureau was doing the best they could with rations to blacks and some whites, too. He said he planned to offer supper as an incentive to attend the schooling.

After an hour, Eliason excused himself and left, but not before leaving two gold pieces on the table. For nearly ten minutes, neither Cordell nor Taullery spoke after watching the black man drive off, waving as he did. Both knew what the other was thinking, and it didn't need further conversation: Taullery was worried about what the town would think, and Cordell was worried about the black children.

Their friendship had begun as children. Taullery was two years older and knew well the bitter agony his younger friend had endured with his maniacal minister father. Once, he stole his father's shotgun with every intention of shooting Reverend Aaron Cordell after he beat his seven-year-old son bloody. The beating, one of many, came with a liberal dose of Bible quotations and wild ranting. Cordell kept Taullery from using the gun.

When Cordell was ten, it was again Taullery who helped him get over the sudden death of a young colt. Discovering that the animal was dead, Rule asked his father why God had taken Blackie. Reverend Cordell screamed that the question was blasphemy and slapped the boy into the side of the stall. He stood over the crying child and roared a Bible verse that made no sense and left, leaving young Rule Cordell to believe that the colt's death was his fault. Taullery told him about a colt of theirs that had similarly died and finally convinced him that he wasn't to blame.

Taullery also comforted Cordell after the youngster learned that his mother had run off with a farmer. His weeping was uncontrollable, much as it had been during the War when a stray dog Cordell had befriended was killed in battle. Cordell couldn't be consoled then either. Taullery was struck by the irony that friends had been dying around them for three long years but a dog got to Cordell's heart and broke it.

When Taullery was a young teenager, his parents died from influenza and pneumonia and it was Cordell's turn to help bring him back from the blackness of grief. An Indian-style, blood-brother ritual, something Taullery had heard about from a frontiersman, became a demonstration of their great friendship. Of course, Taullery was the first to explore the magical wonder of kissing girls, smoking tobacco, and shooting pistols. Cordell became unmatched with a gun; Taullery, with women—until Mary took his heart.

It was logical that their decision to join the Confederacy in their fight for states' rights would be made together. Taullery was drawn to the pageantry of it all; Cordell was pulled by the passion to fight. When he was leaving, Cordell's father exploded into another tirade after Cordell told him he was going to fight for the Confederacy. This time, though, Rule Cordell caught the vicious slap headed for his face and forced his father to sit in a chair. As he left, Rule asked the minister to pray for the South, and for Texas, but the last words he heard from his father were "May you rot in hell."

"It's a long way from Boydton Plank Road, Rule," Taullery finally said, staring at the buggy, now a speck on the horizon. He was referring to the "masquerade battalion" stand they made during their final winter of battle in Virginia. His gaze was broken by two chickens scooting from the side of the house to check out the front.

"Seems like a long way from Texas," Cordell answered, and turned away from the door. "What's the

Bible say? 'I have been a stranger in a strange land.' "

"A lot of folks will be upset by your doing this." Taullery bit the inside of his cheek to give him the courage to say it.

Cordell looked at his friend, and Taullery blinked away the intensity of the glare.

"Upset? Where were they when Padgett hanged Douglas Harper?"

"That's not fair, Rule. What were they supposed to do? He's the law. An' there was Lion Graham looking like a man hoping someone would try something. Come on, Rule."

"Padgett—and Lion—and my father would get along real fine."

It was the first time Taullery could remember Cordell mentioning his father in a long time. He wasn't sure of how to respond, but it didn't matter—Cordell did it for him.

"Men like them become strong because no one stands up to them. They're weeds taking over a field. You can't wish away weeds." He paused and added, "Can't pray them away, either. You have to tear them out with your hands."

Chapter Six

"What's that got to do with teaching Negroes how to read and write?" Taullery closed the door behind them and hurried to catch up.

"Ignorance is the weed I'm going to help pull out. It's the only answer for those people, Ian, and you know that as well as I do." Cordell walked back into the main room, his eyes searching for the Bible he used for church services. He spotted it on a narrow table pushed against an overstuffed chair Aleta had purchased from an estate sale for back taxes.

"A lot of people are afraid of the Africans taking control. I've heard it. I've read it. So have you, Rule."

"That sounds like something my father would say." Cordell held the leather-bound book in his hands. Taullery noticed a slight tremble as his friend gripped it, then remembered that his friend had been mostly unconscious for three days.

"You'd better take it easy, Rule."

"I'm all right. Just a little weak," Cordell said. "I'm going to catch up with Aleta at school. Then I'll go along to see Missus Harper and her kids."

"I think you should rest."

"You going with me—or to your store?"

"I'll ride with you. Mary's there. Then we'll go open up." Taullery paused and said, "There's another Bible in your bedroom—on top of your guns." It was the closest he could get to a direct question.

Cordell never looked up; his fingers stroked the book's leather cover. "Those guns are there to remind me of the man I used to be. Every day I tell myself that I don't want to go back. Every day I touch that Bible and ask for God's help."

"I liked that man."

"He's dead."

An hour later, the two friends rode up to a square, unpainted building surrounded by a split-rail fence in need of repair. There had been little attempt to hide the fact that it had once held chickens. Texas sun slammed against the ramshackle roof like bullets from a giant gun. Even the bare earth crackled beneath the impact. Their horses' hooves drummed the parched land like it was a giant hollow shell. Taullery's wagon was parked on the west side, with two hitched horses tied to a low branch of a scraggly cottonwood. Taullery muttered that he had warned his wife to be careful about leaving the animals unattended. Roving bands of homeless scavengers, black and white, would steal a horse any way they could.

Swinging down from the saddle, Cordell wobbled and grabbed the mane of his gray horse to keep from falling. The animal jumped sideways in surprise and he stumbled forward, landing on his hands and knees. His wide-brimmed black hat sailed toward Taullery. Not pausing to pick it up, Taullery rushed over to find his minister friend laughing.

"You all right, Rule?"

Cordell nodded his head. "Yeah, I was working on my dramatic entrance into the school."

"You'd better let me take a look at that wound, Rule. You're lucky to be alive."

"If I'd had a gun, Douglas Harper would be alive." The proclamation jumped from his mouth before he had time to stop it. His expression soured in recognition of the blurted thought.

Taullery grabbed his arm and helped Cordell to his feet. The storekeeper's mind was whirring with images and things to say.

"If you had, you'd be dead. There were too damn many of them, Rule. An' there was good old Lion David, too." He didn't try to tell his friend that a minister shouldn't be talking that way. He wasn't certain anymore what was the right thing to do. Texas was being pounded into the ground mercilessly and no one seemed able to stop it. What were wishes against guns? What were prayers against absolute authority? What were words against economic ruin? Didn't a man have to find the way the river was running and go with it?

Cordell brushed himself off, his forehead furrowed with frustration. "Forgive me for saying that, Ian. A gun isn't the answer to anything."

"A gun is just a tool, my good friend. You know that. In the right hands, it can do the right things." Taullery looped the reins of both horses over adjacent fence posts. He studied the quiet building ahead while Cordell retrieved his hat. "I'll see if Mary wants to go with me to open the store, her and little Rule. When you're ready to go see the Harper family, you can come and get us. If that's all right with you."

"Sounds like a good plan."

"It looks like it could rain. Would you rather wait until tomorrow?"

"No, I think they need us today. We won't melt."

"All right, I'll bring along two of those English umbrellas I just got—and a couple of slickers, just in case."

Cordell reached into his pocket, retrieved two gold coins, and held them toward his friend. "Let's take along food for the Harpers, too. As much as this will buy."

"I don't want your money, Rule."

"It's Suitcase's."

Taullery laughed and took the coins.

They opened the door to the small commercial structure that had once housed hundreds of chickens, removing their hats as they entered. Immediately, they drew the attention of the closest children. Holding his hat with one hand, Cordell put the finger of his other to his mouth to ask for silence. Giggles and whispers were the response, followed by glances from books at the new distraction. He studied his wife, working with two boys on their subtraction near the front of the class. A stray streak of sunlight sought her face and illuminated it. "She's beautiful," he muttered.

"Yeah, she is. Too damn beautiful for you," Taullery whispered, and nudged his friend with his elbow.

Taullery's wife sat in the other corner, holding their sleeping baby and reading to six younger children, grouped eagerly around her chair.

"Look who's talking," Cordell snapped in a hushed voice.

Aleta glanced at the back of the schoolroom, either from the inner connection that comes from knowing her man was close by, or simply hearing the murmur in the back, or both. Her eyes raced to Cordell's and embraced him. Her smile washed away the dizziness he had hidden from Taullery. She told Mary of their arrival and Taullery's wife looked up, smiled and waved, and returned to her reading.

Brushing the dush from his black suit, Cordell studied the tiny classroom and wondered if schools for the newly freed black children could possibly be worse. Twenty writing tables were crammed into the stifling room, surrounded by the baked-in odor of chicken waste. The walls had been whitewashed when the building's usage was changed, and they provided a smell that actually neutralized the other somewhat. Nailed to the front wall was a makeshift blackboard with the upper corner missing. On it was written in faint chalk the reading assignments for each grade. In the far corner, a potbellied stove sat, unneeded now but woefully inadequate on cold days. At least there were windows—with wooden shutters pushed opened as far as they could go. Hot air was eagerly joining the stale remains of yesterday. But school was nearly over for the year; children would be needed on farms and ranches.

"Good morning, Reverend. My mother said you were very brave at Sunday meetin'. She said you went after those awful Regulators all by yourself." The greeting came from a smiling, freckle-faced girl with brown hair and a faded blue dress.

"Oh yeah? My pa said he was plain stupid to do that. A wonder he didn't get the whole congregation killed. That's what Pa said." A towheaded boy with two missing teeth spit his challenge to her statement.

She stuck out her tongue at him, and he responded with a thrown book. Her hand deflected the missile, and the book thumped on the chicken-waste-stained floor. Aleta stood and asked both what had happened.

"Ernest threw his book at me," the girl replied, folding her arms.

"*Por favor* tell me, Ernest, did you throw thees book?" Aleta's voice was stern.

"Yeah, I guess I did."

"Why did you do thees thing, Ernest—to a girl?"

"He said the pastor was stupid for fighting the Regulators." The girl burst out the accusation, barely containing her triumphant smile.

At the rear of the school, Taullery held his hand over his mouth to keep from laughing, and Cordell avoided catching his friend's gaze for the same reason.

Her dark eyes sparkling, Aleta ignored the girl's outburst as well as the men's reaction, and asked the red-faced boy again. "Ernest, I asked you—why? *Por favor*, please tell me."

His face squirmed with embarrassment; his lips pursed and retreated; his shoulders squeezed against his neck to release the tension. "I . . . ah . . . my pa, he said . . . Reverend, ah, Langford . . . shouldn't of, ah, done what he done . . . Sunday."

With a victorious gleam in her eyes, the brown-haired girl exclaimed, "That's not what he said. He said—"

"I heard you, Margaret. I am talking with Ernest. *Por favor.*" Aleta closed the distance between herself and Ernest, who was trying to look anywhere but at his teacher. She came to his desk and knelt beside it. Her voice was soft and gentle. "Ernest, you have a right to say your ideas, even if it ees something not all want to hear. That ees the beauty of freedom, ees that not so? Many brave men fought for thees right—for you and me. Look at me, Ernest. *Sí?* I cannot hear your head nod."

Ernest smiled and raised his head to look at her. She smiled and added, "But you don't have a right to throw a book at someone, do you?"

He started to shake his head but mumbled, "No, ma'am."

"*Esta bien*. That ees good." Aleta stood and stepped back. "Now apologize to Margaret."

He squeezed both hands together, pursed his lips, and said, "I'm sorry I threw a book at you, Margaret." Under his breath, he muttered, "And missed."

Both Cordell and Taullery heard the final attachment and burst out laughing. Margaret heard it, too, and complained loudly to Aleta, but she already had other thoughts on her mind as she continued to walk toward the front of the class.

"Now, Ernest, I think we should hear from the man who caused thees commotion, don't you?" Her eyes again sought Cordell's as he fought to bring his laughter under control. "Señor Langford, will you please tell the class what you were trying to do last Sunday?

"Oh come on, Aleta, I don't . . ."

"*Por favor*, my husband. I think it ees good for children to know what things are happening. They must hear—to learn."

Slightly annoyed, Cordell cleared his throat. "Last Sunday, an innocent man was hanged. Without a trial. Without any reason, except that he fought for the Confederacy. Like most of your fathers did, I reckon. I tried to get them to listen to reason, Ernest, but they wouldn't. I tried to get them to stop and got hit on the head. I would do the same thing if they came for your pa. You can tell him that."

Angry at hearing the boy recite his father's comment, Taullery stepped forward. "Young man, I suggest you tell your pa that I said *he* was the fool. Next time, maybe, the Regulators *will* come for him. Ask him if he would rather no one tried to help."

The boy's face turned white and tears swelled at the corners of his eyes.

"That ees enough, Señor Taullery," Aleta said.

Cordell rubbed his chin with his right hand and walked toward the boy. Cordell placed his hand on the boy's shoulder and said quietly, "I know your father,

Ernest. He is a good man. I understand why he said what he did." He looked around the room at the small faces locked onto his. "When you go home today, I hope you will hug your mother and your father and tell them that you love them. They are very brave and want the best for you."

His eyes went immediately to Aleta's and sought her soul. She smiled and mouthed, *Bueno.*

From the other corner of the room, a boyish voice asked, "Why don't the Yanks go home and leave us alone?" Another voice: "My momma says you shouldn't ever use that word." A second question from another boy was an echo: "Will they take away all our land?" Then another: "Did you fight for the South, Reverend? My mother says ministers aren't ever soldiers." "Of course he did. All Texans fought in the War." "Why did we lose?" " 'Cuz Lee gave up." "How come you told them Regulators you was Rule Cordell? My father said you did." "That's silly. No preacher would do that." "That's what he said. My father heard it." A final question found courage in the blossoming dialogue: "Why are all the Negroes free to go wherever they want?"

Cordell cringed. He touched the bandage around his head as if the words had struck the wound and reopened it. His mind welled with pain, and he thought of his father. He barely heard Aleta's hushing of the room to silence more eruptions. Instead, he was a boy again, being whipped by a short, portly, and bespectacled minister who saw himself as a singular force of righteousness and intelligence. *"I cannot believe you are the offspring of me, a righteous man. Why has God presented me, of all men, with this sinful connection to my blood. I must drive Satan from your body, my son—it is the only way to save your soul."*

Cordell squeezed shut his eyes to grab his father's image and throw it again behind the closed door in his memory. He pressed his hands together as if to pray, and gazed once more upon the tense classroom. He spoke evenly, his words washing the children with a comfort that rarely entered his own mind.

"Children, this is a time of many questions for us all, young and old, child and parent. God has visited upon us great change. Change that is hard for all of us to understand and accept. Change that sometimes feels like He has forsaken us. That is not so. God loves us all, but he wants us to change. I pray that you study hard to help us with these changes. Texas is depending on you."

He paused, glanced at Taullery, now standing next to Mary and their baby, then turned back to the children who were watching him like he was a new book filled with wondrous ideas. "Know this: Today black mothers and fathers are telling their children the same thing. For the first time, they are free, as God intended. We must help them too. God tells us the only answer is love. We must love one another as we love ourselves. I pray for that."

Taullery blinked away his disbelief at the statement and took a deep breath. He ran his hand lightly across the head of the sleeping Rule Taullery, cradled in Mary's arms.

From the corner of the room, an older boy managed to yell, "Well, I'm prayin' for thunder an' lightnin'—a great big storm to wash away all them Yanks."

Chapter Seven

The two couples rode in Taullery's wagon, with its double row of seats toward the Widow Bauer's house. There was little conversation except for an occasional remark by one of the women about the countryside. The back half of the wagon was filled with food and supplies. The two harnessed, matching bays walked easily across the rolling land, moving to a trot with Taullery's occasional snap of the reins. He had traded for the animals three months before and was very proud of them. In the rear came the two saddle horses, tied to the wagon and finally understanding the futility of fighting the connection.

Spring was venturing across the Texas plains, bringing with it the promise of new crops, the lure of wild flowers, and the threat of summer storms. Even now, behind them, rain clouds attacked the sky, replacing blue with an ominous gray. Wherever the darkness took command, crackles of young lightning bloomed for an instant, trailed by coughs of thunder. Rain would not be far behind.

Each held close to thoughts that had sprung from the classroom and, particularly, Cordell's last words to the children. Cordell had already shared with Aleta the news about Suitcase Eliason wanting them to teach black children at night. She hadn't hesitated in agreeing to do so.

The wagon easily followed a broken line of slump-shouldered ridges, splattered with chapparal, scraggly oak, and mesquite. Here and there, thickets of plum bushes and meandering grapevines snuggled against a low-banked stream. Sand-filled and porous, it was thick with gypsum and not good for drinking. On the far side of the ridge, a series of tight canyons could hide a herd of buffalo, or a war party of Comanches, or a regiment of Regulators.

Finally, Ian Taullery broke the growing tension. "Rule, you've got to quit saying all those things about those Negroes. My God, man, those kids will go home and tell their parents that you want them to love them, for Heaven's sake."

"That is what I want."

Unsure of herself, Mary Taullery listened to her husband's criticism before responding. "Dear, I think Reverend Langford . . . was helping them understand the need to change." Her voice was loud, even if it was hesitant.

"Mary, stay with what you know," Taullery snapped, and slapped the reins across the backs of the two horses to reinforce his anger. Their heads jerked up, and both animals clicked into a canter. "No one wants to change. No one wants Negroes taking over. They're trying to—and they don't have the faintest idea of what they're doing."

Touching her fingers to her mouth, Mary returned to

tending her child on her lap. From the corner of her eyes, she glanced at Taullery but said no more. Baby fingers grabbed for the ribbon strings hanging from her bonnet and dangling close to his little face. She tried to concentrate on the baby and attempted a smile. The corner of her mouth wiggled from the sting of his words.

Aleta placed her hand on Cordell's knee. Incensed by Taullery's remarks, she couldn't hold back her thoughts any longer. "I was *bueno* proud of you, my dearest husband. It ees words that all must hear. Children must know thees change."

"Come on, Aleta, there's not one parent around here that wants to hear about change," Taullery said over his shoulder. He popped the reins again to keep the horses at a canter. "Nobody wants it. Nobody."

"No one said they did, Eee-un. Change comes without the asking. Many Texicans theenk they can turn it away. They have, what you call eet, neck in the sand."

Cordell took Aleta's hand, squeezed it, and smiled. "Head in the sand."

"*Gracias*. Head in sand ees it."

Taullery snorted, but his voice was more gentle. "Can't you just preach on things like the Bible—an' Jesus?"

"In case you hadn't noticed, Jesus taught the need for change—to love your neighbor as you love yourself." He paused, smiled, and added, "Isn't that what being reborn is all about? Changing how you feel."

"All right, all right, I give," Taullery said, throwing up his hands in mock surrender. "But you're going to have everybody mad at you. You just can't keep doing that. You just can't. You've already got Lion Graham after you—and he knows it's you, Rule. He knows."

Without a pause for Cordell's response, he launched into a detailed description about Lion Graham, how their strange-acting boyhood friend had turned into an evil being and how obsessed he seemed about Cordell. Aleta watched her husband closely during the one-sided conversation; he hadn't mentioned Graham to her, but she realized he hadn't been talking about anything since Sunday.

Cordell sensed the movement before he saw them. Instinctively his hand dropped to his side where once would have been a gun. His brain reminded him that he was no longer a man of the gun. From the belly of the ridge erupted six well-mounted Comanche warriors. Short and stout with thick chests, they were transformed on horseback to grace and power.

Three carried rifles, two Springfields and a Spencer; the rest held bows and arrows and lances shortened for use on horseback. All were painted for war; plucked eyebrows added to an appearance of dread.

"Comanches, Ian. To the left." Cordell could have been describing wildflowers, so calm was his voice. "Don't try to outrun them, Ian. Bring it to a stop."

Mary let out a wild wail and held her baby close to her breast. Aleta told her to be quiet or they would all die. Quivering, Mary bit her lower lip to keep from making any more noises. Cursing, Taullery halted the wagon and reached for the rifle lying at his feet. The warriors rode parallel to the wagon but didn't attempt to close in. Fierce black eyes studied the passengers and their four horses. The passengers returned the gaze, barely allowing themselves to breathe. Only Cordell's horse in the rear seemed upset about the situtation, yanking on the tied reins and pawing the ground with its hooves.

One warrior's entire body was painted—half yellow, half black. Another's massive face was colored red, with a white half-moon decorating his left cheek. The apparent leader's face and chest were painted in long stripes of black—the mark of death, and of war. His leggings were striped in black the same way. Four feathers flickered ominously from his hair. Cordell knew it meant he had killed four men in battle.

Across the leader's shoulders was draped an antelope skin decorated with silver conchos and bits of cloth. His striking appearance was reinforced by the glistening black horse he rode. Several others wore antelope skins as breech clouts or war shirts. Cordell recognized them as part of the Antelope band, the fiercest of Comanches, and the same as his late mentor, Moon.

"I don't suppose you have a gun, Rule," Taullery growled. He levered the rifle and laid the barrel across his left arm in the direction of the Comanches. His fingers curled around the trigger.

"I do," Aleta replied, and pulled a revolver from her purse. Cordell was surprised. "There is *mucho* change going on. A senorita must be ready." She smiled at him and held out the gun to him.

He declined and said, "Everyone sit tight. I'm going to talk with them."

"These boys aren't interested in a prayer meeting, Rule. Take the damn gun." Taullery's voice was taut with fear.

Cordell didn't respond. Instead, he pulled the brim of his hat lower on his head, stood in the wagon, and yelled a warning in Comanche to the warriors. "Ride on, warriors of *Noomah*. The great *puhakut* Moon has given me the Thunderbird to ride." He yanked the medicine pouch from under his shirt and held it forward with his fist. A chain of murmuring ran through the war party at such a powerful statement in their own language.

"I am brother to the Comanche Great Mystery and the white man's God." He held up the cross around his neck with his other hand. "I can bring the buffalo—and the antelope—and the thunderbird."

The leader held his hand for the others to be quiet so

he could listen. His face was puzzled, his eyes wary. Cordell knew the Comanche weren't particularly good with sign language, but he supported his statements with sign anyway. Taullery was white, staring at the war party in disbelief that they hadn't attacked. He squeezed the rifle tighter and glanced down to check that it was cocked. A few seconds later, he looked again to make sure nothing had changed in the meantime. Next to him, Mary rocked her baby and sobbed. Blood dripped from her lip where she had bitten it.

Shoving his chin forward, the Comanche leader shouted back, "I am Drinks-His-Blood. I wear four kill feathers. My *puhahante* is strong. My battle scars are honored. I drink my own blood to become even stronger."

Sitting beside Cordell, Aleta understood most of what was being said. She whispered to her husband, "Tell them you ride with ghosts—and the little men." She spoke of a Comanche belief in a scary sect of small, evil men who came out only at night and killed every time they shot with their tiny bows and arrows. It was a powerful medicine that most Comanches were afraid to associate with because one might inadvertently kill someone he cared about.

Through a loud but halting presentation, Cordell continued to warn them of his powers and wondered if they understood anything he said—or if they knew of Moon—or if they believed his bluff about making magical things happen. "Ghosts of great warriors—and the little men, *nanapi*—ride with me. I give you fair warning, Drinks-His-Blood."

The warriors stood in a line, facing the wagon twenty yards away. Upon hearing of Cordell's further powers, the farthest Comanche began to look around, his painted face furrowed in concern. They began to talk among themselves. Their long black hair, decorated with glass beads, silver conchos, and pieces of tin, fluttered along their shoulders as they jabbered nervously.

As he spoke, Cordell studied them. A streak of color lined the central part of each warrior, from the forehead back to the crown. Eagle feathers were attached to their side locks. A braid on each side of their heads was wrapped in beaver fur and highlighted with bright cloth. Adorned with a single yellow feather was a special scalp lock braided from the hair at the top of the head. In the leader's scalp lock was a black feather with a red circle near the top.

Cordell's mouth tightened momentarily as he noticed that the second-farthest Indian was wearing a white woman's light brown dress. A moment later, Mary realized the same thing. She screamed. Cordell cringed, but said in Comanche, "She screams in fear of my bringing forth *nanapi*."

He thought a smile passed over the leader's thin lips.

"She screams in fear of Drinks-His-Blood and his warriors, not your talked-of magic," the leader proclaimed, and made a motion with his hand that included his war party. Tangling from his wrist was a rawhide quirt "The one of which you speak has long ago gone to the spirit world. I not speak his name. His medicine is gone to the other world. We take your horses and your women."

Cordell thought he understood, but the words rolled together in a guttural stream that made it difficult. The warrior nearest the leader raised his bow, slid an arrow into place, and drew it back in one continuous motion. Out of the corner of his eye, Cordell caught the movement of Taullery's rifle to his shoulder.

"Wait, Ian," he whispered. "Wait."

"The bastard is going to shoot at you, Rule," Taullery advised.

"No, no, he won't. If you shoot now, they'll charge us. Wait."

Aleta whispered again, this time telling him to act like he was talking to Moon. Cordell nodded and turned to his left and began talking in nonsensical English sentences mixed with Comanche phrases about ghosts, thunderbirds, and killing the Comanches if they didn't leave quickly. He waved his arms wildly and motioned toward the war party as if he were talking with an invisible person next to him.

Finally, he stopped and looked back at the war leader. As loud as he could speak, Cordell yelled, "Moon says to tell him to put down his bow—or the ghosts will kill all of you. He tells me to warn you first, since you are of his old tribe. Look around you—see the ghosts waiting?" He pointed at a small dust swirl, then another—tiny advance breezes scouting for the coming rainstorm. "He tells me to give you one more warning about the little people. Look around you—see the tiny arrowheads?" His hand made a sweeping motion, taking in the ground in front of them. He hadn't looked, but chances were good at least one arrowhead-shaped rock would be there. "And look at the sky. Moon tells me the thunderbird rides toward me fast. He is angry you question me—and my power. Ride on, Drinks-His-Blood. You are a great warrior, but your medicine is not strong this day. That is Moon's warning. He will not do so again."

Cordell finished and folded his arms over his chest. A skinny branch of lightning flickered across the sky. Anticipating the thunder that would follow, he immediately raised his arms and the sky appeared to respond to his prayer with a menacing growl. As he returned his arms to a folded position, Cordell's intense gaze connected with the leader's wide-eyed expression. A bead of sweat blossomed on the minister's forehead and made its way down the side of his face, pausing at the corner of his eye, before sliding down his cheek. He dared not wipe at the sign of anxiousness, and he hoped the Comanches didn't notice it. To himself, he prayed that this bluff would work and asked for forgiveness from Moon for misusing his name.

As swiftly as the bow was readied, it came back to the warrior's side, directed by the muttered command of the striped-face war leader. Nudging his horse with his moccasined heels, he rode halfway toward the wagon and stopped again. He held up his right arm in a gesture of friendly greeting and said, "We go. You go. I, Drinks-His-Blood, feel the spirits around us and they tell me you speak strong words. Tonight I tell council of 'Talk-With-Thunder' and how he honored Drinks-His-Blood with words of warning." With his last words, he spun the horse around, gave a yip to the others, and bolted over the ridge and out of sight. In the rear of the wagon, both saddled horses stutter-stepped sideways in a futile attempt to join them.

Taullery's rifle barrel followed the retreat and held at the point where they disappeared. No one spoke. Mary burst into a wailing sound that was more animal than human. Awakened, the baby joined her sobbing. Taullery looked at his distraught wife and baby, then back at Cordell.

"My God, Rule, what happened? I can't believe they left. Will they come back?"

"I don't think so, but let's get going—before the storm breaks."

"We should've opened up on them." Taullery snapped the reins over the horses and they jolted into an uneven canter. "We need to get rid of all those red bastards."

"How many would you have gotten before they shot

one of us? Or your baby?" Cordell said. His voice was even but strong.

Taullery's shoulders rose and fell. "Yeah, maybe so. What did you say to them?"

Chapter Eight

Aleta uncocked the gun and returned it to her purse. "*Mi Marido*, my husband, he say have *mucho* power and they must ride away to be saved from eet. Comanche Great Mystery and our God listen to heem. He say he can make the buffalo—and the antelope—and the thunder—come at hees call. He tell them of ghosts and leetle people. He scare them *mucho*." She explained his "conversation" with the ghost of the old shaman they had met years before.

Taullery shook his head and chuckled in spite of himself. "You sure like to bluff, Rule. One of these times, though, you're gonna get called—and you won't be holding crap." He glanced skyward at the advancing rain clouds and popped the reins again to urge the horses faster.

Leaning over to kiss her cheek, Cordell advised the others that most of the ideas were Aleta's.

"Then I'll be careful playing poker with her." Taullery chuckled and asked, "What did he say to you at the end there?" He patted Mary's leg as she forced herself into a calm to concentrate on the crying baby.

Cordell turned his head toward Aleta and motioned for her to answer. She smiled and said, "*Sí*, Comanche war chief said that spirits tell heem that Rule speaks strong words. He called Rule 'Talk-With-Thunder.' He would tell others of thees power and that Rule honor heem by not keeling him. *Per favor*, sometheeng like that."

After a few minutes of silence, broken only by the rumbling of the wagon wheels, Taullery asked, "Rule?"

"Yeah, Ian?"

"What if he'd wanted you to prove you could bring the buffalo?"

"Produce them, of course." Cordell grinned. "There was probably some over the ridge. Usually are this time of the year. I guess I would've told him to go look."

"You think of everything, my friend."

"There wasn't much choice."

Taullery asked one last question. "Did you ever consider taking Aleta's gun?"

Thunder almost drowned Cordell's negative response, and the vanguard of raindrops followed.

"We're gonna get wet, folks," Taullery said. "Rule, there are two of those fancy English umbrellas back there—with the food. Slickers for you and me, too. They're rolled up tight, back in the corner."

"Speaking of thinking of everything." Cordell leaned over the back seat to look, then decided to climb back to the wagon bed.

"Pull that canvas over the food, too, will you?" Taullery said.

"Sure."

"Be sure the flour sack is covered. If the rain gets to it, we'll have a sack of hard."

"Got it."

Taullery concentrated on the horses for moment as thicker raindrops drove their way into the wagon and its occupants. "Oh yeah, see if that sack of coffee beans is covered too."

Cordell held his teeth together to keep from responding. He knew that was his friend's approach to life. Careful. Thorough. Precise. Always striving to be prepared. There was much to learn from Taullery's way, instead of always always relying on instinct and nerve.

"Here you go," he said, handing one umbrella to Aleta, then another.

She gave the first to Mary Taullery, who was complaining loudly about getting wet, and opened the second. Frantically, Mary looked around for the baby's blanket to cover the infant from the rapidly increasing rain. Aleta handed it to her; the blanket had fallen into the back. Cordell unfolded the canvas and spread it over the pile of food, deciding from where he stood that the flour sack was covered. Taullery would have worked and worked at straightening out the canvas to make certain it was perfectly in place, but Cordell thought it would do just fine.

Grabbing both slickers, he started to climb back into the seat but saw a small wrapped bundle in the corner of the wagon. He knew what it was: a rag doll Aleta had made just for the Harper girl, wrapped in a blanket remmant. He picked up the doll and carefully placed it under the canvas.

Pleased that he had seen the special gift, he eased himself into the seat, still holding the raincoats. He helped Taullery into the heavy raincoat as his friend drove, then eased the second onto himself. Of course, his friend asked if the canvas was on straight and if the lid was on tight. Cordell pronounced them both in good shape.

Rain pounded on them, turning the sky into a fortress of water. Their horses in front and back disappeared, then reappeared, as sheets of rain swallowed and regurgitated them. A thin stream of water fell down in front of Cordell's hat, barely missing his nose. He cocked his head to one side, then another, trying to empty the brim of its excess wetness. It was a fruitless exercise, and his brim began to melt.

Taullery had taken off his hat earlier and placed it under the seat where it would escape most of the downpour. He asked Mary to slant her umbrella a little more toward him, and she did. He looked over to their baby and asked if the child was wet. She felt his blanket and whined that he was damp. Taullery frowned and told her to cover the child better with the umbrella. Mary shouted over the rain that she was doing the best she could.

"I'm gonna head for that grove of trees up ahead," Taullery shouted above the rain. "This is heavier than I expected."

No trees were in sight—with or without the heavy rain—but Cordell figured his friend had planned on the trees as a refuge, if needed, before they started. It seemed like an hour, but it was only ten minutes, before they reached the four windblown cottonwoods squatting beside the same stream, now wider and deeper.

Cordell took off his slicker and spread it on the ground under the wagon, then helped the women squat there for more cover. He took the Taullery infant while Mary got herself positioned under the wagon. Aleta asked to hold him after she was sitting beside her, and Mary was happy for the relief, immediately telling Aleta about the woes of raising a child. Taullery wrapped the reins around a sturdy branch and added his raincoat alongside Cordell's. The intense minister checked on the tied saddle horses, allowing them enough slack with their reins to graze near the wagon. Neither seemed interested. Their ears lay against their necks; their bodies were soaked with fresh rain. Silently he wished he had covered the saddles and decided to loosen the cinches to give their backs some air. The leather would need to be soaped and oiled after it dried out. He shook his head and returned to the wagon.

All of them squatted under the belly of the wagon and sat on the men's slickers. The women's umbrellas were propped outward as a wall to cut off the slanting rain. They sat, watching the downpour from between the gaps in the umbrellas. Taullery griped about not being well prepared, Mary was certain her dress was ruined, and Cordell began to laugh.

"What's so funny, Rule? We're soaked," Taullery said, pulling on his coat.

"Well, only a few minutes ago we were worried about dying. Now we're complaining about a little rain."

Taullery smiled. "Yeah, I guess you're right. 'Course, you'd think a fella with your kind of connections with the gods an' all could have kept it from raining until we got to the Widow's place."

"I'm a little rusty in the connecting department," Cordell replied with a faint smile.

His mind was wrestling with whether it was right for him to have used his short relationship with Moon to send the warriors scurrying. What would the old man have said if he were here? Should a man of the cloth—a Christian minister—be promising such things as "riding the Thunderbird" and "bringing the little people"? It probably saved their lives—or at least some of their lives. Still, guilt chewed at the corner of his thoughts. Cordell's attention was drawn to a squatty shadow beneath the farthest tree. How could a shadow be there now?

As the rain settled around them, his mind returned

to the Comanche camp just south of the Red River, where he and Taullery had been welcomed on their way to War. Their hunger had stolen away any concern about what they might encounter there. But the Indians had welcomed the two young Rebel soldiers-to-be and told them their shaman had foretold their coming, and that he wanted to see Cordell.

The dampness of the ground brought again the shaman's lodge, thick with the odor of healing herbs swirled together with sweetgrass smoke from a tiny fire in the middle of the lodge. Near the dying old man was a bowl of half-eaten pemmican, dried cherries, and pecan nuts. Scattered around the buffalo-skin structure were Moon's spiritual possessions: a sacred rattle, a drum, a medicine pipe bag on a tripod and draped with colored cloth, a large leather bag filled with medicines, and a black iron kettle holding owl feathers. He remembered the old man saying the owl was Mother Moon's messenger.

How strange an encounter. The experience had burned itself into his mind, even though he had rejected the old man's teaching as so much feeble rambling at the time. Ultimately, it had changed him—and saved him from himself. Not just the closeness to a Comanche holy man, but Moon's very words. The young Rebel and the old Indian had connected like father and son, even though Cordell knew none of their language at the time. Even today, he often felt the shaman's presence but never shared the thought with anyone, not even Aleta. He had decided it was God's way of giving him an experience of what a father should be like.

After the two smoked the medicine pipe, the old shaman began to speak in broken, singsong English, as he watched smoke trails embrace the moon watching through the gathered lodge poles at the top of the tipi, laced together and tilted slightly backward. He told the young Texan of the ways of the Comanche, of their love of horses, of their training as warriors to never leave a comrade for the enemy to torture or mutilate, of the sacredness of the buffalo.

On and on he talked, trying to communicate the essence of his nomadic life as if it had to be planted within Cordell. The holiness of the number four. That resurrection was not uncommon. How some shields were sacred to thunder and lightning. That every man could be his own priest and guide his own way to the afterworld. How the selection of a man's medicine was the most important and sacred event in his life. How the Great Spirit was everywhere and in everything, and that a Comanche was connected to all other living things.

He told him that he would soon depart for the afterworld that lay beyond the setting sun. There he would enter a great, lush valley where all warriors were young, all horses fast, and the buffalo plentiful. The birds were beautiful there, and so were the women. Eventually, like all others, he must be reborn of the Mother Earth to keep the power of the Comanche strong and unbroken.

Looking into the young man's eyes, the shaman said, "Mother Moon watches over me tonight. She has done so for many moons. She has given me the power to see what most of The People cannot. It is my strength—and my curse. She told me of your coming."

As if to allow this unfathomable thought to sink into young Rule Cordell's mind, Moon inhaled more smoke from the pipe, stroking the long stem like it was alive. "You are to be a warrior in the *Taibos'* great battle about men with dark skins. Your road will be hard. It will be long and lonely. Men will follow you into battle but not know you. They will fear you and the death song from your iron sticks. It is so."

The next time Moon stopped talking, Cordell actually

thought the old man had died in front of him. The shaman's head nodded and came to rest on his frail chest. His body gave a long sigh and the medicine pipe fell from his hands. But as Cordell touched him, Moon retrieved the pipe at his lap and continued as if nothing had happened. "I have seen my next road. It is straight. The ancients are eager to have me join them. It is well, but I need your help."

A harsh cough followed that ripped through Moon's shaking frame. He coughed again, and Cordell hugged the old man to ease the pain. For the first time in years, the young man prayed. He prayed for the old man to live. The coughing became less frequent and finally stopped. Moon patted Cordell on the shoulder and thanked him for his caring. "I am a worried old man. Mother Moon tells me the God of the *Taibos* has grown strong. I have already talked with the Comanche spirits, and they are satisfied with my coming. But my old ways may not be enough, and I have not met the *Taibo* God. He has chosen others to talk to. I would like to enter the other world with the power of your God at my side as well. Will you talk with this *Taibo* God—for me? The spirits tell me he rides close to you."

He handed Cordell the medicine pipe and Cordell repeated what he had seen the shaman do earlier, pointing the pipe in each direction, the four Winds, and to the ground, Mother Earth, and to the sky. At each point, he drew on the pipe and exhaled sacred smoke. All the while, his mind raced for the right words to say. Out came the Lord's Prayer. It was as if his mind were linked to God and all he had to do was open his mouth.

"*Aiee*, Mother Moon says your talk is strong. Listen! She tells me you walked the black road when a small *tua*. The Voice tells me you are the son of a father who wraps the *Taibo* God around him but does not see this

God. He is a cruel father, unworthy of your love. Ah, this is so."

Cordell's surprise at the old man knowing about him was tempered by his assumption that Taullery had told him of the situation, but he wasn't certain when this could have happened. Before he could ask, Moon said solemnly, "You must forgive him, your father. You must open your heart and let the pain flee from you. Not now. You are not ready, my son. You will know when it is time. You will quit running—from yourself—and be ready to let the *Taibo* God take you where he wants you to go. Moon will watch over you if the spirits are willing. And your God does not mind."

After that, Moon gave the young Texan two gifts: a stone earring and a small pouch with a leather neck thong. "Here. These are for you. I have made them for you. The rock is a piece of Mother Moon to protect you. In this bundle is the medicine of the owl to guide you. It is well. I must go. The spirits are calling."

In return, Cordell went to his saddlebags and retrieved the Bible his mother had given to him, the only thing he had to remind him of her. He handed the book to the old shaman. With both hands, Moon held it above him so that a beam of moonlight could kiss the leather cover.

Pulling the book to his chest, Moon said, "My son, in the spirit world, our time together now is as a lifetime. It is so. When this strange fighting between the *Taibos* is over, and when the fighting with your father inside you is over, you will tell others of your *Taibo* God. It is so. I ask that you also remember the ways of the Comanche. The spirits have given me little time to tell you. Promise me you will learn more."

Moon tried to stand and leaned on Cordell to maintain his balance. He looked upward and waved his arms, as if he were gathering the faint moonbeams sliding through the poles and holding them next to his heart. With his left hand pressed against his heart, he reached out with his right and placed it on Cordell's shoulder. "Whenever you pray, my son, I will hear you. My sons have gone ahead of me to the spirit world. I have no sons in this world to care for. My spirit will watch over you. It is so. Ask for the thunderbird and it will fly to you. It is so."

"I think the rain's let up. We can get going again." Taullery's words broke into Cordell's remembrance. The lithe minister immediately checked for the shadow by the tree. It was gone. Silently, he thanked Moon's spirit.

"Sounds good to me. How about you ladies?" Cordell answered. He felt the side of his head and pulled down what remained of the soggy bandage. For the first time, no pain was there.

Mary snapped, "Well, it's about time. This is terrible. Just terrible. Worse than Sunday even—and that awful Captain Padgett."

Cordell acted like he didn't hear her, but his eyes caught Aleta's and she shook her head slightly in disbelief.

Chapter Nine

White tendrils of smoke wandered into the bluing sky as the wagon pulled alongside Widow Bauer's ranch. Once it had been prosperous; now it was showing signs of neglect. A candle beckoned from one of the angular front windows. Shadows within told they were seen.

In addition to a main house of adobe, there were a number of other smaller buildings surrounded by a rock fence sprouting weeds in several places. A large barn and a cabin, once holding Mexican ranchhands, were positioned at the southern edge of the ranch yard. Nestled close were an outhouse, a stone cooling shed, and a sturdy-looking corral. Twenty feet from the corral was an old well.

Neither Taullery nor Cordell had known the late Alexander Bauer well. Thrown by a horse, he had been dead for ten years. His widow had given up ranching during the War, after her two sons left to fight and never returned. Supposedly, Old Man Bauer never owned slaves, preferring Mexican vaqueros. Mrs. Bauer lived alone on the property, no longer attempting to control any pastureland. Any of her cattle not run off by Comanches roamed wild across the near prairie. Most, however, had been rebranded by more aggressive ranchers.

"Ian, there's that wagon—of that awful Russian." Mary's voice rang across the land. Taullery snorted his dislike.

Visible from the back of the house was an unmistakable wagon. Piled high with pots, pans, brooms, and cooking utensils, it had to belong to the huge man everyone knew simply as "the Russian"—a friendly trader who traveled from settlement to settlement, selling or trading, sharpening knives, bringing the news from throughout the region, and helping others for the sheer joy of it. His two wagon horses—one dappled gray the other sorrel—were standing quietly, still hitched.

In addition to kitchen goods, almost anything might be found in his traveling warehouse: Eggs, nuts, jars of jam, cages of chickens, or perhaps a container of goat's milk or wrapped cheese. Old jewelry and bottled medicines. Bolts of bright cloth and all kinds of guns. Canisters of spices and condiments. Saddles and leather to repair them. Large knives and small, old and new. All very sharp. Books, crockery, music boxes, toys, pressed soaps, and clocks. However, he never carried tobacco or whiskey. No one knew where he got all the things he carried; some said it was stolen merchandise purchased from gangs ravaging the South. No one said it to his face, however.

Many thought he knew more about what was really going on in this part of Texas than any newspaper. Certainly, he rarely met a stranger—and, if so, that person rarely stayed one for long. Whenever he stopped at a homestead with children, each child got something free, regardless of whether the parents bought anything or not. Cordell liked the man; his huge joy for life matched his massive frame. It wasn't surprising to see that "the Russian" was here. The huge man would have learned of the Sunday tragedy and gone immediately to help.

"The Russian's" real name was Caleb Shank, and he wasn't Russian. He wasn't even foreign-born, having grown up in Georgia in a small town outside of Atlanta. A few folks in town thought he fought in the War, but no one said where, or for which side. But someone, somewhere, thought he looked like a Russian, with his long black hair and heavy beard, and the description stuck. He never seemed to mind. There was also another tale that wouldn't go away, of his killing two men in a bar fight, breaking one man's neck with his bare fists and stopping the other with a knife thrown across the room.

Taullery guided the wagon horses toward the barn as the front door burst open and a tree-sized, hatless man sprang from the house. With him came two laughing Harper children. Long black hair bounced on his shoulders, and the sun caught the glimmer of four gold rings on the fingers of his right hand and a large gold ring with a green stone on his left. Both hands were constantly moving as he talked. Strained buttons on his faded shirt had nearly lost the war with his thick chest. Black hair blossomed from the neck of Shank's shirt and ran across the back of his hands. A heavy beard, sprinkled with gray, covered most of his face, leaving only an oft-broken nose and bright, happy eyes. His red-stained, leathery face and hands were testimony to constant sun exposure, but his complexion didn't tan.

Caleb Shank headed immediately for the wagon, singing a song that only the children understood and that he probably had just made up. His body weaved in rhythm with the words and his gruff voice added emphasis where it wasn't needed, bringing contagious laughter from the children each time. Leave it to kids to see beyond the beast to the real man inside, Cordell thought as he removed his slicker and tossed it into the wagon bed. *Kids know. They really know. Did the kids at school believe what I said?* The question was a windswept tumbleweed through his mind and was gone.

Grabbing the hands of both the little boy and girl, he began to half-skip, half-dance toward the barn. His mule-eared boots thudded against the soggy ground, spraying mud in all directions. That only made him roar with laughter. If one looked closely, scars on both sets of knuckles told a story of a man used to fighting. Inside his shirt, down the back, hung a throwing knife in a sheath held by a rawhide thong around his neck.

Mary Taullery wondered aloud, "What's he doing, running the way he was around with the children? Shouldn't they be inside with their mother?"

"Mary, they need some relief from that awful pain. He's giving them a great gift, the gift of laughter." Cordell's tone indicated he didn't want her to say more.

"Ho, my great friends, yo-all are a grand sight." Shank's greeting was as large as his countenance. "Reverend Langford, t'is your prayers they be needin' too. I see you caught the rain."

"I think we caught every single drop, my old friend. Caleb, it's great to see you." Cordell's returned greeting was equally warm. He jumped down from the wagon, helped Aleta down, then Mary and the baby, and headed for "the Russian" with his hand extended.

"Aye, a bear hug is called for, I reckon," Shank announced, and wrapped his tree-trunk arms around Cordell and squeezed. The minister hugged back, gasping for breath at the same time.

Seeing Aleta, the big man released Cordell and made an exaggerated bow to her. "My, my, the minister, indeed, has much to be thankful for. Mrs. Langford, you are proof that prayers are answered."

Aleta laughed and returned the greeting with a smile on her face. "You never change, Senor Shank. You make thees senorita weak with such pretty words. *Mucho gracias*."

Stepping to the side, she introduced Mary Taullery and their son. Shank connected the baby's name with that of the late Rule Cordell. "Rule—a Texas name to be proud of. Is it after the great Rule Cordell?"

Mary nodded and forced a smile. "It is good of you to play with the children. They need to laugh." She avoided looking at either Cordell or Aleta, and glanced back at her husband, who was unharnessing the horses.

"Shucks, ma'am, that ain't no big thing. I jes' hate seein' kids goin' long-faced. They's cried enough, I reckon."

Cordell asked about Mrs. Harper and her children, and the big man shared what he knew of the situation. They had been forced to leave their land this morning when a band of Regulators arrived with the official papers. Captain Padgett led them from his war wagon. The new owner wasn't there and Shank wasn't certain who it was, but thought it was a stranger from up north, maybe a cousin of Captain Padgett's. Lion David Graham, the pistol-fighter, was there too. After Shank helped the Harpers finish packing, the family left with Mrs. Harper demanding her children not cry. They arrived here early in the afternoon, missing the rain by only an hour.

"A brave lady she be," Shank continued. "She never said a word to that son of a bitch Padgett. Beggin' your pardon, preacher. But each time she carried something to the wagon, she gave that crippled bastard a stare he couldn't meet. No sir. Her children worked right with us—and not a sniffle among 'em. Great kids they are, by God. Sorry, preacher. All the time, Padgett and his men, they watched—and they laughed."

"One of them yelled to her that a widow needed some lovemakin'—and words about how he was gonna do it to her." His heavy face turned crimson. "Forgive me, Preacher Langford, but I jes' couldn't take that. I walked over and yanked the silly fool from his horse and hit him. 'Fraid I broke his jaw. Lawdy, it felt good. Sorry, preach."

"No need to ask for my forgiveness, Caleb. But you were playing with fire," Cordell said.

"Yah, Padgett, he told that pistol-fighter something—but I heard Lion tell him that the man deserved it. So they left me alone."

"The good Lord needs more like you—so does Texas." Cordell put his hand on Shank's shoulder and turned back to Aleta. "Why don't you go on in, honey. You and Mary. I'll help Ian with the horses and the food."

"*Sí*, my husband. I weel get the doll for Rebecca."

"Sure. She's going to love that."

She kissed him on the cheek and headed for the wagon. Red blossomed at the edges of Cordell's white collar. For the first time, he was aware of how wet her clothes were. They clung to her body and accented her ample bosom. He glanced down at his groin, and it had obviously responded to his wife's appearance.

From the wagon bed, Aleta lifted the cloth doll from under the canvas. Neither the wrapping nor the doll was damp. Silently, Cordell thanked God for making him see that was it well covered.

Walking over to her, Cordell said quietly, "You're soaking wet, Aleta. Do you need to ask the women for something to wear?"

She looked coyly over her shoulder at him. "I am fine.

Just a little damp. Does my husband see something he does not like?"

Cordell grinned. "Nope. I see everything I love—but I don't want anybody else to see it."

She looked down at herself, smiled, and pulled the wet blouse away from her breasts, then grabbed the edges of her skirt and shook it vigorously. Deciding that only time would help with her clothes, she laid the doll back on the wagon bed and reached for Cordell's discarded slicker.

"How's that, Reverend?" Her words came like falling snowflakes as she slipped on the raincoat and buttoned the top two buttons.

"Well, it might be a little warm—but I like it." He smiled.

"Bueno." She kissed him again on the cheek and picked up the doll, cradling it like a real child. "Be *pronto*. Mrs. Harper needs you."

Cordell agreed, and she headed for the house. Halfway there, she stopped and looked back over her shoulder. He was watching his arms folded. Her eyes made love to him. Then, she continued, almost skipping.

Unaware of the interplay between Cordell and Aleta, Shank squatted beside the children, who were clamoring for his attention. With joy in his voice, the big man told them to hide and he would be "it." Giggling and yelling, they both ran in the same direction toward the barn. He shut his eyes and counted loudly and slowly. The numbers weren't in any known sequence, with a few words like "chicken" and "saddle" thrown in for good measure.

Cordell watched him as he removed the saddle from his gray horse. It was impossible not to smile when one saw "the Russian" with children. He ran his hand across the mantle; it was damp. He shook his head at the saddle soaping that lay ahead. Maybe tonight, after they were home.

Taullery had already turned out the wagon horses, wiping them down carefully with a mostly dry saddle blanket from the wagon bed. He filled the water trough with several buckets of water from her well. Cordell led the unsaddled riding horses into the corral.

"Your red is limping. Right foreleg, Ian." Cordell pointed in the direction of the animal's slight limp.

"Hmm, probably a stone bruise. There was some mean ground we went over early on," Taullery answered. "I'll check it. Will you get some grain from the wagon? Four nose bags are there too."

"Sure. Does it matter which horse gets which bag?" He tried to hide the smile that followed.

Taullery started to answer, caught Cordell's grin, and shook his head. Instead, he asked, "Is 'the Russian' going to help us bring in the food?" His voice carried irritation. "You know they say he sells stuff from gangs. That's why he sells things so cheap."

"I think he's busy right now—with more important things." Cordell ignored his friend's expression of jealousy. He resisted commenting on the fact that Taullery also bought merchandise from men who could hardly have owned it legitimately.

"Some of that stuff is real heavy. I'm afraid the flour got wet some. Are you sure it was covered?"

Cordell grimaced at the question, then went to fill the eating bags from the buckets of the grain shoved into the right corner of the wagon bed. He couldn't help wondering if his friend had ever gone anywhere unprepared. Springing easily into the wagon, he glanced at the flour sack and tried to remember if the canvas had covered it completely or not. His fingers pushing against the sack told him what he didn't really want to know: A portion of the sack was now hardened paste. Further poking indicated, however, that most of the flour was fine. Satisfied, he headed for the grain buckets.

In the corral, Taullery kneeled and ran his hand along the injured leg of his horse. His light pressing on the long tendons brought no response as he moved downward. A good sign, he told himself. Raising the hoof, he touched the soft pad surounded by an iron shoe and the horse pulled it from him in pain.

"Looks like a stone bruise all right." Taullery released the horse's leg and shook his head. "It'll be all right in a few days, I suppose. We should've been watching the trail more closely."

"For rocks?" Cordell said as he attached the first bag to his gray horse's head and the animal began chomping the grain enthusiastically. He walked over to the sorrel, slid the canvas bag over its nose, and began tying the attached strings around its head to hold it in place.

"I'll take the grain for the bays. They don't take well to anyone messing around their heads," Taullery said.

"A bit fussy, huh?"

"No, just, well . . ."

"Fussy." Cordell handed over the remaining feed bags and returned to the wagon.

Stacking one box of canned goods on top of another, he lifted them and started for the Bauer house. Half-skipping with the two Harper children chasing him, Shank came around the side of the barn and headed directly for the minister.

"Brought you some help with your things," he said. "Mighty good help, too."

"It's mostly food for the Harpers," Taullery said tartly, looking up from his two bay horses.

Shank ignored the tone and bellowed, "Well, how's that for neighborly generosity? Michael an' Rebecca, let's get at it."

Eight-year-old Rebecca immediately went to Cordell,

holding the boxes, removed two cans, one in each hand, and trotted toward the house, proud of her contribution. She glanced over her shoulder at Cordell, smiled, and continued. Shank wondered aloud if little girls learned coquettishness from big girls, or if it was something built into them. Shoving his damp hat back on his head, Cordell chuckled and said it was a good question.

Twelve-year-old Michael stared at the black-suited Cordell, blinked away his indecision, and asked, "Preacher, are you going to pray over . . . my pa—and my uncle? Ma said you'd be a-doin' it soon as you could. They're dead, you know. They hanged my pa—with a rope." He tried to state the situation without showing any emotion, but a whimper got past his determination and a loud wail burst through his young resolve.

Grabbing the boy with bearlike arms, Shank held the sobbing boy to him and stared at the horizon for an instant. "That's all right, Michael, me boy. That's all right. Your pa was a fine man, a fine man—an' he'd want you to be the head of the family now. Come on, now."

Chapter Ten

Cordell saw himself in the grieving boy, laid the boxes on the ground, and came over to them. Kneeling beside Michael, his mind raced for words. Something from the Bible? Something more than . . .

"I'm sorry, Michael. I was proud to call your father a friend." Cordell hid his frustration at not saying something more meaningful. "A brave man who fought for Te—"

"They hanged him. I—I s-saw . . . it. One o' them Regulators held me an' made me. He said my pa was a traitor—an' I should see what happens to traitors. Pa looked at me, at all o' us, and tried to say . . . he loved us. They kicked the hoss he were on a'fer he could get out all my name. Pa's face went all purple—an' he kicked his legs an' . . ."

Cordell glanced at Shank's face; the big man's eyes were welling with tears. Pushing back the anger that wanted to express itself, Cordell knew the boy needed to tell someone what he had seen, as awful as it had been. Silently, he let the boy describe watching his father cruelly hang. Each word tore itself from the twelve-year-old's soul. ". . . an' his eyes went all starey . . . an' he . . . his pants were filled with . . . everythin'. He couldn't see . . . us no more."

With a long sigh, Michael stopped talking and hung his head. In a soft voice, Cordell said, "Michael, I want you to do something for me, will you?"

The boy's lips pursed, and he rubbed his eyes. "W-what?"

"I want you to shut your eyes. Close them, will you?"

Michael sniffed back the fullness in his nose; his eyelids fluttered and closed.

"Good, now . . . I want to you to see your father coming home from the War. Remember? Did you run out to hug him? He told me about coming home to you and your sister and your mother. How wonderful it was. Do you see him coming, Michael? Tell me about it."

Michael nodded his head affirmatively. A tear burst through the closed eyelid and escaped down his cheek. "I—I saw him comin' up the r-road—an' I ran out to him. He were a-walkin'. I knew it were him when he were just a stick o' a shape. On that ridge, quarter mile away."

"Do you see him comin' down that road again? Look, Michael. Look, Michael."

Michael's head nodded slightly.

"Is he hugging you now?"

The boy's head moved affirmatively again. He sniffed away emotion. "I—I r-ran an' ran—an' I were all outta breath when I got to him. H-he grabbed me an' held me so tight I couldn't hardly breathe. It was the bestust I ever did feel, I think. He started in a-singin'—an' I yelled. Then Ma came, a-holdin' Becky's hand."

"Yes, it was wonderful. Whenever you think of your

father, I want you to think of that time, Michael. Because he will always be with you. Always." Cordell swallowed away his own emotion and continued. "Squeeze your eyes real tight. If you do, you can feel him hugging you right now. Feel it—can you feel his love all around you?"

"I—I love you, P-Pa."

"I love you, Michael," Cordell whispered. "That's what he's saying. I can hear it, can you?"

Michael nodded, and tears streamed across his shining face. Shank wiped his eyes with a huge fist, his wet face a big mirror of the boy's.

"I—is there really a h-heaven?" Michael stuttered.

"Yes, Michael, there certainly is. Your father is there now—an' it's a wonderful happy place to be. He's very happy there—but he misses you and Becky and your mother. One day, a long time from now, you'll see him again there—and he'll be waiting to hug you again."

"P-promise?"

"I promise, Michael."

From the corral, Taullery yelled about the progress with the wagon. "Hey, you guys gonna get that wagon unloaded today? Or do I have to do everything?"

Cordell put his hand on the boy's shoulder and Michael exploded into him with a fierce hug. The impact knocked the minister off balance, but he caught himself with his right hand against the ground. With first his left arm and then both, Cordell returned the hug. Patting the boy on the back, he said, "Sounds like we'd better get to work, huh?"

"Yes sir."

They stood and headed for the wagon with Shank trailing after them like a huge puppy, his face still wet with tears. Without losing a stride, the big man pulled a folded, but dirty, rag from his pocket and blew his nose loudly three times. The loud honking behind them brought surprise, then a chuckle, from both Cordell and the boy. Pausing to examine the nasal contents in the rag, Shank wiped his nose vigorously, then ceremoniously refolded the rag and put it back into his pocket. His half-skips quickly caught him up with the minister and the boy as they reached the wagon.

Without warning, the image of his own father's self-righteous wrath seeped into Cordell's mind. He wished his recollection of the man could include such a hug as did Michael's memories, but he couldn't recall any emotion from the man except rage. His mother was the only goodness in his small world back then, and she had run away with another man one night and left him alone with the evil man. Her leaving made the senior Pastor Cordell more bitter, and he took it out on the boy with nearly daily beatings.

Actually, the only enduring thing from Cordell's mother, besides her gentle ways, was his name. "Rule" was her choice, a doleful wish to make her only child become nobility. His father hated the name and called his son "Aaron," his middle name. But "Rule Aaron Cordell" was written in the family Bible before he knew, and even his beating couldn't make her change it.

Cordell shook his head to help push the torturous memories into a black hole of his mind, reminding himself that the boy had been forced to watch his own father be hanged. Distorted images of Captain Padgett and Lion Graham lingered in mental shadows. He hated them for what they had done to this boy, to this family. He should forgive, as the Bible said, but he couldn't.

"You know, I may not have covered the flour sack good enough during the rain." Cordell put his arm around Michael and forced concentration onto the wagon. "But don't tell my friend, Ian, over there, will you? He's a real stickler on things like that."

Michael smiled back. "It'll be our secret, sir."

"Great."

"S-sir, will you come to see—us, me, sometime?"

Cordell was surprised by the question, blinked, and said, "I'd like that a lot, Michael. Why don't we make a promise to each other? Once a week, we'll get together—and talk, or go fishin', or go ridin'. Maybe your mother will let you come over to my place and help with the horses."

"Really? That would be swell, sir." Michael's face brightened.

"Let's shake on it," Cordell said, and held out his hand for the boy to grab.

Stepping behind them, Shank laid a huge paw on each shoulder and pronounced with a friendly growl, "I think you boys is plannin' some fun. Hope you can deal this ol' 'Russian' in on it."

Cordell looked at Michael, smiled, and said, "Tell him, Michael."

Beaming, the boy explained their promise to be together once a week, and Shank immediately asked if he could join them. Both agreed that it would be grand if he did, and they began unloading Taullery's wagon with enthusiasm. Shank expressed gratitude for Taullery's generosity, and Cordell didn't mention he had paid for the supplies. Michael told Cordell that the big man had already given them food and other needed items from his mercantile wagon. Shank was embarrassed by the approval from Cordell that followed.

After completing the transfer of boxes and sacks of food into the house, Shank and Taullery stayed outside and Taullery asked to see Shank's merchandise wagon. The big man told Taullery about Cordell's conversation with the boy and said he had never heard a minister say such soothing words. He also knew about Cordell trying to stop the state police last Sunday, even making up the name of a dead outlaw so they would take him instead.

Shank shook his head in wonderment as he recounted what he had heard. Taullery wanted to tell him about his friend's real past but resisted. Shank had a well-earned reputation for spreading news—of all kinds. He wasn't vindictive, just talkative, brought on by so much time alone, traveling from ranch to homestead to small settlement.

Taullery acknowledged that his friend was an intensely caring man and changed the subject. Fleeting pictures of Cordell wildly leading cavalry against entrenched Union forces rushed across his mind. His measured response was to ask where Shank got various items in the wagon; the big man's answer every time was a trade. Cash money was hard to come by. He survived through an ingenious system of bartering that only he completely understood.

Finally, Taullery brought up their earlier encounter with the Comanche war party but changed the outcome to their being threatened away by his rifle. Shank observed that the Indians would soon have trouble existing since the buffalo hunters were destroying the great herds. Taullery thought the sooner both were gone, the better. After discussing the disastrous state of the Texas economy, Shank asked if Taullery knew that a black man—Jacob "Suitcase" Eliason—had bought the closed boot factory.

Taullery acknowledged that he did and cursed the thought that the Negroes were taking over Texas faster than the Northerners. His voice trembled for an instant before retreating into a more controlled tone. In smoldering words, he announced that Eliason had asked the minister and his wife to teach black children at the factory, and he thought it was a great mistake. Shank's eyes narrowed, but he said nothing, changing the subject by asking what Taullery thought was the best way to sell boots.

Meanwhile, Cordell went to the main house with Michael to see his mother. At the doorway, Michael went in first. Before entering, Cordell brushed off his still-damp coat and removed his hat, limp from its bout with the rain. Recalling his telltale arousal after Aleta's sensual departure, he glanced down to make certain that his pants weren't gathered around his groin. They were fine, but he straightened the cloth anyway before entering.

A sense of feminine warmth permeated the house, mixed with a sadness not easily defined. To the casual observer, it was an elegant home; to the more observing eye, signs of neglect ate at the corners. Michael stepped beside him, eager to find his mother and hopeful his closeness would keep the minister moving along. But Cordell was drawn to a magnificent hand-carved wood mantel over the fireplace. Cradles of dust in inlaid patterns of wild flowers only added to the appearance of texture and shading. Definitely Mexican in design, the mantel controlled the entire room with its quiet beauty.

Too impatient to wait any longer, Michael grabbed Cordell's hand to accelerate their travel and said his mother was waiting. Cordell wanted to look further but followed the boy to the parlor off the main room. He heard Mary Taullery before he saw anyone. Entering the parlor, his gaze took in Ellena Harper in a large wood-framed chair, talking quietly with Aleta wearing the slicker, Mary Taullery, and Widow Bauer. Mary had changed into a solemn black dress with a matching bonnet. To Cordell, the funeral apparel seemed artificial in contrast to his radiant wife still in her rain-soaked garments. In the corner, Rebecca was playing quietly with her new rag doll.

When the young minister and her son stepped into

the room, Ellena Harper burst into tears. Michael rushed to comfort her, proclaiming that he wouldn't let anyone hurt their family again. He also blurted out the promise from Cordell to be with him weekly, but forgot to add Shank was invited too.

Kneeling beside the weeping woman, Cordell took her pale hand with his left hand and held Michael's with the other. "Mrs. Harper, I am so sorry. Your husband was a good man, and I will always cherish his friendship."

"Thank you, Reverend. You were very brave to try to stop those Yankee killers. Forgive me, but I only wish you were good with a gun. They deserve to die. I'm sorry, I shouldn't . . ." She pulled her hand from his and covered her face with both hands to hide the anguish that followed. Michael awkwardly hugged her. She patted his arm and thanked him.

Cordell's eyes sought Aleta's. She, too, was crying. Mary Taullery was sniffling behind a lace handkerchief. Only Widow Jenson seemed removed from the sadness, staring at the doorway, alone in some moment of her own from yesterday.

"God has a plan for them—as he does for all of us," Cordell heard himself say. "I—I would be lying to you if I asked you to forgive them—for I cannot."

He shut his eyes and began to pray aloud, asking for God to grant His great peace of mind to all of them, and to comfort the Harper family in such an awful time. An "Amen" followed from his lips. Widow Jenson muttered "Amen" without changing her gaze, and so did Aleta. Ellena Harper mouthed the closing, but no sound emerged. Mary Taullery said strongly, "Praise God that he does so. Amen."

Cordell felt terribly inadequate and wanted to leave the room. He wanted a gun. Beads of sweat attacked his forehead. His head wound began to throb. He wanted to attack something. Anything. Anyone.

Silently, he prayed for forgiveness for thinking so, then heard his father say, "*Who gave you this right to take a life? Only God has that right. Those who take another's life will be plunged into almighty damnation. Yea, verily, I say unto you, it is the word of the righteous God Almighty*." General Stuart followed behind his father, saying that to attack a great enemy was to live. A dying Moon told him everything a man did was a prayer. Johnny Cat Carlson, the dead outlaw leader he had once befriended, told him to quit caring about people who were born to be walked on.

Cordell opened his eyes and saw Michael peeking at him. The boy touched Cordell on the shoulder and whispered, "I know you tried hard, sir. Don't know anybody who would've charged them Regulators the way you did. You 'bout got yourself kilt too. Heck, you're not supposed to be good with a gun, sir. You're a preacher."

Chapter Eleven

A new-born sun, unsure of itself in the early-morning sky, found Rule Cordell already working with a young bay gelding. Aleta was inside preparing breakfast. Tonight would also be her first class with the black children Eliason had gathered at his factory. She was excited about the new experience, especially so since Cordell was going to join her.

Eliason had assured her there would be at least twelve black children waiting. Two white townsmen had visited Rule and Aleta at home to discourage this teaching endeavor, but had been sent away with Cordell's defiant words ringing in their ears.

It felt good to lose himself in work, to leave the responsibilities of the spirit for a while and reconnect with the concerns of this world. Anticipation of a good meal added to his contentment. Trying to stay in the saddle of a green horse was no time to be thinking about anything else. Any praying should have already been done.

An eager sweat bee, awakened by the fragile dawn, tried to surround the bay's head all by itself, then gave up the task to encircle Cordell's. With a swift slap of his opened hand, the insect fluttered to the ground. He stared down at the stunned bee and muttered an apology, reminding himself that it had as much right to the land as he did.

A week had passed since their move to the Jensen place, and they were settling nicely into the small cabin behind the big house. True to his word, he had ridden over to see Michael—and the boy's mother and sister—yesterday. They had gone fishing and caught enough for everyone's supper.

Cordell's mind jerked from the sweet time with Michael to his father's cruel punishments when he was a child. A timid ray of sun across his face triggered the hateful memory of being forced to stand outside their house for several hours on a frigid winter day when he forgot to refer to his father as "Right Reverend." Frostbite nearly consumed his hands and toes. Then he saw his father slap his mother across the face. Twice. Three times. Blood crept from the corner of her lip, but she said nothing. Not a whimper. It was the last night that either Cordell or his father ever saw her. Even now, he wondered what became of her and if her new life ever included any thoughts of him.

He shook his head. That was long ago. Another world. Another lifetime, it seemed. This was now. Shaking his head brought a brief pain. The head wound bothered him only occasionally, usually when he was tired at the end of the day, or when his head was shook hard by the jolt of a bucking horse, or when he moved it vigorously.

With soothing words to the nervous horse, he checked its new shoes. Purchased from Taullery's store and nailed on as they were, most ranchers called them "good 'noughs." They weren't nearly as effective as having a blacksmith use an anvil and bellows to heat and shape the shoe to the horse's foot. But taking a horse into town took time—and money. He had rasped the edges off yesterday. Taullery wouldn't have liked the result, but Cordell thought they looked fine.

Yesterday, as planned, Cordell had delivered the four gift horses to the Evanses. Each had been ridden at least twenty saddles and were broke to the slicker and rope; they would be excellent working horses for any rancher. He was proud of the way they had responded to his training, and the thought of giving them to the family that had so generously helped him and Aleta made him feel good all over again. The look on Jacob Evans's face was all the payment Cordell needed. Slapping his hands together in appreciation, Evans had yelled for his wife and sons to come to the corral, and they were equally appreciative. Mrs. Evans invited Cordell to stay for supper, but he begged off, saying that he had to get back to work on a new stallion. The oldest Evans boy wanted to know if he needed help, but his father, Jacob, reminded him of the chores already assigned.

Satisfied, he curled himself easily into the saddle, his spurs jingling softly. A gunshot rattled the horizon. He settled into the stirrups and concentrated on listening. Maybe he had heard wrong. The young horse shook at the strange presence again on its back, then stood quietly. Patting its brown neck, he complimented the horse on being quiet. The animal's alert ears spun toward him to gather more information, but its rider was preoccupied with watching the shadowed prairie.

No other sounds of shooting came across the land. One shot? Probably someone trying to shoot a prairie grouse or a rabbit, he mused to himself. The shot came from the east, where three other small homesteads stretched across the rolling land. Sound could travel quite a distance in the early-morning air, he reminded himself, and LeRoy Breen, his farthest neighbor, liked rabbit stew. He grinned at the man describing such a meal the last time they were together. It was at least a month ago, after church services. Mrs. Breen came every Sunday, but not her husband.

A second shot cracked the silence, followed by another and another, growing into a string of explosions. Aleta came to the back door and stepped outside. She wore an apron over her leather riding skirt and white peasant blouse. Her frown was a knowing one; somewhere a gun battle was under way—and it was heading toward their home.

"Rule, can you see anytheeng? What ees it, *por favor?*"

"Don't know, Aleta. Wait a minute, there's a rider—see? Against the sky. Just a speck. Could be headed this way." Cordell held his hand above his eyes to help him see. "He's still a long way from Breen's, I think."

"There has to be more than one, Rule."

"Yeah, I know, one's all I see—so far." He turned back to her and she was gone.

Within a minute, she returned with one of her pistols pushed into an apron pocket. In her right hand was a Henry rifle; in the other, his old field glasses. The guns were from the bedroom display, the field glasses from a kitchen drawer. Gunshots were linked together now, like an oncoming train. Seeing her with the weapons tore at the promise to himself that he would give his life to God and leave violence behind him. The sight upset him more than the shooting.

"I don't think you're going to need a gun, Aleta," Cordell said as he swung down and walked toward her to retrieve the binoculars. He led the saddled horse by the reins, and the animal shook its head joyously to be relieved of the strange thing on its back.

"Maybe not, my love, but eet is *bueno* to be ready, no?" Aleta's smile was less than full. "Not all vaqueros ride for good." She handed him the glasses.

He didn't answer, walking to the edge of the corral closest to the distant silhouette. Initially, the horse balked at the change in direction, but Cordell talked it into joining his advance. Holding the reins in one hand, he stared into the glasses, blinked, and looked again, rejecting what his eyes were telling him in the uneven morning light.

"It's Billy Rip's sister! It's Lizzie!" Cordell exclaimed without looking away, using the Civil War nickname for Bill Ripton, then the youngest scout in his patrol.

"Elizabeth Ripton?"

"Yeah, what the . . . a bunch of riders are after her. My God, Regulators! Why?"

Carrying the rifle, Aleta ran from the house to Cordell's side. He handed her the field glasses and swung into the saddle.

"Where are you going?" Aleta held the glasses, but was watching him instead.

"I'm going out to see what's going on."

"I go too." She started to put the field glasses into the apron pocket containing her pistol. Realizing it was full, she shoved them into the other empty apron pocket instead. Her eyes were hot with the threat of oncoming battle.

"No, you stay here."

"Take thees gun." Her face was stern. She held out the rifle with both hands.

He hesitated, swung onto the horse's back, and said, "All right. Give it to me. But, please, go back into the house."

She handed him the Henry as he rode past and spurred the horse into a gallop.

"*Escuche!* Listen! Rule, my love, they are not coming

to hear a sermon. *Por favor*, you must shoot, then pray, eef you want to help her." Aleta's words caught his ears as the big-shouldered bay crow-hopped once, in response to the jab of the rowels, lowered its ears, and stretched out to run.

He was headed for a long, swollen ridge, a giant dismembered arm stretching out across the flat land. It was naked of growth, except for defiant batches of buffalo grass and a trio of scrawny trees on the far southern lip. Side by side, the wind-shoved trees stood, like three skinny cowboys standing together, chatting and watching the prairie.

The big gun was comfortable in his outstretched arm, and he urged the bay into a smooth run, eating up the distance between himself and his fleeing friend. Suddenly, his mind told him that he was carrying a weapon again. His eyes turned from the land to the hand gripping the Henry. Anger swept through his body. His own hand had betrayed him. He raised the gun to fling it away from himself, away from what it meant.

Then he glanced back to Lizzie Ripton. The fourteen-year-old Ripton girl was in clear sight now, nearing the farthest in the string of homesteads. A more confident dawn highlighted her against its chest-thumping color. Her ballooning dress was transformed into giant heaving lungs on both sides of her charging horse.

She was riding bareback with only a bridle and reins. Her torn bodice was half red, her right breast exposed. Hair braids flopped on her back in rhythm with the wild ride. Suddenly, she slumped, holding on to the horse's neck. One rein danced loose in the wind. He could see the patrol easily now without the aid of field glasses. They were a black shape oozing across the plain, five riders spitting bursts of orange flame a hundred yards behind her. The firing was less frequent now, as Lizzie's fine horse lengthened its lead in spite of the uneven movement of the rider.

Leave it to Billy Rip's sister to have good horse flesh under her, Cordell thought, and lowered his arm and the rifle. Silently, he told God that nothing had changed; he just had to help his friend, that's all. He asked for understanding. His words were clipped in rhythm with the pounding of the strong-striding bay.

Ahead was the middle of the ridge, offering the most protection. He would dismount there and fire over the heads of the Regulars. Hopefully, Lizzie Ripton would realize it was someone friendly and come his way. Hopefully, the warning shots would be enough to turn away the Regulators. Hopefully. He asked God for understanding again.

Approaching the land swell, he reined in the bay, but the horse didn't want to stop, savoring the wonder of running. He pulled harder on the reins, but the animal had the bit in its mouth and decided to keep going, ignoring his physical and verbal commands. Realizing the animal could easily bolt past Lizzie Ripton and into the advancing patrol, he pulled the reins to the left side and held them there, forcing the horse to turn sideways.

In spite of the need for urgency, he had to be patient. Yanking the horse too hard would likely make the animal fall, possibly injuring both of them. He forced himself to concentrate on bringing the animal into a gradual circle behind the ridge. The rifle was in the way, but he rejected the passing thought to drop the weapon and get it later. Instead, he laid the barrel, with his right hand, against the opposite side of the horse's head to reinforce his left fist's rein pull.

A wide jerky circle began to take shape, with the bay fighting the tightly held reins and frantically seeking an opportunity to race once more. Then another circle, this time smaller; then another and another. Each time the circle shrunk and the animal's gallop changed into a lathered trot. Finally, it came to a begrudging stop at the northernmost slope of the ridge.

He inhaled and exhaled the tension. Sweat bubbled on his forehead in contrast to the coolness of the early morning. He felt like he'd been in a fistfight and took another deep breath to regain his mental balance. A splatter of gunshots brought him back to the need for immediate action. He glanced in the direction of the patrol. He doubted they had seen him; they were still too far away and their concentration was on their fleeing prey.

Worried that the animal would try to bolt again when he left the saddle, he jumped down anyway. Shooting from its back would make for a guaranteed runaway. Holding the reins in his right fist, he hurried back to the middle of the ridge, then cocked and aimed the rifle. There was no time to wonder what the green animal would do when the weapon roared.

The Henry jumped slightly in his hands as he fired. Rearing in fearful response, the frightened horse tried to pull away from the rifle's roar. He barely looked at the bay, knowing only more exposure to gunfire itself would eventually calm the animal. The pull against the reins in his fist made aiming difficult, but he wasn't trying to hit anything anyway. Realizing that the big gun had a tendency to jam, he levered new cartridges carefully, a task he had learned the hard way. In between shots, he waved at Lizzie to come toward him.

He didn't think the young girl saw the motion as Cordell concentrated more shots over the heads of the Regulators, who showed no signs of responding to his firing yet. The faces of the five men were beginning to define themselves as they raced after the young girl. If they kept at their same direction, both Lizzie and the Regulators would pass fifty yards in front of the ridge, slanting toward the south. If she made it that far.

Movement behind him was sensed before heard, and he spun around with his rifle readied. It was Aleta riding her paint horse and carrying the other rifle in her hand. Gone was the apron, and in its place was a pistol belt and holstered revolver. Stray sunlight recoiled from the pearl handle. Long black hair flamed behind her like a wild Comanche on the warpath. Her skirt was flapping like a huge bird above her thighs.

There was no time to be angry or to waste words about her going back. He pointed in the direction of the ridge where it swelled highest and returned to firing at the Regulators. He wasn't certain, but he thought they may be gaining on Lizzie and fired again over their heads. A streak of red on the flank of Lizzie's horse explained the shrinking lead. Cordell fired again over the heads of the patrol. For the first time, shots were returned in his general direction.

Chapter Twelve

Aleta's running dismount would have been the envy of any fighting man. Her well-trained paint stood quietly where the reins hit the ground. But she knelt on top of them for assurance it wouldn't be frightened away. She cocked and swung the Henry to her shoulder in a single motion, and her first shot knocked a Regulator from his saddle.

Cordell stared at the riderless horse with its flailing stirrups and exclaimed, "Aleta, you just shot a man!"

"*Sí*. You want to save Elizabeth Ripton—or jes' say you tried. You must stop them now, Rule. She weel not stay on her horse *mucho* longer." Her words were calm, like she was asking him how he wanted his eggs for breakfast.

Without waiting for his response, she levered the Henry and fired again, but missed. Cordell's own answer was to fire three shots himself, over the heads of the remaining four riders. Yells of concern erupted from the Regulator patrol. Agitated faces searched the ridge for their unknown attackers. One man pointed at the ridge where Cordell and Aleta continued their long-range assault. Cordell fired over their heads again; Aleta levered three shots into the pack and another Regulator fell.

As the man flopped unmoving to the ground, Aleta shouted "Vamos!" and fired again at the falling rider. Returning gunshots spit dirt on the crouching Cordell. Together, the remaining three Regulators shouted hoarse encouragement to each other and charged toward the ridge, now less than fifty yards away. The embankment thumped with lead from their rifles. Aleta's first shot missed, but her second drove the lead rider tumbling from his horse.

Cordell fired twice; his second shot caught the rider low in the stomach, driving him backward and out of the saddle. The man's released rifle held in the air for an instant before thudding to the prairie. Cordell watched the result with her eyes wide. He had intended to shoot the horse.

Aleta stood. The remaining Regulator aimed his rifle at the suddenly appearing target and two bullets spit their songs of death around her. Coolly, she levered a new cartridge into her Henry, raised it to her shoulder, fired, and missed. She cocked and fired again, but the gun was empty. Closing on her, the Regulator recocked his shiny Winchester and aimed, grasping the reins in his left fist where it held the barrel. Aleta reached for new bullets in her skirt pocket, shoved one into the loading tube, and looked up as the man's face exploded into crimson. His riderless horse raced wildly onward, clearing the ridge and continuing past them. Limp smoke from Cordell's rifle told the rest of the story. Stillness came again so fast that it made both Aleta and Cordell freeze in place. To her face came a faint smile. To Cordell's, a great sadness.

Knowing he had no choice but to stop the man, Cordell studied the other downed riders scattered about the prairie. None were threats any longer, he decided. Only one was standing, dragging a broken leg and holding his bleeding stomach. Four of the horses had bolted toward where they had come from. A lone brown horse stood with its head down, badly winded but unhurt otherwise. Closer was an unmoving Regulator, facedown in the dust, Aleta's second victim. Spread-legged on the ground near him was the man Cordell had accidentally shot, holding his crimson stomach with both hands. Ten feet to his right was the man Cordell had just killed. The dead rider's face was a red ball. The part-time minister held his hand to his mouth to hold back the anguish rushing through him. He hadn't wanted this. He wanted to lead others toward a peace he had finally found within himself. He wanted a new life, a new beginning.

Aleta's rifle roared twice more and the only standing Regulator crumpled, twitched, and moved no more. She yelled in Spanish that they would kill no more innocent men. Cordell shuddered, thought of Lizzie Ripton, and looked in her direction. Twenty yards from the three scrawny trees guarding the end of the ridge, the young rider's wounded horse stood. Unmoving. Heaving its last gasps.

Lizzie lay across its back, her right shoulder and shirt sleeve drenched in bright red blood. The homespun cotton dress was ripped open; torn cloth and one braid caressed her pink breast. Cordell avoided looking at her body and sought her face. She was pale, in spite of long days in the sun; light brown curls stuck to her damp cheeks and forehead. Across the bridge of her nose, a patch of freckles appeared more prominent than ever. She was half woman, half child—and all Ripton, resembling her older brother and father with the same thick chin, deep-set eyes, and high cheekbones.

An uneven sigh foreshadowed the animal's collapse as it sank to the ground. Another groan followed and the horse lay on its side. Lizzie disappeared, like she was connected. There was no attempt to kick free; no reaction at all. Only her right leg, with no sign of her dress, was visible, and it could just as well been attached to the horse, so little did it move.

Cordell rushed to the south slope as fast as he could lead his balky bay. He laid down his smoking rifle and wrapped the reins around a branch on the first tree there. He quieted the horse, disturbed by the smell of blood and death. After a few shivers, the animal lowered its head and Cordell ran on to the fallen girl.

"Lizzie! It's me, Rule. Lizzie, are you all right?"

A thin voice answered, "Captun Cordell, I'm mighty glad to see you, suh. Mighty glad. They's dun in my mare. Goddamn 'em to hell."

Cordell couldn't hold back a smile. He hadn't heard her curse before, but it was exactly something her older brother would have said. Even sounded like him. A closer look at Lizzie's horse wiped the smile away; the fine animal was nearing the end. The caring thing would be to put the horse out of its misery, but that should be Lizzie's decision if she was able to make it. Cordell raced around the downed horse to see that her left leg was trapped under the unmoving mount.

Lizzie's admiring gaze followed Cordell's advance, and she spoke through clinched teeth, trying to hide the roaring pain. Her bleary eyes sought his, and she made no attempt to cover herself. "Was a-comin' fer yo-all's he'p, Captun. Them Regulators dun got us surrounded. They's a-sayin' Billy's a criminal—an' Ma an' Pa are . . . criminals cuz they's hidin' him. Padgett's a-wantin' us out—so's some carpetbagger kin have our place, I reckon."

She stopped talking, unable to talk more until she could replenish the breath that had left with her words. It took all of her concentration to inhale new air. Cordell took off his shirt, grabbed the sleeve where it was sewn to the main part, and yanked hard. Then again. Seams released their hold and he pulled the freed sleeve from his arm, folding it quickly several times. Kneeling beside her, he covered her exposed bosom with his shirt, then placed the small pad of sleeve over the bullet wound in her shoulder. He took Lizzie's right hand and placed it over the pad. "Hold that tight, Lizzie. You're leaking."

Lizzie's eyes followed him as she complied with his request, continuing to inhale deeply. A weak smile entered her face, and he patted her head gently. She didn't appear to realize her leg was pinned. After a long, leathery gasp, she continued her description of recent trouble.

"They came after us a while back, Captun. Fer taxes. Wanted to throw us off'n the place then. Pa said we wasn't leavin' nohow. Said we'd come up with the money some way. Eight hundred dollars. Eight hundred dollars! Yah know, Captun, our folks dun built that place from nuthin'."

Lizzie paused again, pulled in fresh air that seemed to be vanishing through the bullet holes in her body.

"Don't know how they did it, b-but my folks got the money an' dun paid it all. Made that fancy Captain Padgett real mad, but he went away. 'Til yesterday. They sneaked up on us. Two o' 'em caught me in the barn—and they tried to . . . Billy heard me yellin' an' came a-runnin'. Whipped 'em both, he did."

Lizzie inhaled for a breath that wouldn't come fast enough, swallowed, and wiped away a tear before it could run.

"Take your time, Lizzie. Where are Billy and your folks now?" Cordell said.

"We's holed up in the house. Ma an' I were loadin'—an' Pa an' Billy were shootin'. During the night, Billy an' I sneaked to the barn an' got Sally hyar. Thought I got away without 'em seeing me. Billy tolt me to ride for yo-all. So that's what I were a-doin'."

"You think they're still holding out?"

"Pa said we had plenty o' bullets and water. An' he didn't think they'd burn the place. That'd just make fer more work fer the new owner. Leastwise, that's what Pa thought."

"How many men does Padgett have?"

"Billy said you'd ask that." She smiled and shifted her weight to her left arm, realizing for the first time that Cordell had covered her with his shirt. "You didn't have to use your shirt, Captun. I didn't mind. Really. Billy said there were twenty-four. Twenty-six, countin' Padgett an' a city feller."

"We're going to get you to our house where you'll be safe—and we can take care of you."

Lizzie's eyes indicated she didn't like his use of "our" and "we." Her gaze went beyond him for the first time in an attempt to see if his wife was with him. Then she remembered more of her story.

"I almost forgot the worse part, Captun. They dun shot Whisper. His wife is poorly, and he came fer a poultice Ma makes. He went outside to talk with Padgett. Said the law would protect us. Wouldn't listen to Pa or Billy. Mighty fancy words he threw at 'em, Captun. I dun heard most from the window. You'd a been real proud o' him, Billy said."

Cordell couldn't believe what he was hearing, and the air caught in his throat and wouldn't go anywhere. "That skinny city fella with Padgett dun kilt him—ri't front of our house. Coldest eyes I ever did see behind them spectacles."

"Lion Graham." Cordell's pronouncement was a hiss.

"N-never heard his name. But he pulled a shooter from his purty sash an' shot Whisper. Ri't in midword. Three, four times he shot Whisper. Then he l-laughed and said he were tired of all the windying. Then Padgett shouted fer us to give up. The shootin' started ri' after that."

Cordell squeezed his eyes shut to stop the pain. It wasn't real. It couldn't be. It wasn't fair, not after all Whisper had gone through during the War. Whisper was a good man. Honest and strong. A flash of Whisper Jenson at a patrol campfire, questioning their next move, roared through Cordell's mind. What would happen to his family? Cordell touched the medicine pouch hanging from his neck, under his shirt, and made a silent promise to his wartime comrade: Whisper's family would be cared for. The face of Lion Graham came to him, and he shivered. It angered him that he felt such a twinge of fear. How could a small boy become so mad?

Shaking away the darkness in his mind, he concentrated on the next task, getting Lizzie freed from her horse. He sat on the ground beside her and put both boots against the horse's back, his knees nearly doubled.

She watched the daring Confederate leader that her brother had told her about so often and she had met at their house. Her crush was hard to conceal, even when she was weak from loss of blood. She wanted to touch his face, but it hurt to move her arm. "Heard yo-all a-firin' at them. Do appreciate yur doin' it, I sur do, Captun Cordell. I reckon yo-all are the bravest man I know. Billy said you'd know what to do."

"When I say go, Lizzie, you pull your leg out. Can you do that?"

"Sur nuff, Captun Cordell. Holler away. This hyar

mare, she dun give me all she had, I reckon."

Pushing against the dying horse, Cordell managed to lift its back slightly and Lizzie Ripton pulled on her trapped left leg, bracing herself with her good left arm and driving with her right boot against the animal's back. Nothing happened. Cordell gasped and released his legs, emptied of strength. They would need Aleta's help too.

He stood and yelled for her to come. Lizzie frowned but was too weak to complain. Aleta was walking through the downed Regulators, leading her paint horse. She paused, a look of irritation on her face, and mouthed *"Uno momento."* A revolver in her hand made it clear what she was doing: making certain none of the attackers were alive. Cordell sighed and knew she was right, even if it hurt to see and think about.

The ridge was too far away from the other homesteads for anyone to be able to determine who had helped the young rider or who her pursuers were. Of course, even at a distance, it was obvious Aleta was a woman, but he couldn't worry about that. His mind was turning to ways to disguise what had happened. Eventually, Captain Padgett would send out more riders to find out what happened to the first five.

It wouldn't take much of a tracker to end up at his ranch. What could he do to misdirect them—without putting a neighbor at risk either? How long before more would return? He didn't think it would be any sooner than tomorrow morning. But if Captain Padgett wanted it so, their return visit to the ridge could come before nightfall.

A plan of sorts was taking shape in his mind as he watched Aleta cross back over the ridge, leading her paint. He would try to create the appearance of an outlaw band waiting in ambush and then riding off to the south. After Lizzie was freed from her dying mount,

Cordell would walk their horses back and forth several times along the back side of the ridge to create the illusion of many waiting there. His own layered footprints would add to this picture as well.

Next, he would let them see horse tracks riding off to the south, straight from the bottom lip of the ridge, like the "gang" might have been from the border. He would hold Lizzie in the saddle in front of him. They would head for a dry creek bed that slid diagonally across the land. It was a half-hour away, but riding through the rock-lined creek bed would be enough to lose any trackers—especially if they weren't expecting the riders to swing north again.

Before leaving the rock cover, he would muffle his horse's movement with pieces of his shirt tied over its hooves. That should make their return to the ranch nearly impossible to follow. With any break at all, the wind would do the rest. All of that misdirection would take time, and Lizzie's wounds were serious. She would need to heal and regain her strength. That meant keeping her hidden in their home. That was a different problem, one to worry about later.

Cordell thought the young girl could handle the ride after the bleeding was stopped. Or was he trying to convince himself of that fact because he was afraid of Regulators coming to their home? His chest rose and fell as he contemplated the answer to that question, watching Aleta come toward him. *If anything ever happened to Aleta . . .* He stopped his mind from pursuing that line of thought and raced to others more pressing.

If the Regulators returned before he erased the tracks, he could simply say that he and his wife had ridden out to see what happened, and that the gang had already left. That answer helped relieve the tension within him somewhat. Part of him wanted to bury the dead men and pray for them. He struggled with the thought of leaving that to others who may or may not come. It wasn't just a religious act, he admitted to himself. It would be a way to hide the fact that Lizzie was alive.

No, his mind challenged, it wouldn't. The state police would dig up the graves to see which bodies were there. An empty hole would mean Lizzie was alive. A single mass grave would make it even easier to discover the truth. Better for the Regulators to think she ran off with an outlaw gang. Thinking through how best to protect the Ripton girl—and to hide their own involvement—was much more comfortable to think about than what he was going to do about the Riptons. Was he going to ride there—and do what? Was he going to let Whisper's death go unchallenged? Or was he going to stay out of it and hope for the best?

Billy Ripton had sent his sister for Captain Rule Cordell, not Reverend Rule Langford. But why should that make him give up his new life? He had made it clear to his friends that "Rule Cordell was dead." That wasn't just to escape his outlaw past, although that was certainly a good enough reason. No, it was to also make it clear his life was forever changed. So why did Padgett have to be his problem? Other than breaking into his church service, the Regulator leader hadn't bothered him—and he knew Lion Graham only by reputation.

Hadn't he talked of peace every Sunday, of looking ahead to better times, of building a community everyone could be proud of? Wasn't he doing his part by helping build a church? His stomach churned with the agony of not wanting to deal with the thought of returning. To battle. A battle that would make him an outlaw again—or a dead man. It wasn't what he had planned for Aleta and himself. It wasn't fair to ask him to give it up.

No one should ask that of him. No one.

Chapter Thirteen

Aleta joined him after tying her own horse to the middle of the three trees. Just seeing her made him feel better and shoved the idea of going after Padgett into a mind shadow. As she inspected Lizzie's wounds, Cordell told about the Regulators surrounding the Riptons' house and Lion Graham killing Whisper, as well as his plan to cover their intervention at the ridge.

Looking up at him, Aleta said with an impish grin, "Elizabeth is becoming *mucho* woman—or did the great Rule Cordell not notice?"

He frowned and pointed at his shirt. Without further comment, she agreed with the idea of making it look like a band of outlaws waited. Such easy agreement surprised him a little, but he hid it in a cough. With a fierce smile, she suggested some touches of her own. They should take some tobacco and cartridges from the dead Regulators and spread the items behind the ridge, as if left by the waiting gang.

She would leave her own sombrero. It was a man's anyway. To make her point, she removed the hat and tossed it toward their horses. Her paint horse watched it sail past his head without moving; Cordell's green mount reared and nearly snapped off the branch holding its reins. The sombrero came to rest against the middle tree. Then she told him to place short sticks inside his two spurs and let the ends touch the ground. When he walked, it would leave tracks like someone was wearing large-roweled Mexican spurs, something he didn't wear.

Her face glowed with anger and a strange sense of accomplishment. "If you want to leave a *mucho* picture, my sweetheart, we can scalp thees bastards—an' make them theenk eet was a Comanche war party."

"I can't do that, Aleta. We have done enough killing today."

"T'is better they die—or our young friend—or us? They weel come back, you know thees." Aleta stepped back to the wounded girl and knelt beside her. "Or weel you ride to help your friends—and take the fight to these bastards." It wasn't a question.

"Let's stay with covering our tracks. For now. After we get Lizzie freed, we'll leave new ones. There's time before you need to leave for school." Cordell motioned toward Lizzie and the downed horse. There was no need to put the animal out of its misery now; the fine mare was dead. Tears trailed from Lizzie's eyes, and Cordell knew it wasn't from the pain of her wounds; it was from the realization that her horse had died.

With Aleta's help, Cordell was able to pull the trapped girl from under the dead horse. Lizzie Ripton attempted to stand and reach for Cordell, but wobbled into a heap at his feet, barely conscious.

Aleta leaned over and felt her forehead. "She has fever. You must hurry her back to the house. Get her water."

"What about riding north—to the creek bed first?"

"No. No time. Take her to the house. *Pronto*. She ees too weak for long ride."

"What if they come before I get back?"

Aleta smiled again and shrugged. "They come. We have guns. No?"

"I can't . . ."

"Does Rule Cordell not go to help hees friends?"

"Rule Cordell is dead. He died when the South did."

"I think, maybe, he is not," Aleta said, returning to her horse. "I think, maybe, he just waits—in your head."

In minutes they were headed back to their ranch house with an unconscious Lizzie Ripton slumped in front of Cordell, his torn shirt buttoned around her. The minister's eyes returned to the ridge often as they rode. A triumphant sun had taken control of the lower horizon. Anyone could see their trail to and from there, made more obvious by early-morning shadows. Each time he looked, Aleta chuckled and told him not to worry so. That was the extent of the discussion about the gun battle. Each disappeared into thoughts neither wanted to express.

As they neared their small ranch, she turned in the saddle and faced him. "The first time I saw you, I was pulled to your courage. You were alone—and the Yankees came for you in that cantina. You were not afraid. You were a warrior. You will always be a warrior."

"That was a long time ago, Aleta—and I *was* afraid. It just didn't make much sense to show it. Now I only want peace."

"Peace comes only to warriors who fight for it."

At their home, Rule Cordell eased from the saddle and let the unconscious girl slide into his arms. Lizzie Ripton's weight was that of a dead man, and Cordell took a step back as the full impact came to him.

After several steps, he found a rhythm and carried her easily toward their house. The saddled bay was freed in the corral, along with Aleta's saddled horse. Aleta hurried to open the door, holding both rifles in her arms. Cordell rushed through the house and laid Lizzie on their bed. From the window, golden fingers of sunlight sought the young girl's head and caressed her sweating hair.

Aleta returned their guns to the special altar. "I weel clean the guns later. We weel need them, I think."

She was immediately by Lizzie's side with a filled cup of water. Dipping her fingers into the cup, Aleta ran them along Lizzie's lips. The girl's eyes fluttered as she tasted the wetness and fought for consciousness. Aleta moistened her fingers in the water again and repeated the wettening. Lizzie mouthed "Thank you" and balanced herself unevenly on her elbows. Carefully, Aleta helped Lizzie drink a little from the cup itself. Lizzie choked, then asked hoarsely for more. Aleta allowed her to sip once more from the cup, quietly telling her to drink slowly.

After Lizzie gradually drank the entire cup, Aleta left again and returned with two bowls. The larger held water for cleaning; the smaller, a strange compound kept on hand for wounds and cuts. It always hurried the healing. Cordell wasn't certain what was in the salve, except for beeswax, vinegar, and several different herbs. The medicine had been handed down for generations within Aleta's family. She removed the girl's bloody dress, then cleaned and dressed her wounds. A nightshirt of her own and a damp cloth on Lizzie's forehead completed the medical treatment.

While Aleta worked, Cordell stood in front of the waist-high cabinet with its array of guns, gingerly fingering first one revolver, then another. He hadn't said a word since they entered the house.

After touching the dried rose, he said aloud, "They killed Whisper, my friend. They are trying to kill more of my friends. How long do we have to pay for losing? Someone has to stop them." He paused, and his fingers caressed the Dean & Adams .44 revolver taken from a Yankee scout near the War's end. "Why does it have to be me? Don't they understand I don't want to fight anymore?" Picking up the double-action gun, he spun it easily in his hand, letting it come to rest in his fist, ready for firing. He stared at the English-made weapon and laid it down again like the gun was boiling hot. A passage from the Old Testament rolled from his clinched teeth. " 'He shall return no more to his house, neither shall his place know him anymore.' "

Aleta watched him from the bed but said nothing. She pretended to be finishing with her first aid.

"If I go, they will come and take our home. I—I may n-never see you again." He closed his eyes and stood with his arms at his sides.

"Why do they have to know who you are?" Her words were soft. A prayer.

Cordell's shoulders rose and fell. "How can I do that?"

"I do not know. Eet was a bad idea." She stood and headed for the kitchen, humming a Mexican tune he could not place.

Turning, Aleta stood in the doorway. "Our breakfast ees cold. I weel warm it now, Captain Rule Cordell."

"Something to eat sounds mighty good." He ignored her reference to his real name and what it implied.

His beautful wife was not being realistic, he told himself. How could one man stop many and not be recognized, much less killed. Getting involved was tantamount to returning to the outlaw trail he was so eager to leave behind. It meant going against what he professed as a minister. His gaze took in the sleeping

Lizzie Ripton. She looked like a small girl asleep in their bed, and he thought of Billy Ripton and his parents. The Riptons had risked their lives to hide him while he recovered from his father's gunshot. He told himself that he had repaid them with gift horses as well.

Blinking away his frustration, his attention became caught on the minister's robe hanging from a peg on the wall, next to a Mexican hand-carved dresser. On its top lay the cross he wore on Sundays and the special white collar. He looked away. The ache in his stomach swirled and he decided it was just hunger. Walking into the kitchen, he realized their meal of tortillas, eggs, and bacon remained on the counter where she had left it before they rode to help Lizzie. Only the coffee smelled like it was ready.

Aleta turned toward him. Her face was glowing. Her eyes eagerly sought his.

"I thought you were—"

His question went incomplete as she interrupted, "I am hungry for you, Rule Cordell."

She didn't wait for his answer, rushing forward and wrapping her arms around him. Her hands held his face as she sought his mouth with her tongue. The return to battle had unleashed a fire for this man, as if for the first time. Passion rippled through their embrace.

He pulled away from her. "I can't bear the thought of losing you. I just can't."

His eyes caressed her, and she smiled. A devilish smile. Her hands slid from his face down his chest and rested at his belt buckle. Her eyes were an invitation. They dropped together to the floor, entangled in their desire to be one body. Their hands rushed to rid the hindrance of the other's clothes and to enjoy the other's nakedness. She popped apart his pants buttons and reached for his corded manhood. Greedily, his hands unbuttoned her blouse and his mouth sought her freed breasts. She moaned and arched her back as he entered her. Unnoticed, a fly buzzed around their intertwined bodies before moving on to the windowsill and finally back into the afternoon air.

A half hour later, they lay half naked and exhausted. Aleta's head rested on Rule Cordell's shoulder. Neither wanted to return to the world. Aleta rose first; her blouse lay open on her arms; her skirt was wadded around her waist; her undergarments were flung across the room. Re-dressing, she focused on their waiting food on the counter instead of him.

"*Por favor*, please forgive me for trying to get you to do something you do not want to do, Rule. I love you—and I do not want anything to happen to you. You are right. It ees not fair that you should go to the Riptons'. It ees not your fight."

Cordell stared at the ceiling, making no attempt to put his clothes on. He didn't respond.

"I weel get us somettheeng to eat now."

"We're supposed to start Suitcase's school tonight."

She turned away to hide a smile at what she thought was a last objection to his going to the Riptons'. "Do you wish to stay here, instead? Eet is not necessary that you go there with me. I weel go there, by myself, without you. Eet is *bueno*."

Her eyes were bright with purpose and continued to avoid connecting with his. She fiddled with a plate of cold tortillas.

"What about Lizzie? Shouldn't one of us remain here—to watch her?"

"I theenk not so. She must sleep and heal. I weel care for her wounds again *mañana*."

Propping himself up on his elbows, he told her that he had decided to help the Riptons. "Good, I'm going to the Riptons'. I have to. They hid us after my father shot me. We can't turn our backs on them now. I'll fix up the ridge first, like we planned, then go get Ian. He'll want to go too." His stomachache disappeared as he spoke, and he began rebuttoning his pants.

Her attention was apparently on cutting up an apple for their breakfast, but her eyes wandered hopefully toward the ceiling as she continued her conversation of misdirection. "It ees not your fight, this problem with the Riptons. Whatever happens will be so. You would be few against many."

"I spent the War that way."

"*Sí*, I know." Her voice was soft, her eyes frozen on the ceiling.

Putting on his shirt, Cordell said without emotion, "If I go, our lives will be changed forever. I will be a wanted man—again."

Unable to hold back any longer the emotions she felt, she dropped the knife and spun around. The blade clanged off the counter.

"*Sí*, you might become a wanted man—again, my Captain Cordell."

"That doesn't bother you? I thought you said . . ."

"*No importa*. It doesn't matter. As long as I am with you, I care not what happens. I know you must do thees. But I believe you can—without theem knowing who does it."

"B-but I am a man of God now."

"*Sí*, do you think your God wants you to stand by while your friends are killed and their lands are taken?"

"But . . ."

"There are many ways to serve God. Teach children. Plant corn. Train horses. Build a home. Love your wife. Fight for friends." She ran her fingers across her lips, then repeated the movement on his. "Thees Padgett ees a coward. If he becomes afraid, he weel leave the Riptons alone. You must become many and scare him away. I theenk Rule Cordell knows how to become many."

"You mean, like the trick we pulled on the Yanks with that empty breastworks?"

"*Sí*. Cannot the outlaw gang that saved Lizzie come after Padgett?"

He laughed out loud. Shaking his head, he said, "I think you've been stringing me along. You've had this all figured out."

Her face recoiled in a wide smile. "I weel worry about you, *mi marido* . . . my husband—but it ees right."

Without waiting, she left the room and returned a few minutes later with two gunbelts, each carrying a holstered revolver, as well as his rifle. Surprised at her swiftness, he nevertheless thanked her and took the weapons. After propping the rifle against the counter, he put on the cross-belted handguns, the ones he'd worn last on the outlaw trail. The weight on his hips felt strangely good, but he denied the sensation to himself. Aleta's face glowed as she watched him lift first one .44 Colt, then the other, from the holsters and check the loads.

"They are fresh, my captain." Her eyes narrowed, and she gave the advice that had been churning in her mind for some time. "You must become the thunder that comes in the night. Thunder is never seen but warns of the coming storm. Padgett will run from the storm he sees in hees mind."

He stood without speaking, absorbing her analogy. Then he nodded agreement and she smiled again. Her face was total relief. Disappearing again, she returned with his black long coat and a crimson scarf that had once belonged to her mother.

"No one knows what thunder looks like." She handed him the coat and scarf. "Thees coat will hide your frame. Thees scarf will hide your face. You become a son of thunder."

Chapter Fourteen

The idea of disguising himself hadn't occured to him, but he quickly acknowledged that it made sense. He thanked her, took the offered items, and held the scarf in his hand while he put on the coat.

"What's this?" He pointed at the dried rose inserted in the coat lapel. The stiff flower came from their gun display. A petal fell when he slipped on the coat. The tiny reddish shape dribbled along his sleeve and floated to the floor. Watching its descent brought a swirl of old memories.

"For luck, my captain, please wear the rose. You wore it when I first saw you." She hesitated and opened her left fist. Her eyes studied the small object there, not daring to meet his gaze. "You should wear this, too. It ees good medicine. Moon weel see that you come back to me." It was the Comanche stone earring given him long ago by the late shaman.

Slowly her eyes rose from her hand. His mouth was

a thin line of disagreement, matching the frown embedded in his forehead.

"Please, my love. Please."

With a shrug of his shoulders, he took the earring and placed its small rawhide loop over his ear. He touched the tiny pouch beneath his shirt in a silent tribute to the dead shaman, then began to roll the scarf in a ball to carry in his pocket. But she insisted that he try it on first and took the scarf from him without waiting for any response. Both were giggling as she wrapped the red cloth around his nose and mouth and knotted it in place. The silky ends streamed halfway down his back. As she stepped back to admire her work, her eyes sparkled.

"I theenk we should make love again, my *capitan.*"

He chuckled. "You just like a man in uniform."

She laughed deeply. "No, I just love you."

"I love you, Aleta. I will be back."

"I know thees."

They embraced, holding each other close. A kiss became a long, soul-searching exhange of tongues. As they finally pulled away, their eyes did all of the communicating. She wanted to say something about Lion Graham but knew it was not the thing to do. Her only words were those of advice. "Do not wear guns into town. Someone weel remember." He nodded agreement. Neither could say "goodbye" for fear that it could bring bad luck.

After a hurried meal together, standing at the counter, Cordell went outside while Aleta gathered her things for her regular school. He unsaddled the green bay and readied his buckskin, a ten-year-old gelding with a steady attitude. Quickly, the rifle sheath was strapped on and the Henry shoved into place. He tapped its walnut stock for emphasis.

A heavy pole, once a corral section piece before it rotted on the end, was tied with a lariat behind the horse. The bouncing sliding weight would remove most of the horse tracks from their ranch as he rode toward the ambush ridge. After adding the pole, he walked over to Aleta's horse, standing quietly against the corral fence, and rechecked its cinch.

The swish of the door turned him toward the house. Aleta burst through the doorway with his saddlebags packed with food and supplies. He tied on the bags, they kissed goodbye, and she galloped away first, waving as she rode. At her waist was a holstered revolver—a last-minute decision on her part. Cordell hadn't objected. Her class would be waiting, but she wouldn't be more than a few minutes late.

Minutes later he headed toward the ridge, riding in a zigzag pattern that would look like wind had bruised the land. It would be hard to read anything from the result. His mind rattled through the ideas for creating misdirection at the ridge. Establishing the presence of a "gang" now took on added importance. It would provide the start of an imaginary army seeking Padgett.

After planting the various "left behinds" in place and stomping around to add the impression of many men, he would ride the horse back and forth to the north, creating the illusion of a gang coming and going from that direction. Eventually he would circle through the creek bed and back to the house to check on Lizzie, then leave to get Taullery.

Morning haze had laid its thin hands along the land as he realized that their earlier hoofprints ceased to exist a hundred yards from the ridge. As he rode closer, his eyes caught wagon tracks coming from the north and returning, just like he planned to do. The tracks umistakably belonged to "the Russian." One of his mules had a split shoe; the other dragged a right rear hoof slightly. The trail was a book to anyone who could read sign and knew the wandering merchant. Yet the giant man had evidently ridden the wagon back and forth over the same area repeatedly to create the illusion of many men with horses and wagons.

What was more surprising was the appearance of the ridge itself. Cordell reined in his buckskin and took in the sight. Ineed, it looked like a small army had waited there. Boot prints went everywhere. Empty cartridges were strewn nearly the entire length of the incline. A canteen with a busted strap lay on the ground. A pistol and a single spur caught his eye, then a discarded bag of tobacco. Cordell knew the man collected empty cartridges for reloading, as well as discarded merchandise of every kind. Aleta's hat was gone, but in its place was what appeared to have been a stand of rifles, judging from the marks in the ground. It had to be the work of the eccentric merchant.

Definitely, the impression was the one that he, Rule Cordell, had intended to create. Only better. Why would Caleb Shank, "the Russian," do this? Why would he risk getting involved? The only answer was that he came upon the scene, read what had happened, and decided to protect Rule and Aleta. Shank was counting on the fact that if his wagon marks were recognized, it would be viewed as a natural coincidence—after the battle, not a part of it.

Cordell swung down and removed the dragged pole and left it. Because of the rotting end, the wood actually looked like it had been there for a long time. After recoiling his lariat and tying it to his saddle, Cordell rode around the north end of the ridge, past the three forelorn trees, Lizzie Ripton's dead horse, and onto the flat land. The bridle was gone, leaving only a large brown mass of what had been a magnificent animal. That wasn't all that was missing. All of the dead Regulators were gone, too. Even the winded horse had left—or Shank had taken it with him. He didn't let his thoughts remind him of the two men that breathed no more because of him.

The latest tracks indicated that the wagon headed north, back the way it had come. Caleb Shank had evidently hauled the bodies away, but why? There was no value in pondering what had happened, so Cordell kicked his buckskin into a lope north toward the creek. The ends of his long coat flipped up as he next pushed the horse into a gallop. He was in a hurry to complete the swing back to his house and get to town. Ian Taullery would go with him, he was certain. Maybe his friend would have an idea about what to do when they got to the Riptons' place.

Something more than riding in with guns blazing. That would end in the Riptons dying—and them too. How could they trick Padgett into thinking a large outlaw gang was after him? Aleta's idea made good sense; now he had to figure how to do it. Taullery would have some ideas. He was the best at finding things nobody else could. During the War, he was always the best-dressed and helped keep the outfit well-fed, well-armed, and well-mounted. Taullery always found a way to get what they needed. That comforting thought sat with Cordell as he rode.

An hour later he returned to their ranch, after swinging wide through the dry creek. It wasn't really necessary, but somehow it felt right to complete at least a part of his strategy. Lizzie Ripton was sleeping soundly when Cordell checked on her. Just seeing the young girl made him even more certain of the rightness of his commitment to help the Riptons.

Passing by the gun display, he paused and decided to take the Dean & Adams revolver along as well. He shoved it into his back waistband and went outside. He switched saddles from the steady buckskin to the new roan stallion purchased from "the Russian." Not as steady as the buckskin, of course, but the big roan could outrun anything he'd seen. He might need speed more than calm, he decided. He eased into the saddle, and the horse was into a smooth, ground-eating stride in seconds.

Dulling unseasonal heat shredded the few clouds into thin gauzy strips, and he slowed the horse to a walk that it didn't like, tossing its head in defiance. Cordell slapped the horse on its neck with his reins and the animal quieted. As he passed the adobe warehouse that served as the community church, he wondered if his fledgling parish would survive. A wagon drawn by a six-hitch team of mules was being loaded by three men. A teamster in a derby waved and Cordell returned the greeting, not recognizing the man. Movement of goods was a sign the region's economy was taking shape again, if barely.

He couldn't help feeling the building should be used for God's message alone. It needed to be closer to town as well. Maybe the town would undertake such a commitment if it had a better preacher, he self-assessed. If Padgett or his men identified him, the fledgling parish would have no choice but to replace him. He didn't consider that the same would be true if they killed him. He bit his lower lip in recognition of the one-way path he was taking. There was talk of using the building in the winter to hold a lyceum, a literary society, for weekly debates, lectures, and songfests. He thought it was a great idea, but now neither winter gatherings nor Sunday services seemed important at the moment. Rather, he needed to come up with a way to fool Padgett into thinking he was "many," as Aleta put it.

Dismissing the church's concerns, he growled, "What Clark Springs needs is a real church—and a real minister." His stallion spun its ears backward to assess what its rider wanted that it wasn't doing. Chuckling at his spirited self-conversation, Cordell patted the horse's neck to ressure the animal. "You're doing fine, boy. Doing fine." The stallion's ears returned to normal but took the sign as an indication it could run again. The horse yanked on the reins and gathered itself to gallop. Cordell discouraged the movement with a pull on the reins and they stayed at a walk. The horse reminded him of the stout mounts he had ridden during the War and on the outlaw trail afterward. The big roan was a bull, for sure, but didn't seem to show many of the unruly attributes of a stallion. Cordell was pleased with the horse's performance so far.

He was also pleased with himself. His statement about the town needing a real minister produced no sense of defeat or sadness. Only a renewed ache where he had received the blow Sunday. Removing his hat, he rubbed his hand along the back side of his head to ease the pounding. It didn't help, and he replaced the hat.

His decision to help his friends was a morning fog around his soul, leaving him determined but happy. If he were honest with himself—except for being with Aleta—the early days of the great War when the South was winning were the happiest days of his life. His purpose was clearest then his cause to a young Rebel warrior noble and grand. All he had to do then was fight and ride—and he was very good at both.

In bright memory, Cordell saw the gallant General Stuart again, resplendent in his newest uniform, a black-plumed hat and a red rose on his lapel, leading his vaunted cavalry against too-slow Union forces. Cordell would have followed him anywhere.

He was jerked back into the day as silhouettes of three riders abruptly rose on the horizon. They were headed his way. Sunlight reflected from the middle of one rider's chest. Cordell guessed it was a badge. Were Regulators already backtracking to see what had happened? Had Padgett reacted that quickly? Had they come directly from the ambush ridge? It appeared like they may have. Why? Why wouldn't they ride north in the direction of the tracks? Had they seen through the fake signs? Maybe they were on an unrelated assignment. Had they seen him yet? He shook his head to clear away the remnants of yesterday. It wasn't smart to let his mind wander at times like this. Jeb Stuart had taught him better than that. He touched the rose on his lapel and studied the advancing riders.

Chapter Fifteen

Rule Cordell pulled his wide-brimmed hat lower and rolled his shoulders. He was certain it was Regulators and they had seen him. It would be foolish to ride in another direction. That would only invite suspicion and pursuit. He pulled both revolvers from their holsters and shoved one into each coat pocket. They were too far away to see the precautionary move. He gathered his long coat with one button to hide his gunbelts.

A deep breath took away the jitters and he nudged his horse into a lope toward the advancing Regulators, now in full view. He wasn't certain why he felt they had come directly from the ambush ridge, but he did. Were they looking for him?

As the distance between them closed, he recognized the closest rider immediately as being a part of the Sunday assault in his church. Besides being fat, the man was distinctive because he carried his pistol on a looped thong around his neck, letting it hang in front of his stomach on a ring from the butt. The other two looked familiar, too. Cordell's mind raced through blurred faces coming at him at the ridge, then earlier at the church. Yes, they had been at the church when Padgett came after Douglas Harper. They were talking to each other, possibly about him, but he couldn't make out the words. The guns in his pockets were reassuring. He shut off the ache from his head and tried to concentrate.

A blond-haired Regulator with greasy spectacles stared at Cordell. Like the other two, his rifle lay across his saddle for immediate use. At thirty feet, his eyebrows shot upward and his mouth opened in recognition.

"Hey, y-you're that preacher! W-what are ya doin' here? Ain't no prayer meetin' 'round here. Whar's yur preachin' collar, anyhow?" The other two men snorted their approval of his remarks and reined their horses to a stop. All three men laid their hands on readied rifles but didn't lift them. Cordell decided the movement was intended only to intimidate.

" 'Afternoon, men. Did you boys need some praying over?" Cordell reined his stallion to a stop ten feet closer. The big horse stutter-stepped, eager to keep moving, but finally stood. Still annoyed at the command, the horse pawed the ground and sawed on the taut bit. Cordell pulled on the reins to stop the belligerence and reinforced it with a nudge of his spurs. The horse raised its head and froze in place, just like his easygoing buckskin would have done. He patted its shoulder to reinforce the behavior. The next move was theirs.

The large-bellied, sweaty Regulator with a double chin responded. "Ride on, preacher. Before we forget who you are." His shirt buttons were struggling to hold against the advance of his stomach as he leaned forward in the saddle. The hanging revolver bounced against the saddle horn.

Cordell swallowed the anger he felt. They made no attempt to open the trail for him to pass and he made no attempt to ride on.

The third Regulator's narrow face was pulled by sleep, hate, and too much whiskey. His whiskey-laden voice was thin and hesitant, like it was coming through an iron pipe. His eyebrows were wirey and seeking space away from his forehead. Cordell vaguely remembered hitting him with his fist at the church.

"Who are . . . you . . . this time?" he snarled. "Clay Allison . . . or have you decided to be . . . Bill Longley?"

Derisive laughter swarmed around Cordell, who smiled but said nothing.

"Say, what do ya know 'bout a girl that escaped from the law this mornin'. Looks like some gunnies was a-waitin' for 'em. Reckon they be headed north afterward." The question and explanation jabbed at the air. It came from the blond Regulator; the others called him Mason.

"Afraid I don't know what you're talking about." A part of Cordell was pleased they had bought the signs left by "the Russian"; another part wondered if the statement was designed to catch him in a lie.

The heavy Regulator straightened in the saddle, and his hanging gun rose with the reaction, flopping against his rolling belly. "You mean to say you didn't hear any gunshots this morning? Ain't you got a place close by? It was a whole bunch of riders. Rebs, I'm betting. Or maybe Comancheros. They blasted away while our boys were chasing a fugitive. Must've been ten or twelve. Shot down our boys in cold blood, they did."

The other two Regulators chuckled at his use of the word "fugitive," and Mason added, "Yeah, an' Padgett was fit to be tied when them hosses came a-sketterin' back. I thought he were gonna explode hisse'f."

"Nobody could've stood up to that shootin'," the fat

man said defensively, and turned back to Cordell. "I asked if you heard any gunshots this morning, preacher."

"Yes, I did. Many. It sounded like they were coming a long way east of us. Couldn't tell from my corral what it was." If they pursued the matter, whatever tracks from their house remained could be explained as coming out afterward to see what had happened. "But that's not what your friend asked me. He asked if I'd seen a girl or a bunch of riders on this trail. I haven't seen anyone on this trail, except you three." It wasn't the question, but it was a truthful statement, Cordell acknowledged silently to himself.

"Hard to figure how they knew we was comin'—an' where. Had to be that gal led 'em right into a trap all set an' waitin'. Yessir, that's what I think. Looked to me like they'd been there awhile, from the signs. Had wagons too." As the heavyset man continued, he searched his right shirt pocket for a cigar, jabbing fat fingers into the stretched-out cloth. "Hell, they even carried off our dead. They was all gone. You didn't bury anybody, did you, preacher?" He withdrew a half-smoked cigar from his pocket, jabbed it into his mouth, and started a search for a match.

"Not today."

"You're mighty . . . uppity for . . . a Bible-thumper." The narrow-faced gunman snarled and handed a match to the fat Regulator. "How come you ain't got on . . . a preacher collar? Hey . . . what's with that damn . . . dried flower . . . stuck on your coat? Did that good-lookin' Mex gal of yours . . . give it to you?"

The fat Regulator chuckled, his belly bouncing his hanging pistol back and forth, then grabbed the gun, scratched the match on its barrel, and sucked flame into his cigar.

Mason, the blond Regulator, smiled wickedly. "I'll

bet she's a hot one. Yessiree, probably needin' a real man 'stead of . . . whadda ya got 'round yur ear? Be that thar a rock? What the hell!"

"If you'll move aside, I'll be on my way. I'm certain you've got important business to attend to."

"Now . . . don't be in such . . . a hurry, preacher," the narrow-faced man wheezed, nudging his horse forward. "We figured to . . . check out each place nearby . . . an' make sure nobody's . . . hiding that gal. She's wanted . . . you know. So . . . why don't you just turn around . . . an' head back to your place. We can start there. Wouldn't surprise me if you had her hidden there. Along with some o' them gunnies that got our boys.' "

Mason grinned and laid his hands over the rifle in front of him. "Maybe yur fine Mex gal'll need some tendin' to." He looked at the others for approval. "Sur beats the hell outta trailin' after them Johnny Rebs. That's jes' what they want, I reckon, to have us come after 'em. We got ourselves enough to tell Padgett. " 'Sides, I wanna spend a little time in town a'fer we head back."

The other two nodded agreement.

"Scoutin' the territory, that's what we're a-doin'. That's what we dun did at the tail end o' the War, chasin' down yella Johnny Rebs. 'Course, you wouldn't know nuthin' about War, would ya, preacher?" Mason added his own nod to the others in tribute to his assessment.

Pulling his cigar from moist, blubbery lips, the heavy lawman squinted at Cordell. "You haven't asked who the girl is. Ain't you curious, preacher?"

Cordell's slow-coming smile was laced with contempt. He patted his stallion's shoulder before responding.

"No."

Looking at each other, the three Regulators waited

for more, but Cordell was rubbing his horse's ears and paying no attention to them.

The heavyset man threw the cigar toward the ground. "What gets me is why a preacher man is riding a fine horse like this one." He couldn't hold back his interest in the roan stallion any longer. "I reckon you won't care if we take it along with us. Official state business an' all."

"Sorry, I'm headed for town."

"So what? Whatcha gonna do, preacher? Give us a prayer?"

"Wouldn't think of it."

Cordell wrapped the reins around the saddle horn and slipped both hands casually into his coat pockets. His stallion snorted, raised its head, and stamped its front hooves authoritatively. Cordell reached for the reins with his left hand, hoping the animal wouldn't act up. His pressure on the wrapped leather was enough to return the horse to quiet, and he returned the hand to his pocket.

Staring at the minister, Mason reached into his vest pocket with his left hand and withdrew the makin's for a cigarette. His right hand remained on the rifle until he was certain the weapon was positioned well enough to rest on its own. With both hands, he deftly rolled a smoke and returned the sack to his pocket, then moved his right hand back to the rifle. A match crackled into flame from the strike against the weapon. He inhaled and let white smoke slip from the corner of his mouth. Cordell watched the ceremony without comment.

Finally, the blond Regulator spoke, with thinner strings of smoke bristling from his yellowed teeth. "Ya know, I don't believe all that religious crap you boys dish out. Jesus, Moses, Adam and Eve—nuthin' but silly fairy tales." He patted the rifle. "I believe in this hyar."

Cordell smiled.

"Ain't nuthin' much that riles you, is thar, preacher?"

Cordell leaned forward in the saddle, keeping his hands in his pockets. "How you choose to go to Hell is your own business."

"What?" Mason choked on just-inhaled smoke and the fat lawman laughed, his belly bubbling with emotion.

"Come on . . . Mason, let's get goin'. We've . . . got to report . . . back to Padgett . . . by tonight," the lean-faced Regulator urged. "An' I ain't about . . . to go ridin' up . . . the ass end . . . of that gang."

"Jes' a minute, Lester. Ya bother me, preacher, like an itch I cain't git to." Mason eased his rifle from his saddle and aimed it at Cordell without moving the weapon to his shoulder. "Lion Graham keeps a-tellin' us that you really is Rule Cordell. Says he knew you in one o' them Bible places somewhars. What 'bout that, preacher?"

"Oh hell, Mason, Graham's always talking crazy about livin' in some other time. Who cares? More important, preacher . . . you hit me . . . in the face." The narrow-faced man studied the stoic minister with renewed suspicion. "I don't like . . . getting hit . . . in the face."

"Wal, ya kin call it crazy if'n ya want—but now he's a-wearin' a flower an' sportin' outlaw-fast hoss flesh. Thar's only one man I hear tell that liked wearin' hisse'f a flower. Rule Cordell." The blond Regulator cocked the hammer on his rifle. "Just who the hell are you anyway, preacher-man?"

The narrow-faced man's hand curled around the rifle across his saddle and added, "I think . . . you'd better pull your hands outta . . . your pockets . . . an' get down."

"Sure, boys, anything you want." Cordell leaned back

and raised his pockets toward them, as if freeing his hands. Instead, orange blasts erupted from the coat. His horse reared in fright but came down in place, tossing its mane, while Cordell held tightly with his legs and continued firing with both guns still in his pockets. A lone button sprang from its position holding the coat together and the front separated, immediately giving him more flexibility with the hidden guns.

Mason's eyes widened and he grabbed for his chest as Cordell's first two bullets ripped into him. The blond lawman's rifle bounced off his saddle and exploded, sending lead hissing past Cordell's head. The narrow-faced Regulator raised his rifle and fired too quickly. The bullet creased Cordell's left arm, driving the gun from his hand. A split second later, the minister's return shots spun the lawman sideways. Cordell yanked the revolver from his right-hand pocket and a second shot punched the Regulator from his horse. Wild-eyed, the animal bolted with its strirrups flapping like a giant bird that couldn't get off the ground.

Cordell's stunned left hand regripped the Colt in his left pocket and withdrew it, emptying the gun into the falling man. A click of the hammer on an empty shell registered in Cordell's mind as he turned his attention on the remaining lawman. He snapped a shot at the heavyset rider with his right-hand Colt and missed. Slowest to react, the fat Regulator lifted his rifle and fired as Cordell's horse jumped sideways at the continuing roar of gunfire.

Cordell's frightened stallion reared again and screamed its fear. A blur of reddish gray and hooves. Dropping the spent gun, the sometime minister grabbed the saddle horn with his bloody left hand to maintain his balance as the frightened horse froze in place on its hind legs, standing nearly straight up. The fat-bellied Regulator's bullet tore through Cordell's flapping coat.

The lawman hurried to lever another shot, but the gun jammed. Frantically, he dropped the rifle and grabbed the pistol dancing wildly on his stomach from its neck cord.

With the stallion's front legs still lashing at the air, Cordell kicked free of the stirrups, pushed away with his left hand, and jumped down in one smooth motion, landing a few feet from the rearing animal. The surprising move caught the Regulator firing at an empty saddle. Cordell's revolver roared three times in a continuous string of sound, lead, and smoke.

The heavyset man's head snapped backward, like it was on a hinge. Already dead, he went to his knees, then folded headfirst into the ground. Freed of its rider, the stallion crow-hopped and bucked away. Cordell paid no attention. Realizing his second Colt was also empty, he shoved the gun back into its holster and reached for the third pistol in his waistband.

"I'm Rule Cordell," he growled, cocking the gun and pointing it at the downed men.

None moved, and he relaxed. Silence came as suddenly as it had left. Acrid gun smoke encircled the three dead Regulators and two of their horses. The third mount was barely in sight. He examined the three men; none was alive. Satisfied his adversaries could harm him no more, he returned the British pistol to his waistband and reholstered his first dropped Colt. He had no energy to reload his weapons, even though he knew he should.

After a few minutes of letting his mind and body absorb what had just happened, he began to examine his wound. A slice along the upper sleeve of his coat was wet with his blood, and smoke snorted from both coat pockets. For the first time, he noticed that his big roan had not bolted far and was eating grass twenty yards away. Taking the wadded-up scarf from his smoking pocket, he shoved it into his coat sleeve where the bullet had struck. It would have to do for now. His assessment was that the wound was not serious, only bloody and painful. Cut flesh was angry and puffing.

Wary of what his horse might do, he walked slowly toward the grazing animal, talking low and gently. The big roan snorted and stomped but didn't run, and allowed him to take the wrapped reins from the saddle horn without trotting away. He reassured the horse, calming it into lowering its head. "You're all right, boy. Steady now, we've got work to do."

Leading the stallion back to the dead men, he went to the closest body and lifted it onto the closest horse. He kept both his stallion's reins and the Regulator's reins in his numb left hand, leaving his right hand and arm free to do the heaviest part of the task. His stallion balked and tried to back away from the smell of death, then gentled and lowered its head.

It took a while, but he finally got the other two bodies across the saddle of the other remaining horse. Roping the bodies in place took longer than he expected. He stopped often to let the weakness of lost blood and the realization of what had happened pass and wipe the nervous sweat from his reddened face. Satisfied the bodies would stay in place, he slapped the rumps of the animals and sent them galloping toward the Riptons', where they had come from.

"Consider this the first roll of thunder, Padgett," he said, watching the frightened horses pound into the distance.

Chapter Sixteen

Rule Cordell leaned against his stallion, letting spent energy seep back into the hollows of his soul. The pounding in his head returned, or his mind allowed him to be aware of it. The horse was steady, as if it understood the weakness of its rider. For a moment, he was back in Virginia and his cavalry had just finished a successful attack against Union forces. His mind returned him to the reality of the day.

Another blow against Padgett and the Regulators had been struck, whether he liked it or not. Padgett had lost eight men today; the crippled leader would be forced to send out another scout team to determine what had happened. He could wait and ambush them; the thought registered only brief consideration. No, he needed to hit Padgett closer; the Regulator leader needed to feel that he was not safe anymore, not even when surrounded by his own men. That was a big task for him and Taullery.

Old uncertainties trailed the recharge of energy. A young Lion Graham entered his mind briefly to charge him with not playing fair and running away. A lashing by Cordell's violent father followed. Stunning his only son with vicious slaps to his reddened face, the evil minister screamed that the young Rule Cordell was just like his mother and would never amount to anything. But the embedded nightmares were quickly followed by Aleta's last reminder to take off his guns before entering town. "My God, Aleta, I miss you already," he muttered.

With a long sigh, he unbelted the weapons and squatted. The stallion stood quietly beside him, and Cordell wrapped the reins around his leg to leave both hands free. His mind kept running away to the contentment he felt as a minister and wondering if he would ever know that feeling again. In the midst of feeling sorry for himself, the memory of Moon came to him. The old Comanche shaman once again reminded him that, for the brave man, "life was the point of an arrow. Flint was only a piece of rock until much pounding made it into a sharp weapon. Welcome the challenges of life, my son, for they make you strong."

He felt the medicine pouch hanging beneath his shirt, then remembered his stone earring. Aleta hadn't mentioned it, but the earring, too, should be removed during his town appearance. He lifted the small loop from his ear and placed the earring in his pocket. He looked at his long coat and decided to leave it on. Better than seeing his bloody shirtsleeve. No one—except Taullery—would notice the coat's bullet holes. The Dean & Adams pistol would remain in his waistband. And the dried rose would stay on his lapel, he determined, glancing down at the stem and its few hardened petals. He didn't care what anyone thought. It was long past caring about that.

Talking with Taullery would help him focus, he told

himself, shoving new bullets into the open chambers. It always did. His ever-practical, perfection-seeking mind was a salve to Cordell's impetuous, intense style. After reloading the two Colts, then wiping off occasional smears of blood, he unwrapped the reins, rose a bit wobbly, and placed the gunbelts in his saddlebags.

An easy lope took him past the busy sawmill and the empty base-ball field that had been the scene of many epic battles against neighboring towns. Cordell and Taullery loved the game as much as anyone. The rooftops of a string of two-story buildings teased the skyline. He was almost to town.

Clark Springs was like a hundred other Texas towns, born of a welcomed source of water, nurtured by men and women who toiled the land, and surviving because of sheer will. It wasn't really home, Rule Cordell realized as he entered the busy main street, but what was? Wherever Aleta was, that was home, he told himself and smiled.

Rhythmic sounds of the blacksmith reached Cordell as a rumbling freight wagon and an outrider passed him headed the other direction. The black-coated minister waved at the skinny blacksmith turning the yellow-hot end of a horse shoe into shape and the sweating man nodded a return greeting. Leaning against a fence enclosing the blacksmith's work area was a one-armed man in faded Confederate pants and kepi cap. He waved too, then went back to intensely watching the blacksmith. Next was a stable with a pair of black horses being readied for someone, followed by a string of false-fronted buildings.

Cordell spotted a man pushing a wheelbarrow, piled with rock, along the planked sidewalk toward an unknown destination for no apparent reason. He wheeled his load past several men without saying a word. Cordell couldn't help wondering where the man was going with his load or what he expected to achieve. At that moment, a freight wagon pulled by oxen rumbled onto the main street from an alley and shouldered its way past Cordell in the other direction. Cordell reined in his horse hard to keep from colliding with the wagon. The driver grunted an apology between snaps of his bullwhip and splattered curses.

Passing three riders he knew, Cordell didn't notice the nicely dressed older woman watching him from the porch of the unpainted boarding house. He trotted alongside a lead-gray-painted, one-story building with a lengthy sign proclaiming "Real Estate, Insurance & Loan Agent & Attorney-at-Law. William H. Giles." Squeezed next to it was the Benning Home Restaurant, also a one-story structure; then the bank; and the year-old headquarters of *The Clark Springs Clarion*, the region's newspaper. Cordell liked the editor, a fiery young man from Nebraska.

A few other retail establishments announced their services with signs of varying levels of professionalism and weathering. At the far end of town was a stone well, offering the community a continuous flow of cool spring water and a permanent point of reference to its name. A lone cottonwood guarded the well with long, drooping branches that could knock a man off his horse if he wasn't paying attention when he rode to get water. Flanking the well, at the corners of the street, were three saloons and a pleasure house, probably doing more business than the rest of the stores put together.

Near the center of town, Cordell pulled up next to the hitching rack in front of Taullery's General Merchandise store. Behind him, two buckboard wagons clanked past each other in the middle of the street. A well-dressed couple strolled toward him on the planked sidewalk. He didn't move, letting a wave of lightheadedness pass. His left arm was throbbing.

"Well, good afternoon, preacher. What brings you to town?" Mayor William H. Giles said with little enthusiasm, as he stopped in front of Cordell. White spittle took its usual position in the corner of his mouth after his salutation. "Did you hear shots a while back—out your way?"

His response was a lie. "No, I didn't hear anything coming in." Cordell didn't like the man, yet he knew he should try to do so. Giles was quickly becoming an influential force in the region. His holdings, like his presence, came after the War, and for little more than back taxes. In the case of one of the ranches, the original owner was arrested and hanged for treason by Captain Padgett. Cordell had heard the rumors that the previous hotel owner tried to hide Rebel holdouts shortly after the War ended and was finally led away by Federal troops. One rumor had Rule Cordell and Johnny Cat Carlson hiding there for a while, among other notorious Confederate outlaws. He didn't know what happened to the other ranch owner.

"It is good to see you in town, Reverend Langford." His wife's greeting was considerably warmer. The pudgy woman's gaze sought Cordell's as part of the welcome. Always a fashion leader, she was dressed in a matching, light-blue silk skirt and O-shaped bodice gathered tightly at her waist. A white cheissette collar, white gloves, a wide black belt, and exaggerated full sleeves at her elbows completed her dress. Her hemline was a daring four inches off the ground in front and dragging the ground in the back. A matching bonnet with a curled ostrich feather, dyed blue, set off brown ringlets pushed around her fat face. She wore as much makeup as most prostitutes; Taullery thought she had been one.

"Afternoon, Mayor . . . Mrs. Giles. It's a beautiful day, isn't it?" Cordell said, not answering the mayor's question. He tugged on the brim of his hat, then swung down from the saddle and slipped the reins over the rack. He was glad to have heeded Aleta's advice about his guns. The mayor would be among the worst to have seen them.

"A trifle warm. But it's always so in Texas, I fear. Going to do some trading at Taullery's, I see," Giles responded, satisfied with his self-analysis of Cordell's mission to town.

The heavy-jowled man's voice was curious and polite. He had heard this Southern minister's preaching several times and wasn't certain what to make of it. Northern friends suggested keeping an eye on Reverend Langford, in case the sermons began to take on renewed pleas for succession. Last Sunday's outburst was a further indication of a potential problem.

Swallowing a twinge of fear, Giles said in his most mayoral tone, his eyebrows climbing toward his hairline before flattening. "I must say I was taken aback by your brawl with state police officers—during services, no less. What were you thinking, Reverend? My word, you even said you were a dead outlaw."

"Justice." Cordell walked past them to the store. The ring of his spur rowels on the board sidewalk was music.

"Did you hurt your arm, pastor?" Mrs. Giles asked, her round eyes locked onto his coat sleeve.

Cordell stopped in midstride, turned back, and smiled warmly. "Why, thank you, ma'am. That's nice of you to notice. Actually, it's an old coat, I'm afraid. Kinda torn in places. It's comfortable, though."

"But, but, that looks like—blood."

"Oh, it is. Hit a corral post, working with a young horse a week ago." He turned back and continued walking.

"What did he say?" Giles asked his puzzled wife.

"He hurt himself on a corral post—some time ago."

"Oh. That's too bad." A smile crawled into the corner

of Giles's mouth and stayed there. "Reverend, I trust last Sunday was something we won't see again. Your position—even though it is part-time and, perhaps, temporary—requires considerable restraint. I didn't like the situation either, but we must support our police. I'm sure you agree, upon reflection. Perhaps you can apologize next Sunday."

Cordell stopped again, this time in front of Taullery's store window. His reflection was that of a man Giles didn't know. A man with such intensity in his eyes that the mayor braced himself unconsciously for Cordell's response.

Cordell turned around, and his voice was as syrupy as the mayor's had been. The softness surprised Giles and he didn't catch the subtlety of the message. "Much must change before next Sunday. 'They that saw in tears shall reap in joy.' " Completing his statement, Cordell spun back to the window, lost in thought.

Encouraged by what he termed a most agreeable response, Giles moved to sweeten things. "By the way, my foreman at the Lazy K says we need horses. I told him that I was certain you had the best for sale."

If Cordell heard the remark, his manner didn't indicate so. Giles started to repeat it, then decided to resume his walk. He was pleased with himself, taking Cordell's silence as a further indication of wanting to cooperate. Money had a way of doing that, he thought and chuckled. Mrs. Giles kept pace but glanced over her shoulder at the minister; her face was a question mark.

"Maybe we should take up a collection to buy him a new coat, dear. You know, being a minister like that takes a lot of time. He doesn't get anything for it."

"Well, he'll soon be well paid, my dear. Haven't seen a preacher yet that couldn't be turned by the sight of gold."

"Did you see that old, dried rose?"

"What? Where?"

"An old dried rose—on his coat lapel." She glanced back again at Cordell, who was looking in the store window.

"Goodness, how silly." Giles thought about looking too, but decided against it. "Well, you know preachers. Look, dear, there are the Atkinsons. I need to talk with him. His place butts up to the Harpers'. Come along, now. You can ask them about a coat for the preacher if you've a mind to. Langford's a good man, even if a bit hotheaded and impractical."

Cradling his wounded arm with his other, Cordell read the new hand-lettered sign in Taullery's store window: "Trades accepted for hard goods, clothing, or guns. Gold only for food. No Colored People Allowed." Cordell grimaced and glanced at Mayor Giles and his wife, who had stopped to talk with another couple.

Eager sunlight pushed its way inside the small store as he entered. A gray world of pungent smells rushed at him. The captivating perfume of freshly ground coffee danced with aromas of tobacco, bacon, spices, oils, salted fish, soaps, vinegar, pickles, and the satisfying scent of leather goods. Everywhere he looked were carefully displayed goods. Taullery hadn't wasted an inch of space. Definitely, this was the town's center of attraction, the saloons and whorehouse notwithstanding.

The room was thoughtfully arranged for shopping, with kegs, sacks, and barrels of cooking staples and groceries on one side, and dry goods and hardware on the other. Some things were available only with Taullery's personal assistance, but he allowed customers to touch and feel most merchandise. Even the rafter beams carried heavy pots for cooking, as well as hams, slabs of bacon, and sides of mutton. Of course, Taullery was usually moving through the store, straightening items and restacking them to fit his perfectionist eye.

Two women were examining an exhibit of crockery, highlighted by a complete set of fine French china, likely something traded for more practical things. Cordell couldn't hear what they were saying but wasn't interested anyway. He didn't see Taullery waiting on anyone or sitting on his high stool in the rear next to his tall desk, like some crowned prince viewing his court. Perhaps he was in the back storeroom. Cordell knew he kept an open jug and tin cups for selected male customers to enjoy. That was likely, and he headed for the rear of the store.

The pain in his arm was growing more intense, but he tried to ignore it. There was no time for pain now; he and Taullery had to ride to their friends before it was too late. Cordell slipped past separate areas displaying farm and ranch tools, containers of coal oil, ropes, hats, boots, spurs, and gloves. Tables were crammed with canning jars, candles, kerosene lamps, blankets, flat irons, copper boilers, stoneware water dispensers, coffee grinders, and clocks. Even a baby carrriage. Cordell smiled. Even better stocked than the last time he was here. How like his friend to gather an array of homestead treasures to rival any Northern store. If Taullery's store was any indication, the region must be doing better, he told himself.

A small section contained rifles and handguns, gunpowder, and ammunition. He couldn't help pausing to stare at two shiny Model 1866 Winchesters. He had heard about this improvement over the Henry repeating rifle, with the loading from the side instead of the awkward tube beneath the muzzle. He wondered if it jammed as easily as his Henry, then shook off the thought and moved on. Several saddles and bridles lay across empty barrels, with an open box of "good 'nough" horseshoes next to them. He glanced down at the box and mentally assessed if he needed more at home.

Taullery had created a special medicinal section in the far corner. A stray beam of light from the only window in the back accented a collection of patented medicines, along with several kinds of croup syrups and salves for babies; a half dozen bottles of variously labeled female remedies, worm destroyers, and stomach bitters; but mostly home remedies of Epsom salts, cod liver oil, opium, paregoric, camphor, and snake root. Cordell couldn't help looking to see if any reminded him of the salve Aleta made. They didn't. He wished he had some now, for his arm and his head. A pain drove through him, as if it recognized his closeness to medicine. He grimaced and walked on.

Chapter Seventeen

Across a long table was a colorful array of bolts of cloth. Rule Cordell walked around the woman examining a roll of calico. On the wall behind the table were displayed bonnets, ready-to-wears, sewing patterns, and boxes of needles, thread, and thimbles. Even pairs of black silk gloves and green gauze veils. Self-conscious, he held his right hand over the bloody slit in his coat sleeve. But it wasn't necessary. The woman's expression was distant as she imagined herself at a fine place in a beautiful gown.

Close by were boxes of cigars, tobacco plugs, and a few sacks of shredded Durham tobacco on its own stand. Shoved into a corner were Bibles, school books, a lone volume of Shakespeare's plays, two poetry books, and a leather-bound Robinson Crusoe novel. The books were propped up by a box of canned oysters on one side and a case of whiskey bottles on the other. This was the one thing that seemed out of place. Cordell couldn't help smiling, and he muttered, "Maybe there's hope for Ian yet."

Four chairs in a semicircle around a cold potbellied stove, in the center of the store, served as a meeting place for men waiting on their wives. A half-filled cracker barrel completed the area, with a small handwritten sign reading "For customers only." Two farmers rested there, chatting about the weather and, in hushed tones, about problems with Northerners. One spat tobacco juice at a box of cold ashes and missed twice. Both stopped their conversation to acknowledge Cordell as he walked toward the back. He nodded, and they returned to their discussion.

Ten feet away and directly in his path was a tall, pale woman staring at him. She balanced a copper bowl in both hands but appeared to have no real interest in it. Cordell had the feeling she had been watching him for some time. She didn't look familiar, but he didn't know all of his parishioners well yet. Light-blue, crystal-like eyes didn't seem to go with her straight black hair, cascading over her shoulders and nearly reaching her waist. She could have been twenty or forty, he couldn't tell.

A simple homespun dress was accented with a necklace of thin silver holding a bear claw mounted in a gold and silver band. He continued toward her. It was the most direct way to the back room. She didn't blink or acknowledge his approach; her eyes were locked, like those of someone in a séance or a daydream. Maybe he had mistaken daydreaming for staring at him, he told himself.

He stopped a few feet in front of her and touched the brim of his hat, and turning his left shoulder slightly away from her, said, "Good afternoon, ma'am. I'm Reverend Langford."

Her gaze met his, but she said nothing.

"You haven't seen the owner—Ian Taullery—have you?"

She shut her eyes for a long breath, opened them, and met his attention with a knowing glint. A tremor was barely visible at the corner of her mouth.

When she spoke, her voice was soft and low, like words echoing from a deep well. "Why are you here? You are thunder. You are lightning. You are a storm to clean the land."

Instinctively, Cordell reached out to touch her arm, as if it would stop her announcement. "I think you have me confused with someone else."

She repeated the statement and stared at his face. "Why are you here? You are thunder. You are lightning. You are a storm to clean the land." She hesitated and added, tilting her head to the side, "But someone comes . . . from another time, he comes . . . seeking the storm . . . to destroy it."

He stepped back to keep the words from reaching him. "I—I am a man of God."

She said no more and looked down at the bowl, aware of its presence for the first time. He couldn't hold back the shiver that shot through him. He took another step away from her, grabbed his aching arm, and hurried on. As he passed, she muttered in a singsong voice, "God brings thunder and lightning. God brings the storm to clean the land. But someone comes . . . from another time, he comes . . . seeking the storm . . . to destroy it."

He started to respond but didn't. He guessed she was one of those so-called séancers who seemed to be thriving in the South since the War. He wasn't sure why, but there were more important things to worry about. When he reached the back storeroom door, he looked back. She was gone. A shiver went through him again. The copper bowl rested on a table, apart from a cluster of canned goods. To Cordell, all the light in the room rushed to huddle against it. He wondered if anyone else saw it that way.

Cordell stood next to the closed storeroom door, trying to refocus on his mission. From the rear, Taullery's voice could be heard if Cordell concentrated. There was another voice. It was a woman's. Cordell didn't think it was Mary's. Too cheerful for her.

"Ian. Ian Taullery. It's Rule. Ah, Rule Langford. I need to see you." His voice was low to avoid attracting attention.

Out of the corner of his eye, he saw a small boy tiptoe over to the cracker barrel, grab a handful, and dash away. Inside the storeroom, there was sudden silence, then scuffling noises, a woman's giggle, and finally Taullery attempting to sound businesslike.

"I'll be right out, Reverend. I'm, ah, helping a customer."

"You can help me anytime." The woman's voice was a whisper, followed by a giggle.

"Shhhh."

The door opened and a tall, golden-haired woman with painted sloe-eyes, wearing a dark green, fitted dress, stepped out. Her clothes were wrinkled and a button had been missed at her bodice. She smiled warmly at Cordell without stopping and waltzed through the store, pausing to fondle an apple in a barrel before putting it back. Taullery came through the doorway a few seconds later. He was fiddling with his collar.

"What's up, my friend?" Taullery asked as casually as he could.

"I could answer that it's something in your pants, my friend," Cordell replied. "But I've got more important things to talk about it."

"At least you didn't say 'bigger.' " Taullery's grin was wide. "Ah, you won't mention this to Mary, will you?"

"Mention what?"

"Thanks." For the first time, Taullery concentrated on his hard-faced friend before him. "What happened to you? You've been hurt." Taullery touched Cordell's coat sleeve. "And what's with the rose? You look an awful lot like a man I used to know." He pulled back his hand as if the coat was hot. "My God, your coat pockets—they've got holes blasted through them! Did you shoot guns through them?"

"Yeah. Had a little run-in with three of Padgett's men. I'm all right, they're not."

"Are you sure? You look a little pale." Taullery wondered why his friend had been carrying guns again in the first place. What had happened?

"It's just a scratch, really."

At the store's front entrance, the woman turned her head to see if Taullery and Cordell were watching. Pleased that they were, she winked and went outside. Cordell waited for his friend's attention to return to him, then explained what was happening to the Riptons, including Lion Graham killing Whisper, Lizzie Ripton being wounded, the cover-up at the ridge by Caleb Shank, and the gunfight on the trail with the three Regulators. He didn't mention the strange woman in the store but wanted to.

As they talked, Taullery examined his own dark blue coat and vest, removing an occasional strand of hair. "I hate hair. If Mary'd let me, I'd shave it all off of me." He chuckled nervously. Cordell shook his head, chuckled in response, and resumed his story.

When Cordell was finished, Taullery's first reaction was a criticism of the traveling merchant, saying "the old Russian" just wanted to strip the dead men of things he could sell.

Cordell frowned and pushed the hat brim back on his head. "I doubt that, Ian. He's a friend. A good one, I think. I'm riding to Riptons now to see if I can help. Will you ride with me?"

"Right now?"

"Right now."

"Rule, I've got a wife and baby and . . ."

"That didn't seem to be slowing you down earlier."

"Oh, come on. That's different. What are the two of us going to do against an army of Regulators? An' you know Lion's going to be there too."

"We're going to make them think they're outnumbered." Cordell's expression reminded Taullery of another time in Virginia. The gunfighter-turned-minister explained what he had in mind.

Taullery glanced around the store to see if anyone was close enough to hear their conversation. Satisfied, he said, "This isn't Virginia, Rule. We got lucky then."

"We'll think of something," Cordell said. "We always do."

Taullery took a deep breath. "I can't leave the store."

"We'll go after you close."

"These clothes aren't for riding—or fighting."

"You can go home first and change.'

Oily, yellow light bled across Taullery's taut face, his furtive eyes avoiding Cordell's steady gaze. He looked away like a man not wanting to be trapped against the truth. What came out was close. "Those damn Northerners are just looking for a reason to take away businesses from Southerners. You know that. I can't be trotting around, butting into everybody else's business."

"Billy Ripton is our friend. Whisper was."

"That was then, this is now, Rule. Hell, you're the one always talking about forgiving. Let it go." With a shrug, Taullery went on to explain that he was in the back room closing a deal to purhase Lady Matilda's small pleasure house at the far end of the main street. He and another businessman had gone together to make the purchase. He didn't want anyone knowing, and he didn't mention the name of his partner. Cordell didn't ask.

"I take it that was Lady Whatshername."

"Matilda, yeah." Taullery glanced left and right to assure himself no one was close enough to hear their conversation. "Mary doesn't know about it yet—but she won't complain about the extra money. I'll make more from that whorehouse than I do from this whole store. Can you believe that?"

Cordell studied his taller friend without judging him. They had been through too much together to do that. What he had just heard was something he never expected. He told himself to be understanding, this was his best friend since childhood. It had taken him a while to recognize the need to take a stand. Taullery would come around. He always did. It was just his way to be more methodical, to examine every nook and cranny before making a move.

Before he could respond, a ruddy-faced farmer sauntered up to the general store owner and pronounced loudly, "Quite the she-bang yo-all got hyar, Taullery. Yo-all got any tobaccy plugs?"

Taullery pointed in the direction of the tobacco table without speaking. Not recognizing Cordell at first, the farmer jerked slightly when he realized it was the minister.

"Well, howdy, Preacher Langford, didn't expect to see yo-all hyar."

"Nice to see you, Eb." Cordell extended his hand. The farmer attended church occasionally; his wife rarely missed.

"Why, thank ye, preacher." He shook Cordell's hand without meeting his eyes. The farmer's grin revealed four missing teeth. "Glad to see yo-all be up 'n' around after that tussle with . . . Captain Padgett." His voice dropped to a hoarse whisper on the Regulator leader's name.

Cordell nodded and the farmer left for the tobacco offerings, glad to be away from such close proximity to a minister.

Taullery spoke first. "Tell Billy I'm real sorry about his problems. You need any medicine for that wound—or the Ripton girl? Just take what you want. No charge."

"We're doing fine with some salve Aleta makes."

"Well, I've got 'Dr. Rober Byer's Anti-Pain Plaster.' Best there is. Even the drugstore doesn't have it." Taullery was staring at a display of dishes on the far side of the room. "Just a minute, I've got to do this."

Without waiting for Cordell's response, he strode across the store and straightened a stack of plates, then repositioned two sets of coffee cups and saucers. On his way back to Cordell, he turned to examine his work; satisfied, he continued.

"Sorry, Rule, I just can't stand to see such a mess. Makes my back crawl."

Cordell smiled. "What about it, Ian? You want to go with me to help the Riptons?"

Taullery took a deep breath to let the anger building within him find a better route than yelling at his friend. "No, Rule, I'm not—and you shouldn't either. You're damn lucky they didn't hang you after you yelled out your name. Padgett'll come with all his guns to find out who killed all his men. Dammit, you aren't making sense."

An awkwardness slithered between them, separating the two old friends as they had never been. To Cordell, it was a heavy bullet in his chest. At that moment, he realized things between them would be forever different. A fury swirled within him, but it came out as a forced chuckle. The back of his neck prickled and bile came to his throat that wanted out. Taullery joined him in laughter, hoarse and furious. He, too, knew what had happened. He had made a choice to turn away his oldest friend. There wasn't anything else to do but laugh. Neither would cry. Their eyes stung with memories.

"All right. Give my best to Mary and little Rule. I'll see you when I get back." The smells and sounds of the store were suddenly stalking him, and Cordell knew he must leave before he blurted out something he would regret later. He shouldn't have expected Taullery to drop everything and go with him. He told himself that Taullery had changed, but his mind shoved the thought away.

"Doesn't Aleta's school with those Negroes start tonight? I thought you were going with her." Taullery's face changed with the new subject.

Cordell said she was going to handle the teaching alone tonight while he went to Ripton's. Taullery's reaction was slow water coming from an old pipe.

"Say, maybe that black friend of yours could help the Riptons. Suitcase has more money than any white man I know."

Cordell spun away from Taullery. He bit the inside of his cheeks to keep from talking.

"Don't forget to get a jar of Dr. Robert Byer's Anti-Pain Plaster." Taullery's voice boomed across the store as Cordell opened the door and stepped back into the aging sunlight. "It's the best there is." He walked to a table to pursue a forced realignment of canned goods. With a can in his hand, he straightened and bolted toward the door, nearly knocking over an incoming woman. He reached it as Cordell swung into the saddle.

"Wait, Rule, take one of the new Winchesters. Please . . ."

Chapter Eighteen

Rule Cordell hesitated, then kicked his horse harder than needed and was in a full gallop before he passed the town's well. He never looked back. Taullery watched his friend until he disappeared over the rolling horizon, shook his head, and went back inside the store.

A few miles out of town, Cordell shook off the feeling of rejection, accepted the fact that he should have taken Taullery's Winchester, and tried to think through what he could do to stop Padgett. Aleta's suggestion of creating the illusion of "a gang" was taking root in his mind. He would use the night as his ally. Some ideas were taking shape, depending on what he found at the Riptons'—and how many Regulators.

Ahead, late-afternoon sun washed over the hard prairie and painted a layer of gold on the underbellies of clouds. Darting among the gilt-edged fluffiness was a red-tailed hawk, appearing like a copper dart. To Cordell's right was a small box canyon where dark shapes indicated that wild longhorn were grazing. Beyond was a belt of rolling hills, distinguished only by a thin topping of yellowish rock, and connected to a line of blackjack, post oak, and juniper stretching for miles across grassy plain. Scattered longhorn and sagebrush were interrupted by gatherings of wild flowers. Over the second rise was the Ripton ranch, rich in water and grazing land.

He cleared a washed-out buffalo stand and saw a wagon in the distance. It was not moving, off to the right of the trail. Even though it was only a gray shape, he knew it was Caleb Shank. Was the strange traveling merchant waiting for him? How could he know? Or was this just a coincidence? After all, the man traveled all over this area, selling his wares and trading for more.

Wary of what the big man wanted, Cordell's right hand slid inside his coat and moved the English pistol from the back to a quicker position in his waistband; the gun butt was inches from his belt buckle, resting on his left hip. His further assessment assured him that the waiting merchant was alone and both hands were visible. Still, the sight of the man who had altered the tracks at the ridge unsettled him. Not because of his size, though.

Although Shank stood six feet four and weighed at least two hundred and fifty pounds, he was no bigger than the Confederate infantryman who had called Jeb Stuart "a fancy-dressed coward." That had triggered a vicious "soldier's fight" between Cordell and the confident bully. Afterward, Taullery offered to split his winnings with his victorious friend. He got twenty-to-one odds from many of the big man's comrades. Cordell wasn't able to move well around for three days.

The Reb however, was in a hospital for two weeks with cracked ribs, a severely bruised stomach, and a broken jaw. Taullery wasn't surprised that his friend whipped the much bigger man. He'd seen Cordell win bare-knuckle fights all the time back home—partly because his father made him work like a dog, adding hard muscle to his lithe frame, but mostly because Cordell had an intensity that drove him beyond pain, beyond reason. That and a devastating left jab. But Cordell wasn't expecting a fight with the big merchant. The day had already brought unpleasant surprises. His stomach was churning from not knowing what Shank intended to do with his knowledge of what happened on the ridge—and if that included recognizing that he and Aleta were there.

Cordell eased the stallion into a walk to give him more time to study the situation. The powerful animal surprised him by sliding into the slower gait without resisting. Shank sat on the wagon seat, smoking his pipe with a hand intertwined in one of his suspenders, and looking for all the world like a man enjoying the silence of the prairie. His two unmatched horses looked like they might be sleeping, barely acknowledging Cordell's approach. The huge man waved his hand in a friendly salute as Cordell headed toward him. Cordell wondered if the greeting was to any rider—or in recognition of him specifically.

Shank's dark eyes brightened and a wide smile took over his black-bearded face as Cordell closed the distance between them. "Good afternoon to ya, Reverend. Bin a-hopin' you might be comin' along."

Cordell reined in his horse beside the wagon and Shank motioned toward the bounty in the back of the wagon. Sunlight gingerly sought the rings on each finger of his gesturing right hand. Piled behind him, on top of the regular assembly of cooking utensils, jewelry, foodstuffs, clocks, toys, medicines, and clothing, were the weapons taken from the dead Regulators at the ridge.

Three Winchesters were particularly evident, and so was Aleta's hat.

"Came across some interestin' stuff this mornin', don't ya think? Look at them fancy new 'Chesters." Shank looked at the new items as if seeing them for the first time. A faint smile flickered under the thick hair on his upper lip.

"I see," Cordell responded without showing any emotion in his voice or his face. Was this a subtle attempt to blackmail him?

Taking the pipe from his mouth, Shank continued to smile as he spoke. "Reverend, I do reckon I kin read sign 'bout as well as any man. No offense, but not far from your place, two folks dun stopped a bunch o' Regulators from catchin' up to somebody. By the looks of the brand on a fine dead hoss, I'd say they was a-chasin' one of the Riptons."

Cordell said nothing, but laid his right hand on top of the saddle horn, inches from his pistol. From this angle, he doubted the merchant could see what lay inside Cordell's coat. It didn't matter; the move didn't appear threatening. His stallion snorted its impatience and pawed the ground. Cordell's left fist pulled on the reins to quiet the animal. His eyes studied the huge man, who folded his arms over his massive chest, straining the fibers in his faded shirt even more than normal. Cordell remembered that the man carried a throwing knife in a sheath held by a rawhide thong around his neck, down the inside back of his shirt. He didn't appear to have a gun of any kind close to him, although Cordell couldn't see his back where a pistol might be shoved into his waistband. If his reputation with his fists—and knife—was accurate, Shank probably rarely used one, Cordell guessed.

If possible, Shank's smile became wider. "Say, that be the he-hoss I traded ya, ain't it? Lawdy, that's a fine-lookin' animal. Does he do like he looks?"

"As good as any I've ever been on. A mite edgy, but that's to be expected. He can eat up the miles, though."

"Yessiree, a fine one—an' I reckon you'd be knowin'. Thought o' you the minute I laid eyes on 'em. Don't act staggy or nothin', do he? Yessirree," Shank said, and returned to his tale of the morning like it was one continuous statement.

He explained that signs of a battle were discovered while making his regular rounds. He changed the appearance of the ridge so it would look like the ambush had been done by many men. "Figgered I could be a mite o' help by changin' the slant o' them signs," Shank said, making imaginary marks with his hands. "Make it look like a whole bunch o' owlhoots were a-waitin'. How'd I do?" The question carried no accusation, more like a man asking to have his performance evaluated.

Shank was eager to talk, explaining that the real signs indicated a woman had helped turn the Regulators away, judging from the smaller-sized boot prints. Either that or a small man. He was certain it was a woman, though, because the hat left behind smelled sweet inside. It was in his wagon now, for that reason. He thought someone else might come to the same conclusion.

But he was impressed that she walked among the downed riders and did most of the final killing where it was needed. At least, the smaller footprints indicated she was the only one who got close. He figured she realized a wounded Regulator would've had a closer look than those who ran and might identify them. He observed that such a woman was well worth keeping and followed it with a chuckle. Cordell licked his lower lip. Obviously Shank knew it was he and Aleta. Should he admit as much?

"Caleb, I'm a preacher and a horse rancher, not a gunfighter. Why are you telling me this?" Cordell leaned forward in the saddle, fingers brushing against the butt of his hidden pistol. His eyes narrowed, waiting for more.

Rubbing his beard with his right hand, Shank looked away, as if selecting what he should say next. His heavy eyebrows locked together in a long frown. Thick shoulders rose and fell. That choice had been made when he left the ridge and decided to wait for the minister. His heartfelt speech was rambling but clear. The unwarranted hanging of Douglas Harper and the cold-blooded murder of his brother had disturbed him greatly. He grieved for the children and for their mother. He was certain Padgett had an arrangement with a buyer who wanted the Harper land. He didn't know who that villainous person was. Yet. Of course, proving the connection in a court would be unlikely, even if a fair Northern judge could be found.

Relighting his pipe brought an awkward silence as Cordell showed no inclination to respond. A few hearty puffs delivered a stream of new smoke and more explanation followed. He considered getting a petition signed by area landowners to have Padgett removed from office. But he knew people would be afraid to sign, because they wouldn't believe Governor Davis would act on their demand, leaving them exposed to Padgett's revenge.

He puffed again, frowned at the pipe's lack of response again. Searching for a match preoccupied him with a successful discovery coming from his pants pocket. Cordell smiled at the big man's easy distractions but wondered what the talk had to do with him. Did he expect Cordell to push for a petition from the pulpit? It wasn't a bad idea, but it wouldn't help the Riptons now.

Showing signs of nervousness as he got closer to his conclusion, Shank swallowed, rubbed his nose, and drew deeply on the pipe. His voice wavered, and the announcement hurled itself toward Cordell with all the anger that had been building within his massive frame.

"T-that s-sonvabitch Padgett—an' his rattlesnake Graham—they've bin hurtin' good people long 'nuff. Bin a-hopin' somebody with . . . the doin' in 'im . . . would stop 'em. When I saw the sign, I knowed it were you I'da bin waitin' fer. Had me a feelin' when I heard 'bout you a-fightin' 'em in church." He paused again, tried to swallow but his throat was too dry, coughed, and summed up his thoughts. "Unless I'm mighty wrong, you be a-headin' for the Ripton place. I want to go along—if you'll have me." Relief shimmered in his eyes, then changed to concern for the reaction he might get.

Something in Cordell told him that he needn't be cautious around this man. Shank was trying to be a friend. Nothing more. Shank's reasons for helping were sincere. His offer to go along to Ripton's ranch was genuine, if not realistic. Cordell's right hand dropped to his side and he sat up straight.

"Thank you, Reverend, for the trust." Shank nodded toward where Cordell's hand had been.

Involuntarily, Cordell looked at his waistband, then back at the merchant, and grinned. Shank's smile was hopeful, and he used the moment to add some levity. Returning his pipe to his mouth, the eccentric merchant explained that he had buried the dead Regulators in a single grave not far from the battle, but in a place Padgett and the others weren't likely to think of. It was right next to an old Comanche burial ground. He laughed out loud telling the story, and Cordell had to smile in spite of himself.

Shank planned on giving the weapons and saddle gear away to anyone who needed them, first making sure none could be identified. He certainly didn't want to hand off a problem to someone. With no urging from

Cordell, he explained how a change of pistol handles took away most distinctive marks. He always had extra walnut handles in the wagon. There was one Colt with the trigger guard removed and the sight cut off, so he left it in the grave along with the original marked handles. Rifles were no problem unless the stock had been carved upon. If they were, he used a hot running iron to change initials into other letters or symbols. With saddles, branded identification was changed the same way or the marked piece was replaced. It was a thorough exercise, and clearly one Shank had done before, Cordell noted to himself.

Shank was suddenly quiet, and Cordell knew it was his turn to talk. He explained what had happened with the Ripton girl, about Padgett trying to force the Riptons from their land, Lion Graham shooting his friend Whisper, about Aleta going on to her day school and starting Eliason's school for some black children tonight, and that he was on the way to the Ripton ranch. He skipped over Graham being a boyhood friend and his run-in with the Regulator scouts. Instead, he told about planning to go with his wife tonight to the factory, but that she had insisted on his riding to help the Riptons.

"I reckon she kin take care o' herse'f ri't smart-like," Shank observed, and winked.

"Yeah, I think she can. Still, there's been strong talk against it."

"Heard that. Hard to figger some folks an' their hate."

Shank told of Eliason coming to him secretly and paying for food and supplies for several black families, as well as pairs of good boots. The successful black businessman didn't want them to know it was charity. Agreeing, Shank accepted knife sharpening and other work projects in return for the goods, as Eliason wished. In return, Eliason gave him some boots at no cost; they carried minor flaws because they were made in initial trial runs, after Shank reopened the factory. The talk focused on the problems of Texas for a few minutes, with Shank finally getting up the courage to ask what had happened to Cordell's arm. He told about the run-in with the three Regulators and that his handguns were now in his saddlebags, another suggestion from Aleta.

"I've always made it a habit never to ask a man about his back trail," Shank observed, unwrapping his reins from the brake handle. "But I reckon there's a lot of gun behind yours, Reverend. Made me remember your friend, Ian, a-callin' ya Rule a time or two."

"That's my middle name. James Rule Langford. I used to be called 'Rule' some when I was a boy." Cordell spoke through gritted teeth.

"Reckon so. Fella I remember wore a rose like that, come to think on it. Near the tail end o' the War, I ran into him, a Reb cavalryman—name of Rule . . . Rule Cordell. I was with Longstreet. In Virginia, it was. This hyar Rule Cordell was the wildest-lookin' son-of-a-wolf I ever seed. Made me wonder how we ever got beat with men like him." Shank fiddled with the wagon reins, staring at his fingers as they manipulated the leather strips.

Cordell was rigid in the saddle. He was angry at himself for letting Aleta pin the flower on him. What was he thinking? Even the mayor's wife had commented on it.

"Never met him, mind ya. Jes' saw him from a ways off. He'd jes' fooled a whole Yank division into thinkin' they was a-facin' a dug-in bunch o' Rebs. Fact is, he an' his scouts was only three. Three, mind ya. Kept Longstreet's flank from bein' chewed up, he did. 'Masquerade Battalion,' that's what they called it. Yessirree." Shank shook his head, enjoying the reminiscence, not looking at Cordell. "Didn't realize 'til later that he was a Texican. Wondered why he didn't ride with Terry's Texas Rangers, ya know, the Eighth Texas Cavalry. Guess he had his reasons."

Cordell rubbed his mouth with the back of his left hand and waited.

"Ya know'd, he saved a lot o' Reb lives that day. Maybe mine. Wished I coulda thanked him personal-like." Quickly, Shank added, " 'Course, Rule Cordell is daid now. Got hisse'f kilt along with another wild'un, Johnny Cat Carlson. Must be two years back, I reckon."

Cordell pushed his hat back on his forehead, and his grin matched Shank's earlier smile. "Don't know about this 'Rule Cordell' fellow, but I do thank you for your help on the ridge, Caleb. You did a much better job than I would have." He paused and added, "But I think this is a job I'd better do alone."

"Your friend, Ian, he wouldn't go with you?"

The question hurt, and Cordell's face showed it. "Oh, Ian couldn't get away. Pretty short notice. It's all right."

"King o' the piddlers, that's what I call him. Always a-piddlin' with this thing or that. Fancies hisself gittin' rich." Shank didn't look at Cordell as he made his observation, then looked up and saw Cordell's pained expression and added quickly, "Ain't nuthin' wrong with that, o' course."

"I'll be seeing you, Caleb. Thanks again." Cordell turned his stallion back toward the trail, and the horse was eager to be on the move again.

"Wait, Rule, er Reverend . . . please, I shouldn't be a-paintin' your friend thatta way. Ian Taullery's a good man. Jes' a mite particular 'bout things. Reckon I could learn from that myself."

"That's all right, Caleb. Nobody knows what a pain in the butt Ian can be at times. Still, he's my oldest friend. We grew up together." Cordell's eyes flashed with the thought that he shouldn't have revealed that connection.

Shaking his head excitedly, Shank pleaded, "I kin help ya, Rule. Really. This ol' man is mighty good with a knife—and a fist, if'n I do say so myself. Might fool ya how quiet I kin be, too. Dun spyin' fer Marse Robert an' Longstreet, ya know."

Cordell reined in the horse, and it didn't like the change in orders and shook its mane. "Caleb, I figure the best way to make Padgett leave is to scare the hell out of him. Aleta came up with the idea of making him think there's an outlaw gang ready to kill him if he doesn't leave the Riptons alone. I think she's right and he'll find a reason to ride away. If I do it right, they won't know it's me either—What do you think?"

"I think I be havin' a wagon full of stuff that'll make one hellva of a gang."

"So do I."

"Kinda like that masquerade battalion, ya know? But . . ."

"But what?" Cordell's eyes narrowed.

Shank yanked the pipe from between his teeth. "Why don't we jes' sneak up an' cut the bastard's throat? I kin do it, Ru—Reverend, jes' as sure as yur a-sittin' there."

Cordell cocked his head to the side. The same idea had passed through his mind earlier. "Thought of it. But killing him will only bring more law in here. Swarming all over to find out who did it. I figure if Padgett backs away on his own, there will be peace, sort of. At least, it's a start. Then we'll find who's pushin' him along."

"I'm with ya, Rule. Any way ya want to play it."

Cordell leaned across the saddle with his right hand fully extended. Shank grabbed it enthusiastically. Cordell's fist disappeared within the big man's own.

Chapter Nineteen

Outside of town in the other direction, Aleta approached the darkened boot factory. Only yellow light from a single window welcomed her. A defiant grove of cottonwoods loomed grotesquely to the far side. Surrounding the small building was a hedgerow of unruly bushes, except for a fifteen-foot gap that served as an entrance. On the back side, the bushes deteriorated into scattered growth, linking with the more robust bushes on either side. The original owner had been fascinated with the unruly vegetation for reasons known only to him.

She saw Eliason's black buggy and mules before she saw him. The carriage stood at the corner of the unpainted structure closest to her. What appeared to be a double-barreled shotgun poked its head up from the seat. Then she saw Jacob Henry Eliason, the black businessman, sitting in a chair on the factory's wooden porch, smoking a pipe. She waved, and he stood to greet her.

He laid his pipe on the planked porch beside his chair and removed his hat. His gray suit and black cravat matched the growing shadows. Fading sunlight found the gold chain across his vest and caressed it before leaving. He walked quickly to the steps, holding the hat in his left hand.

"Good evening, Missus Langford. Right good to see you tonight." He was enthusiastic but couldn't hide his concern. "Where be the Reverend?"

She reined her horse at the rack and swung easily from her saddle, her split leather skirt flopping against her thighs. Eliason tried to avoid looking there, but admired her riding like a man instead of sidesaddle. His gaze couldn't miss the gun at her waist. She wrapped the reins around the crossbar, removed a large canvas bag from the saddle horn, and quickly explained about Lizzie Ripton. She could think of no reason to hide the situation from a friend. Eliason's expression was unreadable.

"So the preacher is headed for the Ripton place." He returned his hat to his balding head.

"*Sí*. He rides first to hees friend, Ian. They will go together."

Eliason hesitated before asking if she really thought Taullery would accompany the minister. Aleta's response was immediate and positive. Eliason's frown indicated that her enthusiasm was not well-placed, but he said nothing.

Instead, he rubbed his graying beard with his right hand and asked, "What does your man expect to do there?"

"He weel get Padgett to leave theem alone." Her chin raised slightly as she finished the statement.

Eliason's smile was instantaneous. "How's he going to do that?"

It was Aleta's turn to smile. "He has hees ways."

"I figured as much." Eliason's chuckle shook his lean frame. "Still, I hope he rides careful. Padgett won't care if he's a man of the Lord or not."

"Are the children inside?"

Pleased by her change of subject, Eliason described the waiting class: fifteen children ranging in ages from six to twelve. He swallowed and added, "There's also Zachim. He thinks he's thirty. He won't stay if you don't want him to—but he badly wants to learn to read and cipher."

"That weel be fine." She unbuckled her gunbelt and pushed it into the bag.

"May I help you with that?" Eliason reached for the bag.

"Thank you, Mr. Eliason. It ees things for the children."

"I figured as much."

Neither mentioned the gun as they stepped inside the factory. Two wall lamps cast their proud light on three rows of desks occupying a freshly swept area next to a front window. All but three contained children, their eyes bright with interest and fear. Standing in the corner was a tall black man with his arms behind his back and his eyes down. Watching from the dark were worktables scattered with leather, tools, and boxes of readied boots. A slate board was nailed to the wall in front of the desks, and a scratched teacher's desk and chair completed the schooling section.

Stacked on the desk were two piles of *The New Texas School Reader*, books written during the War, along with small individual slates and boxes of chalk. He apologized for the desk's appearance, then explained the children had already been fed supper here.

"Hope this will work for you, Missus Langford. It's all I could find. Nothing, I'm afraid, for the younger children." Eliason's voice was uncharacteristically tentative. "Figured you'd be wantin' to do the passing out of the books an' such."

"Thank you, Senor Eliason. It ees *bueno.*" Her smile was wide. "Thees ees better than my, ah . . ."

"White folks' school."

"Sí."

It was Eliason's turn to smile. Then he put his hand over his mouth to cover his words. "Missus Langford, some of these children don't know their last names." His eyes flickered in pain and anger. "Thought you should know."

"Oh, thank you, Mr. Eliason. They are beautiful, aren't they."

"My friends call me 'Suitcase.' "

"Thank you, Suitcase. I am very glad to be here. My husband . . . wanted to . . ."

"I know he did. Where do you want this?" He raised the bag to his waist.

"Oh, just put it anywhere. On the desk ees fine."

Without further discussion, she stepped to the front of the desks. "Good evening, children, I am Missus Langford—and I am here to help you learn how to read and write."

"An' cipher?" a yellow-shirted boy with two missing front teeth asked.

"And cipher."

He shook his head authoritatively.

"Thank you for coming, Zachim. I appreciate you being here to help me with the children."

Zachim's head snapped up and his face slowly registered the significance of her gesture. He mouthed, "Thank ye, ma'am."

She invited him to join her at the front of the class. Reluctantly, he edged forward with his eyes watching his new boots. A gift from Eliason. He paused at her side with his back to the children. "Missus Langford, I cain't read no letters. No numbers, neither."

She put her fist to her mouth, faked a cough, and whispered, "You weel."

He smiled and stepped behind her, alongside the blackboard. Smiling, Eliason slipped quietly outside. Nightfall had sweetly come, like a young woman tending her flower garden. Instead of savoring the spring evening's gentleness, he went immediately to his carriage and lifted the shotgun from the seat. After checking the loads, he clicked shut the gun, picked up a small sack of extra ammunition, and head back to the front porch.

He had hoped Reverend Langford would have joined them. Threats against this school had grown more intense each day. A few steps from his vehicle, he stopped, chewed on his lower lip, and returned. He lifted the scarred suitcase with his free hand from the carriage, looked around as if he expected someone to be watching, and resumed his return to the porch with one hand holding the suitcase, the other his shotgun. He chuckled to himself that he was becoming a real worrier in his old age. But he liked the security of having his legal papers close to him. Always had. It was a good idea for a black man succeeding in a white man's world.

Words on a piece of paper weren't really on his mind. It was the part-time minister who had become his friend. Something told him Reverend Langford was more than a Bible-thumper. He sensed it before Sunday's awful conflict and was certain of it after. That had convinced him of his hunch to ask Aleta to teach black children. This minister was all warrior, he was sure of it. In the back of his mind, the name "Rule Cordell" crept forward to gain attention, but he dismissed the notion as nothing more than an impassioned man doing anything he could to save another.

He leaned back in the chair, scooting it sideways to fully place himself in the darkest shadow. Maybe he was just geting old, he told himself, set the suitcase beside him, laid the shotgun across his lap, and looked for his pipe. It was lying a few feet away, right where he had left it. But placing the stem in his clinched teeth released a shiver. Why? *How silly,* he thought, and reached for a match in his vest. Another strange worry shot through him, and he instinctively removed his fingers to pause at the handle of his shoulder-holster revolver. The concern left, and his eyes sought the thin moon sliver tacked to the dark sky. He didn't need to smoke right now. It was greater satisfaction just knowing he had done something to help. Even if it was just fifteen children—and a thirty-year-old man.

Inside, Aleta was thrilled with the hunger to learn she was finding among the children. She was particularly drawn to an eight-year-old girl eager to answer every question. Mary Ann's cheery voice was music. Without appearing to do so, Aleta quickly assessed the academic level of each student, distributing the slates to every child and the books to the older ones.

She made a special announcement of suggesting Zachim sit beside a twelve-year-old boy named William James to help him. Zachim realized she was giving him a way to learn without the humiliation of being so much older than the class. His face beamed with joy when she gave him a slate and a book. He wiped away a tear with his fist, and she blinked away a responding emotion.

Under her direction, the class began to recite the alphabet as Aleta drew the letters on the blackboard and the children wrote them on their own slates. She worked through the alphabet, giving the class an opportunity to tell her what each letter was. Mary Ann had given most of the letters so far.

"Right . . . 'M.' Let us all say it together. 'M.' *Bueno!* Ah, very good. Now—after 'M' comes?"

The same yellow-shirted boy jammed his hand in the

air and she called on him, pleased to have someone respond beside Mary Ann. "*Sí*, David Duane, what ees the letter?"

"I hear tell your man dun fi't them Regulators—during church. Be that the truth of it? Heard you was a-fi'ttin' them too."

Aleta's half-smile was less a response to the request than the annoyance of interrupting her lesson plan. "What you heard was true. Now, who knows what letter comes next?"

David Duane's hand shot up again, a fraction ahead of Mary Ann's.

What was left of her smile vanished. "*Sí*, David Duane?" She knew his response wouldn't be "N."

"Is yo-all ag'in all the Yanks?" David Duane's face was earnest, his eyebrows propped to reinforce his concern.

"Let us concentrate on the alphabet for now," Aleta said.

"But, Missus Langford, my Momma says them Regulators are hyar to make sure we'uns gi't our . . . just doin's."

Aleta folded her arms. "Your mother ees right. That ees what they should be doing. Last Sunday, they took an innocent man and hanged him. What if they did that to your father?"

"I don't have no Pappa. Some white men in sheets burned our house—an' kilt him."

She nodded and tried to think of something to say. The class was staring at her. Waiting. Their eyes told her that they wanted reassurance their new teacher wasn't suddenly something evil.

"That ees why you must learn all you can. That ees what your pappa would want." She forced a smile, but it was trembling and thin. "The more you learn, the more you can do, and the more you will know who will really help you—and who says he does, but really does not want you to get better."

The silence that followed was sliced by Zachim's intense speech. He stood from his crouched position beside James William. "Chil'un, this hyar fine lady—and her good man—they's on our side. You best be knowin' that. I dun seed that Captain Padgett and his bunch. Don't you go believin' they's hyar to he'p us. They's a-wantin' to he'p theirselves—an' that's all. David Duane, you tell your Momma to come an' talk to me about it. She's wrong as the devil attendin' Sunday meetin'."

Outside on the porch, Eliason heard the discussion and the resumption of the alphabet recitation. Just the sound of learning made him feel good. He muttered to himself, "School is the best fort there is." His mind caught a rustling sound to his left, a noise that shouldn't be there.

Sliding from the chair to a kneeling position, he returned his pipe to the porch and raised the shotgun to his shoulder, pointing it in the direction of the sound. He waited for more indications of movement and was rewarded with rustling to his right. No one out there was a friend, he was sure of it.

With his right hand on the trigger and gripping the shotgun, he reached inside his coat with his left hand and awkwardly drew the pearl-handled revolver from its shoulder holster. He placed the gun at his knee and silently cursed its silver plating for the reflection it gave away in the moonlight. His attention was drawn to the nearby suitcase. Impulsively, he grabbed the handle and hurled it as hard as he could over the side porch and into the night. It sounded like the luggage landed in the hedgerow bordering the small building. He tried to calm himself by joking that a little scratching wouldn't hurt anything that hadn't already been marred from wear. He would hunt for the suitcase later—after this, whatever it was, was over. Silently, he chastised himself for being so jumpy but returned his attention to the night. Down deep, he knew it wasn't a joke and he wasn't hearing things. He listened again for shuffling but heard nothing.

His two vest-pocket derringers were always ready but only good in close quarters. He saw the movement—or thought he did. Lighter-colored shapes moving in the darkness. But nothing definitive enough to shoot at. How many were out there? Would they really shoot with children inside—and the wife of a minister? Should he warn Missus Langford? He remembered her gun.

Crack! Crack! Crack! Crack! Orange flames cut into the night and he felt lead hammer against his chest and stomach. His shotgun exploded as his fingers closed in response to the impact. Bullets crashed around him. His head jerked sideways and his hat went flying. Sickening thumps of lead found his lean frame. He fell backward, grabbing wildly for the revolver at his feet. Blood covered his clothes. Blood was in his eyes. His mouth. He couldn't see. Unable to move, he stammered, "Save . . . the children!" Three more shots rang out. A confident cry followed.

"We've got the black bastard. Take the school! Come on!"

Inside, Aleta's first reaction to the gunfire was calm. "Zachim, put out the lamps and stay away from the window. Children, get down on the floor. Now." She grabbed the bag beside the teacher's desk and pulled free the gunbelt and holster. Pulling the revolver from the leather sheath, she slung the gunbelt over her shoulder.

"There ees a back door. I saw it. Everyone follow me. Quickly, children. There ees not much time. Stay low."

Children sprang from their desks and scurried in the

direction she pointed. Zachim hurried past Aleta, toward the door.

"No, Zachim, thees way!"

"I must go help Mr. Eliason."

"No, Zachim—they weel kill you too!"

He opened the door and gunfire filled the space. Slammed backward, he spun awkwardly on one foot, then fell. Blood seeped from his chest and stomach. An ugly crease along his forehead was crimson and widening. He pushed up on his elbows, then on his trembling arms, to stand again. He got to his knees. Five more shots rammed into him. He gasped and collapsed.

Aleta took a deep breath, turned over three chairs pushed against a long assembly table to block their path, and urged the closest child to keep his head down. In the middle of the moving string of children, Mary Ann spun and ran toward her desk.

"Mary Ann, come here!"

But the little girl never hesitated, returning to her desk. She grabbed the book and slate and ran back, carrying them like they were precious and easily broken. A bullet creased the windowsill and skidded toward the floor a few feet from where she had stood.

"Teacher, I couldn't leave them." Mary Ann held the book and slate away from her chest and then returned them with a hug.

"I know, sweetheart. I know," Aleta assured, patting her on the back. "But let us keep going, all right?"

"Yes, teacher. Are you mad at me?"

Aleta tried to smile. "Of course not, Mary Ann. I think you are wonderful."

With her pistol pointed at the entrance, Aleta kept glancing back as she guided the children half-crawling, half-running into the darkness of the factory. The porch filled with heavy boots and cursing. "Shoot 'em again, right between the eyes. Both of 'em. That black sonvabitch thought he was as good as us."

"I—I didn't think a-anyone was s-supposed to get hurt." The voice was thin and choking.

"Nobody did. Come on, let's git them colored kids. If'n we kill a few, the rest o' them will be too damn scared to do this no more."

"Yeah. Let's do it."

"I want that Langford woman, too. She's too big for her britches."

"She needs a real man to teach her some manners." Guffaws trailed the statement.

The same choking voice warned the others. "I—I'd l-leave her alone i-if I were you. You don't know Rule."

"Rule? You mean Preacher Langford? Who the hell is afraid of some damn Bible-thumper?"

"H-he isn't a minister, not r-really. He's . . ."

"Come on—before they spread out in there and are hard to find."

"We kin always spot thar eyes. They's the onliest thing that's white. Them an' their teeth."

Laughter followed the five men as they entered the factory, brandishing pistols and rifles. White sheets, with holes cut for seeing, covered their heads and shoulders. They swarmed into the empty schooling area, kicking over desks and tossing left-behind books and slates to the floor.

"Write a message on that damn blackboard. Tell them no more of this."

"I can't write."

"Mayor, you do it."

"Shut up, stupid. You're not supposed to use anybody's name."

"Sorry."

"Where the hell did they go?"

With a motion toward the main part of the factory,

the five men rushed into the tables. Behind them three more entered, eager to find something to shoot at. Just inside the back door, Aleta watched the children dash for the row of bushes lining the creek behind the factory. To William James, the oldest, she had quickly given responsibility for seeing that the others followed him. They were to hide in the creek bed on the far side of the trees. She would meet them there and take them home. The boy's eyes shone with the pride of leadership.

"I ain't scared, Mrs. Langford. I ain't scared o' nuthin'." William James folded his arms defiantly.

"I know you aren't, William James, but the others are. So you keep them real quiet—and wait for me in the creek bed. All right?"

"Ya gonna shoot 'em? Did they kill Mr. Eliason—and Zachim?"

"Go on, William James. We can talk about it later."

"Ya sur you's a-comin'?"

"Yes. Go." She looked back at the advancing band of hooded men, then again to the vanishing children. William James was making certain they were close beside him. He looked up and met Aleta's eyes for an instant before she turned around to wait.

Darkness in the main factory area was contributing to a slow advance. At the front of the charging mob, the clan leader stumbled against the first tipped-over chair and fell headlong. Unable to catch himself, his sheet mask caught on the leg of the second chair and was yanked from his face. His sneering face was contorted with wild-eyed surprise and his pistol discharged as he hit the floor, driving a slug into the roof.

Even in the dull blackness of the building, Aleta recognized Mayor Giles. She gasped as the realization hit her mind. Under her breath, she muttered, "Colonel Bulldog." Angrily, he got to his feet with two men helping him. He cursed and yelled for his mask and quickly recovered his head. They started through the factory again, this time with a different man in the lead. Fourth in line, Giles urged them to move faster.

With a cocked revolver, Aleta stood beside the opened door. Waiting. Everything in her wanted to shoot, but she knew her gunfire would only speed up their discovery of the back entrance. The children needed all the time they could get. She shut her mind off to the possibility that there were more clansmen waiting in the back. Calmly she stood as they worked their way through the gauntlet of turned-over chairs, boxes, tables, and equipment. So far, they hadn't seen her or the door. They were less than twenty feet away when the man at the front of the band realized where she was.

"There! There's a goddamn back door—and the Langford woman's getting away with them kids!"

"L-let 'er go. It's t-too late. C-come on, w-we've done enough here."

Without looking back, the first hoodsman snarled, "What the hell's the matter with you? We came to put a stop to—"

Aleta's pistol roared twice, then three times. The first intruder buckled and fell, and the intruder next to him spun sideways. Returning gunfire strafed the door, but she had already slipped through it and into the night.

Chapter Twenty

None of the sixteen Regulators, camped on the Ripton ranch—nor their wheelchair-bound leader or his hired killer—paid any attention to the red Comanche moon taking control of the darkening sky. None noticed, either, that a shadow in the long buffalo grass, across from where they were bedding down for the night, was actually a man lying motionless. Watching. It was Rule Cordell.

His prone position was alongside the creek meandering past the Ripton ranch, about thirty yards from the Regulators' evening campfire. Downstream, it fattened into a year-round pond, used daily by Ripton cattle. His face and hands were rubbed with dirt to minimize his appearance. His spurs had been removed and left behind with his stallion and Shank's wagon over the closest rise and hidden by a thicket of young cottonwood trees that took their stand near the same creek. Ample grass would keep the horses quiet and content.

The Regulators' small camp was sheltered from gunfire from the dark main house, lying in the belly of a wide dry creek bed that had once held the stream passing near Cordell. Shallow banks provided a certain structure to their encampment. Overhead, more cottonwoods provided shade. The fire's soft crackle carried the wonderful sound of warmth. A wimpering wind brought the sweet aroma of coffee, as well as the sharp smell of green wood smoke. A man with a bandaged head, sitting around the campfire, was likely one of the men Billy had beaten.

Cordell's arm pounded with each heartbeat, but it wasn't bleeding. For once, his head was clear and without pain. He wanted to move, to stretch, but knew he dared not. He had long since rebuckled on his handguns and returned the warrior's stone earring to his ear. Shank had asked about the earring and Cordell had told him it was a gift from a Comanche shaman. The merchant was hoping for more, but Cordell made it clear he intended to speak no more about the gift or the giver.

The weight of his guns at his hips and the soft dangling pebble fueled the strange fire growing within him. A flame that was both cold and hot at the same time. He swallowed, but his own saliva did nothing to quench it. Out of habit, he touched the medicine pouch hanging beneath his shirt and glanced at the dead rose resting on his lapel. For the first time, he noticed that most of the petals were missing.

Six state lawmen were already asleep, stretched out behind high-cut banks; four more sat around the campfire, talking and passing a bottle of rye whiskey. Cordell figured they were waiting to take their turn at guard duty. Four more were stationed as night guards at key points around the perimeter of the Ripton house. Caleb Shank was somewhere on the far side of the ranch yard, studying the guard setup from that angle. Cordell trusted the big man to make good judgments—even though it meant being quiet. Shank had talked nonstop for most of their ride, telling war stories and explaining in great detail about Cordell's "masquerade battalion" battle in Virginia.

Another Regulator guarded their string of horses held back among the rear guard of cottonwoods; he was fighting hard to hold back sleep. Fifty feet away, a fidgety man stood watch beside Captain Padgett's unhitched wagon. With the mounted Gatling gun pointed toward the Ripton house, it rested like a giant beast where the creek bed broadened to become the advent of a gentle valley made for grazing cattle. Captain Padgett was in the wagon, sleeping. Cordell knew they would have to take control of the rapid-firing gun if they were to have any chance of success.

Cordell figured the Regulator leader hadn't used the big gun yet—and didn't want to. The value of the property would be diminished by the storm of bullets it belched. The crippled Regulator leader was sleeping in the wagon on a padded cot. Cordell couldn't see him, only hear his steady snoring. The glow of the campfire barely licked the wagon or the guard standing out front.

Not far from the horses was a gathering of saddles and tack, and just to the north were at least twenty rifles, carefully stacked against and around what was once a stone fence pillar. Next to the guns were two large barrels; he assumed they held water. A makeshift cooking area was nestled between them. Cordell hadn't yet seen the pistol-fighter, Lion Graham, but assumed he was around and wished he knew where. It was possible Graham was one of the men already asleep. A part of him wanted to talk with Graham, to try to understand the man who had come from the boy he knew. Yet he knew that such an encounter could not happen. Not without gunfire.

Everything was muted and uneasy after a day of unsettling news for the Regulators. First had come the likelihood that the Ripton girl had eluded them with the return of riderless horses. At dusk, three more came galloping into camp; two carried the three dead Regulators that Padgett had sent to determine what had happened. Furious about the second setback and the Riptons' stubborn refusal to surrender, he had become so upset that he couldn't talk and finally ended his evening downing most of a bottle of whiskey.

The Riptons' tenacity touched Cordell greatly. He marveled at Lizzie Ripton managing to escape at all. They were holding the main house like a fort, with both parents and Billy shooting effectively whenever a target took shape. Since he had been there, only sporadic gunfire had occurred, mostly from Regulators trying to unnerve the family. So far, the Riptons had been holding their own well enough that Padgett hadn't risked an all-out attack.

Why should he? No one would come to help the Riptons and the family was cut off from water, so it was only a matter of time before they would be forced to surrender. Shank thought the intended owner might be a wealthy Yankee rancher near Dallas; the man had been buying property with tax liens right and left. Cordell thought it could also be Mayor Giles. Whoever it was, they figured Padgett was offered a "finder's fee" for running the Riptons off. Cordell reminded himself that the would-be purchasers were as guilty as Padgett—and it was likely his Regulators didn't know about the deal, only Padgett's word that the family was hiding a wanted criminal.

He continued to study the Regulator camp, deciding on the moves he wanted to make, repeating them in his mind so he could perform them quickly and quietly. War had taught Cordell the power of being patient and waiting, in addition to the added force of doing the unexpected. The patience part had come more easily to his friend Taullery, who liked to know everything about a situation before making any move. Patience had not come easily to Cordell, whose every instinct was to attack, but he had learned the value of waiting.

Since heavy dusk, he had been stretched out sixty yards from the main building, but at an angle where he could see the entire ranch and the Regulator camp. Cordell rubbed his eyes to push back weariness that wanted control. When he and Shank separated, after sharing some food from the wagon and Cordell's saddlebags, the decision was to meet back at the horses when it was completely dark and decide on their next move.

From his position beside the creek, Cordell had examined the structures that made up the Ripton ranch: a house and large barn, a small bunkhouse with windows patched shut, a blacksmith shed, two corrals, one quite small, and an oddly shaped toolshed. Iron Creek, or Clark Creek as some called it, slowly crossed this side of the open ranchyard, providing a pathway of tall green cattails, fat buffalo grass, flowering yucca, and an occasional cottonwood tree and elderberry bush on both sides of soft black banks.

Closest to the house was a patch of blossoming buttercups, larkspur, and bluebells; Cordell guessed young Lizzie Ripton had tended to the wild flowers on her own. They were shaded by a grandfatherly cottonwood that was bent with age. Against their front porch, three small clumps of wild roses were thriving. The buildings were constructed of planked lumber and adobe. No rawhide outfit, that's for sure. Old man Ripton had tried to put down some deep roots, Cordell thought.

Glimpses of people moving inside the main house, and shadows flickering on the walls, disappeared with darkness. But never had there been any substantive silhouettes for targets. The family was too savvy for that. Sneaking into the main house had crossed his mind, but it seemed like a waste of time. He would like to see the family—and especially Billy—but this wasn't the moment for it. And it was too big a risk, likely pinning down Shank and himself. They would go there later and tell them of the plan.

Into his mind came the tall, pale woman from Taullery's store. She held the copper bowl, shut her eyes, and reopened them. He heard again her pronouncements: "You are thunder. You are lightning. You are a storm to clean the land." . . . followed by "God brings thunder and lightning. God brings the storm to clean the land. But someone comes . . . from another time, he comes . . . seeking the storm . . . to destroy it." What a strange woman. Where had she come from? Why had she said those strange things? Was she talking about Graham as the one from "another time"? What was Graham's insistence about their being together in another life as Roman soldiers? Did Graham believe in reincarnation? Is that what the woman meant? He should've asked Taullery if he knew her, or anything about her. When he had the chance, he would describe her to Shank; the merchant knew everyone in the region.

Aleta had used somewhat the same terms to describe how he should get Padgett to leave. "Become a son of the thunder." That was eerie. Just a coincidence, he assured himself. Aleta was describing how he should go about this attack. Thoughts of her made him homesick, and he tried to keep them from his mind. She would be home now, he thought, and tried to concentrate. Instead, he mentally kissed and held her until a particularly shrill laugh from the campfire took him away from her.

Daring moves were entrenched in Cordell's experience. In June 1862, he had been a part of General Jeb Stuart's unparalleled cavalry ride around McClellan's entire army. Deep in enemy territory, Stuart's twelve hundred gray-clad riders had humiliated McClellan's one hundred thousand troops. They had killed Federals, burned wagons, captured horses and guns, provided Lee with vital information for the successful Seven Days campaign that followed—and, most important, demoralized the North and given a great lift to the South. Stuart's ride was in all the Southern newspapers.

Unlike his mentor, Cordell didn't need praise nor seek it. Even though it didn't make much sense to him, he had obeyed the gallant general's orders to repeat the ride around the Union army again in October and partly again in June the following year. Unfortunately, Stuart's third attempt meant he was absent when Lee badly needed his eyes during the early days of Gettysburg. Cordell had never understood why Marse Robert had insisted on fighting there. It was clear, from the start, that his subordinate officers had mishandled the situation, giving the Union force the high ground uncontested. Later, when the South was fighting on without hope, grain, or bullets, he realized that the great leader knew Gettysburg was their only real chance to win. Time was definitely not on their side. Just like the Riptons.

Cordell's "masquerade battlion," as the Federal ambush became known, was partly a result of his training with Stuart and partly Cordell's stubbornness. If things went right tonight, he planned on repeating the concept with Shank's help. The big merchant seemed eager to try his hand at creating fake riflemen, spouting about the various items in his wagon that would prove useful.

Finally the remaining lawmen drifted away from the campfire and rolled into their sleeping blankets. Still Cordell waited. If his calculations were correct, the guards would change at midnight. He would wait until the new sentries were settled in before returning to their horses and wagon. At ten minutes past midnight, four Regulators wandered out of camp toward their preassigned positions. Two others headed toward Padgett's wagon and the string of horses to replace the guards there. None spoke, preferring silence to having to make talk. A few minutes later, the replaced guards from the positions nearest their ramp headed directly for their bedrolls.

Cordell sensed the other sentries coming before he saw them. Three Regulators, returning from guard duty, walked within ten feet of him without realizing their closeness. They were yawning and talking about a blond whore they both had known, and about who might have been responsible for today's ambush of their fellow Regulators, and whether there would be any whiskey left for them. He drew a gun in case they actually walked into him, leaving no choice but to fire. The three men passed him. One man stepped a foot from Cordell's shoulder; his voice was clipped and sarcastic. Where was the fourth?

There! The last Regulator had stopped to relieve himself in a shallow ditch in the middle of the east side of the ranch yard, only twenty-five feet from the house itself and next to the nurtured growth of wild flowers. Now he was moving again, holding his rifle like it was very heavy. Cordell watched him but avoided connecting with the man's eyes. He had known of instances where men actually felt such surveillance and reacted out of some long-forgotten instinct.

Satisfied the four men were interested only in sleeping, he crouched and worked his way back along the creek line until he felt comfortable walking. In the darkness, he could see that Shank had already returned and was cutting on something in the back of his wagon, using a large-bladed knife. A welcoming nicker from his stallion was louder than Cordell would have wished, but he went immediately to the horse, rubbed its nose, and led it to the creek for a drink. He wanted to loosen the cinch but knew it wasn't a smart thing to do. They might be coming back fast.

"Whatcha think, Reverend?" Shank whispered, as he watched the part-time minister care for the stallion.

Retying the horse, Cordell removed his saddle lariat and joined Shank. "They're all asleep now—except for the guards. I think we should go first to the house, like we planned, then get Billy Rip an' finish this."

Shank nodded agreement. "Found some hats—for our 'battalion.' " He chuckled and held up a handful of wide-brimmed hats. "Wish I had more. Bin thinkin' we're gonna need somethin' to make 'em stand up. I gathered up some heavy 'nuff branches but couldn't find 'nuff."

The same idea had been churning in Cordell's mind, but he hadn't decided the best way to create the appearance of many men in the darkness. It wouldn't take much, just a shape. He popped the lariat against his leg as he considered their options.

"See these hyar?" Shank lifted a piece of broom he'd cut. His heavy eyebrows jumped around with a life of their own. "These'll go in the ground real good. We kin stick hats on 'em. I thought slidin' a burlap sack over one would look like a man in the dark too. What do ya think?"

"You're way ahead of me, Caleb. That's perfect. But we'll have to work fast—and quiet."

"Gotcha. Ya wanna kill them guards 'round the house—a'fer we talk with the Riptons?"

They discussed the options with Shank definitely more inclined to eliminate the four guards than Cordell was. They decided on knocking out only the man on the south side to allow them easier access to the house. If Billy Ripton agreed, he would join them in "surrounding" the Regulators with their props.

"Are we takin' them guns with us now? Them 'Chesters is all loaded an' ready." Shank pointed to the weapons in the wagon. "What 'bout these hyar sacks an' hats? Hellfire, I almost forgot. Got one o' them things ladies use to make dresses on. That oughta make a good'un." He pushed aside some boxes to reveal a full-size dress form.

Cordell chuckled, and Shank slapped him hard on the back.

"We'll get the stuff for the dummies later. Let's take two Winchesters and some boxes of bullets—for now. That'll give Ma and Pa Ripton more firepower. You can put the other Winchester to good use. I'll use my Henry."

Shank motioned toward heavy canvas containers hanging from the sides of his wagon. "I'm figgerin' those folks could be needin' some water. I kin take two o' these water bags. Fixed up a mite o' extra grub, too. An' lead." He waved his ringed right hand in the direction of two packed leather pouches near his feet, one with food tins and the other holding boxes of bullets.

Agreeing, Cordell laid his lariat on the ground, took a stubby pencil and a folded sheet of paper from his shirt pocket, and wrote in a scrawly handwriting, unlike his own: "Padgett—Leave the Riptons alone or we will hunt you down and kill you."

He showed it to Shank, who studied the note, rubbed his bearded chin, and handed it back. "Ri't good sentiment. But I think it should be signed, ya know'd, give this hyar gang o' ours a name. Make it sound real an' all."

Grinning, Cordell thought for a moment, then wrote, "Sons of Thunder." He showed the note to Shank, who reviewed it a long time before commenting again. His eyebrows danced along with the reading. " 'Sons of Thunder,' eh? Got a nice ring to 'er. T'were a couple o' boys from the Good Book, weren't they?"

Chapter Twenty-one

Shank's observation surprised Cordell. It was true, but that hadn't occurred to him. He smiled at the irony of a would-be minister overlooking the linkage to a New Testament reference to two of Jesus' disciples. Shaking his head at his own lapse, Cordell told him about Aleta's analogy of thunder being an unseen warning of a coming storm—and the need to become a "son of the thunder" to accomplish the rescue of the Riptons without being discovered. Since it was the two of them, "sons of thunder" simply sounded right. Then he told the big man about the woman in Taullery's store and her reference to thunder and storms. Shank's eyes widened with the news of the seer, and Cordell wasn't certain he should have shared the encounter.

Shank ran his hand through thick black hair. "Wal, that'd be Eagle Mary. Part Comanche, part witch. Let's be hopin' she dun seed it right. Las' time I heard tell o' one of her seein's, a fella north o' hyar up 'n' died. Nobody knew from what."

"Sorry I brought it up." Cordell shoved the note into his coat pocket.

Nodding his head in agreement, Shank started to walk toward the water sack and stopped. When he turned back to Cordell, his eyes were wallowing in tears. "Reckon I should oughta tell ya somethin'. I ain't exactly goin' after Padgett to help these good folks. Ya see these hyar rings?"

In choking sentences, he explained that the four rings on his right hand represented each of his four children; the bigger ring on his left was in memory of his wife. His entire family, living in Georgia, had been killed during the War, their home burned. The Yankee officer in charge of the brutal assault, he later learned from a search of newspaper accounts, was Padgett. Shortly after that, Padgett himself was wounded and lost the use of his legs.

"I be a-carryin' a heap o' hate—an' a heap more o' sad inside me fer a long time. Bin a while since I could sleep a night through—without seein' my kids an' my wife . . ." He turned away, unable to finish.

Shank's anguish slammed into Cordell. He stepped back, caught his own emotions, and moved toward the big man, holding him by the shoulders. Cordell could feel Shank trembling. His hands covered a third of Shank's upper arms. The massive merchant was dissolving with pent-up sorrow.

"Caleb, I'm very sorry. I wish I could take away your pain—but God doesn't give us men that power." He looked into the big man's face, washed with hot tears. "All I know is this—an' I know it to the tips of my toes. They are happy. Very happy. They're in a joyful place—with no pain, no worries, no wants. Except one. They want you to know this, and that they'll be waiting on the other side. When it's time, you'll all be together again. Until that time, you'll always see them in every sunset. Every bird singing. Every gentle rain. Every pretty flower. I promise."

Shank stood with his head down and his shoulders heaving. His response was barely audible. "I—I c-can't . . . quite see their faces . . . no more. I—I . . ."

Cordell was about to tell him the same idea that he had shared with the young Michael Harper, about shutting your eyes and re-creating a happy moment, but realized Shank wouldn't be able to do that. Glad it wasn't the first thing out of his mouth, Cordell responded in a voice that was nearly as quiet as Shank's.

"You know, Caleb, that's God's way of letting us know they are well. They'll always be in your heart, but not in your head." He didn't know if it made sense or not, but it seemed right to him. He had lost a mother, but not to death—and a father, to hatred. It was the only common link he could draw on. Cordell was silent, waiting to see what his big friend would do next. The part-time minister felt like his vitality had been drawn from him and into Shank.

Shank rubbed his eyes with huge leathery fists and Cordell released his hold on his shoulders, not sure what would happen next. He couldn't wait much longer to move on Padgett and his wagon, with or without Shank's help. Slowly, the big man looked up again. His eyes crackled with pain, and his cheeks and beard were lined with wetness, but he smiled. A smile of contentment. The expression puzzled Cordell.

"Didn't think no preacher'd ever make me feel so good. Thank ye for them words. They's like one o' them spring rains, all sweet an' gentle, makin' ever'thin' green an' nice."

Cordell winced. He wasn't certain he would be able to return to the pulpit. Not after today. Men of God didn't shoot people. He swallowed and couldn't bring himself to silently ask for forgiveness. Instead, he said, "Let's do this for your family."

"I'm ready. Thank ye."

To emphasize the point, Shank grabbed a lariat and the two large sacks of water. Without further word, he headed toward their planned drop-off point. Cordell couldn't imagine how Shank would be able to handle both water sacks, but he carried them like a man holding two dead chickens. Cordell picked up his own lariat, slung it through his left arm and over his shoulder, then lifted the two rifles from the wagon, the pouches of ammunition and food from the ground, and followed Shank. Shank again suggested they take out all four guards. He reminded Cordell that it would make things easier when they started the "gang" attack; they wouldn't have to worry about one sneaking behind them.

"Remember, these boys is figgerin' on killin' some good folks—an' takin' their fine home." Shank summed up his argument, waving the water sacks as he talked.

"Are you worried I'm going to hold a prayer meeting?" Cordell glanced at him as they crossed the creek over a chain of flat stones, left there by the Riptons for that purpose, and eased through a cluster of cattails and tall buffalo grass.

"Nope, jes' didn't want ye to be chewin' on yourself 'bout gittin' rid o' these bastards. Ya know, it were Jesus himself who sent all them coin-changers a-packin' out of the temple. Dun had himself a whip too."

Suddenly Cordell froze. Something touched his right knee! His pistol jumped into his hand as he looked down. A big-eyed, yellow cat stared back at him. The Riptons' cat. Exhaling the tension, Cordell moved his foot to convince the animal there were other adventures more worthwhile. Now, where was the guard on this side of the house? Had he moved? Had the man seen them? No, he would have shot or yelled out.

A solitary line of sweat crossed Cordell's tanned face. He was thankful for the black sky with its mere handful of weak stars. Touching the buckskin pouch beneath his shirt, he prayed silently. He gave no thought to the irony of invoking two very different spiritual actions.

"Damn cats have a way of sneakin' up on a man, don't they?" Shank observed.

"I know why they were here, my friend—and I agree with you, we should take out all four." He pointed in the direction of the ditch near the house.

Shank stared in the direction Cordell aimed. "Ya think . . . ah, Rule Cordell coulda handled Lion Graham? If'n he were alive, I mean."

The darkness hid Cordell's frown. He had asked himself the same question over and over since last Sunday. "It'd be awfully close. Neither would have wanted to live on the difference, I reckon. Guess we'll never know, though, will we—since Cordell's dead."

"Huh? Oh, yah, no, we won't, I reckon."

After an awkward silence of several steps, Shank began describing the guards. It was like a military briefing, Cordell thought. All four carried Winchesters and belted handguns; the rifles wouldn't be cocked, only levered, or at least that's how they were when he left. The farthest guard, on the west side, was impatient and bored with the whole thing; Shank thought he would be inclined to let his mind drift. Both the north and south guards had a routine of walking they went through, repeating it over and over. The east guard was very nervous and would be the greatest problem because of it.

Shank's gaze was intense; Cordell fought to regain energy. They slipped into the ditch and crouched there to study the situation. Cordell pointed out a dark spot where one of the first guards had urinated so Shank wouldn't lay anything in it. The big man hefted the heavy water bags toward the southern end of the small earthen bowl and laid them there. All the time, his dark eyes sought signs of the guard posted on this side of the house.

The man wasn't hard to find, and Shank's assessment of him was right. The guard was in constant movement around a tree. Even normal night sounds were bothering him. The murmuring leaves in the cottonwood were ominous conversations. He would whirl first in one direction, then another, at imagined advances. Worse, he was carrying a cocked Winchester, with his finger on the trigger. If they attacked the guard now, it was likely his finger would squeeze the trigger the instant Cordell or Shank hit him, assuming either could get that close without being seen. That was a chance they couldn't risk.

Settling into a crouch, they let some of the guard's jittery nerves burn off naturally, watching from a mere twenty feet away, but careful not to look the edgy guard in the eyes. Cordell guessed the early guards—the first and second sets—would be the weakest men. The best ones would take the harder parts of the night when sleep beckoned to every sentry. He counted on them not expecting any problem so early in the evening, if they were concerned about an attack at all.

About Cordell's size but slighter, the guard wore two belted guns—one with the handle forward, the other toward his back. Both holsters were tied down. A light-colored derby, a dirty neckerchief, too-tight pants, and a woolen vest that glistened with remains of a greasy dinner completed the man's distinctive appearance. Cordell decided that the nervous guard would respond favorably to some "company." If the sentry thought someone was coming from camp to talk with him, he might relax.

It was worth the gamble. Waiting longer just increased their being seen. He motioned for Shank to stay in the shadows and the big merchant complied, his eyes wide with concern. Without a murmur, Cordell circled around to position himself as if coming directly from the sleeping camp. Remembering Aleta's advice, he pulled the folded-up scarf from his coat sleeve where it blotted his wound and tied it around his mouth and nose. The smell of his own blood hit his nose, and he coughed. His arm burned from the movement but didn't bleed again. He looked up at the guard but knew the slight sound wouldn't carry that far.

He should have suggested that Shank wear a mask too. The thought jumped into his mind. Would the big man think of wearing something to hide his face? Probably not. Cordell stared into the darkness as if he would be able to check on his big friend. He reclosed the gap of thirty feet between the nervous man and himself without another sound. Pulling his hat brim lower to partially cover his eyes and shadow his face, he drew a revolver and kept it at his side.

The two-pistoled sentry was facing the ranch house, the sleeping camp to his back. The guard's cocked rifle was now cradled in his arms with his fingers out of the trigger area. He was watching the same yellow cat that had surprised Cordell earlier. Rubbing its back against the tree, the scrawny animal was a welcome diversion for the man.

Snapping a match to life with his left hand to simulate lighting a cigarette, Cordell declared his presence in a soft, offhand manner at the same time, trying his best to imitate the drawl of one of the Regulators who had passed him earlier. He pushed the coiled lariat back in place on his shoulder as a way to help him concentrate on the voice. "Don'cha shoot now, ol' friend. Thought you might be likin' some company. Couldn't sleep."

The guard flinched slightly, but the reassuring voice

was a comforting sound in the lonely night. He turned and said, "That you, Bobby Joe? Glad to have the—"

"If you whisper, I'll blow your head off."

Cordell's gun barrel lifted the man's chin to attention, as the dark-coated gunfighter's left hand slid between the guard's rifle hammer and the readied bullet in the chamber, and his fingers grabbed the gun itself. The move was a blur. It would be enough to keep the rifle from falling and keep the gun from going off if the guard made some sudden move to fire it and warn his friends. Cordell's instinct was right, as the guard's arms jerked upward in response to Cordell's terrifying command, releasing the gun.

"Good boy. I'll take the rifle. Easy-like. Don't move," Cordell growled. "If there's any noise at all, you won't be around to see the fun. Understand? Nod your head."

The nervous guard nodded excessively; a dark stain spread across the groin area of his pants. Cordell pulled the weapon free, his left hand still blocking the hammer's intended path. Smoothly, he uncocked the gun without moving his own from the guard's neck. With the rifle in his left hand, Cordell delivered a blow to the back of the guard's head with his revolver barrel. A stuttered groan followed, and the man collapsed into Cordell's arms. His lariat wobbled from his shoulder and trailed the sagging guard to the ground.

A glance at the sleeping Regulators revealed no movement, nor did he hear any sounds from other parts of the ranch yard. Cordell reholstered his Colt and retrieved his fallen rope. Even their short conversation hadn't carried over the night sounds. He didn't think it would.

Cordell dragged the body to the tree and strained to hold the unconscious man in place while he lashed him there with his lariat. Shank appeared from nowhere to help. Like elks at a water hole, they looked up frequently to make certain no one had discovered them. From afar, the guard would appear to be on duty. Tossing the weapons on the ground away from the body, Cordell replaced the handguns with a rock in each holster. In the shadows, they would easily pass as gun handles from a distance. He crossed the sentry's arms, like they were folded naturally, and held them in place with quick loops of his lariat.

"I'll git a stick to look like a rifle—in his arms," Shank whispered, and disappeared.

The guard's neckerchief became a gag tied tightly around his mouth, in case he became conscious too soon. The gash in his skull was bleeding, but it wouldn't show in the darkness. Several lashings around the man's nose held his head up. Cordell didn't want one of the man's friends coming to see if the guard was sleeping on duty.

Behind him came a low growl. "What the hell? Raise your hands, mister, and turn around real slow."

Chapter Twenty-two

Cordell's hands eased skyward. He hadn't seen any movement around the camp. Where had this man come from? He had to be one of the other guards from around the house. Silently, Cordell cursed himself for being so careless.

"That's the first part, mister. Now turn 'round . . . real slow-like. Reckon I dun caught myself one of those bastards that dun shot up our boys today. Glad I needed a smoke from ol' Jeff. Did ya kill him?"

Cordell turned slowly toward the man. A thick handlebar mustache couldn't quite hide the guard's missing teeth in his victorious grin; a cowhide vest was too big for his thin frame. Moonlight slipped along the barrel of his Winchester; Cordell had already noticed that the hammer on the rifle wasn't cocked. A bullet had probably been levered into the chamber and the hammer eased down, so it wouldn't go off accidentally, Cordell decided. A sign of a more savvy guard.

That would be the only edge in Cordell's favor if he decided to draw his pistol. Could he draw and shoot before the man pulled back the hammer and fired? Cordell's mind raced for a decision of what to do next. He knew he wouldn't let himself be disarmed, but shots would bring the whole camp. Where was Shank? The thought rammed into his mind.

"Wait 'til I show you to the Captain. He'll be real happy to string you up." The grinning guard laid his thumb on the hammer. "Pull down that red mask, fella, so's I kin . . ."

An iron hand over the guard's mouth held in the rest of the words as a big knife ripped across his exposed throat. A gurgle was the only night sound. Shank's huge frame took shape behind the crumpled man.

Cordell watched him, breathed deeply to release the tension, and whispered, "Thanks, Caleb. Not too many options left for me."

"Yeah, had me a feelin' ya was a second or two away from pullin' leather. Thought for a swallow he were that scarey sonvabitch Lion Graham. Haven't laid eyes on that bastard, have ye?"

"No, I haven't, but he's around here, I'm sure," Cordell said, helping Shank drag the lifeless form into the ditch.

The mention of Graham's name brought a twitch to Cordell's face. He saw the killer's eyes and they became his father's. He hitched his shoulders to rid himself of the image and heard Shank say he thought that the guard was just coming over to pass the time and didn't realize anything was wrong until he got close. Shank identified him as the guard watching the north side of the Ripton house. He remembered the mustache and vest.

"Didn't think 'bout hidin' my face." Shank stared at Cordell's red mask. "Ya think it's worth my doin'? Not many folks are big as this ol'man. Cain't put a mask over my whole body." He chuckled at his joke.

"It can't hurt, Caleb. Have you got a handkerchief or something?"

A dirty handkerchief from Shank's back pocket was soon stretched across his wide face.

"Nice mask," Cordell teased.

" 'Bout like puttin' lace on a pumpkin and sayin' it's a table," Shank growled, and showed him a thick branch he'd found to add to the first guard's folded arms, to simulate a rifle.

Cordell folded his own arms. "Caleb, we don't have much time. We won't try to put this other guard back 'on duty.' He wouldn't be seen from camp anyway. I think they'll change guards in an hour. Maybe less. We've got a lot to do before then."

Shank smiled, and the expression lifted his entire face. "Good 'nuff. How 'bout me sendin' the last two your way. That'd be a mite faster."

"What do you have in mind?"

"Whiskey."

Minutes later, Shank crawled away toward the guard on the south, after placing the stick into the unconscious guard's arms. From the ditch, it appeared to be a rifle barrel, Cordell thought. Shank's guttural whisper in the direction of the unseen guard was barely audible. "S-shay, we got . . . s-some Tennessee sippin' whiskey . . . over hyar. Wan' s-some? Come on. We's all on the east s-side . . . down in that low s-spot thar."

Cordell grinned at the presentation. It sounded just like somebody who'd been drinking. A rush of heavy footsteps followed an interested "Damn right I do. This night's got me bored."

Cordell lost the moving silhouette in the darkest shadows but followed the sound of the man advancing. He wasn't certain where Shank went, but the guard passed where Cordell thought his friend was hiding, came to the the east edge of the ditch, and stopped. Cordell stood and waved his arms to direct his entry into the shallow embankment. The man wasn't more than fifteen feet away. In the darkness, neither man was much more than a shape.

Reinforcing his gestured welcome, Cordell said enthusiastically, "Over here, man. It's real good stuff."

"All right!"

Casually holding his rifle in his right hand at his side, the guard cut straight down the incline. He misjudged the drop-off and slipped, let go of his gun, and staggered to keep his balance. His gun came to rest three feet away. With a long curse, he picked up the rifle as if it were part of his plan of entry.

His head turned first one way, then the other. "Where the hell are you, Jeff . . . Levi? Can't see crap out here. Damn near fell on my ass."

"Right here." The crack of Cordell's pistol barrel on the man's head punctuated the statement.

Before Cordell could pull the unconscious man into the deeper shadows, another silhouette appeared at the top of the ditch.

"Hey, you bastards better save some of that for me, goddammit."

Standing upright beside the downed guard, Cordell waved at him and the man half-ran toward him, stopping only four feet from Cordell.

"Hey, you're not . . ."

"Drop the gun."

The stocky guard with a black cloth patch over his left eye hesitated, and Cordell cocked his pistol. A menacing crackle in the night.

"If you shoot, you'll have Regulators all over your ass," the guard snarled. His one good eye almost glowed in the darkness.

"Better take a closer look, friend," Cordell said confidently. "We've got your friends surrounded. We can start the ball anytime. You want to go first? Might as well—you won't be around for the end."

The man's face paled and his lone eye widened with a brown eyebrow that arched in fear. He dropped the rifle and it thumped on the ground, sending gray puffs of dust over his mule-eared boots. Unsuccessful with one approach, the guard tried another.

"Hey, we ain't regular lawdogs. The boss spreads around the money he gets for running off sorry-ass Rebs like these here. I'm sure he could use some more good guns. I'd be happy to put in the word for ya. Say, you look familiar? Ever been down Rio Bravo way?"

"Not interested. I remind people of a lot of men, especially when they're staring at my gun."

"W-who are you?"

"They call us the Sons of Thunder."

"T-the Sons of Thunder?" The guard squinted at Cordell, trying to see him more clearly.

"Where's Lion Graham?" Cordell kept his face in the shadows. His sense told him that the one-eyed guard wasn't going to challenge him without a clear edge. Maybe the man would talk.

"Lion Graham? That crazy sonvabitch. How would I know?" The thick-chested guard rocked his hands back and forth in a nervous rhythm, like a schoolboy reciting. "Padgett has to keep him around because . . . well, the man with the money wants it that way. Graham gives me the shivers." His right hand inadvertently brushed against the handle of his belt gun. He jumped at the slight contact and rushed his hand out and away from the pistol. "S-sorry. Sorry, I . . ."

"Take off the gunbelt. You wouldn't want me to mistake what you're doing." Cordell's voice was actually soft.

"Yeah, you're right." The guard's hands shook as he struggled to release the leather strip from the belt buckle.

"Who runs Padgett?"

"What?" The gun thudded at the guard's boots.

"Who runs Padgett? You said there's a man with money who wants Graham with you."

The guard shrugged his shoulders. "Hell, I dunno. Never saw him, never heard his name. All I know is he's the one who tells us who to go after—and tells Graham who to kill."

"Is that what happened to Whisper Jenson?" Cordell's question had an edge and and his gentler tone was gone.

"Yeah, I heard the big man was worried about Jenson rallying the folks around here." The guard motioned with his hands to simulate the killer's jerky manner. "But Graham, he's crazy. Talks about being alive at different times. Ya know, back in history. Rome an' all that. An' he keeps talking about seeing a dead man an' wanting to kill him—for real. Rule Cordell, ya remember him? A real heller. Got hisself dead two years back. Him an' a whole gang, I think."

Above them, a large shadowed figure appeared. Cordell knew immediately it could only be one person. Shank's earlier observation about a mask not doing much to hide his identity was probably right.

Shank's growl explained his appearance. "That's the last one. How you doin'?"

"We're fine. All of the boys ready?"

"Who . . . ah, yeah, they be ready whenever you give the word. All thirty o' us. We's itchin' to cut down a few o' them Regulators. Who's this sorry ass?"

The guard found enough courage to comment, "You boys are playing with fire. That's Captain Padgett down there, you know. Head of the state police."

Shank replied first. "Hellfire, dun thought it were Saint Patrick. Wonder if Padgett is up for skeedaddlin' outta hyar."

Shank stomped into the ditch like it was level ground, heading toward the standing guard who was still facing Cordell. The big merchant's sagging mask had slipped below his nose and now barely covered his mouth. Cordell motioned for him to raise it, but Shank wasn't paying attention.

"What are you going to do with this guy?" Shank stopped just behind the eye-patched guard.

"Got any thoughts?" Cordell asked.

Shank's answer was to tap the man on the shoulder. When the guard turned around, Shank's right fist exploded into his face. The savage blow drove the man off his feet and he tumbled into the top bank of the incline, hit it, and slid back down without knowing.

"Will that do?" Shank asked, shaking his hand to relieve the pain. Shank's hand ran across his face, pulling the mask down to his chin. His fingers stopped at his neck and scratched it. He didn't appear to remember the handkerchief was even there.

"Looks good to me. You think he saw you?" Cordell asked as they tied the two guards' hands and legs with their own pants belts and gunbelts and gagged them with their own neckerchiefs.

"Naw, he never saw nothin' around my fist. Why? Would you kill 'im if he did? I figgered you wanted the boy to be able to tell Padgett a few things—when he comes around."

Cordell didn't answer. He shoved two of the guards' handguns into his waistband. The action felt like the old days when he carried four or more revolvers into battle. He told Shank what the guard had said about not knowing where Graham was and about Padgett being controlled by another man. He didn't see any benefit in telling about Graham being after him.

Just to make certain Billy Ripton—and the Ripton family—knew friends, not enemies, were close by, Cordell crawled beside the lone, glass-enclosed window and whistled a low shrill sound, much like a hawk screaming. He and other Rebel scouts with him had used it to signal to each other when they were sneaking up on something. He whistled, then waited for a response. Waited. Nothing. Precisely, he whistled again, a little louder this time. Still no response.

Surely Billy could hear that, even if he was sleeping. Maybe he was wounded and not able to respond. He would try again. There! There it was. Faint but distinct. Cordell whistled again; this time the signal indicated that Billy was to stay where he was, they were coming his way. The answering whistle was stronger this time; Billy Ripton understood.

Cordell hurried back to the waiting Shank. "Come on, Caleb, let's go see some nice people."

"You betcha." Shank lifted the water sacks and scaled the incline like it wasn't more than a stair step in town. Cordell gathered the sacks of food and bullets and the two wagon Winchesters. Lizzie's cat reappeared, meowed its curiosity, and followed them to the back door, where they laid down their supplies, knocked, and waited. Inside were sounds of scuffling feet, muffled voices, and, finally, the unlatching of the heavy door. The door opened slowly, only an inch.

At the last moment, Cordell remembered his mask, pulled down the scarf, and tried to smile. Billy Ripton stood in the doorway, holding a Spencer repeating carbine taken from a dead Union soldier during the War. His eyes were bright, but fatigue hung to his sunburned face. He was heavier than the last time Cordell had seen him, but it was the same energetic boy who had ridden with them as an underage Confederate cavalryman. His homespun shirt was dark at his left shoulder; dried blood speckled his neck.

"Oh Lordy be, it is you. Thank God, it's Captun Cordell, Pa. He's here!"

And the door swung open wide and the yellow cat scooted ahead of Cordell and Shank into the house.

"Better git in quick, Captun, a'fer them Regulators see ya. Thar be four 'round the house—all the time." Billy glanced down at the streaking animal and chuckled. "So that's whar yo-all's bin, huh, Belle? Yo-all bin with the Captun."

Cordell stepped inside and waved for Shank to join him. The big man entered, ducking his head to clear the door frame. When Billy Ripton saw the big man, he realized what he had said. "Oh my, I . . . ah, how are you, Reverend . . . Langford. I'm sorry I . . ."

"That's all right, Billy Rip. This is Caleb Shank, a good friend—an he's been trying not to call me that all night." Cordell turned toward Shank and grinned.

Shank chuckled, and his eyebrows danced. "Wal, I didn't want to be a-stompin' on your back trail." He paused and held out his hand to Billy. "I were at Longstreet's when you came a-ridin' to warn him—while the Captain hyar did his playactin' with them Yanks. You boys did a heap fine job that day."

Billy's proud glow was evident even in the dark.

Shank cocked his head to the side. "By the way, t'ain't nobody out thar now, 'ceptin' an owl or two."

Cordell snapped, "But there are plenty waiting in that creek bed. We only took out the four guards close to the house."

"Well, come on in. I reckon Ian's out thar somewhars too."

Chapter Twenty-three

Cordell avoided the question until he was inside, then only muttered that Taullery couldn't come on such short notice. In the grayness, he could see a potbellied stove, a washstand, and a rocking chair now occupied by the sitting cat. Strangely, the aroma of fresh baked bread hung in the air, mixing with the sharp odor of gunpowder.

In the adjoining room, he noticed that a large knife lay on the red coals in the kitchen stone fireplace. Only the blade was being heated; the wooden handle rested on stone and was wrapped in a rag. He surmised that the knife on the fire was Billy's idea. It was a trick they used during the War. If not too severe, a wound could be cauterized with a hot blade and the soldier returned to action.

Billy apologized for the darkness as his father, Eldon Ripton, stepped forward from the shadows. He was an inch shorter than his son, his frame thinner, his hair nearly gray, and his shoulders bent slightly, but the resemblance was obvious. Unlike his son, however, the older man's manner was stern, self-righteous, and humorless. In his reddened hands was a Confederate Enfield rifle with the "CSA" plate embedded in the stock.

"Ri't glad to see you, Captun." Eldon Ripton held out his hand. "Whar's our Lizzie—she got to yo-all, I reckon."

After the greeting, Cordell explained about Lizzie Ripton being wounded but being cared for by his wife. Eldon's only response was a frown. Cordell didn't mention Aleta being at the school for black children but told about stopping the Regulators chasing her and Shank covering their tracks. He omitted any reference to Ian Taullery and outlined quickly what they intended to do next. While he talked, Shank went back outside and brought in the water bags, food pouch, and weapons.

"Ya got any lead to go with them fine-lookin' guns?" Eldon Ripton asked.

"Sure 'nuff," Shank replied, and dragged in the pouch of bullets.

"That might do us, I reckon."

"Them's Winchesters, Pa."

"I know'd what they are, son. Bin a-seein' 'em pointin' at us." Eldon's square jaw pushed outward as if to challenge his enemies to try again.

From another room, Tallie Mae Ripton, Billy's mother, quietly appeared. She held a pistol at her side. Her simple cotton dress was stained with blood; Cordell thought it was Billy's, not hers. Her wide, flat face had lost its youthful beauty years ago, but her bright eyes were defiant. Billy had her eyes and so did the youngest Ripton child, eight-year-old Jeremiah Ripton, coming a few steps behind her. A long-barreled Navy Colt dragoon was carried proudly in both hands.

Mrs. Ripton studied Cordell without speaking. Disappointment was evident when she finally addressed him. "Pastor, I'm real sorry to see you back in this. Thought you'd given up the gun for . . . better things."

Removing his hat, Cordell swallowed before answering. "Mrs. Ripton, your enemies are my enemies. I think the good Lord wants me here—with my gun. If he doesn't, I guess he'll let me know."

Rolling her shoulders, she started to say something else, but Eldon Ripton barked, "Tallie Mae, what kinda talk is that? Captun Cordell came to he'p us. There'll be time enough for prayin' an' sech when this be over an' dun with. Goodness, woman."

Embarrassed by her husband's remarks, Tallie Mae Ripton wiped at her dress as if it would remove the bloodstains. She spoke with her eyes down, raising them slowly to meet Cordell's. She had been drawn to him ever since he stayed with them after his father shot him. "We're nigh outta cartridges—an' food. Ain't had no water for two days. I did bake us some bread. Last o' our flour. Jes' finished. Be proud to share it with ya." Her assessment of the situation was expressed without emotion; the last sentence was her version of an apology.

"Captun—and the Russian hyar—they dun brung us some . . . o' all three, Ma." Billly said, forcing enthusiasm through his weariness.

"That's mighty kind of yo-all." She brought the gun to her bosom and held it there with both hands, then realized it emphasized her breasts and returned the gun to her side.

Steppping in front of his mother, Jeremiah Ripton said matter-of-factly, "I bin doin' the loadin'—but I kin shoot."

"I'm sure you can, son," Cordell replied, meeting the boy's intense gaze. "If we're lucky, maybe we can get these Regulators to go away—and stay away."

"Yo-all gonna shoot 'em all?" the boy asked, his eyes reinforcing the question.

Cordell glanced at Billy, then at both Ripton parents, before returning his attention to the youngest son. "No, we're not, Jeremiah. Even if we were lucky enough, and that's hard to imagine, the state police would come after you even harder."

"I—I don' understand. What did ya come fer, then?" Jeremiah was close to crying but bit his lower lip to keep the tears away.

Kneeling, Cordell explained the strategy of making the Regulators think they were surrounded by superior numbers, and letting Padgett decide on his own not to continue with his attack, and why it made sense. He talked to the boy as if he were an adult and the only one in the room. Jeremiah listened without saying a word. When Cordell finished, the boy asked only one question:

"Can I be one o' the 'Sons of Thunder'? Please?"

Shank roared and the others smiled, except for Cordell. He put his hand on the boy's shoulder. "You already are. Better yet, you're a Ripton."

Jeremiah beamed and asked, "So I can go with you?"

"I've got a special job for you, Jeremiah, if your folks agree. You're going to man one of these windows, so they won't think yo-all have left the house unguarded."

"But I . . ."

"This new Winchester is for you to use," Cordell went to the doorway where the weapons and supplies lay. He picked up one of the rifles and returned. "You and your mother will each take a window and fire as fast as you can—straight up into the air, when we give the signal."

Jeremiah received the gun like it was precious jewelry, then turned to his mother for her approval. Her wan smile was the best she could do. She mentioned that she hoped her one windowpane would survive the ordeal.

Eldon Ripton responded first, turning toward Cordell. "I don't git it. Why we don't jes' cut 'em all down? They shot our Lizzie—an' they're a-tryin' to kill us an' take our home." He raised his right hand toward his own face, balling it into a tight fist. "We dun built this hyar ranch, Captun, outta nothin' but red clay and rock. I already dun paid 'em eight hundred dollars in taxes they said I owed. Had to borry it from that damn Yankee bank in town."

"Pa figgers on makin' a drive with some o' our cattle. Git us some cash money," Billy added. "Thar's word o' others doin' it an' makin' good money if they git through."

Cordell's face flushed with frustration, but it disappeared as he realized the strain Eldon Ripton was under. "I understand how you feel, Eldon, but if we kill a company of state police, you and your family will be blamed, you'll be wanted—and you'll lose your place anyway. You'll have to run—and keep runnin'. Is that what you want?"

"That's purty hard talk. Yo-all were a-ridin' the owl-hoot trail once, I do believe."

"Yes, I did. But I didn't have a family—or a fine place like this."

"Sounds like you've bin a-chewin' on this awhile." The elder Ripton rubbed his chin. "Thought you an' your lady dun kilt some Regulators yourself today."

Shank waved his arms and added, "He didn't tell ya about the three he had to fight this afternoon, when they came a-lookin' fer yur girl."

"That how you got that bloody sleeve, Captun?" Billy asked.

Cordell nodded and frowned at the big merchant.

"That puts 'em down to sixteen, plus that bastard

captain—an' that gunfighter o' his'n. Billy dun whupped a couple earlier, too," Eldon assessed.

"Saw one of them at their campfire—with a bandaged head." Cordell shoved his hands into his gunbelts.

"Pa, remember Captun Cordell's the one that dun outsmarted all them Yanks," Billy said, his eyes pleading for his father to understand. "We dun it by settin' up all kinds of dummies, makin' 'em think they was facin' a load of Rebs."

"This ain't Virginia, boy." Eldon Ripton shot a look at his older son that immediately stopped him from saying more, then turned to Cordell again and demanded, "Yo-all think Padgett's jes' gonna up an' ride off—if we do this hyar fake soldjur stuff?"

"I think it's your only chance. But you'd better decide quick. We've got to do it before they switch guards." Cordell crossed his arms and stared at him. "The Sons of Thunder will get the blame for the dead Regulators so far, not your family."

Eldon Ripton looked down at his worn boots, then over at his wife. In the gray light, Cordell thought the man looked twenty years older than he was. She nodded slightly.

"Let's do it, I reckon," Eldon muttered. "An' God he'p us."

"Reverend, will you please . . . " Tallie Mae started and hesitated, ". . . lead us in a prayer—before yo-all go?"

Annoyed by the idea, Cordell started to respond that they didn't have the time, but something in him stopped any words that were coming. He held his hat in front of him with this arms extended and bowed his head. The others followed his action.

"Lord, we know you are always near and that you are never sought in vain. Guide our minds now as well as our hands—and grant that we will have peace again on this beautiful land. Amen."

"Amen" was echoed by everyone in the room; Shank was the loudest. Billy hugged his mother, and Cordell brought her the second Winchester. Eldon grabbed her hand and turned to leave, but she held it an instant longer and their eyes met in an embrace. Shank rushed out, rubbing his eyes.

At the doorway, Cordell was the last one to leave. He turned back to young Jeremiah and said, "Remember, when you fire, I want you to shoot into the air. Don't look out the window. You stay under it and poke the gun up an' out the window. If you shoot straight out, you might hit one of us. Got that?"

"Yessir."

"Good boy."

"You're not a'scar't o' that Lion Graham fella, are ya, Captain?"

Cordell's attempt at a smile was more of a grimace. "Only a fool wouldn't be, Jeremiah. He's killed too many men who knew how to fight."

"B-but you're better than he is with a gun, ain't ya?" Jeremiah's eyes pleaded for a positive response.

"I don't know about that."

Jeremiah's face contracted with disappointment, then his eyebrows flickered and he pronounced fiercely, "I think you are. I think you're the best there is."

Cordell hitched his gunbelt to adjust the two handguns there, in addition to his holstered Colts and the Deane & Adams pistol in his back waistband. It was an unconscious reaction to the boy's praise. He pulled back from the door and walked toward the rocking chair. "If it's all right with you, I'm going to take along . . . Belle, isn't it? She's been a big help so far. That all right with you?"

Jeremiah's face was a puzzle. "S-she gonna be in any danger?"

"No more than she has been, Jeremiah."

"Wal, she's Lizzie's cat. It don't matter much to me."

Picking up the cat, he headed back to the door. Belle nuzzled his arm, and Cordell scratched its ears. Tallie Mae met him there and laid a gentle hand on his shoulder as he paused there. "Rule, please forgive me for what I said earlier. I . . . had no right."

"Tallie Mae, there is nothing to forgive. Good old Caleb reminded me that it was Jesus who drove the coin-changers out of the temple with a whip. I reckon a simple preacher can fight for his friends."

"Bless you, Rule Cordell." She sought his eyes. "You should let me look at your arm first."

"Thank you, ma'am, but it's all right."

Hurrying through the night, the four men worked their way back to the merchant's wagon, carrying with them the guards' rifles. The other three were surprised to see Cordell with a cat, but he didn't seem inclined to explain. From the tailgate, Shank distributed hats, burlap sacks, broomsticks, gathered branches, and the few remaining pistols. Cordell gave his two guard revolvers to Billy. They decided to set up in three positions: Billy Ripton would take the west side, far enough back from the dry creek bed so that it wouldn't be easy to see; Eldon would be on the north where the creek bed slanted to the east, with the sleeping Regulators in front and below him; Shank would man the Gatling gun; Cordell would direct Padgett. It was decided to leave Shank's dress form behind because it was too awkward to carry.

Cordell instructed the Riptons to lay the rifles and revolvers in a straight line, each gun a few feet from the next, and spread out the dummies as best they could. He recommended they hold a pistol in each hand as they moved. It was easier to shoot them quickly. The idea was to fire as rapidly as possible, from as many different places as possible, once the "attack" began. Cordell insisted on firing only for effect, unless there was no choice. The two Riptons left with the understanding of the need to be quiet yet move quickly.

Returning to his earlier watching place at the creek bank, only this time with the cat in his arms, Cordell again studied the wagon guard, catching only glimpses of the other sentry standing at the far end of the string of quiet horses. It would take Shank a little longer to get over there, he guessed. The trick would be to take out both men without alerting the other—or worse, the entire camp.

The lateness of the night was having a definite effect on the wagon guard. He was leaning against the wagon, relaxed with his arms folded. His rifle also lay against the wagon at his side. Cordell couldn't see the man's eyes from under his pulled-down hat brim, but thought he was awake. Curling along the creek until he was behind the man, Cordell slipped next to the wagon on the east side. He stood, holding his breath.

The guard hadn't moved. Three quick steps and Cordell tossed the cat in front of the man's feet. Belle landed alertly and hissed her indignation at the activity. The guard jumped and reached for his rifle as Cordell's pistol thudded against the man's skull. The only sound was a rush of air from the guard's mouth as he sank to the ground—and Belle's sweet meow. A toss of the man's handgun into the shadows was followed by Cordell's boot kicking the rifle so it slid to the ground. Fascinated by the movement, the cat bounced toward it for closer observation.

"Good work, Belle."

Out of the corner of his eye, he saw a Regulator standing in midcamp. Cordell hadn't seen him before. How long had the man been standing there? Cordell squeezed the handle of his pistol in his fist, readying himself for the man's response. Instead, the Regulator yawned and proceeded to urinate on the ground a few feet from his blankets. Finished, he turned back to his bedroll without so much as a glance around.

Behind Cordell was a padded advance, and he whirled to meet it. Caleb Shank waved him off with a big grin.

"Nothin' like a man peein' to git ya a little nervous, is thar?" Shank whispered, and slapped Cordell on the back.

There wasn't time to worry about anyone noticing the missing guard or taking the time to tie him up. By Cordell's estimate, men could be stirring in camp within minutes, readying themselves for the next guard shift.

"What about the horse guard?"

"I reckon it's real hot whar he be."

Cordell grimaced, but there was nothing he could do about the situation now. After removing the pegs holding the tailgate hinges in place, they went to the front of Padgett's wagon with the cat trailing after them. Shank gave Cordell a push up into the driver's seat. Without a sound, the big man disappeared and returned minutes later holding a sack filled with more cut-off broom handles and burlap strips. Cordell gave a lift with his hand under Shank's shoulder, surprised at the huge merchant's agility.

Both stood quietly, looking down into the enclosed wagon at the sleeping Padgett and the Gatling gun on its platform a few feet away. Out of the night came the yellow cat, sliding next to Cordell. He shook his head in reaction to her unexpected reappearance.

"Looks like the Sons of Thunder dun growed another," Shank said with an impish twist to his mouth.

"Maybe so."

Cordell stroked the cat's back, and it curled upward to enjoy all of the encounter as the gunfighter returned his attention to the wagon's interior. Padgett's wheelchair was bolted into its special place in the corner of the wagon, poised like an iron panther. Lying on the floorboard next to it were his carefully folded uniform coat, pants, and hat. One of his twin beaded holsters, hanging from the chair arms, was empty, the gold-plated gun resting on Padgett's stomach, his open hand across the pearl handle. Beside the wooden-framed cot was a small dressing table with a scattering of papers and an inkwell, anchored in place. The walls of the wagon were planked and lined with rifle firing holes; the fold-down ramp for the wheelchair was curled against the tailgate.

"Ya know, thar's a Reb over Fort Worth way, lost his arm an' his leg a-fightin' for the Cause," Shank whispered, staring at Padgett, appearing peaceful in his long underwear. "Ever' time I see him, I git a catch in my throat. Should oughta feel the same 'bout Padgett, but I don't. Jes' want to strangle the bastard."

"If this goes right, it'll be even better."

Chapter Twenty-four

"Would ya mind if'n I took a close-up at that bastard a'fore we git at it?" Shank's idea of a whisper rattled around the wagon enclosure as they swung quietly over the buckboard into the wagon bed.

Cordell's shoulders raised in response. He didn't answer, only waving at the merchant to do what he wanted. He winced at the pain that shot from his arm from the sudden movement. Shank stepped toward Padgett's bed. Belle watched and then came bounding down with them.

"You're not going to kill him, are you?" Cordell asked, half watching the cat explore the wagon's interior, half focused on his friend's request.

"No sir, I dun promised ya. 'Sides, I know what we're about," Shank responded, patting his back where the throwing knife waited. "Not that I ain't had it cross my mind a time or two."

Cordell looked up at the dark sky, trying to judge the

time. Weariness throbbed at him, and he rolled his neck for comfort. An owl saluted as it flew across his path in search of dinner and he watched it sail past the softening moon. Belle stopped her exploring to watch the bird's flight, then returned to her review. Cordell's scan of the area revealed a line of in-place shapes of differing sizes across the two ridges where the Riptons were working. His silent approval followed: The shapes looked real. He was surprised himself at how much they looked like crouching men. Billy Ripton waved. He and his father were ready.

"Did ya see this hyar?"

The question jolted Cordell back to the wagon. Shank was shuffling through the papers on Padgett's table. "Look hyar, Rule. It's that sonvabitch Giles. You were right. God damn him to hell. Er, sorry, Reverend."

Cordell stepped over, urging his friend to keep his voice down. Cordell's eyes continued to search the area around them for signs of movement, but saw none.

Shank waved a paper in front of Cordell. "This hyar's a deed—to the Harper place. Giles's name's on it, big as ya please. Padgett must gonna file it fer him. He's one o' the witnesses. Don't know the other'n."

"Let's see." Cordell scanned the gray document, then folded it and placed it down in his pants pocket. "We'll deal with this later. I have the feeling the mayor is going to be generous and give the place to Missus Harper and her kids."

Shank grinned as he continued to flip through the stack of wanted posters and government reports. "Well, look at this. Hyar's one fer the Riptons' place. Giles dun signed it—all it needs is Ripton's mark. Reckon Giles is after the Ripton place too."

"I'll take that one too."

Shank doubled over the document and handed it to Cordell, who added it to his pocket.

"Come here, Millicent. I need you." A breathy command from the sleep-talking Padgett made both men jump.

Shank held back a giggle with his hand to his mouth. Regaining his composure, Shank headed for the wheelchair and emptied the bullets from the holstered revolver. Standing over the sleeping leader, Cordell lifted the man's limp hand, withdrew the gun on Padgett's stomach, and emptied the bullets into his own pocket, joining the folded deeds. He tossed the gun to Shank and the big merchant shoved it into the other holster. The cat stood on its hind legs with front paws resting on the top edge of Padgett's cot, then jumped and landed on the police chief's stomach. He made a strange noise but didn't wake up.

"All right, give me a hand. We'll get the king into his throne—and get this thing started." Cordell motioned toward the sleeping leader. "First, pull up your mask. It won't do you much good around your chin."

Shank chortled and pulled up the handkerchief, forcing it over his nose. He lifted the cat, handing it to Cordell, and yanked the crippled leader from his cot and sat him in the wheelchair. Padgett shook his head and struggled to gain control of his mind.

"W-what the hell! What's go . . ."

"Shut up, Padgett—or you're going to die right here." Cordell growled and shoved a pistol into the man's cheek. He held Belle in his other arm. "We're the Sons of Thunder—and we've come to bring you a warning. Listen real good, Padgett, it'll only come once. You leave the Riptons—and the other good folks around here—alone or you personally will have to deal with us."

"What? Who the . . . My men'll k—"

"Careful, Padgett, I don't think you were listening good enough. Let's try again."

Padgett's bloated face was twisted with red fury, but his eyes were filling with fear. His right hand edged slowly toward the holstered pistol on his chair arm.

"Please do," Cordell growled. "It'll save us the trouble of watching you for the next year."

Padgett's hand grasped the chair arm and went no further. Cordell motioned for Shank to get the Gatling gun ready—partly to hurry their presence to the sleeping Regulators, but mostly to keep the big man's distinctive shape in the shadows.

"Here's what's going to happen," Cordell said as he pushed Padgett's chair toward the tailgate after releasing the cat to the wagon floor. Belle jumped from Cordell's arm to the wagon floor. Padgett gripped the other chair arm, swallowed, and stared straight ahead. "We're going to wake up your men—and then it's up to you what happens next."

Cordell pushed the tailgate and it swung, crashing to the ground, followed by a blur of yellow and the wheelchair lumbering down the ramp with Cordell controlling its speed. He watched Belle disappear into the darkness and knew he shouldn't be paying attention to a cat at this moment.

With a wild Rebel yell, a distinctive high-pitched war cry that made the whole night shiver, Shank opened up with the Gatling gun, rotating the six-barrel cylinder with the hand crank and aiming it at the same time. Six hundred bullets a minute ripped into the darkness. His first target was the stack of rifles. A torrent of lead savaged the weapons, sending a shower of wood and golden sparks in all directions.

The ridge came alive with a continuous bracelet of orange flame. Cordell could see the Riptons firing and running from one position to the next, but knew no one else would notice. Deep within his soul came his own Rebel yell, and it was matched by a similar scream from

Billy, both so loud and piercing that the sounds themselves seemed to have lives of their own. Louder and higher they hollered, with a fierce triumphant swell. From the house came spurts of gunfire. Behind him the roar of the Gatling gun was a windmill of whining bullets.

As planned, Shank fired the weapon only to the east, where no one was. Along the dry creek bed, Regulators jumped from their beds or dove for anything resembling cover. A silhouette produced a handgun and fired once. Returned rifle fire silenced him. Another ran for the scrambled rifles, but Cordell's pistol fire in front of him discouraged the idea and the man stopped and held up his hands.

Into Padgett's ear, Cordell announced, "When the firing stops, you can tell your men they can ride out of here—without us shooting at them. And without their guns. Or they can fight and—you guess." Cordell moved Padgett's chair directly in front of the wagon, a few feet from the unconscious guard. In the midst of the shooting, Cordell suddenly wondered where Lizzie's cat had gone. His study of the darkness didn't reveal any clues to the little animal. Hopeful the cat hadn't gotten in the way of a stray bullet, Cordell waved for Shank to stop and he finally did. Heartbeats later, the rest of the shooting stopped. Two more shots came from the house, and then silence.

Most of the Regulators were standing with their hands up. One man, in yellowish, torn long johns, was attempting to climb out of the embankment next to his bedroll. Another sat on his blankets with his legs crossed, looking like he was waiting for instructions. A third was inching his courage and his hand toward a gunbelt next to his bedding. Cordell thought it was Billy's rifle that spat into the ground a foot from the weapon, and the man jumped up and stood at attention.

"Do it now, Padgett. Tell them not to shoot—and to leave their guns behind."

Clearing his throat, Padgett yelled, "Don't shoot. Don't. Go to your horses, men. We're leaving. Now." His mouth curled downward to meet his jutting jaw; his beady eyes flickered a mixture of hate and fear.

"Tell them—no guns."

"Ah, leave your guns. Do it. And don't nobody do anything stupid, ya hear me?"

A scramble for the horse string erupted as Padgett's words echoed in the night. Cursing and yelling, men in various stages of dress ran for saddles or simply mounted bareback. A lone gunshot came from the house, and Cordell figured Jeremiah had gotten excited or just wanted to shoot again. Galloping horses accented the darkness. A frightened bay with a loose saddle bouncing under its belly ran and jumped down into the dry creek bed. After streaking through discarded blankets, clothing, and pistol belts, the lathered animal returned, stopping a few feet from Cordell and Padgett. Lowering its head, the horse seemed to be asking for assistance. Cordell shoved his left-hand pistol into its holster and walked toward the exhausted horse. His other gun was pointed at Padgett.

"Easy, boy, you're all right." Cordell patted the horse on its wet neck, swung the saddle upright, and yanked tight the cinch. "Tell your men to leave horses behind for the dead and wounded. Your guards will need them when they wake up too."

"T-the guards aren't dead?" Padgett's voice cracked.

"Two are. The rest are just coldcocked. We'll put all of them on horses and send them your way before we ride on." Cordell slapped the horse on its rear and sent it trotting back up the incline to the disappearing horse string.

Padgett hesitated and yelled out the order for all the

horses not ridden to be left behind. His fists opened and closed. Cordell walked back, redrawing his second pistol and watching as he moved. "Where's Lion Graham?"

Pagett's eyes blinked. "I don't know. The coward probably was the first one outta here. He only likes shooting when he's the only one with a gun."

"Somebody better come and hitch up your wagon—or you're going to have a slow roll home," Cordell suggested, kneeling behind the chair with a pistol in each hand.

"Alex! Nelson! Bring the trace mules, goddammit!"

"Good boy."

Cordell caught the glimpse of metal among the trees and fired twice with both guns in its direction. A yelp and orange flame snapping at tree leaves followed.

"The next one hurts you, Padgett."

Rolling his shoulders, Padgett screamed, "Goddammit, I said no guns. Get on your goddamn horses and ride out." Under his breath, Padgett muttered, "Enjoy this, you son of a bitch. The state of Texas won't rest until you're hanging from a cottonwood."

"No, the state of Texas won't rest until law enforcement is in the hands of good men," Cordell snapped, his gaze centered on the horses and the crazed exit of the Regulators. "Oh, and don't forget to tell Giles he's next on our list."

Padgett stiffened. "What? Who? Giles?"

"Tell the mayor we expect him to sign that deed back to Mrs Harper."

"What deed?"

"The one on your table—and now in my pocket."

"Hell, he won't do that."

"You tell him. We'll see that he does," Cordell said. "Oh, and tell him the new Ripton deed has been burned. Tell him not to try that again."

Behind them, Cordell could hear Shank shuffling

around, talking to himself. A thump on the wagon floor was distracting, but the big merchant quickly assured Cordell that he was fine. Two Regulators appeared, wearing only boots and hats over their long underwear and leading the eight matching mules. Neither said a word as they began hitching the animals in place, but they were obviously anxious to get away. While they worked, Cordell told the Regulator leader that the "Sons of Thunder" would leave him—and his men—alone as long as they stayed away from the people in the region.

"Do you understand, Padgett? Say it, real loud."

"I understand."

"What do you understand, Padgett?"

"I understand if I leave the Riptons alone . . ." Padgett's face was plastered with fright. His hands trembled, and he gripped the wheelchair arms to steady them.

"And?"

"Ah, and other people around here, ah, I will . . ."

"Live."

". . . live."

Padgett's voice cracked with the last word, and his body rose and fell like a giant hand had lifted and dropped him. He heard creaking sounds, and a quick glance told him Shank was finished and coming down the plank. Cordell motioned for him to go toward the house. Satisfied his friend was beyond recognition, Cordell ordered the two Regulators to come around and push their leader back into his wagon.

Standing behind the wheelchair, Cordell yelled out fake orders into the night. "Rattlesnake and Panther Patrols, check the camp. Bear Patrol, the horses. Black and Rose Patrols, hold the perimeter."

Chapter Twenty-five

Rose Patrol? He laughed to himself at the name, but it was the first thing that came to mind. The Riptons wouldn't know for certain what he wanted, but that was all right. The yelling was for Padgett's benefit. He planned on checking the area himself after Padgett was gone. His little performance completed, Cordell withdrew the note from his coat pocket and placed it in Padgett's right hand. The Regulator leader stared at the paper as if trying to read it without opening the folds.

"Just a reminder of what we told you. Wouldn't want you to forget, now would we?" Cordell growled.

As soon as Padgett was in place and the tailgate raised, the wagon lumbered off. Shank came out of hiding and stood beside Cordell.

"Watch this," Shank said with a slap on Cordell's back. "Ever' one o' them six big barrels is jammed with broomsticks an' flour sack strips. Nice 'n' tight. It ain't gonna be purty."

As they watched, the wagon came to a sudden stop only twenty yards away. Moonlight caught the Gatling gun swinging into position toward them. Cordell looked at Shank, but the big man was standing confidently, his chest swelling with pride at what was about to happen. They could hear Padgett urgently barking orders. There was an odd thumping noise, followed by a biting explosion, then another, then another. A man screamed, and Padgett cursed. Red and gold sparks billowed from the wagon, outlining the black Gatling gun, followed by hungry lips of flame.

"Think we'd better see if Padgett gets outta thar?" Shank asked. The tone of his voice indicated he wasn't in a hurry to do so. "Sur wouldn't want them fine mules to git hurt none."

A "meow" distracted Cordell from the wagon, and he spun toward the soft sound. Beneath one of the Regulator blankets across the creek bed was a tiny yellow head.

"Belle—there you are!" Cordell holstered his guns as he hurried toward the cat. "Be right with you. Got to make sure she's all right."

Shank turned to watch Cordell and shook his head. Chuckling, he headed toward the wagon. Popping open the hinge locks, he pulled the tailgate down with his left hand, his rifle held in his right. Staring inside, he saw flames giggling around the edges of the silent Gatling gun; a broomstick extended two inches from one barrel, with a burlap tongue crackling with flame. Sprawled against the back wall was the blackened shape of the gunner.

Padgett sat in his wheelchair, still in his underwear. Reflection glittered off the gold-plated pistols in his lap. The man's hands lay on the wheelchair arms and made no attempt to reach the weapons. In his right fist was Cordell's note, still unread. The other Regulator was nowhere in sight. Shank rubbed his chin, forgetting the handkerchief that crossed his mouth and yanking it down. Behind him came Cordell, carrying Belle.

"I don't think Padgett's going to burn, do you?" Cordell asked.

"Not hyar, anyhow. What do ya wanna do?"

"You gather up the men. I'll see that the fire's out—and Padgett's on his way again." Cordell motioned for Shank to stay in the shadows and pull up his mask. The big man frowned, then realized what Cordell was indicating. Shank chuckled and pulled the handkerchief back into place.

"Here, take Belle with you. Have . . . the Rose Patrol . . . go and tell the Riptons everything is all right, that Padgett has decided to leave. For good. Those good folks will be wondering what's been happening. Be sure they know you're friendly before you get too close." Cordell winked. "When I'm through here, I'll join the patrols checking out the area."

"You betcha. You'd better check out Mistah Padgett's fancy pistols first, Ru . . . er, ah, they might be refilled, ya know." Shank frowned at his close call at calling Cordell by name, took the cat, and rambled away, talking to himself.

With three strides, Cordell bound up the ramp and went directly to Padgett. Shank's suggestion was a smart step—and one he might have overlooked. He took the two golden guns and tossed them up and onto the driver's seat. Swiftly, Cordell beat out the scattered flames with his long coat. A glance at the motionless gunner told him all he needed to know about the man.

Cordell's arm was aching and bleeding again by the time he returned to Padgett, and his head was throbbing again. The Regulator leader's eyes were glazed, and he appeared in shock. Cordell realized that not much, if any, of their contrived dialogue may have registered in his dazed mind. Regardless, the layering of a story of an organized force after him should have the necessary effect.

"One of your men is dead. The other ran. There's no one to drive your wagon," Cordell said, standing in front of Padgett.

The crippled man nodded without looking up.

"I'm going to drive you—out to some of your men."

"W-why?"

"Not sure. Maybe it's to let you know we're men of our word. You stay away from the people around here, we'll stay away from you."

"S-Sons of Thunder?"

"Yes."

"A-are you one of those S-Southern clans everyone's talking about?" Padgett raised his head slowly.

Cordell pondered the question. "No, we're not. Just a bunch of . . . men who believe in the law behaving like the law should."

"You were the ones that hit my men earlier, weren't you?"

"We were waiting for them." Cordell walked to the tailgate ramp.

"How'd you know . . . they were coming?"

At the bottom of the ramp, Cordell lifted the end board and answered as he closed it. "We've been watching you for weeks, Padgett. We're good at it. We'll be watching you to see if you're smart enough to move on."

With a snap of the reins, Cordell took control of the wagon and it pulled away. Minutes later, he stopped at the trees where Shank's wagon and his horse waited, positioning the vehicle so Padgett couldn't see the big merchant's wagon. Cordell tied his horse's reins together, looped them through his arm so the stallion would have to trot alongside the wagon, and started again. Padgett sat in his chair, bracing himself for the jostling of the wagon. They rode for at least a mile, maybe more. He could hear men yelling for the wagon to stop and knew they were only yards away.

"Shoot the bastard driving the wagon!" he yelled. "He's one . . . of the Sons of Thunder. Shoot him!"

He heard no shots, only the sounds of someone bringing the horses to a stop. "Whoa. Whoa, boys. Whoa."

After the wagon jerked to a stop, he heard the squeak of someone getting down from the driver's seat, then the clink of the hinge locks being removed. Down came the tailgate, and three Regulators greeted him. Two were in long johns, the other fully dressed.

"You all right, boss?"

"I told you to shoot that sonvabitch. Bring him here," Padgett snapped.

"There's nobody up there, boss," the stocky Regulator answered. "Them reins was held down with a big rock. We wasn't sure you were even in hyar."

The tallest Regulator held out two gold-plated revolvers. "Got your guns, though. They was next to the rock."

Padgett glared, and the third man mumbled, "At least they didn't kill us all. Must've been forty of 'em. Where'd they come from?"

Furious, Padgett started to say something, then remembered the note in his fist and looked at it. He fumbled to open the paper and studied the few words scribbled there.

"What ya got, Captain?"

"Never mind," Padgett said, staring at the note. "Get the men together, we're heading for headquarters. We've got better things to do than worry about these Riptons." The three Regulators glanced at one another in collective relief.

After walking through the abandoned Regulator camp, Caleb Shank, Billy Ripton, and his father were nearly back to the dark house. Eldon was talking about the new Winchesters and how well they worked. A few steps away, Shank released Belle because it wanted down. He watched the cat scoot away, then returned to sharing the joy at the outcome of the night. Billy laughed as he described his difficulty with shooting a pistol with his left hand at the same time as he fired one with this right. He marveled at Cordell's "masquerade" idea and compared it favorably to the Virginia war episode, indicating that the only major difference was fake cannon. Shank made no attempt to point out that the Confederate masquerade had kept an entire Union sneak attack at bay for hours.

Using his words with care, Eldon admitted that Cordell was mostly right about what would happen. He expressed greater satisfaction at getting to shoot at the Regulators when they went for their guns. Both Riptons were surprised at the Gatling gun exploding and puzzled by Cordell's orders about the patrols. They weren't certain what they were supposed to do and wondered if it was secret code they had missed. It was Shank's turn to laugh.

Reaching the house, they expressed surprise that neither Jeremiah nor Tallie Mae had come outside to greet them. Billy surmised that they didn't feel they should leave their posts. Grumbling about the foolishness, Eldon knocked on the door and it swung open. Jeremiah was standing there with a sickly look on his face. He stammered for them to enter. Eldon Ripton led the way and the door slammed shut behind them.

"Drop your guns, you simpletons. The little party's over." Lion David Graham stood where the open door had been, holding Tallie Mae next to him with his left hand over her mouth, and pointing a six-gun at the surprised men, then toward her temple. "If you move wrong, she's dead."

In the shadowy light, the killer appeared ghostlike, with his gray suit, short cape, and derby—and his pale skin—blending with the room's dullness. Only bespectacled eyes, a black goatee, narrow eyebrows, and two black-handled revolvers stood out. Around his waist, a gray silk sash held the second gun.

Billy reacted quicker than his father or the big merchant. Swinging his rifle toward Graham, he barked, "Thar's three o' us—and only one o' you, mister. What are you gonna do now?"

Graham fired his pistol and Billy spun sideways, staggered against the wall, and fell. Tallie Mae struggled, but Graham yanked her tighter and jammed his gun into her ribs.

A wicked grin crossed Graham's face. "Next time you'd better have your gun cocked before you threaten someone, idiot." For emphasis, he cocked the pistol, savoring the metallic *click-click.* "Now there's only two of you. Want to try again?"

Wide-eyed, Jeremiah blurted, "I—I'm s-sorry. H-he was gonna shoot M-Ma if'n I didn' let you in. I'm s-sorry." His face twisted and the tears came.

"That's all right, Jeremiah," Shank assured, and let his rifle fall to the floor. Turning his back to Graham, he knelt beside Billy. The big man yanked off his handkerchief and pushed it against the young man's bleeding right shoulder. Billy grimaced as the pain reached his brain. Eldon dropped his rifle, then two pistols, from his waistband, and held his arms up so high his fingers brushed against the low ceiling.

"My goodness, you're a real gunslinger, aren't you, Ripton? Any good with those six-guns? Or are you as pathetic as that stupid, one-armed friend of yours? What was his name . . . oh yeah, Jenson. Had a funny voice. Died funny, too. Laugh, Ripton."

Eldon shook his head negatively and choked out sounds imitating a laugh.

"Of course, you aren't any good at laughing either." Graham growled into Tallie Mae's ear, "Is this cowardly fool your husband? What a shame." His attention moved to Shank. "Don't worry, big boy. I didn't kill him. Just matched up his shoulders. I always hit what I aim at. I don't want him dead—yet. He may be the one with the answers I want. One of you has them. After that, who knows? I may just let you all alone—or I may not." Graham chuckled at his comment and paused, his eyes narrowed. "Wait a minute—I don't think you believe me when I say I hit what I aim at."

A second blast from Graham's revolver ripped through the tension of the room, and Shank's left ear blossomed in crimson. The big man screamed and grabbed for it.

"See?" Graham said, and recocked his revolver. "You won't miss that little bit. Not much, anyway. Now do you believe me—or would you care for another demonstration? How about this little fool's right eye? Or maybe . . ."

"You made your point. Leave the boy alone. What do you want to know?" Shank responded, holding his bleeding ear and grimacing. His pained eyes tracked the handles of Billy's revolvers extending from the young man's waistband.

Graham saw them too. "First, big boy, take those pistols and toss them this way. One at a time. Real slow."

Shank withdrew one revolver and threw it toward Graham. He took a deep breath and reached for the second.

"Remember the little lady here before you try something stupid. She dies, then I'll kill you before you can even get that hogleg aimed at me. I thought you believed me. How disappointing."

Graham fired again, and Billy's left hand, lying outstretched on the floor, jumped and a red hole appeared. Billy groaned and grabbed for his hand. "Y-you son of a bitch! I'll . . ."

Shank's shoulders rose and fell. He eased the gun from Billy's waistband, holding the handle by just two fingers.

Returning his first pistol to his waist and withdrawing his second, Graham snarled, "Now, all I want is your friend in the black coat. That's all. One of you is going to tell me where he is—and what his name is." The words slashed like a jabbed knife. "Who wants to live?"

Chapter Twenty-six

"Thar's thirty o' our men outside a-comin' up the hill. You'd better git yurself gone," Caleb Shank advised, continuing to hold the handkerchief against the blossoming hole in Billy's shoulder while he held the young man's hand tightly to stop the bleeding. His own ear dripped red tears, but he ignored it.

"You're talking to Lion David Graham now, clown—not Padgett and his band of fools. There's nothing out there but some hats on sticks." Graham's eyes bore on Shank's face, and the big man blinked and looked again at Billy's bleeding shoulder. The young Ripton was dazed but trying to regain his thoughts.

Graham swung his revolver toward Eldon and told him to lock the door. A shiver wouldn't release its hold on the Ripton elder as he walked over to the door, closed it hard, and lowered the lock beam in place.

"I see you can do something right," Graham snarled.

"Now, once again, where's the man in the black coat? And what's his name?"

Swallowing the last of his courage, Shank said, "Wal, sir, the last time I laid eyes on him, he were a-drivin' that wagon o' Padgett's, with that crippled bastard in it. Calls himself . . . James."

"Don't give me that crap."

"That's the God's truth. Watched it myse'f."

"What kind of fool is he?" Graham asked, his forehead rolled into a puzzled frown. "That means Padgett's men will get the fun of killing him—not me. That's not right. What was his name? I know it wasn't James. I need to know. We will meet again—in another life." He laughed.

Shank glanced away to the open window, where Jeremiah had done his shooting, and stared into the blackness framed by the rough-cut wood. *Is Rule Cordell really dead?* he asked himself. *Where is he? Graham was right. It was mighty foolish to be drivin' that wagon into Padgett's men. My Gawd!* Breathing came hard as the thought of Cordell being dead pushed bile upward from his stomach. Determination kept it from coming further.

A soft patter came from the darkness and Belle sauntered into the room, her nose high in the air. Graham's gun swung to meet the noise, then moved back to Tallie Mae's head. From the angle of its advance, the animal had entered through one of the open windows used for shooting earlier.

"I hate cats," Graham said, and aimed his gun at the curious animal.

"Shoo, cat. Git outta hyar!" Shank yelled, and waved his arms.

Graham's gun jumped in his hand. Belle yipped and flopped to the floor.

"Oh, not you, Belle," Shank moaned. "Rule'll be heartsick."

"What did you say?" Graham shoved Tallie Mae in the back so violently that she fell into Shank.

Her eyes were wild as she lifted herself from him. Graham again drew his first pistol with his left hand and screamed, "Stay down, bitch. Don't move, Ripton. Get down on your knees, big boy. You too, kid." His shrill laugh haunted the room.

Jeremiah choked to keep from crying as he crawled next to his mother. Squatting on her hands and knees, she patted his hand to reassure him. Eldon swallowed hard and slumped to the ground, awkwardly keeping his hands raised as he did. "Don't shoot, mister, don't shoot. We was jes' followin' orders, that's all. Captain . . ."

"Shut up." Shank's command snapped Eldon into silence.

Graham snarled, "Oh, so that's how it's going to be. Well, boys and girls, we're going to play a little game, then. I'll ask a question and you'll give me an answer. If I don't like the answer, one of you will die. Not a shoulder, or an ear, or a hand—one of you will die. Then we'll play again. Got it? Now, what was the name of the man in the black coat?" Graham's eyes burned into Eldon, and the tall man pleaded with his gaze at his wife.

She shook her head negatively, and Eldon whimpered and said, "I—I d-don' know."

Shaking his head to clear it of the swelling pain, Billy put his hand on Shank's chest and whispered, "Ya gotta try."

"Hold this," Shank muttered, and the wounded man held Shank's blood-soaked handerchief. The big merchant shifted his feet so that he could spring at Graham as soon as he got the chance.

Graham took a step toward Eldon and placed the barrel of his right-hand pistol next to Eldon's trembling head. "Was he that preacher over in Clark Springs?" His voice suddenly became soft and gentle. "Come on, now. Your friend is dead. You heard the big man. He drove Padgett's wagon—to his men. Bang. Bang." He mimicked shooting his gun, laughed again, and shook his head.

Terrified, Eldon looked at Shank, who mouthed "No." Graham stared up at the ceiling. The cocking of his pistol ripped through the room.

"Well, all right, Ripton, if that's the way you want it."

"N-no, p-please. I-it w-was C-Captain Rule C-Cordell. H-he's bin a-hidin' as the preacher, l-like ya said." Eldon whined and covered his head with shaking hands and squeezed his legs against his chest to shrink himself into a ball.

A strange squeal gurgled from Graham's mouth. Graham's voice was thin and wistful. "We were Roman soldiers once, you know, in another life. Back in Jesus' time. I figure that's why Cordell became a preacher. I killed then—with a sword."

Shank didn't look up. He didn't know which was more terrifying, Graham's haunting eyes or the jibberish coming from his twisted mouth.

"Big boy, tell me this." Graham broke into Shank's mind. "You think Padgett's men are good enough to kill Rule Cordell?"

"No suh, I don't."

Graham giggled gleefully and said, "I don't either." His voice had changed to that of a boy wishing for a pony. "So you think I can still kill him."

"I think ya kin try."

Graham's eyebrows rose in surprise. "I killed a man. In San Antonio, it was. No, no, it was Houston, for those same words." He swung the revolver toward Shank and the merchant's mind raced toward his dead wife and family and told himself he would be seeing them again. "Naw, you've given me hope, big boy. Rule Cordell will be mine to kill. Besides, Giles hasn't put a price on you. Yet." Graham's gun returned to Eldon's head. "Now, the Riptons, that's another story. I get five hundred apiece for you."

The silence was slapped away by Eldon's whimpering. "P-please, don't kill us. P-please. I—I dun tolt ya what ya w-wanted to know. It's Rule C-Cordell."

"I'll bet you'd sign over the deed right about now, wouldn't you, Ripton?" Graham drew the second gun from his red sash, cocked it, and placed the black-handled revolver alongside the first. Both barrels touched Eldon's shaking head, inches apart. A cackle that sounded like wind whipping against an old water pump followed.

"P-please, it's all w-we have."

"Why the hell do I care?" Graham said, and glanced at Shank. "Big boy, I said I'm not going to kill you. But if you try what's in your face, I'll drop you before you take two steps. Now, don't make me a liar. I don't like killing people for free."

The corner of Shank's mouth trembled. Giggling, Graham turned again to Eldon. "Don't wet on yourself, man. That's awful." His laugh was shrill once more. "Hell, I don't have a deed for you to sign anyway. You'll have to wait until I bring Padgett back. Oh, he'll be spitting mad to learn you fooled him." Graham glanced again at Shank, who was holding Billy's hand to stop the bleeding. He felt like Graham could read his mind and squinted to think of something other than the unsigned deed in Cordell's pocket.

Graham continued, cocking his head to one side, then the other to illustrate his dilemna. "Of course, if you're all dead, he can buy this wretched piece of land from the tax man. I don't know why he wants it so much, anyway. Crazy, isn't it? Oh, but it's a terrible burden for me. Deciding. Should I kill you now—or wait until later?" His chuckle was shortened by a hard knock at the door.

Everyone jumped at the sound, including Graham. His eyes flashed, and he pushed both guns against Eldon's head and whispered, "Ask who it is."

Shank responded, "I'll do it." Without waiting, he stood, threw back his shoulders, and yelled, "Who's thar?"

A slightly disgusted voice responded, "It's Rule. Open the door."

Graham's frown at Shank's presumptive action popped into a wide, toothy grin. He motioned for Shank to open the door. Shank hesitated, and Graham aimed his revolvers at Tallie Mae and Jeremiah.

"I'm a-comin', Rule," Shank said loudly as Graham stepped away from Eldon and positioned himself against the wall where the door would open and conceal his presence.

"Thought ya'd have that big black o' yurn a-runnin' hard fer home an' your pretty Rebecca." Shank slowly lifted the lock bar from the iron frames and let it slip from his fingers. Cursing, he regrasped the beam, raised it free, and laid it aside. Taking a deep breath, he swung open the door, hoping Cordell had realized something was wrong because of his obvious misstatements.

Shank stood without speaking, gulping air to stabilize the fierce thumping of his heart. After a few seconds, Graham sprang around the door to see what was going on. The doorway was empty. He took a cautious step forward to peer outside. Nothing. Nothing but darkness. And only the sounds of the night greeted him.

"What the hell did you say to him?" Graham sputtered, spinning back into Shank. Graham's face was swollen with madness. "Where is he?"

"I'm right here, Lion."

Graham's revolvers were a blur toward the open window behind him. Cordell's first two bullets struck the killer in the chest and stomach almost the instant Graham fired. Graham's own lead ripped wood from the frame next to Cordell's head, powering splinters into his cheek and cutting through the thong that held his stone earring. Cordell fired again with both Colts, as the freed earring bounced inside. Black holes appeared in Graham's forehead and cheek. His body buckled as his head snapped backward and he staggered through the doorway and onto the porch.

A strange squeal gurgled from his open mouth. Graham fired his right-hand gun, but the barrel was aimed at the night sky. The gray-suited killer tried to shoot again, but his finger wouldn't squeeze the trigger of the gun in his left hand. His eyes wouldn't focus. Where was the one man he wanted to kill? He crashed against the railing and spun toward the sound of Cordell rushing toward him.

Cordell fired again at Graham's vest, turning it crimson, and pounding him as he staggered on the porch. Moonlight danced across the killer's revolvers as they hung by themselves for a moment in the air, then thumped on the wooden porch. He slipped to one knee and grabbed for the railing post. His quivering hand couldn't hold on, and he crashed to the ground on his back.

Shank couldn't move, stunned by what he was seeing. He had been an instant from rushing at Graham and probably dying in the attempt. Unnoticed, the ear wound dribbled a line of red down his coat. Mumbling something that sounded like "Amen," Tallie Mae hurried to her wounded son. Tears dissolved her face into a blister of water as she lifted Shank's reddened handkerchief Billy held against his shoulder and patted the wound herself. Jeremiah stood and watched, trying to hold back the vomit. He couldn't, and raced for the open window where Cordell had been. Eldon lay on the floor, afraid to look at the dying Graham. Finally, his gaze met Tallie Mae's and she tried to smile; he could only nod.

Outside, Rule Cordell waited beside the rasping Lion David Graham. Cordell holstered one smoking Colt but held the second revolver cocked in his right fist. The killer's eyes stared at him through blood-soaked eyelashes. For an instant his face became that of Cordell's father, then disappeared. Graham coughed, and blood splattered on his chin and cheek. "I—I w-was supposed . . . to k-kill you, l-like before. N-next time, I—I . . ."

"I didn't want this, Lion, we were friends—once. We played together, remember? You, an' Ian, an' me. I don't . . ."

"I—I always w-wanted to be y-you. E-everybody thought you were the g-great fighter, t-the leader, t-the b-best." Blood flooded from Graham's mouth and he choked on its heavy flow. "I-if I k-killed you, I would be the one t-they all looked to. K-killing w-was the only thing I w-was good at. I—I killed you b-before, you know, w-when we were Roman soldiers."

"That was play, Lion. We were playing like we were Roman soldiers. Don't you remember? It wasn't real."

"N-no, I r-really did. A-another l-life. W-we . . ." Graham's face froze and his eyes saw nothing.

Cordell's own eyes sought the sky and his shoulders sagged. How could a long-ago friendship go so bad? He saw Lion David Graham and himself again as boys, running and pretending together along a creek. Ian Taullery was there, too, as always. Both he and Taullery were quicker and stronger than Graham then. He saw the three of them practicing with an old gun. Why did he think things would ever change? Why did he think the guns would leave him alone? Why did he think he could live any other way?

Somewhere inside of him, a thought trickled through his other emotions: He couldn't have beaten Graham in a fair fight. Shank's warning had made the difference, allowing him a split-second edge. Another thought rushed behind the first, pointing out that Graham would have probably killed him if he had entered the room unsuspecting. He shivered at the prospect and looked down at the still mass that had been both childhood friend and obsessed enemy.

"Forgive us, Father, for we are killers of men," Cordell said, and turned away.

Tallie Mae's attention was drawn to Cordell as she tended to Billy. For the first time, she understood how much he had sacrificed emotionally to come to their aid. He had broken all his promises to God. He had turned his back on his commitment to leave the gun behind. He had emotionally left the ministry to fight and kill. She wanted to hold him tight to her, to kiss him, to give herself to him. The lustful instant passed and she regained her composure, returning awkwardly to patting her son's shoulder wound.

"W-what happened, Ma?" Billy's eyes fluttered open. Each breath brought new pain to his shoulder and hand.

"Captain Cordell is what happened, son. It's all right. We're safe."

Eldon crawled over to his wife and oldest son, and pronounced, "Got blood all ag'in the wall, Ma. It's gonna be mighty hard to git off."

Her husband's observation snapped Tallie Mae Ripton into action. She stood and took over. "Eldon, you get us some wood so we can get the fire going strong again. We'll need hot water to clean Billy's wounds. His hand's shot clear through, but I can't tell if lead's in Billy's shoulder or not. May have to dig it out. Jeremiah, you find me some rags. Clean ones. Look on the back shelf. Up high."

"B-but, Ma, he k-killed B-Belle," Jeremiah blurted, staring at the unmoving yellow form against the dark wall.

"Yes, I know, son. Better Belle than us. We'll bury her later."

"What'll Lizzie say?"

"She'll cry, just like we've been doin'. Now go, Jeremiah."

"I-is Billy gonna d-die?"

"No. But he's hurt bad. Now go, Jeremiah."

Chapter Twenty-seven

Cordell stepped to the doorway and watched the boy scurry into the other room. Brushing off his shirt, Eldon pushed himself slowly erect. "Howdy, Captun Cordell. You was a mite slow gittin' hyar. Too bad about the cat." He hurried past Cordell to gather wood, paused in front of Graham's body, started to kick at it, then lost his nerve and walked wide of the still form.

"Sorry. I didn't get here sooner." Cordell entered and stopped next to Shank. "You saved my life, Caleb. I'd have walked into his guns without your warning. Thank you."

"Hot damn, I was a-hopin' ya was a-listenin'." Shank's eyes were welling with tears of released tension. "I couldn't think o' nothin' else." His breath came long and hard, pushing back the wall of emotion that wanted out. "Lordy, it's mighty good to see ya, Rule."

"What did Eldon mean about the cat?"

"Graham dun kilt Belle, jes' fer spite." Shank was

surprised at the look on Cordell's face as the words hi
him. He aged ten years in an instant. A moan tried t
come out, but Cordell clinched his teeth and squeeze
his eyes shut.

"Ohhhh . . . not you, Texas. Not Texas. Pray for him
soldier, please. Please. Pray for Texas. God, not Texas
Isn't Whisper's arm enough?"

A wobbly Billy heard the name, and his pain-fille
mind clicked to a bloody Virginia battle where
Cordell-led cavalry caught a Union force by surprise an
forced their retreat, but the intense leader lost his dog
Texas, and couldn't be consoled afterward. Their com
rade, Whisper Jenson, had lost his arm from wound
during the "masquerade battalion" skirmish.

"Captun . . . I'm sorry 'bout Texas," Billy said softly
"He went down, fightin' at your side. Them Yanks is a
runnin' hard, Captun."

Shank couldn't comprehend what was happening. H
rubbed his ear and realized the bottom lobe was gone
leaving crusty gristle. Had the shot affected his hear
ing—or did Cordell call the cat "Texas"? Didn't he re
member its name was "Belle"? Of course he did. Wh
was this "Texas"? Or was he talking bout the state
Didn't he know Whisper Jenson had been killed—b
this mad killer, Lion Graham?

Understanding only that Cordell was trapped in som
personal agony, Tallie Mae rushed across the room an
hugged him. The greeting brought new tears to her pal
face.

"T-they're gone, Captain. An' that awful man is dea
Y-you saved us. You saved us all."

His eyes still closed, he hugged back, fighting an ol
agony that had broken free. "B-Belle came to me . .
as I was walking to the house. S-she was t-trying t
warn me, I guess. S-she ran off. I—I didn't know."

"Of course you didn't, Captain. Belle saved us to

That devil killed her—instead of shooting one of us."

"I—I lost T-Texas. He was a fine dog. H-he didn't deserve to die." Cordell trembled, opened his eyes, and looked away, his hands at his sides.

She touched his face gently and studied its hard features. She was drawn to this gun warrior in a way she knew she shouldn't be. Here he was in her arms so close, so strong yet so vulnerable. He smelled warm—a mixture of gunsmoke, blood, dirt, and the musky scent of manhood.

Red-faced, she brushed the front of her skirt to ward off the surge of emotions that had sprung loose again. Embarrassed by her feelings, she changed the subject. "I—I didn't see that awful man come in. All of a sudden, he was behind me. I—I thought he was going to kill all of us."

Cordell tenderly wiped her cheek with his hand. He felt only an overwhelming tiredness, so strong he could barely stand. A deep breath, then another, brought in enough energy to fight off the spreading weakness. Sleep wanted him, now that the tension of battle was leaving and the ache of Belle's death swam through him. His shoulder pounded its own need for attention as the adrenaline of battle sank from him.

"How bad is Billy Rip hurt?" Cordell asked, looking blankly at her.

She stared back and reached for his arm, wishing they were alone, then forced herself to look at her older son and bring back reality.

Watching the encounter, Shank answered, "Wal, he ain't gonna be liftin' nothin' fer a fair piece. Gonna take time to git his hand back, too. Good thing it's his left, I reckon." The big merchant searched his coat pockets for his pipe and added, "Had me the feelin' Lion know'd ya, Rule—even a'fer Eldon dun said yur name. You were the only one he wanted. Woulda kilt us all otherwise. Said somethin' 'bout killin' ya a'fer. Crazy words." He found the pipe, happily slid it into his mouth, and started another search for matches in his pockets. "He know'd we was a-fakin' how many we had."

Tallie Mae turned toward the big merchant, her hand holding Cordell's arm. "I almost forgot, Mister Shank. You were very brave—to help Billy like you did. Is your ear hurt badly? Please let me clean and bandage it." She glanced back at Cordell, who was looking at Shank. "And you too, Captain—your arm."

Cordell looked at his coat sleeve, shook his head, and said, "I'm all right. You tend to Billy—and Caleb."

"Shucks, this ain't nothin'. Never did have purty ears nohow," Shank replied, and held up his open palms to express a need for a match. "Anybody got a match?"

"Sure we do. Bring some matches too, Jeremiah," Tallie Mae said, looking around for the boy but not wanting to step away from Cordell. "Oh, Captain, ah, Reverend—do you think it would be all right to have some light in the house now?" She returned to his face.

"Yes, Padgett is gone. May I see Belle?"

"Of course."

Without another word, she took Cordell's hand and led him toward the dead cat. Both knelt beside the still form. Shank wondered if she had forgotten that her son was seriously hurt. He stepped over to the nearly unconscious Billy, leaned over, and pulled on his shirt where the bullet had entered. He studied the wound and was pleased with what he saw. Most of the fabric was soaked with blood, but the wound itself was coagulating. He pushed Billy's shoulder upright so he could see the destruction on the other side. A crimson exit looked to him like the bullet had passed through. Then, in the wall, he saw the chunk of lead lodged there.

Jeremiah brought him a wooden match along with a

short pile of folded cloth. "I-is Billy g-gonna die?"

"Like yur maw said, nosirree, son, he ain't," Shank responded. "He's gonna be fine. Be laid up awhile, though."

"Reckon that means I'll have to do all his chores."

"Wal, that could be." Shank scratched his beard and laughed as he snapped the match on a shirt button and let its flame bring the half-smoked bowl of tobacco to life.

A few feet away, Cordell slid his hands under Belle and lifted her to his chest. He glanced at Tallie Mae, and she was crying.

"Tallie Mae, Belle's with my Texas now. They'll be waiting for us. I know this. We'll carry Billy wherever you want him—and then I—I'll take her outside . . . if you wish."

"Oh, that's not necessary, I'll take it out later . . . and we can bury it. You stay here and relax with Mister Shank. I'll get some coffee going." She touched his hand and studied his face before standing. She threw back her shoulders to clear her head.

"Thank you, but Caleb and I have some things to do, so it's no trouble taking Belle outside if you would like."

"But Mister Shank is hurt. That awful man shot him—in the ear." The gunfighter looked at Shank and it registered, for the first time, that his friend was hurt. "Forgive me, Caleb, I wasn't thinking. You stay here and let Mrs. Ripton clean that wound."

"Nope, I'd jes' as soon be workin'—an' she needs to be takin' care of that fine son o' hers." Pipe smoke swam around Shank's hat and disappeared into the air. " 'Sides, I kinda like it. Sorta like an earring, don't ya think?" He chuckled.

"Are you a Comanche—or a pirate?" Cordell asked, touching his own ear and realizing his earring was gone.

His gaze sought the floor by the window and saw it lying there.

"Me? I'm one o' them 'Sons of Thunder.' " His belly rippled with enjoyment over his response.

Flustered, Tallie Mae refocused on her son's wound. "Jeremiah, where are my rags? I'll be caring for Billy now."

Cordell turned to her face, and she blushed.

"Tallie Mae?" He said softly.

"Y-yes?" She bit her lower lip, keeping her eyes locked on his. The answer was more than a response.

"Does Billy keep shells for reloading?"

Her gaze was broken by rapid blinking and the realization that she had misread this magnetic man. His passion wasn't about her; it was the wildfire within him, honed by the awful trials of war.

"O-oh, of course he does. A big sack of them." She paused, and her voice glistened with rejection. "Captain Cordell, don't we have enough bullets already? I thought Padgett was gone."

"He is, but I want to make sure he doesn't bother you any more." Cordell looked at Shank as he rose. "He might send back a scout to make sure of things. I want him to—"

"Make it look like the 'Sons of Thunder' is a real bunch, right?" Shank interrupted. "Then they'll tell their boss."

"Yes, it won't take much. We'll put away the dummies, stomp around, and spread out some of Billy's shells."

"How 'bout some cigarette butts, too?"

"Good idea. Do you have any makin's?"

"Got a whole box of tobaccy sacks an' papers—in my wagon."

From the floor, Billy groaned and shuffled his feet in

a vain attempt to stand. "I kin fight. H-help me up, Captun."

Immediately, Cordell went to the young man, knelt beside him, and whispered in his ear. Billy relaxed, frowning but nodding. A half-smile crept across his mouth. "T-they's in a sack . . . under my bed. Jeremiah knows whar. He kin stomp 'round, too, Captun." He swallowed back the pain. "Ya better make some hoss signs too, ya know."

"Good idea, soldier." Cordell held Billy's arm. "Now, you rest—an' let us do some playactin'."

"Yessiree, Captun. Jes' like old times, ain't it?"

Behind him, Cordell heard Shank tell Tallie Mae that the bullet went through her son's shoulder. Quietly, she requested the merchant and Cordell to carry Billy to his bedroom so she could care for him there. As Cordell and Shank carried Billy into the bedroom, Eldon entered with an armful of cut logs and proceeded to build up the fire in the fireplace. He asked if his wife wanted one started in the stove, too, but she didn't. Tallie Mae concentrated on lighting an oil lamp, and its golden light made her glow. She told Jeremiah to pump some water into a bowl while she removed Billy's shirt, then told him to go help Shank and Cordell. The boy was excited about the prospect of being close to Cordell and hurried through his water-pumping task.

After picking up his torn earring, Cordell walked toward the door, holding the dead cat against his chest. His manner was like that of a man awakened from a bad dream. Shank came behind him, holding the sack of shells. He wanted to ask if Cordell was worried about Padgett coming again in force but didn't think this was the right time. Tallie Mae's words of comfort to Billy tailed away quickly as the door shut behind them.

Outside, Cordell took off his long coat and wrapped the little animal in it and laid the bundle carefully on the porch. He glanced at Graham's pistols lying there and kicked them off the wood frame onto the ground. "We'll leave Belle here until the Riptons decide where they want to bury her."

"So ya think Padgett'll come back?" Shank finally blurted, deliberately avoiding looking at the dead Graham.

Cordell's eyes narrowed and his voice carried its earlier strength. "I'm guessing he'll only scout around to make sure we were for real."

"What if he don't? What if he dun comes a-roarin' back?" Shank took the pipe from his mouth and pointed it at Cordell for emphasis.

Staring at the pipe, Cordell said, "They'll run over the Riptons—and us."

Shank's eyes widened and he jammed the pipe back into his mouth. He studied Cordell for a moment. "I see. Wal, what do ya wanna do with this?" He pointed at Graham's body.

"We'll use one of the left-behind horses—and send it running," Cordell said. "That should help keep Padgett off balance. I figure we'd better do the same with any of his men still around. They could become a problem for the Riptons later."

Shank grabbed his coat lapels with both fists. "What are we a-doin' first?"

"Let's make like many."

"Well, sir, we's gittin' good at this make-believe stuff. Let's git 'er done."

Quickly they began creating the appearance of thirty men surrounding the Regulator camp. After removing the dummies and filling in the holes made by the stakes, they brought the sacks, hats, and wood back to Shank's wagon. Their boot prints added to the impression of numbers, in addition to the marks left earlier by the Riptons. Jeremiah soon joined them and was eager to trounce around the ridge, tossing shells from his big brother's sack.

At the wagon, Shank began rolling cigarettes using what tobacco and papers he had left. As soon as one was made, he smoked it and started another, then moved the smoking cigarette into a brass spittoon he found in the corner of the wagon. Standing beside him, Cordell joined in, puffing on one cigarette while he rolled another.

"How many we got thar?" Shank tried to count the butts in the nearly full spittoon.

"Enough."

"What else are we leaving?"

"I've got some food in my saddlebags. We'll spread pieces of that around too." Cordell walked over to where he had left his own horse, checked on the grazing animal, and took a sack containing food Aleta had packed for him. He turned to see Shank coming toward him with Aleta's hat in his huge hands like he was concerned it would perish if he wasn't careful. "Hyar's your lady's hat. I dun fergot." Cordell laid the tie-down thong over his saddle horn and they returned to the spittoon.

Neither man spoke as they made their way to the ridge. Both minds were dull and wanting sleep, but struggling to think of anything that would enhance the impression they needed to leave. A strange hush lay over the dry creek bed below. Discarded blankets and clothes appeared like a blotchy disease on the land. Joining with Jeremiah, they walked along the ridge, tossing cigarettes, food scraps, and shells.

A pistol jumped into Cordell's hand. There was movement near the far end of the camp below them. Shank pushed Jeremiah to the ground and Cordell handed him the Dean & Adams revolver from his back waistband. The big man crouched and squinted into the night, seeing nothing.

"Stay here." Cordell whispered and zigzagged down the incline. He stopped at the bottom of the ridge, studied the spread-out blankets, and looked up at Shank and Jeremiah. "Coyotes." He paused, saw something on the ground, and picked up a small shiny object. Returning to where the big merchant and the boy waited, he held out a state police badge. "Well, pistols, blankets, and clothes aren't the only things they left behind."

"Reckon my wagon'll have some fresh things to trade. I'll git 'em later." He extended the Dean & Adams pistol, handle first, to Cordell.

Cordell shoved the gun into his back waistband, then pushed the badge into the pocket with the folded Harper deed and asked, "You think the coyotes'll get to . . . Belle?"

Shank grunted. "Nope. Too close to the house."

"Jeremiah, why don't you head back an' check with your ma—about burying Belle. We'll be right along, as soon as we can bring a horse to carry Graham. All right?"

The boy wanted to stay with them but nodded approval and skipped toward the house, now glowing softly with warm light. After saddling an uneasy bay left at the Regulator string, they returned to the house and tied Graham's body into place with a camp lariat. Cordell slapped the animal hard and they watched it gallop toward the lightening sky. It was false dawn, but morning wouldn't be many hours away.

"That oughta keep Padgett shook up," Shank said.

"Should I worry the Riptons about the possibility he might return?"

Shank ventured that Tallie Mae should be alerted but no one else. He thought she had the steel. Chewing on the pipe stem in his teeth, he watched Cordell for any indications of interest in the woman and was a little disappointed when there weren't any. After readying the remaining horses, they led them in a wide loop to Shank's wagon, encircling it several times to look like many horses had stayed there. The animals were allowed to stand long enough to leave manure, then they were walked along the "Sons of Thunder" ridge and back. It wasn't perfect, but both men thought the appearance would be sufficient.

Next, the horses were led to each downed Regulator, whether dead or unconscious. Cordell and Shank methodically tied each man onto a mount and sent the horse running. Several horses had to carry two bodies. It was hard work, made worse by their tiredness. Even the huge Shank was having difficulty lifting. A silhouette caught their attention and Eldon's stiff frame took shape against the darkened land.

"Thought ye might be wantin' some help. Tallie Mae's got Billy all fixed up. Bullet went straight through. He's a-sleepin'. She's fixin' some food. Jeremiah's digging a . . . spot fer the cat." Eldon walked toward them, carrying the Winchester crossed in his arms. Both Shank and Cordell noticed that he also had Graham's black-handled revolvers shoved into his waistband. "Say, who do these hyar fancy guns belong to . . . now?"

Shank answered first: "I reckon they belong to yo-all. Thar's some six-guns 'round an' about too. I'd be careful 'bout keepin' any iron that kin be identified, though."

"Ya mean like it havin' a carvin' somwhars?"

"Yeah, anything that makes it easy to tell who the owner was."

Smiling, Eldon rubbed his hand over the rifle in his arms. "Ya think people would think I cut down that crazy bastard if'n they saw me with these?" He patted the revolvers.

"Could be. Most folks would recognize them, I think,"

Shank observed, glancing at Cordell, who didn't appear to be paying attention.

Eldon's smile was thick. "Wal, guess we got sumthin' outta all this, anyway." He looked down at the revolvers and added, "But I don't think we'll be a-keepin' these. Ya want 'em? Captun Cordell? Sort o' a trophy?"

Cordell's glare was the only answer. He looked away from the white-faced Eldon. "Caleb, do you have any paper—and ink—in your wagon?"

"Wal, I reckon so. Why?"

"Just thought of something else to leave behind." Cordell turned back to Eldon. "Eldon, we'll meet you back at the house." The elder Ripton accepted the dismissal eagerly and spun around.

At the wagon, Shank rummaged through his crowded wagon bed and proudly came up with a stack of writing papers, a glass, decorative ink bottle, and fairly new dip pen. "Ain't got no sand to dry it, though."

"Thanks, Caleb. I don't know what I would have done without you," Cordell said, and squatted on the ground. "I can sprinkle little dirt on them if I need to." Quickly, he wrote eight notes, each with the same message: "S. O. T. Meet at shadow tree at 6 tonight. Padgett is at Ripton's." Shank picked up a finished paper and asked, "What's this fer? Whar's the 'shadow tree'?"

"I don't know where the 'shadow tree' is. Thought it sounded nice an' secret. We're going to leave them around, like the Sons of Thunder were an organized band and ordered to be here. Padgett's scouts'll bring them back to him."

"Maybe ya should put 'Padgett, ya better watch out' on one o' them."

Cordell smiled, stood, and patted his friend on the back. "Let's spread the news. They're dry enough."

After folding and leaving the notes in different places along the ridge, they returned to the house. Jeremiah had finished digging a small grave under the elderly cottonwood that protected Lizzie's wild flowers. A hastily grabbed bunch of buttercups lay on top of the filled-in grave; a tiny cross of sticks, held with a leather strip, completed the remembrance. Tallie Mae was standing beside him with her arm draped across his shoulder. He held Cordell's coat close to his chest and handed it to him as he approached. Studying Cordell's face, Tallie Mae said Billy was sleeping. She smiled warmly and asked Cordell if he would offer a prayer for Belle, adding that Lizzie would have selected this burial place herself. She invited them to eat afterward, and encouraged their staying and sleeping. Her eyes darted toward Cordell, waiting for his response.

"I'd be honored. I'm only sorry you can't have a real minister here."

Tallie Mae bit her lower lip and the words came with a choke. "R-Reverend L-Langford, you're the only . . . man, minister I'd want."

They formed a circle around the tiny mound, with Tallie Mae standing next to Cordell on one side, Shank on the other. The big merchant held his hat and his pipe in his hands. With his coat draped over his shoulder, Cordell removed his hat and bowed his head.

"Dear Lord, we give to you the sweet spirit of Belle. This fine and brave cat gave the Riptons much love—and tonight helped us overcome a wicked foe. Please bring her to you and keep her warm and happy. Y-you will love having her close. We've been through much these past days, Lord, give us your peace and your protection—and bless this family and this house. Amen."

The others echoed his "Amen." Tallie Mae laid a wild rose, cut from the bush beside their front door, on top of the other flowers. Cordell removed the rose stem from his coat and placed the remembrance on the grave next to the bright bloom. He muttered something no one else heard, but Shank thought he caught "Texas." Tallie Mae whispered to Jeremiah, and he rushed away.

Eldon said that Cordell and Shank were welcome to sleep on the floor beside the stove where it was warm. Cooking smells from the house were inviting, but Cordell told them he needed to leave. Breathing hard, Jeremiah returned and proudly held out another rose; this one yanked free, not cut. One petal was missing, victim of his urgent handling. Tallie Mae took the flower and placed it in the button hole of Cordell's coat lapel and urged him to stay. The gunfighter studied the rose, thanked her, then rustled Jeremiah's hair and thanked him.

He turned to Shank and held out his hand. "Caleb, I hope you'll stay and enjoy this fine family's invitation."

Shank grabbed it and pulled Cordell to him in a giant bear hug. They patted each other on the back and stepped away, their eyes filling.

"I can't thank you enough for your help, Caleb," Cordell said.

"Wal, I missed out on yur first masquerade party, didn't wanna miss the second," Caleb pronounced joyfully. "Kin I he'p ya take care o' Giles?"

"No need . . . yet. I think Padgett is rattled enough to tell him, especially without Graham to back his play. But I'll see that Giles gets a reminder about giving back the Harper deed. If the fine mayor drags his feet . . ." Cordell didn't finish the statement, rubbing his chest to push away the tiredness. "Been thinking about starting a petition in church—to ask the state to remove Padgett."

Shank grinned. He wasn't sure which pleased him more: the realization that Cordell was going to use his idea—or the fact that Cordell was going back to the pulpit.

"I'm too weary to go nowhar fer a piece. Sur ya

wanna be ridin' now?" Shank asked, putting a large paw of a hand on Cordell's shoulder.

"I'll be all right—and Aleta will be worried about me."

No one caught the slight wince on Tallie Mae's face as Cordell announced his second reason for leaving.

Cordell continued, "An' it might be smart for you to keep wide of Clark Springs for a week or so. Just in case."

Cordell shook hands with Eldon and Jeremiah. Turning to Tallie Mae, she quickly extended her hand and told him to give their love to Lizzie. He wasn't sure if he would share the awful news about Belle or not. She nodded and looked away. With that, the Riptons and Shank turned toward the house and Cordell headed for his horse.

Chapter Twenty-eight

On the ride home, Lion David Graham returned to Rule Cordell's mind as a kid along the creek, but his face was a blur. Cordell's mind found the book about Roman armies in Taullery's house. Did Graham really believe the two of them had lived back then?

Somewhere an owl hooted its own loneliness as Rule Cordell rode alone in the waning hours before dawn. In his weariness, he was reminded of Moon's admonishments that the bird was often a reincarnated spirit. He remembered the Comanche belief in reincarnation; Moon had told him that, too, and the old shaman was a wise man. He touched the medicine pouch under his shirt to honor Moon's memory, then reassured himself that the earring was in his pocket. Dead warriors spent time in a wonderful valley, west of the sunset, where they were young and virile, the land was forever green, and the buffalo were plentiful. Then they returned to

Mother Earth to come again as Comanche faithful to keep The People strong.

"Maybe you knew something the rest of us don't, Lion," he said aloud.

The stallion's ears pricked up to catch the meaning of the words. Cordell recalled Whisper Jenson questioning him once about Jesus not being recognized by his disciples after the Resurrection. Whisper wondered if the reason was that Jesus didn't look the same. An argument for reincarnation, the grizzled lawyer had surmised, enjoying the stunned look on the faces of his fellow Confederate scouts around the campfire.

Ian Taullery was at that campfire, too, and Cordell's thoughts ran to him for the first time since leaving his friend. He smiled just thinking about the reaction his dirty coat would have brought from his friend. It would have been good to have him with them. His absence bothered Cordell more than he knew it should. After all, his friend had a family, a business, responsibilities. Somehow, those excuses soured like old milk in his mind.

His friend was settling into a good life, and here he was—in the eyes of the law—a wanted man. Again. The only difference was that the law didn't know who he was this time. He figured it would only be a matter of days before wanted bulletins for the "Sons of Thunder" would appear. At least they had managed to keep the Riptons from any responsibility for attacking the state police, unless he was wrong about Padgett.

He hoped Caleb Shank would stay away from the region for a while—and not be tempted to tell about the experience. He wondered if any of the Regulators had spotted his huge frame during the fight. That reminded him of the Harper deed, and he touched his pocket for reassurance that it remained. His mind was too tired to focus on how to get Giles to sign it over to the Harper family. He accepted the satisfaction that at least the deed couldn't be filed while he held it.

A soft rain whispered through the leaves, and he watched it blanket the land. He had kept off the main trail to avoid attention or ambush, but his alertness was waning. Raising his head, he let the spray cleanse his face. It felt good, in spite of the growing wetness across his body. Old habits made him check to see that his coat covered his guns. His hands brushed against the cold steel and assured him they were still dry. The storm wouldn't last long. He could already see sunlight shoving away the clouds.

Sleep sang a seductive song as adrenaline from fighting drained away with each pounding hoof. Aleta's hanging hat brushed against his leg as he loped through an uneven prairie. He should've stayed at the Riptons'; only his desire to be with her had spurred him to try returning. It seemed like he had been gone from town for a week—and from Aleta for months, instead of a single night. His mind ran ahead to Aleta and the goodness of seeing her. He rode for minutes with her at his side.

Maybe he couldn't try to give up the ways of violence. An Old Testament quotation rose in his mind: "Teach a child in the way he should go, and when he is old, he will not depart from it." Maybe he was really no different from his father. He was soon lost in a dark time long ago, when his father had killed his pet dog because Texas had wet their rug.

Reverend Cordell beat the dog to death and, almost, young Rule Cordell. The boy had come upon the father whipping the dog with a heavy stick and had dived on top of the bloody, whimpering animal to save it. The minister continued the beating, yelling out Bible quotations. Young Rule passed out eventually and was carried away by his mother, who discovered the cruel punishment barely in time. Only vague wisps remained of being quite ill for a long time and hearing his father tell his distraught mother that their son deserved to die for trying to disrupt him and God's punishment. He couldn't remember getting to bury the pet, and that brought once more the grief of Texas—and Belle—upon him.

Memory relinquished its hold on his mind as the the rain stopped. Black clouds grumbled and rolled on to the north, and the sky reclad itself in a beautiful cloak of blue. Entering a string of cottonwoods and underbrush pushed against a sometime stream called Mud Creek, he startled a sleeping deer and its fawn. The two animals slid silently to another resting place nearby. He watched their retreat with a grim smile.

Streaks of dawn cut brilliant strips of gold through the trees, warning night creatures that the sun was about to take control. He drank deep of the clean air left behind in the storm's wake and felt it lift his tortured mind. Blackbirds sang from the sparse undergrowth in celebration of the rain ending. Life was a joyous thing, he reminded himself. He was wet from head to toe but cleansed inside. For the first time since he had buckled on his guns, he managed a prayer to guide him for the path he had taken. His chest rose and fell in the slow rhythm of his stallion's walk. His head nodded, and Rule Cordell was asleep.

With its sleeping rider, the stallion kept steadily moving down through a shallow arroyo, across a dry wash, and into a kingdom of grass. Two jays followed for twenty-five yards, chewing out horse and rider for not giving them any food. Shadows within the ravine were twisted and angry. Minutes later, the horse passed the remains of an old campfire. Several miles away were clusters of cattle amid patches of heavy buffalo grass.

Jewels of blue, red, and yellow wildflowers decorated the green. Brown shapes were gathered around a water tank beneath a sturdy windmill. A small stream meandered alongside the foothills. All around them, dawn had stripped away the gray with bands of pink, violet, and gold.

Cordell jerked awake as the stallion stutter-stepped to a halt. For an instant he fought through a foggy dreamworld, past haunting images of his father, mother, and childhood friends. His mind finally registered on two horses with their heads down, eating grass, a few yards ahead. A blink later, his instincts took over. He swung to the side of the stallion with a Colt pointed along the horse's neck. Ahead nothing stirred. On one horse's back was the body of Lion Graham. The other had lost its load; two bodies lay sprawled on the wet earth; a partially untied rope dangled from the saddle. A third shape, at first a man kneeling beside the first horse, became a gnarled bush.

Sounds behind him! He swung in the saddle, a cocked pistol in his right hand. Standing twenty feet behind was a baby longhorn calf. The wobbly animal looked at Cordell, then squealed. The calf's mother appeared from the trees and nudged her infant back into the darkness, giving the horseman a scornful look as she did. Cordell shook his head; he had been lucky. Then saw the tracks of a group of riders with a heavy wagon—made since the rain had stopped, by the looks of them.

He forced himself to read the sign more thoroughly. It had to be Padgett and his men. They were headed away from Clark Springs. The tracks came from hillside rock shelving where they probably sat out the storm. Apparently they left their dead behind, probably because it would slow them down. It was possible the horses had arrived after the Regulators left, but he doubted it. Lion Graham was soaked, his gray suit now more of an odd-looking pink.

Cordell's eyes burned from lack of sleep. His insides ached from longing to be with Aleta. His arm throbbed from the trail gunfight; his head had more of a dull pain where the Sunday gun had struck. And his mind stung with a lack of answers of how to stop the insidious raiding of property. His only solution, so far, was the gun—a solution he had vowed to give up. But it did seem good to be helping someone. He hadn't recognized the truth of the sensation until now.

"I'll come back and bury you, Lion. I promise," Cordell muttered, and rediscovered the limp rose on his coat. He couldn't remember how it got there. A new energy spun through him. A squeeze of his legs was all that was needed to bring the stallion into a ground-eating lope. His movement took him along the edge of steep yellowish banks, gashed and torn, that rose abruptly from the creek bank, and followed it for miles. This narrow deer trail would be difficult for even the best tracker to follow quickly. His mind was working again and telling him that he shouldn't leave an easy trail to his home. It wasn't enough to not be seen; he shouldn't lead them to his home, either.

A morning breeze whipped at his wet clothes and began to dry them, but he didn't notice. He could barely wait to hear about Aleta's first night of schooling the black children. Her face would light up, as it always did when she enjoyed something. His first stop would be the school where she would be teaching. And waiting for him.

Another hour passed before horse and rider cleared a stingy, rock-laden pass and headed down into a secluded wide curve in the trail. A downward-traveling stream looped around the turn in the path, or was its cause. From the crest of the clearing, he could see the distinctive square outline of the schoolhouse and its dilapidated fencing. Strings of chimney smoke from neighboring buildings were caught in the late-morning sky, attempting to connect with the fully born sun.

He was surprised to see a saddled lineback dun tied at the rack beside the schoolhouse, instead of Aleta's paint horse. The dun was one of theirs, a three-year-old gelding being readied for sale. Maybe she thought the animal needed work. She could certainly ride any horse they had ever owned.

As he swung down in front of the unpainted structure, it thrilled him to hear Aleta's voice above the excited responses of children. He looked at himself and decided he should, at least, unbuckle his guns before going inside. He would look trail-worn and wet, but her students wouldn't be taking home any tales about the minister wearing guns or some Indian thing. Stuffing both weapons and the Comanche warrior earring into his saddlebags, he took a few swipes at his black coat, still damp from the rain, and started up the creaky steps.

The door swung open and Aleta came rushing out to him. They grabbed each other and held tight without saying a word. "I love you" popped from both their mouths simultaneously, and they laughed and kissed. Behind them, children were peeking out of the doorway, whispering and giggling.

"I theenk school should be let out so we can go home and . . ." Her smile finished the sentence. His eyes agreed. But the corners of her smile dropped and she began to tell him what had happened at Eliason's factory last night. Cordell thought he was going to fall to his knees. He couldn't believe what she was saying. His friend, "Suitcase" Eliason, was dead? Killed by men wearing sheets for masks? Oh God, no. No!

He realized Aleta was trembling, and the tears followed. Between sobs, she told him of the night's terror and how she had used her gun to keep the mob from getting to the children—and that she had wounded two. During the night, she walked them back to the tents their families lived in. One boy knew the way. Their parents were stunned and scared but very grateful to her. Four armed black men had taken her home in a wagon. She didn't know what happened to her paint horse; she didn't want to go back to the factory this morning to look.

Between choking statements about the night's terror, she managed to tell him that Lizzie was resting easily and should be up and around in another day or so. He told her in two brief sentences about the Riptons being safe and Padgett leaving. There was no mention of his "Sons of Thunder" ruse or Lion Graham's death or any other aspects of his encounters with the Regulators. That could come later. She asked why he had returned so fast, riding in the rain, and he mumbled that it was to see her. Her smile fought its way through tears.

Ernest, the towheaded boy with two missing teeth, found his courage and stepped out on the porch. A blond girl pulled on his shirt to keep him inside, but he shook off her attempt and stood with his legs wide apart, staring at the couple. "Mrs. Langford, are you all right? What's the matter, preacher—why is our teacher crying?"

Cordell was too tired to dance around the issue. "A good friend of ours was murdered last night. Jacob Henry Eliason. He was killed by cowards wearing masks."

"He that Negra that had hisself a boot factory?"

"Yes, he did."

"My pa said no black man deserved to own nuthin' like that. Pa said he wouldn't live long."

Chapter Twenty-nine

Anger swelled within Cordell, and he spat, "You tell your pa I said he was wrong. Tell him I aim to find out who did this—and they will hang."

The boy was startled by the response and stepped backward. His face contorted, and tears weren't far behind. "B-but my pa . . ."

"I hope for your pa's sake, he wasn't one of them."

Looking into Cordell's face, Aleta whispered, "Rule, you cannot talk like thees. The children will not understand."

"Maybe they should. 'Suitcase' was our friend—and those men would've killed you, if they could have. Probably the black children, too. Maybe these kids should know—"

"T-they killed another man too, Rule," Aleta interrupted. "His name was Zachim. A-all he wanted was to read and write. T-they killed him when he tried to stop them from shooting down Meester Eliason." She took a deep breath and pushed back the emotions. "I—I was so afraid. I—I didn't sleep all night—b-but I thought my place was here. I am so glad you're home, my love."

A freckle-faced girl ventured slowly onto the porch, ignoring Ernest, who was staring at his feet. She walked beside Cordell and tugged on his long coat. He looked down into wide brown eyes.

"Pastor, sir, did you fall off your horse?"

Cordell couldn't help but smile. His dirty coat would certainly appear like he might have had a problem. "Why, yes—yes I did. This young stallion has a mind of its own sometimes."

"I thought so," the girl said with great satisfaction. "I knew you wouldn't be out riding around with such a dirty coat otherwise. Maybe you shouldn't ride him when it rains." She pursed her lips and fluttered her eyelids. "That's a very pretty rose. Did . . . your wife give it to you?"

Aleta noticed the fresh flower for the first time and cocked her head playfully, waiting for his answer.

"Actually, it was given to me by a nice lady. I helped her family bury their pet cat." Cordell pushed his lapel forward so the rose was emphasized.

"Oh, that's so sad. I have a cat. His name is Rebel. What was the cat's name?"

"Her name was Belle. She was a fine cat."

"How did . . . Belle die?" The girl studied Cordell's face.

Aleta placed an arm around her shoulder. "Margaret, why don't you have the children sit down and weel finish our lesson?"

"Are you coming in, too, Pastor?" Margaret's eyes had never left Cordell's face.

"Well, thank you . . . Margaret, but I have to go see about another funeral. This one is for a friend of ours."

"Oh, I'm sorry. Is that why Mrs. Langford is crying? I thought she might be worried about you being hurt—from falling off your horse." Margaret folded her arms and glanced at Aleta for the first time, then quickly back to Cordell.

"When my cat dies, will you give it a funeral?" Margaret asked, her forehead furrowing into a sad frown.

Cordell nodded. "If you want me to. But let's hope that isn't for a long, long time."

Satisfied, the girl spun and retreated into the schoolhouse, telling Ernest to get inside too. The boy hesitated and followed without a word. Margaret announced authoritatively to the rest of the class that Reverend Langford had fallen from his horse during the morning rain, that he had received a rose for burying a cat, that he was going to give a funeral for a friend, and that everyone should be especially nice to Mrs. Langford because she had been crying about the friend dying.

Outside, Aleta hugged Cordell again and asked if the "cat story" was true. He told her what happened with Belle—and with Lion Graham; then about the strategy to make the state police think they were outnumbered; Caleb Shank's help at the ridge and at the Riptons'; the three Regulators on the road to town; Taullery's refusal to go along; and that both the big merchant and Billy Ripton were wounded. She told him not to blame himself for the man Lion Graham became. He pointed to her hat hanging from the saddle horn and mentioned how the big merchant had returned it.

He gave her the credit for the idea of pretending to be a group and calling them "Sons of Thunder." She smiled thinly and shook her head. She licked her lips to ward off the dryness overtaking them and asked about the dried blood on his coat sleeve, touching it lightly as she spoke. He dismissed the wound as superficial, and assured her that his head bruising was fine as well, then changed the subject to the stallion's performance.

As he rubbed the horse's nose, she stepped to her hat lying against his saddle and fingered it. Glancing over her shoulder to be certain Margaret wasn't close, Aleta told him about Mayor Giles being the lead clansman. Cordell's face told her of its importance, and he explained about having the deed to the Harper land made out to the mayor, the deed to the Ripton ranch readied for their signature, and that he was certain Giles was paying Padgett to run off selected landowners so he could purchase their holdings cheaply and eventually control the entire region. He reminded her of the two other ranches Giles owned, as well as the hotel in town. Then he told her about planning on getting Giles to return the deed to the widow Harper. He wasn't certain how to do it, however, without identifying himself. He had thought of sending a letter from the "Sons of Thunder" along with the deed itself.

"Eet weel take mucho more than letters to stop heem, my love. It weel take Rule Cordell. 'Colonel Bulldog' ees a beast who knows only how to keel and take." She patted her hat without removing it from the saddle horn.

A coldness swept through him and he didn't challenge her remark. Instead, he frowned and whispered, "Are you certain he didn't think you saw him?"

"I do not know that for sure. Eet was dark."

Cordell looked at the schoolhouse doorway where Margaret had returned and was waiting with her arms crossed. He nodded in her direction and Aleta told the girl to go to her seat, that class was resuming immediately. He started to tell her more about the discovery that Giles was the new owner of the Harper place and, likely, paying Padgett to run off the Riptons. Now wasn't the time; she needed to concentrate on her classroom. It wouldn't help to talk about her life being in danger, either.

"Rule, I want to keep Suitcase's school going. We must not stop now," Aleta said, holding his arm. "I want you to go find the parents of those children—and tell them. We have to do thees. No 'Colonel Bulldog' ees going to stop me." Her eyes flashed, and for a moment she was once again the outlaw woman he had fallen in love with the first time he saw her.

"I—I agree," Cordell responded, and then said, "But let's go there together. I'll wait here—and keep watch . . . on your hat. Might nap a little."

"No, you get dry clothes, then go to Eliason's. I weel be *bueno*." Her fingers caressed his tired face. "Do you think they weel come here? I have my pistol—in the desk drawer—if they do."

"I don't know what to think, sweetheart. But if I'd been with you last night . . ." His eyes narrowed and his mouth drew itself into a tight line.

"Quit that, my love. You saved another family. You cannot be in two places. You are very good, *sí*, but not that good, *senor.*" She touched his lips with her fingers and brushed them lightly. "Go now. I weel be *bueno*."

"No, not this time. I'll wait. Those families will want to see you anyway."

"W-what about Suitcase? H-he deserves a Christian burial. Y-you must . . ." Aleta's eyes flashed again as she placed her hands on her hips.

"We'll go together. I can stay wet a little longer. I'm almost dry now."

She stared at him and a soft smile took over her face. She nodded, kissed him on the cheek, and said, "The children and I eat our noon meal outside. I weel see you then, my love." She paused and added, "Do not snore too loud. My class will hear." Chuckling, she disappeared into the classroom.

He stood beside the stallion and listened as she resumed their lesson about American history. She had a fascination for George Washington that always oozed from her presentations. He never tired of hearing her talk of the leader. In her eyes, he was a fearless leader, a caring warrior, who had held a fragile idea in his hands and helped it grow strong. Smiling, he touched her hanging hat and made it swing gently.

Finally, he led his horse to a shaded area forty feet from the schoolhouse and a few feet outside of the surrounding fence. His horse deserved to be relieved of its saddle. After removing Aleta's hat, he loosened the cinch and pulled the heavy frame free, letting it slam to the wet earth. The noise wasn't loud, but it seemed so to his tired mind, and he glanced at the narrow window to see if it had disturbed the classroom. One boy was watching him and secretly waved. Cordell waved back, smiled, and pointed for him to pay attention to his teacher. The boy turned his head toward the front of the classroom.

After looping the reins over a branch, Cordell brushed down the sweating animal with handfuls of leaves, then checked its hooves. He cleaned each hoof carefully with a knife from his saddlebags, especially the ridges around the frog. The head of each hoof rested right on the iron. The shoes were well-fitted and not worn. A good fit, he decided, for store-bought iron. The big horse didn't appear to be winded or overly hot, so he offered canteen water from his hat. The wet coolness felt good when he returned it to his head.

Leaning over, he withdrew his rifle from the saddle sheath and sat cross-legged against the tree. Beside him was Aleta's hat. He cocked the gun, then eased the trigger down and laid it across his lap. The quiet whisper of the tree was both comforting and distracting. His insides churned with despair. He knew certain white people were not happy with the black school, but murdering Eliason—and trying to kill Aleta?

A shiver shot through him and sprung frustration loose upon his mind. He could see the pompous Giles. For a moment, he wanted to ride into town and find him. But every idea he had, no matter the subject, would eventually blossom into Aleta. He couldn't risk leaving her alone again, even though he was relatively certain the mayor would not think she had seen him unmasked. At least, not from the way she told the story.

Noise from the front of the school jolted him alert. Had he been sleeping? For how long? What was the matter? He was barely standing when the children filled the open grassland within the fence, laughing and yelling. Coming toward him was Aleta, trying to look like nothing was wrong, but her eyes told him a different story. At least, they were together.

"Whatcha got that gun fer? Rabbits?" A dark-haired boy was leaning against the fence. "My ma makes a rabbit stew that'll make ya want seconds and thirds. 'Course, there never is that much."

Another boy joined the first at the fence, more interested in having his friend join him than in wondering why the minister was waiting.

His mind slow from napping, Cordell tried to think of a reason for the gun. "I . . . ah . . . I was just cleaning it, son. Hope to go hunting . . . soon."

"Yah, my pa cleans his gun ever' night, I reckon."

"Come on, Tommy, let's eat—and then we can play some base-ball. Mrs. Langford said we could." The second boy tugged on the shirtsleeve of the first.

Tommy looked at Cordell and shouted, "Say, Pastor, ya wanna join us—in some base-ball? It's great fun."

"Why, he'd love to," Aleta answered, coming up behind the two boys. "After he eats. Wouldn't you, dear?"

School was out a few minutes after three o'clock, and

a half hour later, Rule and Aleta Cordell were riding toward the boot factory. Aleta tried to cheer him up by telling him that the children were very impressed with his athletic skill. They were certain no one had ever hit a ball as far as Pastor Langford did.

The distraction was short-lived, and their conversation turned to what they might find. They would bury their friend—and the other man—and see if they could learn anything from the tracks around the building. Maybe Aleta's horse would be there but neither expected it to be. Cordell wondered if their friend had left a will—or any kind of legal description of who should get his holdings. He was certain Giles was after the boot factory. Aleta reminded him that Eliason always kept his papers in a suitcase in his carriage. It would be critical to find the buggy and his documents, they agreed.

As they rode, Cordell began a string of questions that were eating at him. Could he really return to the ministry after this? Wasn't it now a sham? Wasn't there a big difference between using a different name to leave his old ways behind—and pretending to be something he wasn't? How could he face the people in church and tell them about God's righteousness when he, himself, turned to the gun for answers? Maybe they should move on? Weren't there lots of places where no one would care about Rule Cordell?

Before she could answer, they cleared a shallow rise. The unpainted factory building was drenched in late-afternoon sun. Aleta saw them first. People were moving about the wooden front porch of Eliason's factory. A few were standing next to the row of unruly bushes surrounding it. She guessed there were at least fourteen, all black, and mostly men. He guessed they were factory workers. A shout was followed by sunlight reflecting from a double-barreled shotgun, then from a rifle. Everyone stopped to watch the couple approach.

"Whatcha want hyar?" The command was harsh and loud. It came from an impressive-looking black man with a full beard, wearing a too-short suitcoat and a white, uncollared shirt. He appeared to be the group's natural leader.

"I'm . . . James . . . Langford. This is my wife, Aleta. She taught children here—last night. I just heard about this awful thing. Jacob Eliason was a friend of ours." Cordell whispered for Aleta to slow her horse to a walk and kept his hands where they could be seen easily. "We came to bury him—and find out who did this."

"We already know'd who dun it. White folks dun it. Yo-all kin git."

"Shut up, Alexander. That's the white preacher from town. And that's his wife. She was a-teachin' hyar. She saved our chil'un's life." An older black woman with nearly white hair and a huge bosom waved her arms in the direction of the black man giving orders. "Put them guns down, you fools."

Alongside Aleta, Cordell stopped the stallion at the hitching rack, but neither dismounted They studied the tense faces of the men and women in front of them. There were no signs of either Eliason or Zachim.

"Yur lady brung our chil'un home safe las' night, Reverend. We-all mighty thankful for that. Reckon she dun saved their lives. We thank ye, Missus Langford," a younger black woman in a faded gold dress pronounced as she stepped to the front of the porch. "Won't you please get down. Jeffrey, ya go fetch these good folks some lemonade—an' be quick about it."

A stocky man in patched overalls nodded and disappeared into the building.

Chapter Thirty

The tall leader lowered his shotgun. "Sorry 'bout raisin' my gun at ya. I . . ."

"No apology necessary. I would've done the same thing. May we see Jacob?" Cordell responded, leaning forward from his saddle.

"We dun buried him over yonder. They weren't happy 'nuff 'bout shootin' him, they dun had to hang him. Zachim, too. That's Zachim's wife." He pointed to a young woman sitting in the rocking chair with her head in her hands, weeping. Two women stood on either side of the chair, trying to console her.

"We'll take ya over to him. It's them trees yonder. Thought it looked peaceful. Part of his land too." The tall man continued, leaning the shotgun against the porch fence. "Buried Zachim thar too. Figgered Mister Eliason would be partial to the idee."

Taking a deep breath, Cordell swung down. Aleta rushed ahead of him to Zachim's widow. She leaned over, took the woman's hand, and told her what a courageous husband Zachim was, and how much he wanted to learn to read and write. Cordell shook hands with the tall man, who introduced himself as Alexander Morrison, then introduced the others. A glass of lemonade was thrust into Cordell's hand and one into Aleta's.

They sipped on the drinks, more out of deference to the expression of generosity than to any interest in lemonade at that moment. Several men and women took turns telling what they knew about the night, which didn't extend beyond Aleta's experience. Except this wasn't the first time they had been bothered by white-cloaked attackers. No one had seen Eliason's carriage or Aleta's horse. No one had any idea who the attackers were, other than the assumption that they were white men.

The group walked quietly the short distance to the graves. Zachim's widow and the women with her stayed behind. Cordell knelt beside the freshly dug mounds and shut his eyes to cut off the anguish that wanted out. Aleta fell to her knees beside him and began to weep.

"Oh, dear friend, if I had only been here," Cordell blurted.

The large, white-haired woman was suddenly beside him. "Now, don't you go blamin' yurself 'bout this. Ol' Suitcase would be angry. He rated you an' your lady mighty high, he did. Told me so hisse'f."

Cordell stared up at her, his eyes filled with pain. "I'll get them. I promise I'll get them—if it's the last thing I do."

She patted his shoulder. "I think the Lord Jesus talked 'bout turnin' the other cheek." She bit her lower lip and added, "Don' mean to be tellin' ya 'bout your business, preacher."

Cordell stood and took the woman's hand in his. "This school must keep going. We promised him. Will you pass the word? That is, if you want it to."

"Nobody's gonna hold yo-all to that, Reverend. Yur lady's dun bin through plenty." She patted his hand with her left and looked at Aleta.

Cordell released his grip as Aleta rose and reinforced his commitment. "We will be here tonight—and every night."

"With Mistuh Eliason gone, there ain't likely gonna be no money for schoolin'." The large woman rubbed her hands together, studying the nervous movement.

"He paid with his life. So did Zachim. We can never be paid more than that," Cordell said.

"Praise be to the Lord." The older woman raised both hands in the air and began to tell the others.

Cordell led the mourners in prayer as they requested, and the white-haired woman led them in singing "Over the River Jordan." He told them that they must keep the factory—and the school—going in Eliason's honor, and asked if any could handle the management of the concern. Several pointed to the tall black man, Alexander Morrison, and the older woman said Eliason was training him to eventually run the factory by himself.

"May we talk with you a few minutes?" Cordell asked.

"Yessuh. We can have some quiet over yonder." Morrison pointed toward the trees.

While the others returned to the factory, Cordell outlined the situation as he and Aleta now knew it. Mayor Giles was seeking control of land through Padgett—and had used this fledgling secret society to get control of the boot factory. Aleta described seeing Giles unmasked, and Cordell showed him Harper's deed and told about the attack on the Riptons. The key would be Eliason's will, if there was one. Without some legal declaration of ownership beyond Eliason, the factory would be sold. Cordell was certain this was what Giles was counting on. He thought that answer would be found in the suitcase kept in Eliason's carriage.

Morrison understood the seriousness of the situation but could offer no thought of where or what record Eliason might have left regarding his wishes, or where the carriage might have been taken. Tracks disappeared over rocky terrain to the west.

"We ain't got much time, does we?" Morrison's shoulders rose and fell.

"Do you think Jacob had a will?"

Before Morrison could answer, Aleta responded, "Of course he did, Rule. He was a thorough man, a man who planned."

"Well, if they're in the carriage, we have to assume they've been destroyed by now," Cordell said. "Wouldn't Giles go through the suitcase—and burn anything that would pass the ownership to someone else?"

"Yasshu, I reckon so. But I can put together pairs of men to ride through the country looking for the carriage. We ain't got much choice, does we?"

"The women can go too," Cordell responded. "And we'll search in town."

"Before you do that," Aleta asserted, "get everyone to search around here—and in the building. Jacob Eliason was the kind of man who would have hidden it—eef he had time."

"That's a big 'if,' honey." Cordell sought her eyes.

"*Sí*, but he was a beeg man."

"Your lady's right, Reverend. We should look here firstust," Morrison said. "I'll git folks a-movin'. Be good for 'em to quit mopin' around, even if'n they don't find nothin'."

While groups of black men and women searched the grounds around the building, and others explored possible hiding places inside, Cordell and Aleta scouted the outlying terrain and found where riders had gathered.

Bunched-up hoofprints and a few boot-smashed cigar butts were the main signs. Cordell noticed that one of the horses left a print of a rear left shoe with a deep notch at its front. Something glittered within a clump of buffalo grass. Aleta leaned over and picked up a shiny dark blue button. It had come from a man's coat or vest.

"Colonel Bulldog wears a suit like thees," she said, holding the button in her outstretched hand.

"So do a lot of men," Cordell replied. "But it's something."

"The man with a missing button weel have *mucho* to explain, I theenk."

"Yeah, and a horseshoe with a cut in it."

They decided to go home, check on Lizzie, and get some supper before returning for the evening's school. By then, Morrison would know if their search was fruitful. She wondered if her beloved paint horse would ever be found, and Cordell could only offer hope that it would turn up, but his manner indicated he didn't believe the statement. Their conversation continued as they walked back to their horses tied to the factory hitch. Cordell finally told her about finding Lion Graham's body, and that of two Regulators, on his way home. He told of his promise to return and bury Graham.

Their walk back was disrupted by the big, white-haired woman waving at him from the middle of the bushes. Her body rippled like a pebble in a stream. Morrison was beside her, smiling. Cordell's lopsided grin was followed by a wave of his own. Aleta exclaimed, "They've found it!"

"Guess what we dun found?" Morrison yelled, and answered without waiting. His excited voice boomed across the open yard. "Mistuh Eliason's suitcase. Yes-suh, it was in a bush, right over there." The nod of his head was toward the eastern hedge.

An immediate examination of the suitcase's contents

began. Cordell spotted the will as Morrison thumbed through the stack of papers.

"There it is."

Morrison withdrew the document and began to read it aloud. Both Cordell and Aleta were impressed with his skill. He stopped at one point, looked at them, and smiled. "Mistah Eliason taught me." He skimmed through the legal jargon and came to the important considerations: The factory was given to Morrison and three other men; his other holdings were to pass to the white family that raised him, Knox College, and to Reverend James and Aleta Langford.

"Quite a fella, that Eliason." Morrison folded his arms and looked away. "H-he helped me become . . . a real man."

"I think Suitcase would say you already were."

A red ball of sun watched them gallop toward their small ranch, both lost in thought yet clinging to each other's closeness. Rounding the slooping hillside, they saw Aleta's paint horse standing quietly in their corral, still saddled. Aleta whooped her joy, and Cordell withdrew the Dean & Adams revolver from his back waistband.

"They may still be here," he warned, but it wasn't necessary. In Aleta's right hand was her pistol. He cocked the handgun and motioned for her to let him go first.

He rode ahead to the corral gate, studying the house and surrounding area for anything that shouldn't be there. Cordell leaned over in the saddle and pulled the rope latch holding the gate and swung it open. He saw a sheet of paper tied to the paint's saddle horn.

"Aleta, looks like there's a note."

She kicked her horse into a lope through the open gate, reined up beside the paint, and tore the paper loose. A leather thong looped around the saddle horn held a shivering corner of the sheet.

"What's it say?" Cordell asked, closing the gate behind him without dismounting.

"OhmyGod, Rule—they've got Lizzie!"

"What?" Cordell's eyes went immediately to the back door. The lock was lying on the ground.

Aleta raced for the house, somehow hoping the message was a joke. Her dun wandered around the corral, dragging its reins. The paper fell from her hand as she pulled open the door and yelled, "Lizzie? Lizzie? OhmyGod!"

Cordell entered behind her, picking up the note as he stepped inside. Silently, he read its horrible story: "We have the girl. If you want her back alive, let a new owner take over the factory. When the paper is signed, she will be returned."

His face burning with a new agony, he met Aleta returning from the bedroom. Her expression needed no words. Her breath came in halting jabs as she fought herself for control.

"What are we going to do? They'll kill her, Rule." She bit her lower lip and stared at the ceiling, then held him tightly.

Cordell's mind was racing to a place he didn't want to go. Tiredness had disappeared; his thoughts were icy clear. The only people, besides themselves, who knew Lizzie Ripton was in their house were the Riptons, Caleb Shank—and Ian Taullery. Could his friend have told someone else—like the madam, Lady Matilda, or his wife, Mary? Or someone else—like Mayor Giles? His mind pushed further—or was the reason Taullery couldn't go with him to help the Riptons because he was going to be a part of Giles's attack on the school at Eliason's factory? But if that was the case, wouldn't Taullery have also told Giles that he was going to help the

Riptons, and Padgett would have been warned? Or did Taullery simply believe Padgett and his men could handle a lone Rule Cordell?

"Oh no, Ian, not you. Not you," he muttered with his arms around Aleta.

She recoiled from the words. "What do you mean?"

"Aleta, Ian was the only person I told about Lizzie being here—besides the Riptons and Caleb. Obviously they didn't have anything to do with it."

Aleta was silent. She looked into his face as if trying to withdraw more information directly from his mind. Finally, she spoke: "Let's go to town—and see your friend. He'll still be at the store, I'll bet." Her manner was calm; shock had evaporated from her system.

He gazed at her face, inches from his. He loved many things about her; there was an inner courage that was always close to the surface.

"Yes, we must go."

From the display of guns, she grabbed the remaining rifle and a box of cartridges. Outside, Cordell took his belt guns from his saddlebags and rebuckled them around his waist. Aleta tied up her dun, then checked the cinch on the paint, tied on the rifle sheath, and shoved the gun into place. She swung easily into the saddle.

"Where is Moon's medicine earring?" Aleta asked, waiting for Cordell to mount.

"Oh, it's in my pocket. Got torn during the night."

"Let me see eet. I weel fix. For luck."

He frowned but handed the pebble earring to her; she examined it and went inside. Minutes later, she returned with new leather in place. He smiled, placed it over his ear, and galloped toward town.

Most of the stores were closed or closing as Cordell rode down the main street. A half-dozen townspeople remained on the sidewalks, absorbed in their personal activities. Similarly, most of the clouds had disappeared to their secret places in the sky, encouraged by a gentle wind. Only the blacksmith and the barbershop appeared to be fully active. The *ping* of the blacksmith rang even harsher in the silence. The one-legged man in worn Confederate garb was leaning against a low fence half surrounding the hot coals, watching as if it were his responsibility to do so. This time Cordell didn't wave.

Eager to be home, the proprietor of the drugstore was locking up but stopped to watch the black-coated rider pass. He frowned as his observation took in the fact that the familiar man was armed and looked around to see if others had noticed. Not seeing anyone, he quickly completed his locking and scurried down the alley and out of sight.

Cordell was suddenly aware of a tall woman with long black hair studying him. She was standing across the street by herself; her light-colored eyes bored into him. Even if she hadn't been wearing the same dress from the day before, he would have recognized her as the strange woman from Taullery's store. Caleb Shank's description rang through his mind: "Wal, that'd be Eagle Mary. Part Comanche, part witch."

His eyes met hers, and she said in a singsong voice, "Why are you here? You are thunder. You are lightning. You are a storm to clean the land. You have sent the one who came to another time."

He shivered and looked around to see if anyone else was watching either of them. When he looked back, she was gone. Instead, a few feet away from where she had been, two men strutted into view and stopped to watch him with interest; both were reinforced by an afternoon of drinking. Weaving as he stood, the white-haired buffalo hunter spat a thick brown string of tobacco juice and asked his younger companion, a hide skinner, if that was the preacher.

When the younger man acknowledged it was, the hunter spat again and asked why the preacher was wearing guns. Wearing a shapeless hat and mule-eared boots, the leathery-faced companion studied Cordell for a few minutes and finally observed, "Maybe he ain't a preacher no more."

The older buffalo hunter spat and muttered, "Things jes' ain't like they used to be. We shoulda won." With that proclamation, he began walking along the planked sidewalk. Behind him came the younger man, scurrying to catch up. He told the stumbling man that the preacher was also wearing a rose and some kind of earring. They both looked back at Cordell, who had pulled up in front of Taullery's general store. A lamp near the rear of the place signaled someone was still there.

Dismounting, Cordell strode to the door and pulled on it. Locked. He banged on the door, then peered in the display window. The light was out, and only shadowed shapes greeted him. He returned to his stallion and swung into the saddle. His coattails flipped back, revealing his belted revolvers. He flipped off the hammer thong and eased the right Colt up and down in its holster to make certain the weapon would clear quickly. Spurring the big horse into a gallop, he raced to the end of the street and around back. A lilac-watered woman yelled at him from the second-floor window of the whorehouse as he passed. Down on the street, a man in business clothes looked up at her and yelled back. Ignoring Cordell, she waved at the man, who began walking toward the house.

Chapter Thirty-one

Rule Cordell held his breath as he rode around a shallow trench hollowed out under a lean-to used by saloon patrons to relieve themselves. The wind whipped the odor into a reeking wall. Clearing it, he shook his head to cast off the smell and looked down the alleyway. Halfway along the rear side of the main row of false-fronted stores, he saw two silhouettes against the fading sky. Aleta's shape was further distinguished by her returned sombrero. Her black hair lay untied and rested easily along her shoulders. At her waist was strapped a bullet belt with an empty holster sitting on her left thigh. Aleta held the holster's gun on Ian Taullery. Beside them was Taullery's waiting buggy, with the reins of Aleta's paint horse now tied to a wheel. Their simple plan had worked. Before getting close to town, Aleta separated from Cordell and slipped behind Taullery's store to wait. As they suspected, Taullery fled as soon as he saw Cordell coming.

"Your friend, he ees not so happy to see us," Aleta snapped, pushing her revolver against Taullery's back.

"This your idea of a joke, Rule?" Taullery demanded. "I'm late for supper. Mary's expecting me." He withdrew a cigar from his coat pocket, bit off the end, and spit it away. His hands roamed his vest pockets for a match.

"No, it's my idea of justice." Cordell stopped his horse and stepped down in one smooth motion, holding the reins in his left fist. "When did you stop carrying a derringer in your vest pocket?"

"Oh, I forgot. I was just looking for a match. Here, you can have the gun." He reached into his right vest pocket for the hidden pistol.

"Leave it—but your hand better be holding a match when it comes out."

With exaggerated slowness, Taullery withdrew a match, popped its head with his fingernail, and lit the cigar. "Care for one, Rule? Just got 'em in. A real fine smoke. Best in the area."

"I only smoke with my friends," Cordell snapped. "Where is Lizzie Ripton?"

"Lizzie Ripton? Why ask me? You told me she was at your place." Taullery spoke through a white ribbon of cigar smoke.

"Yes, and you were the only one I told."

Taullery's face soured for an instant and returned to its put-upon expression. He pulled the cigar from his mouth. "What's that supposed to mean? When did I quit being your friend? Just because I couldn't leave everything to go riding with you last night?"

"You quit being my friend when you and your masked buddies murdered two good men last night—and tried to kill my wife and some innocent children. An' then kidnapped the Ripton girl. That's when."

"That's crazy, Rule. I'm your best friend, remember?

Or have you forgotten all that we've been through together?" Taullery's eyes burned with anger; his hands went to his hips, pushing back the tails of his suitcoat.

"Don't try it, Ian."

Taullery realized the significance of the move and said stiffly, "I'm not carrying, except for that pea gun. I'm a businessman, not a gunfighter. Like you."

"Let's go to your house, Ian." Cordell growled impatiently. "We're in a hurry." His stallion nudged its nose against his arm, and he rubbed it, then looped the reins over the buggy wheel opposite where the paint horse was tied. "I've got a coat button in my pocket. We just found it at Eliason's factory, where we prayed over two fine men's graves. I'm betting it's from your suit, the one you had on yesterday. How'd you like to bet? I'm also betting we find a sheet with holes in it. What do you think?"

Aleta added, "You have a very distinctive voice, Eee-un. I hear thees voice of yours last night, oh so clear. Just like you are talking now." Earlier, they had agreed to press Taullery hard by bluffing about what they knew.

Taullery swallowed, glanced away, and in a thin voice confessed, "P-please, Rule, I didn't have any choice. Giles said he would have Padgett arrest me and take my store i-if I didn't go along. No one was supposed to be hurt. Giles said it was just to warn you not to hold that school." He paused, swallowed again, and shrugged his shoulders. "Y-you know I don't like the b-blacks trying to take over an' all. I tried to tell you about the 'Knights of the Rising Sun'—an' you didn't want to listen. Rule, they're good Southerners trying to get Northern carpetbaggers out of Texas."

"Giles is the worst kind of carpetbagger, Ian, taking land away from good Texans by having Padgett arrest them—or hang them. Or are you trying to tell me you didn't know that?"

"I—I thought if I went, I could protect Aleta."

Aleta bristled. "I don't remember anybody stepping up to do that, Eee-un. I only remember a bunch of cowards keeling two men and hoping to get me and the children."

Stepping close to Taullery, Cordell stared into the taller man's eyes. Taullery blinked away his concern and looked away. Cordell grabbed Taullery's suit collar with his right fist. His voice sounded like it was coming from somewhere else. "Did you also tell Giles that I went to the Riptons'? Don't lie to me."

"N-no."

Cordell's vicious slap across Taullery's face spun his head sideways and blood spurted from the corner of his mouth. His teeth snapped together so hard that his cigar broke and fell to the ground. "Try it again," Cordell said.

"N-no, I didn't."

A second slap staggered Taullery and he stepped backward, but Cordell held him up by his coat lapels. Taullery swallowed the small end of the cigar remaining inside his mouth and choked.

"I—I t-told him you went . . . to the R-Riptons'."

"I assume he had plenty of time to send someone to warn Padgett." Cordell's eyes bored into Taullery's pained face.

"W-well, y-yes, I s-suppose. H-he . . ."

"Didn't think one man would be much of a problem for all of Padgett's men. You didn't think so either, did you, Ian?"

Taullery swallowed some of the blood trickling from the corner of his mouth and choked on its warmth. "I—I t-told you not to g-go, Rule, remember?"

"I'll always remember . . . this," Cordell said. "Where is Giles now?"

"I—I don't know. Haven't seen him today. I think he went out to one of his ranches. Maybe."

"School is on again tonight. Is your little band planning on joining us?"

Taullery looked back into Cordell's face. "Honest, Rule, I—I don't know. Y-you're not going to do it—y-you can't."

Cordell released Taullery's coat and glanced at Aleta, then back at the nervous store owner. "Did you think a handful of white-sheeted fools would stop us? This time you'll have to face me."

"R-Rule, I didn't know, ah, we were going to the Negro school when y-you came to my store, honest I didn't." Taullery shrugged his shoulders and swallowed to push the biting chunk of cigar farther down his windpipe. "I—I knew Giles wanted the Ripton place, that's all. Dammit, Rule, some of us have to go along with the tide, you know. We can't all be like you."

Cordell's stare was a saber to Taullery's slightly rebounding courage. The taller man rubbed his chin with his right hand, looked at the blood on his fingers, then couldn't decide where to rub it off so Cordell wouldn't think he was going for his vest derringer. Finally, he rubbed his hand against his pants and left it at his side.

"So it was all right for Giles and Padgett to run off the Riptons—as long as you didn't get hurt." Cordell's voice was low and deliberate. "I suppose you knew about Harper before it happened too."

Taullery's entire body tightened. His swelling lip quivered. "Come on, Rule, what was I supposed to do? You were preaching sweetness and light—and made a big deal outta putting away your gun. Even had that silly altarlike thing in your bedroom." His teeth clenched, and he hissed, "I did what I had to do."

"I feel sorry for you, Ian."

"The hell with you, Rule. You'd love to have a store like mine. The best around, instead of that run-down horse farm of yours—and you know it."

Jabbing her gun into Taullery's back, Aleta blurted, "Enough of your sorry crap, Eee-un. Where ees Lizzie?"

Taullery looked down and involuntarily brushed himself off, then put his hands at his sides. For a moment, it looked like he was going to stall. "S-she's in t-there."

"Eef she is worse, I weel put bullets in your knees," Aleta threatened. "Maybe I weel anyway." She pointed the gun at his knee and Taullery winced, then looked at Cordell for support.

Cordell motioned toward the store's back door, and Taullery took out his key and opened it. Inside, grayness controlled the crowded storeroom. He pointed toward the corner where a dark shape lay on the floor. Aleta shoved him out of the way and hurried to the lying Lizzie. Quickly, she removed a tight cloth tied around her mouth and another blinding her eyes.

Blinking at the return of even the low light, the young girl blurted, "Oh, Mrs. Cord—Langford, I—I prayed you would come—before they did. I—I was so scared. It was some awful men . . . with their faces covered with white sheets. T-they were in the bedroom before I knew . . . t-they were all around me. W-where am I?"

"You are safe, Lizzie. Captain Cordell ees here—and Ian Taullery." Aleta looked at Taullery, who grimaced at her positioning him as helping. She untied the heavy ropes holding her hands and feet. She rubbed the girl's wrists and ankles to stimulate circulation. A quick examination of her wound showed it hadn't broken open again. Then a terrible thought crossed Aleta's mind and she whispered, "Lizzie, did they . . . take you?"

A rush of tears preceded her soft answer. "O-one of

them p-played with my b-breasts, but another stopped him."

Aleta turned toward Taullery; her eyes were hot.

Nervously, Taullery mouthed, "It was Giles. I told him to quit."

Aleta's expression was disbelief as she helped the young girl stand. Lizzie was wobbly but apparently not hurt more.

"Thank you, Captain Cordell. Thank you, Mister Taullery. I knew you would come, I knew it," Lizzie said as Aleta guided her to the doorway.

"*Tenga cuidado*. Be careful," Aleta said gently.

Cordell asked, "How is she?"

"She is all right. They tied her *mucho* tight, though, the bastards."

"If we go tonight, she must go with us—can she?"

"I weel tell her thees. She weel be ready. She is a tough . . . woman."

Both men watched them pass, then Cordell turned to Taullery. "Ian, here's what we're going to do. Aleta, Lizzie, and I are going to Eliason's factory. To teach the black kids."

"W-why are you telling me this?"

"Because we were friends—once," Cordell said, studying Taullery.

"I—I'm s-sorry, Rule, I didn't want this. I—I thought s-she would be s-safer here," Taullery blubbered, his eyes wallowing in wetness. "I—I wouldn't have let them h-hurt her. Really, I wouldn't. I convinced Giles y-you'd never think to look here." He swallowed and stared at the darkening sky. "I didn't think you would."

"Just don't tell me that it never occured to you that Giles was after the boot factory too—or that you didn't think Padgett's men would kill me."

Taullery acknowledged that the thoughts had crossed his mind but didn't see how he could do anything about it. Cordell asked him where Eliason's buggy was being hidden. The contrite store owner told him the buggy was out at Curt Keffer's place. Without Cordell asking, Taullery rattled off the names of the other members of Giles clan. Cordell recognized one as the father of Ernest, the towheaded boy with two missing teeth. He shook away the thought of what he should do.

"Giles will learn about the 'Sons of Thunder' when he talks with Padgett," Cordell said, changing the subject, and motioned for Taullery to leave the storeroom. The image of Ernest on the schoolhouse steps lingered in his mind.

"Who?"

"Padgett thinks he was surrounded by thirty gunmen called 'Sons of Thunder.' It was Caleb, Billy and his father, and me. Now he'll know I was one of them."

Taullery chuckled and muttered, "Wish I'd been there. Sorta like old times I'll bet."

As they stepped outside, Taullery turned toward Cordell and said, "I-I won't tell him who the Sons of Thunder are—but he already knows you're Rule Cordell."

"I figured you told him."

Taullery stopped and faced Cordell; his forehead furrowed. "No, honest, I didn't. That killing bastard Lion Graham told him. I was there when he did."

Behind them came the sound of a thick stream of water, followed by a loud belch, and then, the clank of approaching spurs. Cordell stepped sideways so he could watch Taullery at the same time as he determined who was coming. A cowboy staggered through the shadows, trying to button his pants but each movement threw him off-balance. On his third step away from the saloon trench, his own boot came down on the corner of his batwing chap and he stumbled backward, waving his arms furiously.

After landing hard, he looked around, pushed back

his hat and started yelling. "H-Hey! *Hiccup*. W-Where the hell's . . . my hoss? *Hiccup*."

Taullery snickered in spite of himself. He glanced at Aleta. She was helping Lizzie onto her horse and not paying attention. Cordell's face was unreadable.

"Ya ain't seed . . . my hoss, has ya, boys? *Hiccup*. Left 'im . . . ri't hyar." The cowboy stuck his finger in the dirt. "Brown . . . with a white stocking. Right. Front. *Hiccup*. Ah, maybe . . . left."

Without turning toward the drunken man, Cordell pointed in the direction of the main street. "Your horse is probably over there."

"W-well, how the h-hell . . . did he git thar, ya reckon. *Hiccup*."

Cordell walked over and helped him stand. He explained that the cowboy was in the alley, but it didn't register at first. After his third explanation, the drunk said, "Why didn't ya say that . . . the first time, mistah? *Hiccup*. H-how's I supposed to k-know . . . they dun m-moved the damn alley? Bin inside all day. *Hiccup*."

Shaking his head as the drunk meandered through the connecting alley toward the main street, Cordell turned back to Taullery as if their conversation had never been interrupted.

"Lion Graham is dead," he said without emotion.

"You kill him?"

"Not before he killed a cat and wounded two good friends."

Taking a deep breath, Taullery spoke in a soft voice. "I remember the good days, Rule. Remember Brandy Station? All of us with General Stuart passed in review of Marse Robert. God, we all looked magnificent. You and me were riding matched blacks—almost as fancy as Jeb's horse, they were. Lee was going into Pennsylvania, and he praised us to the high heavens. Sometimes. I wish we could go back there."

Cordell listened and pushed his hat back on his forehead. "Yeah, but don't forget the next morning the Federals ripped us apart, coming across the Rappahannock. I never saw so much blue."

"You were awesome that day, Rule. You and the General were everywhere. And ol' Grumble Jones, too, in stockinged feet and long johns, an' no pants. All o' you fighting and yelling for us to keep at 'em. I—I can see you there, no shirt on yourself, with a pistol in each hand. We shoved 'em back across the river just as the sun was setting. I—I never told you—how proud I was to be your friend that day."

"No more than I was to be yours, Ian. Like you said, things change because they have to." Cordell pulled the reins of his waiting stallion loose from the buggy wheel and leaped into the saddle. He stared again at Taullery, who stood unmoving. His eyes squinted into a look Taullery had seen often in battle. "Giles, Padgett—you an' the rest—have two choices: Stop what you're doing to innocent people, or kill me. I don't kill easy. Ask Lion Graham. You'll find him in Rome somewhere."

"I won't tell Giles you found out. I'm going to tell him that I brought her back to you—so you wouldn't be suspicious. He'll buy that."

"Don't say anything you can't deliver, Ian." Without waiting for a response, he nudged the horse and loped to catch up with Aleta, riding double with Lizzie in front.

Taullery watched them disappear, pulled out a cigar from his coat, and lit it. He stepped into the seat of his buggy and yelled at the harnessed animal to run.

Chapter Thirty-two

Seats on the planked pews filled rapidly Sunday. In his black robe, Reverend James Rule Langford greeted everyone warmly as they entered. Once again, Mrs. Tomlinson hoped he would be giving a sermon about the "vices" and rattled off her own list. This time she added book-reading and eating mushrooms. Henry Keller paused to ask if his roan stallion was for sale, and Harney Peale whispered that the minister's wife should quit teaching the black children because it would give the town a bad name.

Rule Cordell felt awkward about posing as their part-time pastor after returning to the gun. His healing arm and head were reminders of the path he had chosen. But the week had gone fast, especially after he decided what he must do. After a long night of talking, Aleta had agreed. News of the tragedy at Eliason's factory and the attack on the Ripton ranch spread rapidly throughout the region. So had tales of the "Sons of Thunder," who were being credited with all manner of deeds. Wanted bulletins appeared offering a five-hundred-dollar reward for information leading to their arrest.

Murmurs of the pistol-fighter Lion David Graham being killed, along with several state police, burned their way through the community. The murder of Jacob "Suitcase" Eliason brought differing opinions, some harsh; nothing was mentioned of Zachim's death. There was even a wild tale circulating about the outlaw Rule Cordell being alive. The schooling of the black children had resumed without incident. Eliason's buggy showed up at the factory one morning.

When Cordell went back to bury Lion Graham and the two dead Regulators, he couldn't find their bodies. He guessed wild animals had dragged them off and scared Graham's horse into continuing its flight. Giles hadn't been seen; neither had Padgett. He hadn't talked with Taullery since the day they retrieved Lizzie Ripton. The Riptons had come and taken her home in their buckboard. Lizzie wanted to stay and help Aleta with the schooling, but Tallie Mae insisted she was needed at home as soon as she could get around.

As he welcomed neighbors and townspeople, Cordell realized his feelings were similar to the ones he felt before a battle. He was ice-cold inside and had to work at smiling and chatting as the parishioners filed into the makeshift church. He was surprised to see Michigan Fainwald, the young editor of the *Clark Springs Clarion*. Cordell couldn't remember him being in church before and wondered why the man had chosen this morning to come. Awkwardly, Fainwald asked if he might talk with Cordell after church, and Cordell agreed. Fainwald took a seat near the back.

The bigger surprise for Cordell was the appearance of Mayor William Giles. Cordell assumed Taullery had told him everything and that the mayor was planning some counterassault on him. Or had Taullery been true to his word and not told Giles of what he knew? Giles sauntered into the morning-lit warehouse with his wife two steps behind him.

The mayor's eyes avoided meeting Cordell's gaze as he honored people with salutations. A knowing smirk settled on his face as he sat on the third pew, his customary seat. His wife was dressed in a bright green bodice and skirt, with a fashionable hair net and a small matching handbag. Her thick petticoats rustled as she swooped onto the pew beside him. Next to them was a young mother struggling to make her three small sons sit still. She eyed the mayor and his wife with concern and returned to quieting her boys.

Widow Bauer was already sitting in her regular position on the front row. Beside her, Aleta sat nervously, tightly gripping a small wild rose in both hands. Aleta caught Cordell's eyes and said, " 'The Russian' is here."

Sliding into the building as unobtrusively as the huge man could, Caleb Shank held two decorative ink bottles and a small sack of dip pens. His injured ear was swollen and scabbed over. Hamlike fists placed the writing materials carefully on a handy crate. He withdrew several papers from his coat, smoothed them with his fingers, and laid them on the crate as well.

After a few minutes of arranging and rearranging, the big merchant nodded his satisfaction at the task being completed and smiled at Cordell in his minister's garb. Cordell's response was a quick grin. He thought it was probably Shank's first time in a church since his family was killed. Shank decided to stand in a corner at the back, next to his presentation. Cordell had invited Shank to Sunday dinner at his house after the service; Alexander Morrison and his wife were expected to join them too. Cordell had invited the black couple to the church, but Morrison had politely declined. Later, Aleta had advised her husband that he was being foolish to think his white parishioners would be comfortable with black people in attendance.

Cordell's attention was drawn to an older woman near the back. He hadn't seen her come in—and couldn't see her face now, for she was leaning over. Probably picking up a dropped hymnal. Something pulled him to her, but he didn't know why. Was she from town? Someone he knew? But his attention was yanked to another woman sitting the next pew over. It was Eagle Mary—and in the same light blue dress she had worn when he last saw her. She was staring at the room's ceiling like she could see through the roof.

He'd seen that penetrating glare before and looked away before she realized he'd recognized her. Why was she here? Today, of all days. He didn't need such a distraction. He forced himself to look at the other side, near the back, where the Harpers sat. Ellena was settled with her arm around her young daughter, Rebecca, while twelve-year-old Michael intently watched every move Cordell made at the front of the church.

Just before the services began, Ian Taullery rushed down the middle aisle and managed to find a seat two rows behind Giles. His face was pale, with beads of sweat along his brow. Mary Taullery was apparently not with him. His face was flushed and, so unlike him, his suit was wrinkled, like he had slept in it. Taullery glanced to his left and realized he was sitting next to Michigan Fainwald. Taullery nodded, and Fainwald responded in kind. Immediately, Taullery began to fidget with arranging his hymnal so he wouldn't have to meet Cordell's eyes.

"Good morning, everyone," Cordell began, judging that it was time to begin worship services. "It is a beautiful day, isn't it. On such a day, I am always reminded that our Indian friends see miracles everywhere." He touched the medicine pouch beneath his robe, brushing against the silver cross hanging around his neck. "We should too. The miracle of a sunrise. The miracle of a swift horse and a friendly dog. Good health and hard work. Yes, hard work is a miracle too, producing a better life for our families. Oh, and the miracle of children. Look at those wonderful faces among us today. The miracle of love. Or the miracle of spring bringing new life." He paused and looked at an old man on the sixth row, cupping a hand to his ear to hear. "And, yes, the miracle of wisdom that comes with age. There are miracles all around us."

Somewhere an "Amen" popped into the room, followed by another. He thought he heard Eagle Mary say *"Nanisuwukaiyu,"* the Comanche word for "miracle," but he wasn't certain; it might have been just the mingling of responses. He glanced again in the direction of the older woman, but her face was blocked by a tall man in front of her.

"There are many other miracles—one, in particular, that I want to talk about today. It is the miracle of caring enough about each other to keep all of us from harm. I would like to open today's worship a little differently. First we will pray together, then I have a story to share." His voice was even and kindly; his chiseled face seemed softer than usual.

He closed his eyes and folded his hands. "Lord, we are gathered together in peace—and to share the miracles that are all around us. We seek the goodness of the land—and we ask only for others to grant us the opportunity to find it." He paused, grimaced, and continued, "Lord, give us the miracle of strength, of courage, and of wisdom, to help each other. Amen."

He looked up and glanced at Aleta, who smiled warmly and glanced down at the rose in her hands to make sure he saw it. "Today, I want to tell you about the 'Sons of Thunder.' You may have heard of them; you may not." Several heads nodded affirmatively. An old man on the fourth row was already asleep. His low snoring was bothering the families on both sides of him. Cordell's steady gaze caught Mrs. Tomlinson, and she mouthed, "Vices." He bit his lower lip to keep from smiling.

"These 'Sons of Thunder' are not the ones you've read about in the Bible, the ones who became disciples of Jesus. Although, from their description alone, I reckon they were pretty tough men." Chuckles flickered across the room, and one loud guffaw. "No, these 'Sons of Thunder' are on a wanted poster. It is the name used by me to try to stop wicked men from stealing the Ripton ranch, like they did the Harpers'—and others around here."

A collected gasp rattled through the church. Giles pretended to be thumbing through his hymnal. Taullery looked like he was going to be sick. Cordell proceeded to tell the audience how Captain Padgett had been fooled into thinking he and his men were surrounded. Cordell gave no indication of who had helped him in this effort. Snickers rippled through the audience, much louder than the earlier response. He told his stunned audience about the attack on the Eliason boot factory and minced no words in describing his feelings about the white-sheeted men who had done it.

He stopped and studied the room. Eagle Mary was now looking at him, her gaze so penetrating that he rolled his shoulders to remove the impact of the stare. The church was hushed. A small child's whisper near the back was a loud announcement, bringing a moment of relief to the growing tension. One couple at the back rose and left. Mrs. Tomlinson frowned and mouthed, "No tobacco." Shank was watching two children squirm on the back row, and Cordell figured it was only a matter of time before the big man went over to them with candy or something to occupy their attention. Cordell's smile barely reached his face before he realized it wasn't the right time to do so.

"It is important that you know something," Cordell finally continued. "First, the 'Sons of Thunder' you've heard about are not the only thing that's not real around here. I am not James Langford. I am Rule Cordell." He waited for the talking to ebb before going on. "Friends helped me escape from Union troops—and to become your minister and to start a small horse ranch with my wife, Aleta. It had been our deepest wish that this would be our new life. That was not to be." His chest swelled with nervous energy, and he exhaled. "We could not stand by and let good friends be robbed of their lands—by an evil lawman, William Padgett, his hired killer, Lion Graham, and their boss, William Giles."

Giles's chin shot up and crimson rose from his collar to his forehead. He stood and snarled, "What kind of nonsense is this? First, this wild story about the Sons of Thunder—and now you're Rule Cordell. You said that last Sunday—when you attacked our state police doing their job. Why should anyone believe you—about anything?"

Cordell smiled. "That's a good point, Giles. I'll let the folks here decide. Padgett hanged an innocent man, Douglas Harper—so you could get his land. Then you had Padgett try to run the Ripton family off their ranch. You and some others attacked the boot factory—and murdered my friend, Jacob Eliason, and another fine man. You tried to kill the little kids going to school there, too—and my wife, who was teaching them." He stared at Giles. "My wife saw you, Giles, when your mask came off."

"That's ridiculous! I refuse to listen to any more of this. . . ."

"Sit down, Giles, I'm not through." Cordell pointed at the mayor.

"I have no intention of doing that. My good name is being smeared by . . . by a man who is wanted by the authorities, who has told all of us lies about himself. You have no proof. I demand your dismissal—immediately. This isn't church, it's nonsense."

"I have the deeds, Giles. I took them from Padgett's wagon." Cordell's eyes bored into Giles, and the mayor hesitated and sat down. His wife whispered at him, and he told her to shut up.

"You don't have to believe me, folks, I wouldn't expect you to." From under his robe, he pulled two documents and held them up in his hand. "Here is the deed for the Harper ranch—with Giles's name on it. And here's an unsigned deed to the Ripton place—with Giles's signature already on it." He stepped forward and handed the papers to Widow Bauer. "Pass them around for everyone to see. I hope they scare you as much as they did me."

Staring at Giles, he told the congregation that he had signed confessions from every man who had attacked the factory. Each man asserted that Giles and two of his ranch hands had been the ones who killed Eliason and Zachim. He mentioned that both of these men had been wounded by his wife. Aleta stood and withdrew folded sheets of paper and handed them to the surprised man behind her.

Without pausing, Cordell explained that he would resign after the service was over, and that he and his wife would be leaving the area, but not before justice was delivered to Padgett, Giles, and his two hands. The other clansmen had agreed to buy books and supplies for the black school.

In the middle of the church, a lanky man slowly stood, raising his hand as he did. "Reverend . . . ah, Mister

Cordell, sir . . . some o' us are a-knowin' about all this. We seed Giles git his other ranches the same way. My friend, Warren Hanks, were hanged by Captain Padgett. Fer nothin'. What'er we supposed to do? He's the law, ain't he?"

Cordell cocked his head to one side. "You're going to have to decide that for yourselves. All of you. That's the miracle of caring about each other I mentioned earlier." He motioned toward the back of the room. "Here's a place to start. My good friend, Caleb Shank, has some ink and pens—in the back. There are two petitions for your consideration. One is for the removal of Padgett as captain of the Texas police force. It will be presented to the governor. The other is for the arrest of Giles for murder and his removal as mayor."

"Well, by God, I'll sign it," the lanky man exclaimed. His was the lone endorsement, and he sat down.

Cordell folded his arms and found the encouraging eyes of Aleta. A few parishioners looked uncomfortable; more appeared angry; several women were sobbing. His gaze returned to Giles. "Oh, and we have a special pen for you, Giles. You are going to sign the deed for the Harper land over to Mrs. Harper."

Giles looked up at Cordell, his face twisted with hate. Over his reddened cheeks spread a cruel smile. "Why would I do that? You're going to be hanged—just like that fool Harper."

Outside, the rush of horses gave an indication of why Giles was confident. The door was shoved aside and state police jammed their way into the church. Morning sunlight brushed against their badges as they fanned out along the back. One started to ask Shank to move away from his crate, studied the big man, and thought wiser of it. Without moving, Shank stood quietly, his hands behind his back.

Captain Padgett was pushed into the warehouse, sitting defiantly in his wheelchair. A different Regulator than before delivered the lawman; his strained arms indicated the task wasn't an easy one. Padgett's beaded-cuff gauntlets gripped the chair rails tightly and his head moved jerkily from side to side, like a rooster checking the barnyard. A few steps behind the wheelchair came a short, portly man dressed in black. His stern face was marked with spectacles; his collar and dark clothes marked him as a minister; his expression was one of cruel satisfaction.

It was Reverend Aaron Cordell, Rule's father.

In a loud commanding voice, Padgett bellowed, "Reverend Cordell, do you see a familiar person here this fine Sunday morning?"

"I see my one failure in life. My son. Rule Cordell. May he rot in Hell for his wicked ways." Reverend Cordell stepped forward as he spoke, slowly lifting his right arm until a pudgy finger pointed directly at his son.

"You're under arrest, Cordell, for the murder of Lion Graham and four police officers," Padgett screamed. "Take him, boys. I want to enjoy a hanging this morning." He smiled, glanced up at Rule's father, and added, "Then we're gonna find every one of you bastard 'Sons of Thunder.' You'll rue the day you ever got in my way."

At the front of the church, Cordell stood with his feet spread apart and his arms folded. Calmly, he said, "Well, dear father, it's good to see you too. I see you've found like company. Quite a trio you, Padgett, and Giles make."

Giles jumped to his feet and shouted, "Padgett, you lost my deeds, you idiot. Get them. They're somewhere in there." He waved his arms in the direction of the middle of the pews directly across from him.

Four Regulators headed for the front. A loud metallic *click-click* behind them stopped their progress. It was followed by a casual command. "If'n you boys go any further, I'm afraid your fine captain is gonna find hisse'f in bad shape. This hyar fella's got a hair trigger. Traded fer it jes' yesterday." In Caleb Shank's fist was a long-barreled revolver that had been held behind his back, and it was pointed at Padgett.

Reverend Cordell snarled at Shank, "You sinful fool. You'll go to Hell for helping this . . . this . . ."

"Son of Thunder." The statement came from another large man sitting next to the Harper woman. In his hand was a Colt revolver. It, too, was pointed at Padgett. "You can count me one o' them Sons of Thunder, Padgett. We've had enough of you—and you, too, Giles."

"I'm a Son of Thunder."

"Me too."

"You'd better figger I'm one o' them Sons of Thunder."

Suddenly the room was bursting with men standing, brandishing handguns, and yelling, "I'm a Son of Thunder." Cordell's mouth opened slightly in amazement. His eyes caught movement on the first pew and saw Aleta pull a gun from her handbag, then a second. Next to her, Widow Bauer was standing with an old dragoon in her hand. Aleta turned toward Cordell and tossed him one of the pistols. Shaking his head, he watched it sail toward him, then stepped aside without raising his arms and let it pass. The Colt thudded on the floor behind him.

"Drop them guns, boys." Shank pointed his revolver at different Regulators. "Unless ya figger a church is a fine place to breathe yur last." The Regulator closest to him hesitated, and Shank's left fist jolted the man in the jaw and he sank to the ground. The big merchant looked at the next man in line and said, "I said now."

Immediately, the militiamen began dropping their rifles and unbuckling their handguns. Padgett screamed for them to shoot. An older, white-haired man on the back pew stepped over the plank and seized a dropped rifle and pointed it at the Regulators. He was followed by another. Reverend Aaron Cordell stared in disbelief at what was happening. He yelled, " 'Get thee behind me, Satan.' " But no one heard him.

"You can't do this," Padgett screamed. "We are the law."

The white-haired man shouted back, "Not in Clark Springs, you ain't. Not anymore."

Cordell walked slowly toward a stunned Giles. "Ordinarily, I wouldn't hit anyone in a church. But for you, I'll make an exception." He stopped in front of the red-faced mayor and his fist flew into Giles's belly. Giles staggered as his wind vanished with the blow, followed by the remains of his breakfast. Cordell jumped sideways to avoid the vomit, and it splattered on the floor and the emptied pew in front of him. Satisfied that the bent-over mayor was finished retching, Cordell slammed his fist into Giles's chin, lifting him off the ground and sending him flopping over the pew.

From the back of the church came Shank's steadying call. "I think he dun got the point, preacher."

Editor Fainwald's excited voice followed. "Leave something for the judge."

Cordell backed away from the unconscious Giles. "You're right. He needs to sign a deed, doesn't he?"

Giles's wife studied her still husband, then Cordell, and huffed, "I can assure you that you won't be getting a new coat from us!"

Cordell didn't see the older woman stand, but there she was, glaring at his father. Her words rang across the tightened room, forcing everyone to stop and listen. She pointed at the heavyset minister. "Yes, you are this fine young minister's father. I should know—I'm his mother."

Cordell stared, disbelieving. It was! It was!

"You are fortunate to have a *real* minister. Someone who really cares," she continued, turning toward the puzzled assembly. "This pompous fool beat his wife and his son, cheated on his congregation by keeping their donations for himself. You, Aaron Cordell, are the one damned."

Sunlight glittered off of the gold-plated pistol in Padgett's fist, drawn from one of the holsters hanging from his wheelchair and aimed at Rule Cordell.

"No, no!" Taullery yelled, and jumped to his feet, drawing his derringer. He fired both barrels at the crippled leader as Padgett's gun exploded. Shank's own blast was a fraction behind. Padgett jerked in his wheelchair and yelped, "Kill him, Lion." He rose, took one short step, and collapsed. Reverend Aaron Cordell turned and ran out of the building.

Cordell rushed toward Taullery, who had taken Padgett's bullet in the chest. He knelt beside his friend and held him close. "Ian, breathe easy now. It's going to be all right." Cordell looked up at the throng of faces gathering close. "Give him air. Please. Back up. Someone get some water. Quick."

"D-don't . . . R-Rule. I'm not going to make it." Taullery's eyelashes fluttered, and he swallowed. His body trembled slightly and his eyes closed.

"Ian? You can't . . ."

Taullery's eyes opened. "I'm sorry I let you down, Rule. I—I can't make the next charge. I wish . . ."

Cordell held the unmoving Taullery to his chest and wept. Aleta was at his side, tears streaming down her face. The rose slipped from her hand and tumbled across Taullery's still face, coming to rest on the bloodstained floor. A lone petal fluttered onto Cordell's hand and stayed there, unnoticed. He didn't hear Mrs. Tomlinson mutter, "He has to stay. He hasn't done his sermon on vices yet."

Hestitantly, Cordell's mother came to Aleta, tears consuming her wrinkled face. In halting phrases, she told Aleta that she had heard about this young minister and wondered if it might be her son. She was staying in town at the boardinghouse. Her second husband, Henry Johnson, had died in the War and her other children were working their farm in northern Texas.

She choked on her sobbing and whispered, "D-do you t-think he c-can ever f-forgive me?"

Aleta blinked, and her chest rose and fell. "*Sí*, your son already has."

Widow Bauer stared at the sobbing woman, then at Fainwald scribbling notes on a pad of paper. "How you gonna write about this, Fainwald?" Her tone was accusatory.

He looked up at her, smiled thinly, and said, "State police captain and town mayor captured in a scheme to defraud community. Mayor arrested for murder."

"What about . . . our minister?"

Fainwald cocked his head to side and returned to his writing. "What about him? I don't see his sermon about miracles as a part of this story."

Holding Taullery's body in his arms, Cordell was aware of Eagle Mary standing next to him. "You are thunder. You are lightning. You are a storm to clean the land." She paused and touched the medicine pouch under his shirt and robe. "*Nanisuwukaiyu*. Moon watches over you. Know this." She turned and left before he could respond. His red-lined eyes followed her departure until he heard Aleta's caressing voice: "Your mother is here, Rule. She wants to see you. There is nothing you can do for Eee-un now, my love. He ees gone elsewhere."

At the back of the church, young Michael Harper ran

over to Shank. "I-is he really Rule Cordell?"

"I reckon so, Michael." Shank watched the Regulators being marched outside by armed churchmen. Several lawmen appeared relieved. None made any attempt to go to their their dead leader. One stocky deputy spat at Padgett's body as he passed.

"W-will the Y-Yanks be a-comin' after him? W-will I ever get to be with him again?" Michael's eyes were filling.

"I don't know, son, he's got a lot o' war in 'im." Shank was distracted by several people gathering around his crate. "Wal, I reckon we don't need no paper signed about Padgett no more."

One bearded man holding a long-barreled Colt said defiantly, "I reckon to sign it anyways." As Shank nodded, the man continued, "Ya was sure ri't about the preacher needin' some he'p today. You reckon we kin talk him into stayin'?"

"Hard to say, Jesse. Might be no one'll believe Rule Cordell's alive."

"Yah, does sound a bit far-fetched—even fer a Yank. Ya kin have this hyar pistol back now."

Michael tugged on Shank's coat to get his attention. "Are you one of the Sons of Thunder?"

"I reckon so, Michael."

"Can I be one?"

"You already are, son. Better yet, yur a Harper."